THE AMAZON—A REALM OF EXOTIC BEAUTY, BRUTAL REALITIES . . . AND DREAMS DARKLY CAST.

ALEX POULSON—His innocence protected him from the pulsing magic that emanated from the deepest heart of the Amazon—until Laura appeared and he learned the meaning of desire.

LAURA WELLMAN—Aristocratic, sophisticated, she came from Hollywood and New York seeking release from a haunted past, eager to embrace a menacing enchantment, weaving a web of irresistible allure.

FATHER BENEDICT—Frank Poulson's depravity filled him with murderous rage. Laura filled him with forbidden desire. How long could he resist the moment of weakness that, for him, meant a lifetime of remorse?

AVRIL—A young English beauty, her world, even in the midst of war, had always been ordered and clear . . . until she returned to Brazil to help Alex find the healing understanding that would free their love—unaware how deeply she'd be caught within the spell. . . .

OTHERWORLD

OTHERWORLD

W. A. HARBINSON

A DELL BOOK

Published by
Dell Publishing Co., Inc.
1 Dag Hammarskjold Plaza
New York, New York 10017

This work was first published in Great Britain by Corgi Books.

Dell ® TM 681510, Dell Publishing Co., Inc.

ISBN: 0-440-16738-8

Printed in the United States of America

First U.S.A. printing—March 1985

ACKNOWLEDGMENTS

My thanks to the following people for kind assistance during the course of this book: Stephen Cobb, winner of the Anglo-Brazilian Society Award, 1980, for his general advice regarding travel through Brazil. J. B. Williams and C. A. Parrott of *Journey Latin America* for so quickly and efficiently arranging my trip to Brazil and the Amazon. Peter Kurtz and my British agents, Iris and Richard Gollner, for useful information and introductions. In Brazil: Jim and Elda Mulholland, Mike and Vanika Royster, and of course Karin and Alexandria Zuhlsdorff, two beautiful ladies.

For general editorial assistance and moral support, my sincere thanks to Alan Earney, Sandi Gelles-Cole, Al Zuckerman, and again, Richard and Iris. Thanks, also, to Shaun and Tanya, my son and daughter, who at twelve and nine years of age, respectively, printed this book out on my word processor as I was correcting it. Finally, as representatives of two indispensable but rarely acknowledged aids to a writer's career: John Munday, art director of Corgi Books, for more than once taking the time to share beers and conversation about the pros and cons of book covers—one of this particular author's pet subjects— and Naren Patel, my very good friend and accountant, without whose expert guidance I would not have survived so many years in this precarious business.

Allen Harbinson
London

For Maria Mayer
Mutti to me

OTHERWORLD

PROLOGUE

The snake was about nine feet long, its silvery-gray scales glistening. It slithered out of the darkness, slowly, silently, rising up and curving down, its flat head moving briefly through moonlight, its forked tongue clearly darting in and out, eyes like small stones, jaws throbbing. The spider, also held in that single beam of moonlight, was unaware, or possibly knew and was paralyzed. It was an enormous spider, a birdeater, leg span covering eight inches, furred body heaving rhythmically, taking its last, precious breaths, one of its eight eyes illuminated between its front legs, as the snake slithered toward it.

Alex's pupils reflected both, expanding to defeat the darkness, to mirror the beauty and horror of the forest's cycle of life and death. He raised his head where he lay, his body swinging in the hammock, looking down at the beam of light on the mud floor of the barren thatched shack. The spider should not have been there—perhaps a tarantula, not a birdeater. The snake, which resembled an enormous, throbbing vein, likewise did not belong there but out in the forest.

He kept looking, not frightened, simply wondering why they were there, listening for the sound of the drums but hearing only silence. The snake's slithering broke that silence, its scaled body sliding across the damp leaves toward the spider.

Did the spider know what was going to happen? Studying it keenly, he thought it did. First motionless, it now moved, its hideous legs bending further, the brown fur on the round ball of its body standing up like fine wire. Fear. And then acceptance. The spider almost seemed to sigh, its body sinking back down between the legs that could have straddled a large plate.

It was doomed and knew it. Alex watched its death from his swaying hammock. As the snake stretched out to its full length, he saw its eyes, dead as the moon, hypnotizing its victim. The spider simply stared back, the fur rippling on its body, seven eyes viewing a prismatic world, the eighth greeting death. The snake's forked tongue darted out, and the spider almost imperceptibly quivered and then seemed to freeze. Paralyzed, it was still watchful, unable to turn its head away, its middle eye forced to stare straight at the jaws of the snake, opening wide, moving forward. The neck of the snake formed an arch, its head hanging straight down, and then its jaws, forming a large, dark, salivating funnel, dropped down over the spider and snapped shut.

The snake swallowed the spider whole, with one languid but noisy gulp, sucking it into the expanding tunnel of its throat and flicking the leaves with its tail. Alex watched, fascinated, wondering at how enormous the snake looked in the thatched hut's small gloom. Then at last he heard the drums, very faint and far away, and he swung his long legs off the hammock and dropped down to the floor.

The snake was bloated with the spider but turned its head to stare at him, its body uncoiling as its tongue again began tasting the air. Hearing the drums, Alex was unconcerned, knowing the magic would protect him. He merely smiled and stared at the rearing snake, his eyes following its wavering head. The snake studied him with stony eyes, its hammer head swaying a little. Then, as if he had actually stared it down, it slithered out of the hut.

He watched the snake disappearing, heard the drums, and felt the cold; he glanced quickly around the old Indian's hut, its stark simplicity amusing him. A miniature palm-thatch *maloca*, its earth floor carpeted with fine-leafed ferns, it was shaped like a coconut shell and held only one person. The old Indian lived simply—in the natural gloom, his bed the earth—and the hammock, stretched between two tall poles, was there only for Alex.

He dressed quickly and easily, not requiring much clothing, first putting on short pants and a plain white shirt, then a pair of light sandals. He did not comb his hair but patted it down with his hands, then turned around, feeling healthy and unafraid, and walked out of the hut.

The plantation was couched in darkness, its buildings blacker than the morning, and all around him, in an enormous outer cloak of silence, were the constant sounds of the forest: the distant chattering of monkeys, the muffled croaking of giant frogs, a birdcall that sounded like twanging wire, generalized slithering and rustling and murmuring, the sibilant rush of the river. He glanced across at his father's house, a wooden building raised up on stilts, shivered as if shaking off a ghost, and then started running.

He followed the sound of the beating drums, breathing deeply, his fists clenched, wending his way between the thatched huts and wooden buildings of the plantation's heart, and then heading straight into the forest where most men would not roam at night.

The soaring trees closed in around him, the crowns above him closely spaced, allowing little light in during the day and now themselves lost in darkness. The forest came alive in darkness, when camouflage was not required, and now around him as he ran, skirting the weblike, tangled liana, were the rustlings of huge rodents, the snorting of pigs and anteaters, the shrieking of monkeys, the basso croaking of outsized frogs, and the ghostly whispering of the large leaves on the damp forest floor where ground beetles and ants and termites moved about in their millions.

Alex felt no fear, his attention focused on the distant drumming, his eyes lifting to glance through the forest canopy high above in that darkness. Up there, in that canopy, was the true wealth of the Amazon rain forest: pigeons and honeycreepers, macaws and hummingbirds, marmosets and cotingas, hornets and stinging bees and wasps and huge bats, more monkeys and numerous snakes, including the boa constrictor. He looked up, unafraid, his eyes scanning the darkness, trying to see through the canopy to the patches of sky above it, seeing a dark, drifting cloud, a patch of stars . . . and then a star that *ascended*.

His heart skipped a beat, but then the trees closed in again, shutting out the sky and its ascending star and deepening the darkness around him. He continued his casual running, lured forward by the distant drumming, that lone star still ascending in his head and illuminating the jungle night. An ascending star. A light. Very high in the sky. Ascending and descending over the depths of the rain forest where no white man, and very few Indians, had ever dared walk. He kept running, his heart beating faster, glancing only occasionally at the forest floor, slowing down only to clamber over the gigantic, entangled liana, but quickly picking up speed again and mostly staring above him.

There was a break in the forest canopy, a patch of stars, then some lights, more lights like the one he had seen before, all slowly rising and falling. He kept his eyes upon them, wondering again what they were, and then that patch of sky slipped behind his head as he kept moving forward.

He was near the edge of the plantation, passing the last of the rubber trees. Then he crossed that invisible boundary where the plantation met the jungle and moved deeper into the untamed rain forest, where the drums sounded louder. A furred animal crossed his path, the outsized rodent known as a paca, and then he saw a snake slithering up a treetrunk toward an unwary sloth. He moved past them, unafraid, concentrating on the distant drums, aware that he might never see who was playing them and feeling a biting loss.

The distant drumming was hypnotic, almost ethereal, unreal, and he felt his heart beating even faster as the forest closed in on him. It was bitterly cold, but he felt warm, the running keeping his temperature high. He drank in the crisp, biting air in deep, healthy lungfuls as he ran.

The darkness was growing deeper, the trees pitch black on gray-black, their great trunks and the clinging liana forming enormous, bizarre forms that soared up and fell away into dark, distorting tunnels. Then a wavering beam of gray light, illuminating a demented hornet, falling past it to encircle a scorpion and spider in a dance of death on the forest floor. He jumped over them, kept running, disturbing *pium* flies and mosquitoes, glanced up and saw the sky, an irregular circle of stars, then other lights, not the stars, rising and falling in silent splendor, then followed the striation down, through the various layers of treetops, down past the writhing liana and the great tangled roots to a clearing that was gloomily lit by oblique beams of moonlight.

The clearing was near the river—he could hear the murmuring water—and through a gap in the forest canopy, a natural window through the foliage, he could see the rise and fall of the mysterious lights, their serene, silent grandeur. The lights were like Catherine wheels, ascending and spinning rapidly, their brilliant outer rings swirling around a darker core, their silvery striations shooting out for miles and turning into great cobwebs. There were a great many of them, forming kaleidoscopes in the starry sky, shooting up from the jungle depths, far north, in the interior; and equally mysteriously, exploding out of the sky itself, first as pinpricks of light, then as dazzling flares that descended in slow, elegant arcs and disappeared in the jungle.

He stared at them, fascinated, wanting to know their true nature, then lowered his gaze back down to the clearing and looked at Peruche.

The old Indian was all alone, sitting cross-legged in the damp grass, wearing nothing but the briefest loincloth, his brown flesh like dried leather. He was rocking back and forth to the rhythm of the distant drums, repeatedly bowing his head over a wooden bowl placed just in front of him, and chanting some indecipherable litany in a worn-out, cracked voice.

An old Indian, *very* old, some said ninety-nine years old, now suddenly sitting upright, stiffening his frail shoulders, fixing his bright eyes on Alex and then nodding his head.

"Sit down," he commanded.

Alex sat down, flicked the blond hair from his blue eyes, and gazed into the wizened face of the old Indian, feeling like a child. In fact he was an adolescent, a very healthy seventeen, but now shivering with the morning's biting cold—and with a certain excitement. He kept staring at the ancient Indian, hearing the far-away drums, thinking of the mysterious lights that rose and fell where he still dared not roam. Would the elusive Yano emerge? Was that part of the ritual? Alex, lean and pale, facing the frail, shrunken Indian, felt the forest pressing in on all sides as if trying to crush him.

"White boy," the old Indian said, his gray hair thin on a shining skull, his brown eyes illuminated in moonlight and reflecting more darkness. "What did you dream about?"

Alex licked his lips and leaned forward, his ears filled with the distant drums.

"A great ball of fire in the heavens. An umbrella of light . . ."

His voice trailed away, as if disbelieving its own offering, and the Indian, his brown body shriveled, smiled a little and nodded.

"That is good," he said. "We both shared the same dream. It is a sign that someone is coming to point the way to your future."

He closed his eyes and murmured something, shaking his head from side to side, then reached down to the bowl between his crossed legs and picked something up. The jungle chattered all around them, the drums pounded in the distance, and the old Indian raised his cupped hands to his lips and kissed what he held in them. Then he looked up again.

"Take your clothes off," he murmured.

Alex did as he was told, quickly removing his shirt and pants, then sat cross-legged, naked and cold, directly facing his mentor. The old Indian raised his right hand, crooked one finger in a beckoning gesture, and then, when Alex had leaned toward him, slipped the chain of the stone amulet in his hands around his neck.

"It was dipped in the bowl of *epena*," the wizened Indian croaked.

"Sniff the *epena* into your nostrils and then close your eyes. No evil will harm you then."

Alex glanced north, through that window in the forest canopy, and saw the lights rising and falling above the unexplored regions. He wanted to find that place—to unravel the mystery of Peruche's smile—but that smile, now illuminating his mind, forced his eyelids to close. He held the stone amulet in his cupped hands, lowered his head, sniffed up the *epena*, then put his head back and breathed deeply and let the dreams take command.

"Have faith," the old Indian said.

Now, out of the undergrowth, out of the darkness of shifting foliage, came swarming the enormous spiders and centipedes and giant ants and two snakes. The spiders formed a rippling carpet, an undulating, furry tide, which first lapped at Alex's feet and then splashed up his legs. The centipedes swarmed over the spiders, the ants over the centipedes, glistening on the furred backs in the moonlight that fell over his pale skin. He shivered violently and then was still, his body covered in that seething mass, and then the snakes, oblivious of danger, their every instinct apparently deadened, nosed through the spiders and centipedes, slithered over the countless ants, and then coiled around Alex's body as it gradually disappeared beneath that hideous coating of insects.

Blond hair and blue eyes. Alex's face was strangely beautiful. His eyes opened very briefly and then closed as the crawling mass reached his lips. He shuddered again, thought of the lights, heard the drums; then the centipedes and ants filled his ears as the spiders covered his head.

Now, in the forest clearing, where Alex was still sitting, two anacondas, their thick bodies covered in slime, were wrapped around a living mound of spiders and giant ants and centipedes, all crawling in harmony.

The drums pounded. The lights rose and fell.

PART ONE:

THE MISSION

1

"She arrives today," Father Benedict said, putting his felt hat on his head and settling himself in the small boat, then raising his eyes to squint up at the Indian who was untying the rope. "In fact, she's arriving in the same boat that is taking Father Symonds away from us."

"An American woman?"

"Yes, Mengrire."

He heard the resentment in his own voice and smiled slightly, with self-mockery, aware that he was being unreasonable, but unable to stop himself. Mengrire, like all the Indians, was clearly very curious, unable to comprehend why a rich white woman would come to the jungle. The Indian pulled the rope free, coiled it expertly around his arm, placed it in the stern of the boat, and then started the engine. The sudden noise was shocking, splitting the forest's dawn silence, and some herons, like a slowly exploding cloud, scattered into the leaden sky.

Father Benedict shivered with cold but knew the heat would come soon enough, burning through the clouds to dry the damp trees and fill the air with an oppressive humidity which, combined with the gray sky and muddy river, made the days strangely slow and lackadaisical, more dream than reality. The boat roared and shuddered a little, then nosed through the rushes in the river shallows, moving away from the rotting wooden jetty at the edge of the missionary camp. It was not much of a camp, merely a random collection of thatched-roof log huts, containing living quarters for four, a first-aid hut, a small store, shower and ablutions, and another hut used for worship. The buildings were crammed together in a clearing by the river bank and dwarfed by the immense trees of the dark and inhospitable rain forest. Father Benedict watched the camp receding, growing smaller beneath the trees until it appeared to be sucked into the black-shadowed, rich green vegetation. He shivered.

thinking of God's immutable handiwork, and turned his eyes to the front.

"There has been talk about the woman?" he inquired of the Indian.

"Yes, Father." Mengrire was sitting in the stern, handling the boat's wooden rudder, the jungle behind him coming right to the edge of the river and sweeping away in both directions as far as the eye could see. "It is said that she has come to steal our images as other white men have done."

Mengrire, a Yanoama Indian, was also a Christian, but had not given up on the need for diplomatic deception. The ploy amused Father Benedict and brought a smile to his cracked lips, his heat-dried, middle-aged features wrinkling with good humor as his head, with its thick-curled black and gray hair, shook slowly from side to side.

"Stop talking like a savage, Mengrire. You can reserve that for Miss Wellman. You know damned well what a photograph is, so please don't act bewitched."

Mengrire was short and solid, his brown chest hairless beneath a loose white shirt, his muscular legs in pants cut to just below the knees, a hand-beaded sweatband around his head. Father Benedict glanced at him over his shoulder, saw his quick, fleeting grin, then turned his eyes back to the front, squinting into the brightening light.

"This woman is not a missionary," Mengrire said from behind him, "and we wonder why she comes to this place if not to save our poor souls."

"She's a photographer," Father Benedict said. "She takes photographs for an American magazine. She is coming to take photographs of us all and take them back to America."

"She does this for a living?"

"Yes, Mengrire."

"You white people are strange."

The engine of the small boat was quiet now, as it headed across the Rio Negro toward the Indian village on the opposite bank about three miles away. The water was humus-blackened, splashing around the rocking boat, flowing away like an enormous lake with dense jungle on either side, but receding until it was merely a thin line disappearing, many miles to the east, into an ominous, shadowy green haze. The water dark, the sky dark, the immense jungle also dark; Father Benedict, his thoughts still webbed with sleep, sensed that darkness inside him.

"This white woman will be a nuisance," he said, "but we must treat her kindly. Like Christians, Mengrire."

"Yes, Father. Like Christians."

Was the Indian slyly mocking him? It was very difficult to say. Mengrire's parents had been Christians and he had been brought up as a Christian, learning the white man's mores and speaking English with unusual fluency and understanding; yet for all that he was an Indian, still bound to certain traits, one of which was a sly sense of humor based on mute, natural arrogance. Father Benedict didn't mind it—in fact it gave him some comfort—and so, with a small smile on his lips, he let the comment pass.

It was cold and he shivered, looking forward to the heat, yet dreading it. He fumbled in the pocket of his light shirt and withdrew a cigarette. You could never get used to the Amazon; its extremes were too ridiculous: by day it was hot and humid, forcing even the jungle to silence, and by night it was as cold as a tomb—and like a tomb, without light. Father Benedict shivered again, struck a match, cupped his hands, lit the cigarette and threw the match into the river, watched it racing away from him. The water was uninviting, oppressively quiet, terribly dangerous, and he raised his gaze from its rippling, splashing surface and looked toward the far bank.

"Bloody hell," he said quietly.

He inhaled on the cigarette, hearing the river splashing around him, his gaze fixed on the solid forest at the opposite side of the river, his thoughts winging in languid loops back to the night he had endured without sleep.

Those damned drums again. And the mysterious lights above the jungle. He had lain in his hammock for hours, in the hut's almost total darkness, listening to the drums and to his own beating heart, until his curiosity overcame his fear and forced him into the night. The drums had seemed very close then—much closer than they actually were—and when he had looked at the northern sky, through a break in the forest canopy, he had seen the lights rising and falling in serene, sparkling grandeur.

"You are very quiet this morning," Mengrire said. "Your shoulders lean in deep thought."

"I'm glad to know that my leaning shoulders are so expressive, Mengrire. And no doubt you can also read my bloody mind."

"A priest should not use such bad words."

"No?"

"It does not encourage respect."

"You don't respect me, Mengrire?"

"I respect you, but others might not."

"My language may sometimes be strong, Mengrire, but it's not really bad."

"Some of the Indians think you blasphemous—"

"They are more Christian than I."

"—but I know that your tongue is much sharper than the feelings you hide."

Father Benedict smiled at that, blew some smoke to the warming breeze, felt the breeze blowing through his hair as it followed the river. *I still have my hair*, he thought. *It stays healthy while my body rots*. He automatically spread his fingers, pressed them down on his fleshy stomach, frustrated that the daytime's relentless heat did nothing to reduce his spreading waistline. Men, he well knew, were in truth as vain as women; even he, a middle-aged priest, was not immune to such vanity.

"Why is my friend, the priest, deep in thought?"

"I'm not deep in thought; I'm just tired."

"You could not sleep last night?"

"No."

"The drumming kept you awake?"

"Yes."

"When the Yano beat their drums in the night, no man can sleep soundly."

That was true enough—for both Indians and white men—and Father Benedict, remembering what he had seen and heard, felt the fear gently shaking him. He saw the green line of jungle far ahead, beyond the broad swathe of water, a gray mist drifting over it. He had been here for six months and had still not gotten used to it; the river was too immense, the jungle too alien, and not even his experiences in New Guinea could compare with its strangeness.

"You were awake also, Mengrire?"

"Yes, Father, I was awake. When the drums pound there is sickness and madness, and we have to be watchful."

"The sick become sicker?"

"And the mad uncontrollable. We Indians have learned to live with it, but we cannot ignore it."

Father Benedict closed his eyes, remembered the drums, the peculiar lights, wondered where conjecture merged into blasphemy, and then opened his eyes again. A broad expanse of dappled water and, beyond it, threatening jungle: *When the Yano beat their drums in the night, no man can sleep soundly. . . .*

"I don't believe the Yano exist," Father Benedict said, looking back over his shoulder at Mengrire and seeing his sly, mocking smile.

"No, Father? Then who plays the drums in the depths of the forest?"

"Some of your fellow Yanoama Indians."

"If ordinary Yanoama Indians were in that forest, you would have found them by now. Why have they never been found, Father? Because they are *not* ordinary, Father; they are the Yano who, though human in form, are possessed by the evil ones."

Mengrire was no longer smiling and his brown eyes were intense; and Father Benedict, seeing the sudden change in him, quickly turned away from him.

"And you call yourself a Christian, Mengrire."

"Yes, Father, I am a Christian. But do we Christians not believe in good and evil? The Yano are now pure evil, possessed by the powers of darkness, and because of that—because of the powers of darkness—they will never be found."

"And the lights?"

"I do not talk of the lights. I close my eyes when I see them."

Father Benedict sighed, shook his head from side to side, then flicked his cigarette over the side of the boat and watched the water devouring it. The river was vast and ominous, a dividing line through the jungle, about three miles wide here, a good seven miles wide elsewhere, its source a tiny brook in the snow-covered Andes of Peru, its mouth, pouring out one fifth of all of the earth's water, situated four thousand miles away, where the jungle met the Atlantic. Truly a mighty river, here quiet, elsewhere violent, hidden danger in every inch of its enormous length, and on the banks at both sides of it.

"Ah, Mengrire." Father Benedict sighed. "I'm tired. *Bloody* tired."

"I think not only from lack of sleep, Father. The tiredness springs from your spirit."

"If that is so, Mengrire, then I blame it on this place. This great river and the jungle combine to drive us poor white men crazy."

"The white men are crazy anyway. They were crazy before they came here. The white men have lost touch with their own spirit, and so cannot see clearly."

Father Benedict glanced up, surprised by the Indian's perception, but then just as quickly looked away again, feeling slightly embarrassed. There was truth in the Indian's words—much more than he cared to acknowledge—and his recent insomnia, which he had blamed on the Yano drums, on the haunting mystery of the lights that rose and fell over the distant jungle, kept him awake not only during those visitations but during the most peaceful nights. In truth, he was haunted not only by the mystery of the distant lights but by the shadows that now fell over his faith and chilled the hope that gave life.

He looked straight ahead and saw the riverbank coming closer, the Indian village taking shape beneath the tall trees and tangled liana. The forest canopy was very high, as much as a hundred and thirty feet, and the dark clouds drifted lugubriously above, as if threatening rain. The cold, which before had chilled his bones, was making way for the humid heat of the day.

"This whole place is cursed," Father Benedict said. "It's the devil's very own hiding place."

"So the priest believes in evil after all?"

"I'm a priest. That's *my* curse."

Something bumped against the boat, rocking it slightly before moving away, and he glanced down to see a caiman, an alligator, nosing silently through the rippling, mud-browned water in search of food. Death stalked the river constantly, often wearing a hideous countenance—death by the stingray, by the fearsome anaconda, by the piranha and crocodiles and giant catfish—and as he watched the caiman gliding away toward some rushes near the approaching bank he again felt that nature's horrors, equaled only by human atrocities, made a mockery of man's attempts to give a meaning to life—and thus, incidentally, also formed a challenge to his own, constantly wavering, Christian faith.

The caiman sank beneath the surface, the water rippling where it had been, and then the rushes in the shallows bent sideways as if alive and sprang back to their original positions as the alligator passed through them. Father Benedict watched carefully, both entranced and repelled, as the alligator emerged from the tall rushes and clambered up the narrow, slippery clay bank to disappear once more into the forest where some animal's fate was sealed. The priest shuddered at the thought, not wanting to dwell on life's realities, and then turned his head to stare at the Indian village that was now directly in front of him, set back from the bank in a clearing gouged out of the jungle.

It was quite a large village, consisting of half a dozen *malocas*, among which, squatting around smoldering fires, were mainly women and children. The *malocas* were large communal huts, each housing three or four whole families, each about three hundred feet in diameter and nearly a hundred feet high, made of palm fibers and dry leaves that had been woven onto a skeleton of poles and shaped rather like gigantic, bisected coconut shells upturned on the earth and grouped in a widespread semicircle beneath the towering trees.

The boat bumped against the riverbank, some water splashing into it, the tall rushes swaying gently all around them, disturbed by their presence. Mengrire turned the boat sideways, letting it rest against the wall of earth, and then quickly looped the rope around a pole that was thrusting up from the river's edge. He used the rope to pull them in, tying the boat close to the bank, and then jumped out and reached down with one hand to help the priest up. Father Benedict disembarked easily, not really needing the assistance, but aware that the young Indian thought him an old man, well past his prime. This thought merely amused him.

"*Obrigado*, Mengrire."

"*Nao tem de que*," the Indian replied, his Portuguese as good as his English, and then turned away and glanced across the clearing, his attention clearly drawn by the smell of cooking food.

Father Benedict followed his gaze and saw the Indians around the campfires, the women making manioc cakes or stirring pots of soup, some old men weaving baskets or sniffing *epena*, the children, mostly naked, simply playing or staring forlornly around them.

There was, undoubtedly, a destitute air about the camp, and Father Benedict knew why this was so: the true Yanoama Indians, with their Stone Age culture, had retreated from European encroachment to the few remaining untouched areas of the rain forest, north of the Amazon; those that had not done so had either been herded into tribal reserves or, as with the Indians of this particular camp, had been recruited to work on the white man's rubber plantations. In a proper Yanoama camp, the able men would have been out hunting, fishing, or making war with rival tribes, and the camp would have been vibrant with activity; instead, the men of this camp were mostly working in the surrounding rubber plantation—the despised Frank Poulson's plantation—and the desolate air of this camp sprang from their unspoken shame. These men did not fight, or hunt for animals, or fish. These men worked as *seringueiros*—rubber gatherers—for Frank Poulson, and their status was little more than that of slaves. Now, at the very thought of Frank Poulson, Father Benedict felt anger take hold.

"Damn that man," he said to himself. "There's no end to his evil."

Mengrire did not reply but started advancing into the clearing, heading straight for the Indians huddled around the fires beneath the towering *malocas*. Father Benedict instantly followed him, his stomach lurching uneasily as, deprived of the cooling rush of the river breeze, he began feeling the clammy humidity. With the heat there were many flies—the *borrachudos* and *piums*—and he had to swat them away as he walked, still not keen to be bitten. An old man stood up to greet him, rising slowly and none too steadily, his dark skin hanging in folds above his loincloth, his shoulders broad, his legs thin. He was wearing large, moon-shaped earrings and had a beaded band around one arm, his hair black and remarkably healthy, his chin beardless and angular. He did not smile when the priest stopped in front of him, but appeared to be friendly.

"It is early in the morning, priest," he said, speaking in Portuguese. "You are welcome, but why are you here so early?"

"You have a sick man," Father Benedict replied, "and his woman wants me to look at him."

"His woman should have called the witch doctor, not someone with white skin."

"The woman is a Christian."

"That will not help her man. The white turd who wants the rubber did great damage and you cannot undo it."

The white that the old man was obviously referring to was Frank Poulson, and even without knowing the details, Father Benedict felt his rage growing stronger.

"What damage was done?" he asked.

"The *seringueiro* was overworked and not given enough food. He spent many weeks in the forest, gathering the latex from the trees, and grew sick from exhaustion and hunger and returned before time. The white turd was very angry—and also crazy with his drinking— and instead of giving the *seringueiro* food, he took a stick to him. He beat the Indian badly and sent him home, and now the Indian is dying."

Father Benedict flushed with rage and had to look away from the old man, letting his gaze rest on the great wall of forest just beyond the thatched huts. That forest went for thousands of miles in every direction and never welcomed man's intrusion. It took little effort to imagine what it was like to work in there, but Frank Poulson, even knowing that, continued to send his rubber gatherers in for too long with too little, and this wasn't the first time that one of them had suffered the consequences. Thinking about it, Father Benedict grew angrier yet, glancing briefly over his shoulder to see the coffee-colored river flowing endlessly, a wall of green at the far side.

"Take me to see this man," he said, turning back to the old Indian. "Perhaps there is something I can do—and there is no harm in looking."

"You cannot help him, priest."

"I stand as much chance as your witch doctor."

"The only way you can help him—or any of the others—is to get rid of that white turd who debauches himself nightly in the big house."

Father Benedict grinned at that, amused by the old Indian's perspicacity. They walked side by side across the clearing, leaving Mengrire to have his breakfast, skirting the various groups huddled around the smoldering fires and eventually reaching one of the now towering *malocas*. If the palm-thatch structure had seemed large from outside, it seemed even larger once they were inside, surrounded by the circular walls and dwarfed by the high, dome-shaped roof that disappeared into the darkness directly above them. The interior of the hut was extremely dim—the opposite side was barely discernible—and the woven palm-leaf hammocks, enough for half a dozen families, were slung between poles that had been stuck in the ground around the larger, supporting poles of the *maloca*. Contrary to popular opinion, even the Indians did not like communal living, and the faces of those peering out of the gloom were unfriendly or lifeless.

Father Benedict followed the old Indian across the earthen floor toward the far side of the *maloca*, where they found the sick *seringueiro* lying in a hammock above the lower hammock that belonged to his wife. His wife was sitting on the floor close by, devoid of clothes, her dark skin flabby, rocking back and forth with her eyes shut, her lips offering a repetitive, mournful litany. Beside her, at a vertical loom, in the process of weaving a hammock, was her daughter, dark-haired, full-breasted, still in her early teens. She glanced up when Father Benedict stopped in front of her, then quickly, and demurely, lowered her eyes again. Father Benedict, with a blush on his cheeks, stood by the upper hammock and stared at her father, the ill *seringueiro*.

The man had obviously been beaten badly with a thick stick or length of bamboo. There were welt marks all over his body, as well as his arms and legs. However, if the beating that had been inflicted upon him had been uncommonly vicious, it did not in fact account for his terrible condition. His face was too thin, almost emaciated, his cheekbones clearly visible through his skin, his eyes much too large and wild with fever, his whole face slick with sweat. He seemed to be suffering from anemia, and when Father Benedict examined him by running his hands over his body, he was certain that his fingertips had felt the spleen's fatal enlargement.

"Does he sweat a lot?" he asked.

The man's wife, who had been rocking on the floor, now stopped and looked up at him.

"He burns and he freezes. First hot and then cold. Even when burning up he cries out that he is cold, and when I touch him I feel the death inside him, trying to claim him."

"Has he been taking his quinine?"

The woman stared at him, perplexed. "He sniffs his *epena*, nothing else."

"I'm not interested in his damnable drug; I want to know about medicine. Did he take his *quinine*?"

"He took only *epena*."

Father Benedict, exasperated, stepped away from the dying man, who had suddenly started groaning and rocking his head dementedly from side to side. His wife climbed to her feet, wiped the sweat from his forehead, crooned soothing words in their own language, and eventually managed to calm him.

"He is dying," she said to Father Benedict, again speaking in Portuguese. "When he dies, if we do not obey his murderer, we will all suffer."

Father Benedict, ashamed to look at her, lowered his gaze and studied her daughter, then quickly returned his gaze to the older woman. There was no doubt that her husband was dying—and now her grief seemed to swallow him.

"The beating was bad," he said, "but not fatal. It is the *malaria* that is killing your husband. Why in God's name did he not take his quinine before entering the forest? You understand? *Medicine!*"

The woman shook her head in a negative gesture, her dark eyes blind with grief. "No medicine," she said. "The white chief gave him no more than the stick that opened his skin to the bone. No medicine. Just pain and hunger!''

Her brown eyes were large and glittering, floating before him in the gloom, wrapping their grief around him and drawing him in through his anger and shame. The shame he felt was for Frank Poulson, for other white men just like him; and though he refused to articulate it, for his own, secret self.

''I'm sorry.'' His own voice sounded mechanical and far away. ''I'm sorry, but I'm afraid there is little I can do. I will send for some medicine and arrange for transportation to a hospital—but I'm bound to say I think it is too late.''

''No hospital! He will not die with white men! He will die in this house, in this *maloca*, and feed the earth of the forest.''

''You are a Christian! Your husband is a Christian! He must die like a Christian!''

''No more! No Christians! We play your game no longer! My husband, myself, other Indians, we play your game, because we know that if we do not make you smile we will not go unpunished. We are not Christians, priest! We are Indians—Yanoama! We accepted your God because you told us to do so, and because we needed your protection from the rubber barons. But what good did that do us? What good did it do my husband? He was sent into the jungle, without food or your precious medicine, and then, when he hungered and turned sick, the drunken white man just beat him. Can you protect us from that, priest? Have you *ever* protected us? And can you protect our daughters''—she jabbed her finger at the kneeling girl—''when that beast who tries to get power from rubber comes and steals them away from us? You know what he does, priest! He shames our daughters and then disowns them! And you, priest—you and your fellow Christians—you simply tell us you're sorry. Well, priest, keep your God from my husband's grave; he will die like an Indian!''

The woman spat at his feet and then turned away from him, her naked body twisting in the gloom and curving, as if in slow motion, over the husband who was slowly dying in the swinging hammock. Father Benedict was startled, then felt wounded and humiliated, and his eyes, with a will of their own, turned to stare at the girl. She was getting to her feet, her body well-fleshed and voluptuous, and then her eyes, ignoring death to lure him in, floated out of his vision. He felt numb and unreal but had the urge to say something, and his jaw opened and closed as his brain raced, stumbling into a silence. He

raised his fist and coughed into it, squinted into the dim light, heard
the wailing of the stricken woman, saw her rocking on her husband's
body, that body which, diseased and brutalized, was surely expiring.

"You must understand," he heard himself saying. "I cannot—"

His proposed apology got no further, cut short by the woman's
wailing and, more bizarrely, by the sudden, staccato, high-pitched
chanting of the old Indian who had led him here. Father Benedict
stepped back a little, staring at the old Indian's raucous mourning, at
the woman hanging over her husband, at the husband as he swung in
the hammock beneath the weight of his wife as if, at the quickening
approach of death, they were making love for the last time. Then,
his heart racing, the chanting and wailing filling his head, he turned
and hurried out of the enormous hut and let the morning light dazzle
him.

It was not all that bright, but his eyes were indeed dazzled,
appreciating the sudden release from the dim light of the hut's
interior and trying to adjust to the shocking expansiveness of river
and sky. He blinked and rubbed his eyes, blinked again and then
walked on, wending his way between the warm, smoldering fires
and the Indians squatting around them. Their very presence was
disorienting, defying sense and credibility: a world war had just
ended—a splitting atom had scorched the heavens—and here, as if
guns and tanks had never existed, as if Hiroshima and Nagaski were
simply dreams of a distant future, these Indians still squatted in the
dirt, their spirits tuned to the Stone Age.

Father Benedict felt suffocated, the river breeze now filled with
heat, and was glad when he reached the murmuring water, where the
air was much cooler. He swatted stinging flies from his face, saw
the biting ants on his boots, remembered the alligator gliding out of
the river and crawling up the clay bank. He shuddered, thinking of
death, of the hideous realities of the life preceding it, and wondered
how to reconcile his faith with his very mortal, unsteady thoughts.

"O my God, I cry in the daytime, but thou hearest not."

The sound of his own voice startled him, making him glance up,
embarrassed, and he saw Mengrire kneeling in the boat, untying the
rope from the post. The young girl from the hut was nearby, sitting
casually on the riverbank, one leg raised, her cheek resting on the
knee, her naked skin etched in bronze. She was not staring at
Mengrire but at him, the white priest, and he knew that she did not
fully understand death—not as something terribly final—but would
understand pain and humiliation if Frank Poulson came for her.

Frank Poulson: an evil bastard. Presuming that evil actually existed. Or if evil did not exist, a former good man corrupted. Father Benedict did not feel charitable and let the anger shake his soul, then, in the midst of his anger, thought of Alex, Frank Poulson's son.

The beauty of innocence. To be corrupted and destroyed? As that man, that degenerate, corrupted and destroyed all he touched.

I am a priest, Father Benedict thought. He affirmed this fact as he studied the girl. She was naked, and the river flowed past her and took his senses away with it. How, indeed, had he helped her father? And in truth, how would he help her? Even now, as he looked at her young body, he felt nothing but anguish. Father Benedict breathed deeply, tore his eyes away from the girl, saw Mengrire standing up in the boat, and managed to glare fiercely at him.

"Don't just stand there, you Christian savage," he said, trying to make a joke of it. "Stretch out your hand and help me aboard. We can do no good here."

The Indian, a true Christian, smiled and stretched out his hand.

2

"You look tired," Father Symonds said, glancing up from the piles of clothing that had been placed neatly around the suitcase on the bed.

"That's what Mengrire told me," Father Benedict replied, stepping fully into the other priest's room and sitting down wearily in a chair behind a small wooden table. "However, Mengrire, clever Indian, thinks my tiredness is of the soul, not of the flesh."

Father Symonds smiled gently. He had a round, almost babyish face, his cheeks as pink as his bald head, his blue eyes, with their good-humored crow's-feet, radiating true warmth. "All the Indians are philosophers," he said, "and think our souls are quite visible. Do you think he was right?"

"No, I'm just tired. It was those damned drums again. I spent half the night on the verandah, smoking cigarettes and studying those strange lights that no one can explain."

"You smoke cigarettes and swear," Father Symonds replied, "which makes you a rather unusual priest, if not a respectable one."

"Do you think I'm a good priest?"

"I think you *could* be. I'm not sure that you are." The older man smiled again, his eyes wrinkling with good-natured mockery; then he sighed and stared down at the bed, examining the clothes still to be packed. "Anyway," he continued, "you should not think of those lights. As a Christian, you must simply ignore them and get on with your work."

"Do you mind if I smoke?"

"No."

Father Benedict lit a cigarette and inhaled with gratitude, realizing that he still hadn't eaten, but not feeling hungry. He blew the smoke into the gloomy air, squinting through it at his fellow priest, deeply saddened that he was leaving this very day to take the boat back to England. Now, watching his small, plump, elderly friend abstractedly putting more clothes into his suitcase, Father Benedict again felt desolated, as he had on the river.

"I've only been here for six months," he said, "but you've been here for fifteen years. It just doesn't seem real that you're actually leaving. I still can't quite accept it."

"You'll get used to it soon enough, Paul. And you'll be better off without me. I'm getting too old for this jungle—I'll soon be needing walking sticks—and I think it will be safer for us both if I tend my garden in England."

Father Benedict, finding it difficult to visualize his old friend in an English garden, inhaled on his cigarette and stared through the mesh wire of the window that looked out on the lush green of the rain forest. Whether forest or jungle it always disturbed him slightly, making him feel that he was living a dream in an alien landscape. Here everything was giant-sized—to some, horrifically so—and right now, as he gazed through the insect-covered mesh wire, he saw the great lengths of liana hanging in loops from the towering trees, forming bizarre, surrealistic limbs that embraced the massive treetrunks and webbed the grassy ground in between like numerous gigantic, inert serpents. It was certainly not like an English garden, nor like any forest he had ever known, and the various life forms in there, and the countless ways in which those life forms died, could be viewed as nothing less than a nightmare beyond human imagining. Were all these creatures God's creatures also? If so, what could He be like? And how could the jungle's ferocity, in truth matched only by human cruelty, be accepted as a manifestation of His wisdom and goodness? Father Benedict blew some smoke out, watched it circling before his eyes, then turned his gaze away from the forest to his old friend. The other priest was still by his bed, putting his clothes in the suitcase.

"Sometimes," Father Benedict said, "I wish I were back in New Guinea. At least the Japanese didn't frighten me like this bloody place does."

"The Amazon frightens you?"

"Yes, I think so. In some way I can't define. Lately I've been very disoriented, and have real trouble sleeping."

"I told you: you must ignore the strange lights. You must not let them prey on you."

"How can one ignore them? They're *there*. I mean, you can't keep your eyes off the sky when you know that they're *there*—

lights rising and falling—lights whose source and nature are unknown and which should not, in rational terms, exist.''

"I know what's going on inside you, Paul: you want to take an expedition into the jungle to find the source of those lights.''

"I confess, I am sometimes tempted.''

"Don't be tempted, Paul. You would be wasting your time. For a start, you would not get any natives to go with you, since all of them are frightened of the Yano, whether or not those creatures actually exist. As for making the journey yourself, there is no question that you would never return, since you would either get lost, get drowned in a swamp or quicksands, get yourself poisoned or eaten by one of the jungle's many predatory creatures, or failing all that, be killed by the reportedly murderous Indians who play the drums.''

"The Yano.''

"Some strange Indian tribe, certainly; let's call them that for now. No matter: whoever they are, they would almost certainly kill you.''

"Do you believe what the Yanoama believe about the lights?''

"No, Paul, I do not—and neither, as a Christian, should you—so, please, let us talk no more about it.''

Father Symonds raised his head just long enough to deliver a firm, steady gaze, and then lowered it and resumed his packing. Sighing, first crossing his legs and then uncrossing them, Father Benedict inhaled on his cigarette, blew smoke across the table, then stood up and stared out through the window at the surrounding rain forest. Little sunlight penetrated, and it was gloomy beneath the trees. Everything was damp and remained so, perpetually rotting and being renewed in a natural cycle of birth and death.

"Anyway,'' Father Symonds said behind him, "you will not be alone for long. My replacement arrives in a month. In the meantime, since she will be staying here for that same period, the American woman, the photographer from *National Geographic*, can stay in this room.''

Father Benedict, aware of the rising humidity, turned away from the many insects trapped and dying in the mesh wire of the window and glanced first at his fellow priest, then at the dimly lit room in which he had lived. It was a spartan room, the walls made of forest logs, a hammock stretched between one wall and a pole thrusting up from the boarded floor, a mosquito net above the hammock and another above the crudely made single bed upon which the older priest's suitcase was now resting. Otherwise, the room contained only the small wooden table at which Father Benedict had been sitting, a couple of dilapidated wooden chairs, open shelves on the walls for clothing, books, and sundries, and a couple of oil lamps for illumination. It was not, to Father Benedict's mind, the sort of abode to which a woman from Hollywood would readily accommodate herself.

"I hope this woman doesn't turn out to be a nuisance," he said.

"Why should she be a nuisance?" Father Symonds replied, pressing the clothes down and then closing the lid of his suitcase.

"*Any* white woman would be a nuisance in this particular area— and a woman from New York via Hollywood even more so."

"This woman is a *professional* photographer, Paul. I'm sure she's traveled a lot."

"Being well-traveled, particularly as Americans travel, does not make one suited to this jungle. All Americans, whether well-traveled or not, like airconditioning, prepackaged food, and their fellow Americans. An exaggeration, certainly, but it's reasonably close to the truth. And frankly, now that you're leaving, I could happily do without having to act as a guide for a photojournalist who will clearly want to show up the Indians for what they are not."

"You judge the woman before she has even arrived, Paul. She is coming here for a month to take some photographs and write an article, after which she will be returning to America. It isn't the first such occasion and it certainly won't be the last, and I'm sure that the woman, whether from Hollywood or not, will be able to look after herself. I think, dear Paul, that the celibate life is making you crusty."

It was a good-natured remark, offered with a gentle smile, but Father Benedict, uncomfortably aware of the truth of it, had to hide his embarrassment.

"Bloody great," he said. "My good friend's final shot is that I'm a woman-hater. Revelation is painful."

He shook his head and grinned sardonically, inhaled on his cigarette, blew a few smoke rings into the air, and watched them slowly dissolving. . . . Yes: dissolving. Like his life: gradually dissolving. A spasm of dread whipped through him, unexpected and disturbing, casting up from some dungeon of his mind some long-buried, forgotten fears. His good friend, Father Symonds, was sixty years of age, but still had the face of a child, ebullient and curious; while he, Paul Benedict, a mere forty, already felt the draining of energy and enthusiasm that normally comes in the twilight years. He was tired of the jungle, tired of living like a primitive, possibly even tired of being a priest . . . and the last thought, verging on blasphemy, was growing stronger each day. In truth, what he resented was the possibility that he had not lived a real life.

"So," Father Symonds said, tightening the last strap on his suitcase and then pressing his fingers into his spine as he straightened his shoulders, "I am ready to go."

"What arrangements have you made for leaving?"

"Are you coming with me?"

"Yes."

"I've said good-bye to everyone except a few friends on Frank Poulson's plantation. I thought we could drive there, shake a few hands, and then drive back this way and on to Manaus. Is that all right with you?"

"That's more than all right: I want to have words with that bastard Poulson."

"Ah, you had a bad time in the Indian camp."

"Yes."

"Let's have breakfast."

Father Benedict threw his cigarette on the earthen floor and stomped upon it. Together, the men left the hut and walked across the flat earth of the mission camp, the great river making a rushing sound to their right, the huts of the modest camp on their left, below the towering trees. They did not walk very far but felt the heat nonetheless.

The mission camp's few wooden buildings were incongruous in the forest's green splendor. Naked Indian children were playing freely, chasing frightened ducks and geese, while their parents, most wearing shirts and trousers or shabby dresses, milled around the entrance to the medical hut, waiting for treatment. Behind the medical hut was the quiet of the rain forest, insuring that there was no breeze to temper the clinging heat.

The older priest entered the mess hut and Father Benedict followed him in, ducking his head as he stepped through the low door. It was cooler inside, but the flies were just as numerous as outside, buzzing hungrily over the long wooden table containing their breakfast: a generous selection of melons, mangoes, papaya, and pineapple, crusty white bread with a syrup made from *assai* berries, a porridge of plantains, and two jars containing *laranja* and *maracuja*—all of it, in one way or another, taken straight from the forest.

Father Benedict, unable to forget his spreading waistline, settled for two large slices of melon and some rich, thick black coffee, then sat down at a small trestle table, facing the other priest. He sighed, picked up his knife and fork, and cut into the melon.

"You're not eating?" he said to Father Symonds.

"No," his friend replied. "To tell the truth, I'm feeling a little tense, and my stomach is upset."

"Because you're leaving?"

"Yes. Because this time it's final. Perhaps because retirement is a sign that the curtain is coming down."

"Rubbish," Father Benedict said, forking some melon into his mouth. "You've a lot of years left in you yet, so don't talk like a dying man."

The older priest smiled, accepting the reprimand. "I stand corrected," he said. "And of course you're absolutely right: the curtain has not yet come down, though I make my excuses. The truth, dear friend, is that I've already been here too long, and now the very thought of home frightens me—as if I no longer belong there. And there *is* some truth in that: this place turns one into a primitive. What's a fish knife to a man who licks his fingers? And can I handle a teacup?"

He smiled at his own doubts, but Father Benedict shifted uneasily, feeling strongly that there was more truth to that statement than his old friend realized. The mission priest was almost a castaway, living a primitive life, so far removed from society and the Church itself that the commonplace rites of civilization were all too easily lost. China teacups and fish knives were indeed long lost luxuries, but much greater was the loss of mental stimulation and the mores of cultivated social life. Father Benedict was not a gentleman—he had manners, but lacked etiquette—yet he felt, more and more, as each passing week drained him, that the little civilized refinements he possessed were being eroded in this jungle, worn away through lack of discipline and enforced order, destroyed by pure lethargy. The jungle's silence drained the mind, the empty mind sapped the will, and in time, as the distance between past and present increased, that modest history which at least offered identity vaporized in the sweltering gloom. Father Benedict hated the place—he was allowed to; it was his penance—and yearned quietly to pack his own suitcase and leave with his fellow priest.

"English tea and muffins," he said. "I'm sure you'll learn to live with it. As for fish, after fifteen years here I should think you've had quite enough of it. No fish, no fish knives to deal with, so there's nothing to worry about." He sliced up some more melon and started digging out the seeds, trying to ignore the flies buzzing around his head in pursuit of his sweat. "But does it really feel that strange to be going back after all these years?"

"Yes, I'm afraid it does. I'm not too happy about it. I mean, I *want* to go back, but I'm not sure just what I'm returning to. Fifteen years is a long time; fifteen years here, even longer. I don't know that I can settle back in England and simply tend to my garden. A family might help—but then I have no family left—and perhaps, in that small cottage in Hertfordshire, I'll simply become a recluse." His blue eyes, normally twinkling with good humor, were now very serious, his brow furrowed, his lips straight. "Be very careful of that," he said. "Don't let this place completely change you. You've only been here six months, yet already you can't sleep at nights, your ears tuned to the jungle. This is a very strange place, Paul. It isn't just another jungle. It is not like New Guinea, nor like any other place on earth, and you must learn to close your ears and eyes to what you don't understand."

"You mean the lights that rise and fall over the interior? Those, and the drums of the Yano Indians?"

"Who may or may not exist," Father Symonds replied. "Yes, I mean the drums—which may be played by some unknown tribe, if not the mysterious Yano—and the lights, which though seeming to defy logic, may yet be explicable as atmospheric phenomena. I mean those—but not only those." He finished his coffee, wiped his lips with his fingers, stood up and clasped his hands behind his back, and then went to the door of the hut to look out at the river. Beams of sunlight, edging around the forest clearing, slanted over his portly frame. "Something happens to us white men when we stay here too long," he said. "We rot in mind and body, go native or simply mad; sometimes compensate for boredom and loss of identity by embracing sin as our closest friend."

"Like Frank Poulson?"

"Yes, Paul." Father Symonds sighed loudly, as if emphasizing despair, then turned back to face the interior of the room but remained in the doorway. The light, spraying out around his body, rendered his face a black mask. "The man is corrupt, Paul. Perhaps irredeemably so. And yet once upon a time, not so long ago, he actually seemed halfway decent. It was this place that changed him, wrapping its evil web around him, robbing him of every belief and turning him into a devil. Believe me, this place can do that; by my faith I would swear to it." The older priest shuddered a little, as if caught in a sudden chill. "So," he said, stepping forward, his kindly face reappearing, beads of sweat gleaming brightly on his bald head as he sat down again, "what happened this morning?"

Father Benedict, no longer hungry, slid his plate away from him, swiped at the flies buzzing around his head, then had a sip of his coffee. He wiped his lips with the back of his clenched fist and then reached into his pocket. "You've just named the bastard," he said. "It's Frank Poulson again." He took a cigarette from his packet, lit it and inhaled, blew the smoke over the buzzing flies, and observed their panic with pleasure. "Another *seringueiro* is dying right this minute—and there's no doubt who caused it." He recounted the story of his visit to the Indian camp across the river, noting, as he did so, the distaste on his old friend's face and feeling his own anger rising again. "I'll have to do something," he finished, inhaling deeply, blowing the smoke out. "And I'll start by seeing Poulson. I'm not going to stand by any longer while that bastard, without reason or rhyme, brutalizes his workers. If he doesn't agree to instantly change his ways, I'll go to higher authority."

"*What* higher authority? There *is* no higher authority. Even the Church has no authority in this place, as already you know. By all means speak to him, but do not expect much; most likely he will just laugh in your face and throw you off his plantation. No one cares about the Indians, Paul. The Church can only do so much. We can say what we want to Frank Poulson, but beyond that we're helpless. And with particular regard to Poulson, our words fall on deaf ears."

"And what when the Indian actually dies? Can we not call it murder?"

The older priest sighed. "Yes, Paul, we can call it murder—but that won't get us anywhere with authorities who will call it an accident. Frank Poulson knows that the authorities are on his side, so no matter how much it disgusts us, we are helpless."

Father Benedict felt the sting of his own impotence, the rancid bile of defeat, remembering the angry words of the Indian woman, her accusations unanswerable. "What are we doing here?" he asked, "if we have no power to act? Is there any point in being here at all, or are we fooling ourselves?"

"The Church does what it can, but must accept its limitations. The world cannot be changed overnight—least of all this particular world with its own obscene rules." The blue eyes looked directly at Father Benedict, gentle yet probing. "But is that what you think, Paul? That you are being wasted here? That because the Church cannot move mountains, it should not even try? If so, then indeed you lack faith of the most fundamental kind."

"I think you have always sensed that in me."

"Yes, Paul, I have."

The candid blue eyes were staring directly and steadily at him, and Father Benedict inhaled on his cigarette, feeling slightly ashamed.

"Maybe you're right." he said. "Perhaps I'm not a good priest. My faith wavers, and I feel like a hypocrite when I try to voice principles. It's like talking into a mirror: the image only reflects one's own words; and in that sense, when I get angry, when I let my rage lead me, when I despise Frank Poulson for his brutal mistreatment of the Indians, I can't do so without feeling a certain confusion over my motives."

"I'm not sure I understand, Paul."

"Frank Poulson has, at least indirectly, killed more than this one Indian. He represents that genocidal movement of which we are possibly a part—even if with the very best of intentions."

"By 'we' do you mean the Church?"

"Yes." Father Benedict, hearing his own weary sigh, suddenly felt considerably older than he actually was. "As we both know, the decline of the Indians *and* their way of life has been caused, in the main, by a threat to which they simply cannot adapt: us white men. First the sixteenth-century Spanish, then the Portuguese conquistadors, bringing firearms, diseases, and Christianity, none of which, we must reluctantly agree, were mercifully inclined. When the Indians were not being killed off by the firearms, they were being wiped out by smallpox, measles, the common cold, and syphilis, while many of the survivors were tortured and brutalized as slaves. Christianity, on the other hand, had its own particular effect: destroying the native culture of those who survived physically, and thus encouraging the death of their spirit. . . . Can you now understand why I have doubts? Even we, with our good intentions, may be contributing to the decline—or disappearance—of the Indians' way of life; by our presence, however much we respect the Indians' traditions, we constitute a very real force for change—a change that could, alas, lead to obliteration. Frank Poulson, then, is not the only criminal; we have all been collaborators."

He inhaled on his cigarette, feeling embarrassed and trying to hide it, then blew a cloud of smoke at the circling flies and stubbed the cigarette out. A line of ants crossed the table, oblivious to human doubt, moving through pools of shadow and light on the untreated wood.

Father Symonds clasped his hands, sliding his thumbs beneath his chin, his right eyebrow raised in a questioning manner, his smile almost invisible.

"To err is human," he said. "And the Church is still human. It exists to do God's work—to bridge the sacred and the profane—but can only do that work through human beings, who by their nature are fallible."

"I know that, Michael. I accept it."

"Then why doubt your faith simply because your church is fallible? And why doubt yourself simply because you cannot judge your fellow man without also passing judgment on yourself? It is not a sin to question your own motives; blind acceptance is worse."

Father Benedict nodded, appreciating his old friend's kindness, but sensible words could not heal the wounds scarring his faith. His doubts went too deep for that, were now too old to be subdued, and their genesis lay far back in that time between childhood and youth. He wanted to tell his friend about it, perhaps pass it on, but this moment, with his friend's sad departure imminent, just seemed like the wrong time.

"And Frank Poulson?"

"Have no doubts, Paul. Your judgment is quite correct. The man is corrupt and growing worse, ruining all he touches. I understand your anger, and that it stems from your concern: it is not only the Indians that you care for, but Frank Poulson's son."

"We've grown close," Father Benedict said.

"I know. And I'm pleased. You treat Alex almost like your own son, and that's something he needs." Father Symonds scratched his bald head, pressed his fingers down upon it, shook it in an almost comic manner, then pursed his lips and let air out. "Such a tragedy it was," he said, "to lose his mother when he was born; yet a miracle that the father is such a brute and the boy magically good-natured."

"Magically good-natured—*and* magical."

"Ah, yes, that also." The older priest stood up, removing his hand from his sweating bald head; he swatted abstractedly at the flies and glanced vaguely around him. It was gloomy in the dining hut, a shaft of sunlight falling obliquely, cutting a thin line through dark shadow and illuminating mosquitoes in the motes of dust that seemed to drift endlessly. "He was a beautiful child," he said.

"Always smiling, at peace. The wife of old Peruche, then alive, stood in for his mother. A large woman, always merry, she loved the boy as her own, and when she died, when Alex was six years old, it was a sad day for all of us. Yet strangely, he was unaffected. He just drew closer to Peruche. And that wily old bird, whether he's a witch doctor or not, led Alex gently through childhood. Yes, there's something magical about the boy—and I don't mean his strange powers."

"I thought you would have disapproved of those."

Father Symonds shrugged. "Not really," he said. "His gifts are of a very minor order—and tempered with sweetness."

"They are magical nonetheless."

"But not necessarily supernatural. The Indians, like certain animals, have retained powers which we white men lost long ago; and Alex, under the wing of old Peruche, is very much like an Indian."

"And you still don't disapprove?"

"I chose to ignore it. Which perhaps is *my* cowardice." Father Symonds smiled and shrugged, raising his hands in a begging gesture. "After a lifetime of observation, there are questions that one simply avoids in case the senses betray one. Leave it only that I think of Alex as a very remarkable and lovely boy, and that I understand only too well your urge to protect him. The sadness, of course, is that he most needs protecting from his own father."

Sensing that his friend was preparing to leave, Father Benedict pushed his chair back and stood up, pressing his hands into the small of his back and stretching his spine. "Damn," he said. "I'm not young anymore, and my bones creak and ache."

"A daily swim in the river is what you need. The piranhas would love you."

Father Benedict smiled at that, briefly warmed by the humor, but as they both walked toward the exit, where the shaft of sunlight poured in obliquely, he thought of the man dying across the river because of Frank Poulson. Should he ignore what was happening? Should he accept the status quo? Or should he, representing the Church, take a stand on the matter? His more experienced friend leaned forward, ducked his head, and left the hut, and Father Benedict, undecided and lacking faith, slowly followed him out. The sun was high in the sky, blazing down between scattered clouds, the light fanning around the clouds and glittering like silver on the river's black surface. Father Benedict rubbed his eyes, squinted into the dazzling brightness, then focused on his short, bald-headed friend whose kindly face gave him hope. He was immediately invigorated, filled with unexpected conviction, and suddenly felt that all his fears would fall away if he took positive action.

"So, my son," Father Symonds said, "it is time I was leaving."

"You've said good-bye to everyone here?"

"Everyone. And I can't stand repeating myself."

"Fine. Let's get going."

Father Symonds moved away, heading toward his own hut, murmuring that he would fetch his suitcase and then come straight back. Father Benedict smiled and nodded. He heard the rustling of foliage, turned his head, and saw the Indian, Mengrire, walking urgently toward him. Mengrire stopped in front of him, pointing one finger across the river; Father Benedict looked across that enormous expanse of dappled water and saw a very thin plume of smoke spiraling above the far bank.

"It is a sign," Mengrire said softly. "The *seringueiro* has died."

3

"It is going to rain," Mengrire said, sitting stiff-backed on the driver's seat, his hands firmly on the steering wheel as he let the wind carry his words back to them. "I can feel it in the coldness of the air. It will rain very soon." The two priests, sitting close together in the back of the Jeep as it bounced and rattled along the crude track, merely glanced at one another but said nothing, both aware that Mengrire's words disguised the anger he undoubtedly felt about the Indian's death. They had just left the mission camp and were heading for Frank Poulson's plantation, the gloom deepening all around them as the forest became more dense, the lower branches of the trees meeting above their heads and cutting the sunlight out.

Father Benedict glanced about him, studying the forest, seeing little, helplessly gazing inward at himself and his conflicting emotions. The death of the Indian, though expected, had still badly shocked him, brutally destroying his brief elation and resurrecting his former doubts. He wiped sweat from his face, not feeling the cold that Mengrire had mentioned, and looked straight ahead at the crude track that snaked through the foliage. The few striations of light were dimming, letting the gray shadows blacken, while the clamor of the Jeep, the tortured banging of the gearshift, punctuated the silence of the forest like some alien, metallic beast.

The forest slept during the day, its teeming life well camouflaged, but Father Benedict, understanding what the lush greenery hid, could not forget the terrible spectacle of pain and death enacted nightly within it and was convinced that the jungle, which was cruel beyond belief, was a microcosm of all life on earth, including the history of man. This was not a Christian attitude—quite the opposite, in fact—but it was, increasingly, one that haunted his dreams and tormented his waking hours.

Feeling guilty and unworthy, degraded by his own reasoning, he glanced sideways at Father Symonds's profile with its flushed, blue-veined cheeks, slightly bulbous nose, and bald head rising out of shrinking hair like an egg in a bird's nest. His old friend's eyes were closed, his head held back to catch the breeze, and his lips were curved in a hint of a smile, part good-humored, part sad. Father Benedict felt anger again, thinking of Poulson and the dead Indian, even angrier that the death should have occurred the day his good friend was leaving.

"I'm sorry it had to happen today of all days," he said. "Right now—and God forgive me for saying it—I could kill that bastard Frank Poulson."

"It's a tragedy that it should happen at all, Paul; that it should have happened today of all days has nothing to do with it."

"I think you know what I meant, Michael."

"Yes, Paul, and I appreciate it—but you really shouldn't be concerned for me, but for that poor Indian's family."

"I'll look after them, of course."

"And that's all you can do. There's no point in brooding further about it; change comes slowly but surely."

Father Benedict was doubtful about that, as with most things these days. "I promise you," he said, "I'll do something. I won't let this thing rest."

Father Symonds opened his eyes to stare at him, smiling more broadly and shrugging. "Do as you wish, Paul," he said. "My time here is over."

"That doesn't sound very encouraging."

"It was not intended as such. I merely reiterate that no matter what you feel, you can probably do little."

"He virtually murdered that Indian."

"By all means try to do something, Paul, but do not expect justice. Justice, in this case, can only come from God, when He feels it is time. In the meantime, if you have your confrontation with Frank Poulson, you may at least unburden your conscience and sleep better at nights."

Father Benedict was startled, wondering what his friend meant. "*My* conscience? Why bring *my* conscience into this? We are talking about the activities of Frank Poulson, not of my minor sins."

Father Symonds stared at him, unperturbed, his smile gentle. "You want challenges, Paul. You want issues to wrestle with. You want them much more than you would were your heart truly peaceful. I accept your anger over this crime, and your general contempt for Frank Poulson, and your despair over the limitations of the Church in this uncivilized place—I accept that your feelings are sincere and the causes are real enough. Yet you brood too much, Paul, concentrating too much on negatives, and I sense that your lack of faith, your increasing cynicism, springs not from what you witness around you, but from your own, secret nature. Your anger stands like a mirror before you, casting back your reflection. It's your own sins you fear.''

Shocked by that remark, uncomfortably aware of the truth in it, Father Benedict averted his gaze from his old friend and watched the forest slip past him: a dark and somber sight, few flowers brightening the light-starved soil. Surveying that gloom, still stinging from his friend's perceptiveness, Father Benedict felt that he was staring into the darkness of his own discontented soul.

"You told me it was no sin to doubt," he said eventually, "and yet that is my greatest fear.''

"You fear your own lack of faith?''

"Yes.''

"Why?''

"Because it gets worse every day, making me feel like a hypocrite.''

"Hypocrisy has nothing to do with it, Paul; you are suffering what most decent men must suffer at some time or other: the loss of emotional energy and conviction, of a sense of direction. *And thy life shall hang in doubt before thee; and thou shalt fear day and night. . . . In the morning thou shalt say, Would God it were even! And at even thou shalt say, Would God it were morning!* Is that not the case in this instance, Paul?''

"Deuteronomy. Yes." Father Benedict smiled uneasily, pleased that his friend understood, displeased that the truth in what he said could so easily disturb him. "That, certainly, is what I feel, but it's more than a midlife crisis; I've had such feelings ever since I joined the ministry, and the Amazon, its silence and strangeness, has simply forced me to think more about them.''

He studied the back of Mengrire's head, watching the Indian's long hair blowing, his dark hands sliding around the steering wheel as the Jeep bounced and rattled. Here: the Amazon. And before that: New Guinea. And before that, in childhood and adolescence, the desert plains of Australia. A single street through a small town, a red dust drifting lazily, people frozen in pools of shadow on their porches, the road shimmering in heat waves. One school and one church, both made out of clapboard, swinging doors on the bar of the one hotel where the sheepshearers gathered. The days were bright and long, filled with silence and silhouettes, and his parents, guarding the doors of the small church, were the ghosts of his history. His father, a stern man; his mother, the obedient wife; both preserved in the fine gauze of his memory and impressed on his spirit. Had they loved him? He didn't know. Only their teachings remained with him. His father had pushed him unswervingly toward the ministry, and then shamed him, when he was still a very insecure young man, into going to work for the aboriginal mission stations. A good son, he had done so, sometimes actually imagining he meant it; but eventually, when the truth was forced upon him, he had viewed his own life as lost.

"If being in the Amazon disturbs you so much," Father Symonds said, "why did you volunteer to come here? And indeed, why have you spent so many years working in similar places?"

Mengrire mangled the gears and the Jeep slowed down dramatically, banged into a liana trailing across the track, then bounced over it and crashed back down again and moved on, growling painfully. Father Benedict, holding on to his seat, felt a chill in the air.

"A good question," he said, "and one that bothers me a lot. Time plays tricks with our memories—we often reinvent our past— but I think I left Australia for New Guinea to get away from my father. He was a decent man, I suppose, but I mostly remember his sternness, his humorless and unbending theology, his puritanical zeal. Please forgive the violins, but my childhood *was* lonely. My mother, either respectful or actually in fear of my father, was a gentle but uncommunicative woman who, though treating me kindly and with care, showed me little emotion. As for my father, he was Victorian, proud of me but hiding his warmth, a disciplinarian with narrow views of right and wrong, of honor and duty. He instilled such virtues in me, fiercely protecting me from all evil, even protecting me from the common mischiefs of other children by keeping most at a distance. So I was fairly lonely—and influenced only by my parents; and even later, as a young man, studying theology in a Brisbane college, I observed my father going to very great lengths to keep me free from corruption. *Corruption*—his word, describing everything unchristian, most particularly those my own age who, no matter how decent, did not announce their faith in ringing tones or go to church and confession. Naturally, then, my friendships were few—and my influences likewise; my father's world was the world that I emotionally and intellectually inherited, and because of that, when I was a young man, I never truly felt the call but simply entered the Church by following the path laid down by him.''

The forest was now much darker, the modest sunlight disappearing, and he heard the distant rumbling of thunder punctuating the spasmodic coughing of the untuned Jeep. He felt a little unreal, the deepening gloom dissolving his senses, while his past, in the form of ghostly images, came alive in his mind: the theological college in Brisbane, sunlight pouring into the gloom, his own room bleak and musky, the chapel Spartan and forbidding, voices murmuring prayers or singing hymns as the clock ticked the hours away. Outside, the sun shone; inside, the gloom prevailed. In the night, when sleep refused to come, he knew the heat of temptation: *thou art cursed above all cattle, and above every beast of the field*. There he lay, a young man in the long night, his flesh chilled by the voice of God.

"So you were doubtful even then," Father Symonds said.

"Yes," he replied, feeling the dampness in the air and knowing that the rain would soon be coming. "Now I see that I was doubtful from the beginning, but at the time, perhaps naturally, I couldn't admit it to myself, and indeed prayed most seriously and often that God might strengthen my wavering faith. I *wanted* to believe, but my doubts prevailed and disturbed me. That's why, when my father encouraged me to go and work for the aboriginal mission stations, I went with a certain amount of relief: if nothing else, I would escape his constant attention and maybe find my own breathing space.''

"So you developed a taste for lonely places, far from civilization.''

Father Benedict sighed, feeling foolish, but still compelled to talk, his gaze focused on the darkening forest slipping past on both sides of him. Here, the Amazon rain forest; and before this, New Guinea, its jungles also dense and forbidding, crushing the heart with its silence. The thunder rumbled again above the treetops; a light breeze shook the foliage.

"Yes," he said, his voice strained, in competition with the noisy Jeep, "I developed a taste for the aborigines' alien culture and the outback's great silence. There was a touch of masochism in this, the need to punish myself for my doubts: in that silence I could admit that I hadn't wanted to enter the Church; admit, also, that I was tempted by worldly goods and pleasures, and felt that by being deprived of them I was missing out on a real life. I felt that I had been robbed of the best years of my life; that feeling persists to this day.''

Thunder rumbled high above the forest canopy and the rain started falling, single drops splashing on leaves and spraying around them to announce what was coming. Father Benedict, hearing that noise in the heavens, thought of God's frightening voice.

"God speaks to me," he said, "from the heavens. It's a clear reprimand."

The older priest smiled, not offended, and nodded judiciously. "Did you believe in Him at that time? Or did you live a complete lie?"

"No, not a complete lie. I believed in Him then. And even now, with my doubts looming larger, I can't repudiate Him. I have doubts, yes—but the belief in Him persists. What I cannot accept, and never could, is that *I* belong to Him."

"If not to Him, then to the devil."

"Not necessarily so. We do not have to give ourselves to one when we turn away from the other."

"But you didn't actually turn away from Him; you simply doubted His nature and your own place in His mysterious scheme."

"My every instinct insisted that He had to exist, but I never felt that I had been called, nor really wanted to be. I wanted to *live*, Michael—to live as other men—and the Church, with the demands it made upon me, deprived me of that."

"Are you suggesting that a priest has no real life?"

"I am suggesting that I was not then, and am still not, cut out to be a priest; that I am a man with strong desires—worse, perhaps even a sensualist—and that my need for *earthly* experiences is stronger than my desire for spiritual purity."

"Such desires are quite normal," his friend replied, "even for priests."

"Yes, I accept that—but it doesn't solve my problem. It is true that most priests have to battle with temptation, but most take pride in fighting that battle, and strengthen their faith by so doing. As for myself, I have no pride—I merely resent what I have lost, most particularly one of life's most sacred intimacies: to share love; to give new life."

The words had come out of nowhere, unplanned and unexpected, and he felt the blush burning his cheeks as soon as he spoke them. He lowered his head, feeling confused, sensing the floodgates slowly opening, the buried secrets of his past pouring out and forming a whirlpool inside him. A few raindrops fell upon him, large raindrops, warm and gentle. Then the introductory drizzle to the rainstorm

sprayed down through the trees. He thought of the small church in
the outback, its clapboard walls bleached by the sun, and around it,
shimmering dreamlike in the heat, the huts and tents of the aboriginal mission station with its beaten inhabitants. The men drank and
slept a lot, their spirits broken, their minds emptied, while the
children played distractedly in the dirt and the women welcomed the
white men. Fat women, drained of life, selling themselves for food
and drink; and he, the mission priest, closing his eyes and turning
away in despair. Father Benedict remembered clearly, just as if it
were yesterday: the tents lamplit at nights, the silhouettes in indecent
motion, the masculine, drunken oaths, the feminine giggles, the
children milling outside—and most vivid of all, that particular one,
the young one, her breasts bared in the sweltering gloom of his
room, her brown eyes luring him forward. In that singular recollection,
clear and brilliant as ice, lay the secret he would never discuss nor
completely accept. Nonetheless, perhaps encouraged by the imminent departure of his dear friend, his voice emerged reluctantly from
his throat, speaking into the drizzling rain.

"I was tempted," he confessed. "I was tempted so many times.
And although I never gave in to temptation, I resented my loss. I
wanted to love and be loved in return; to touch and be touched and
see myself in the eyes of my child. I could not understand why the
Church should deprive me of that."

"And of course, by the Church you meant God."

"Yes, I meant God."

The rain started to pour down, first attacking the forest canopy,
making a muffled drumming sound high above them as it drenched
the great trees. Thunder rumbled and lightning crackled, briefly
illuminating the dark depths, then the rain poured through the branches
just above them and turned into a heavy shower.

"There's no point in stopping," Father Symonds said. "We'd
just get soaked anyway."

Mengrire kept driving, his long hair already dripping, his dark
skin showing through his soaked and almost transparent white shirt,
while the experienced Father Symonds, heading toward the rain of
England, quickly opened a slightly tattered black umbrella and held
it over himself and Father Benedict. The Jeep shuddered as if
stalling, its wheels churning up black mud, and then it growled and
lurched forward again, coughing and banging.

"You'll soon need a new Jeep," Father Symonds said. "This one
won't last much longer." He smiled benignly and nodded his head,

still holding the umbrella up, the water drumming on the tattered black cloth and pouring down all around him. "So," he continued, "you were often tempted but resisted, and yet, even knowing that you did not succumb, you still suffer great guilt. Ah, Paul, dear Paul, like your father you are a puritan, expecting, just as he expected of you, an impossible perfection. Is this logical, Paul? Alas, I fear it's not. You are a mortal man with mortal man's weaknesses, and must learn to live with them. Without vice there can be no virtue, without desire no form of sacrifice, without temptation we cannot transcend our baseness in the light of redemption; and so, my friend, my most mortal friend, you must accept that you are imperfect: that your unclean thoughts and impure desires are what render you human. Without those you would be nothing, truly the child of a soulless devil, but as long as you face them and reject them, you will be on the right path. To be human is to choose— between good and evil, right and wrong—and perhaps your lack of faith, your need to question and doubt, is but a sign that you are more aware than most of the need to make choices. And *choice*, Paul—the ability to decide—is what makes men of beasts."

The thunder rolled again, the voice of God splitting the heavens, and the lightning spasmodically slashed the forest in exploding ribbons of silver. First darkness, then brilliant light, then the black of night again, the rain drumming on the forest canopy and running in rivulets down the foliage, and then pouring out of the shivering lower branches to hammer down on their heads. Mengrire whooped in exhilaration, smacking the steering wheel with one hand, but Father Benedict, leaning forward, keeping himself beneath the umbrella, felt cold and deafened and unreal, his head tight as a drum. The umbrella swayed above him, held in his friend's wavering right hand, but the rain simply poured in around it and drenched them. Father Benedict cursed softly, rubbed his eyes, blinked repeatedly, saw slanting lines of silver, glistening streams and rivulets, the rain dropping from the leaves and dribbling down the writhing liana and sweeping across the dark, winding track along which they were traveling.

He shook his head from side to side, grinning painfully at Father Symonds, but the noise of the pouring rain, of the rolling thunder and the crackling lightning, combined with the Jeep's roaring and the banging sound of the misused gearshift, made him cover his ears with his hands and bow his head even lower. The lightning flashed and he closed his eyes, tumbling down through his dark interior, his

friend's words reverberating in his mind like the cry of a ghost . . .
good and evil, right and wrong . . . to be human is to choose. . . . He
felt the words like physical blows at his temples, making his thoughts
spin. The thunder rumbled again, somewhere very far away, and the
flashing of the lightning seared right through his tightly closed
eyelids, illuminating his mind. . . . Another time, another place,
another storm in a distant night, the lightning flashing outside a
window and revealing brown breasts as they moved, with sublimely
undulating beauty, out of black, shifting shadows. Dark hair and
dark eyes, brown breasts and brown shoulders, sensual shoulders,
the skin smoothly curving down to what could not be forgotten.
Remembering, he shivered, burning the image with his shame,
staring through the smoldering ash of the memory back into the
present. He had come here in flight, running from Queensland
through New Guinea, trying to shake off the tentacles of that night
by purging himself in the jungle. And yet nothing had helped,
neither the Indians nor the Japanese; not even the horrors he had
witnessed toward the end of the war. Those horrors had served their
purpose, making him finally lose faith in God, but they had failed to
erase from his mind the shame that kept him awake at nights.

In flight? From what? From the secret he could not discuss. From
the truth of why he could not face his God nor be true to his faith.
The thunder rumbled far away, the pouring rain gradually stopped,
and then out of the growing silence emerged the dripping of the
drenched, shivering jungle. He opened his eyes and glanced sideways,
saw his friend's abstracted smile, looked away and saw the gloomy,
glistening forest, its great leaves bowed and soaked. He had fled to
this place, trying to purge himself of weakness, trying to forget his
sins in work, in the distractions of the unexplained, secretly grateful
for the lights that rose and fell over the interior, also grateful for the
drums whose rhythms emanated from unknown sources and led to
the manifestation of strange powers. . . . Yes, hoping to distract
himself with those mysteries and that magic, yet failing—and, in
that failure, reliving the past even more.

He rubbed his eyes and looked ahead, past Mengrire's windwhipped hair, and saw that the road here was broader and covered
with tarmac. All around were rubber trees, cleared spaces, and
marked posts, and the sun, breaking through to the forest floor, was
making the rain turn to steam. Mengrire raised his right hand,
putting his thumb through his clenched fist, then put his foot down
and drove on to the heart of the plantation. The wooden houses and

thatched huts materialized in a sunlit clearing, their walls and verandahs hazy behind spiraling clouds of steam, while the workers,
moving back and forth across the tarmac roads, and also caught in
those languorous, drifting, white clouds, resembled faceless specters
in a daylight dream.

Mengrire parked the Jeep in an area reserved for cars, and then the
three of them, still drenched, climbed down to the muddy ground,
Father Benedict already staring at the largest building, which was
Frank Poulson's house.

4

The plantation had clearly been organized along the lines of a Jesuit *aldeia*, with the simple, single-story huts of the workers bordering the roads that intersected at right angles and were spread out around the house of their master, Frank Poulson. That house was, in this case, perhaps with deliberate arrogance, situated in the middle, in a handsome, grassy square where, in a genuine *aldeia*, the Jesuit church would have stood. The huts, made of wood, were now dilapidated—the paint peeling off the planks, the wood itself chipped or crumbling, the holes in some roofs stuffed up with cardboard or a patchwork of bamboo cane—whereas the large house belonging to the *fazendeiro*, Frank Poulson, was, with its ornate brickwork, its colonnades and flamboyant porticos (grotesque Portuguese town baroque), an immaculate pink and blue extravagance clearly designed to intimidate the lowly workers.

Father Benedict, staring at it, felt the return of his rage, but he managed to tear his gaze away and have a good look around him. The rain had turned the earth to mud, the roads and trees were still steaming, and he saw, across the clearing beyond the car park, broad stone steps leading down to the jetty. The river was down there, and the plantation had its own *porto*, served frequently by the paddle steamers of the white traders and the smaller boats of the Indians. Manaus, the nearest city, was ninety minutes upstream; and Father Benedict's mission camp, another stop-in for the boats, was approximately halfway between Manaus and this decaying plantation.

Now, glancing around him, squinting against the blazing sunlight, he observed the Indians who worked the plantation—some listlessly walking about, some playing checkers on their small verandahs, others rocking rhythmically in their hammocks and sniffing *epena*— and he knew that this plantation, like the city of Manaus, had seen the last of its good days and was slipping into oblivion.

He looked at Father Symonds, feeling a depressing desolation, and saw his old friend reaching out to Mengrire and putting one hand on his shoulder. "Well, Mengrire," Father Symonds said, smiling benevolently at the Indian, "you managed to get me here without killing me, so now help me to make my last farewells by telling me where I can find your friend Peruche—and *his* friends— and *your* friends. I want to say good-bye to all my children for the very last time."

"This is sad," Mengrire replied, but with a sly, good-humored grin. "This is truly a cause for much mourning, that our friend should depart from us."

"I'm sure you'll all survive, Mengrire."

"But with heaviness in our hearts. We will pray to God to keep you in good health—and keep us in your thoughts."

Father Symonds smiled at him, shaking him lightly by the shoulder, then removed his hand and offered his smile to Father Benedict, his blue eyes lined with pleasure. "What an excellent diplomat Mengrire is. You should cherish him—and also be wary of him. We have taught him too much."

Father Benedict looked at Mengrire, studying his youthful face, then thought of the girl by the river, her naked skin golden in the morning light. The very thought of her made him blush, though he was guilty of nothing, perhaps simply because he knew that Mengrire had been intimate with her. What did conversion mean when applied to these Indians? Could they, once converted to God, really change their old skins? Father Benedict wasn't sure—and wasn't sure that he wanted it anyway—but now, watching Mengrire's restless gaze, he wondered what he was thinking.

"In the afternoon," Mengrire said, "Peruche stays in his hut, receiving those who wish to come to him for help or advice."

"Like a king," Father Benedict said.

"Like a wise man," Mengrire replied. "Though not a Christian, and still practicing unchristian magic, Peruche clings to his modesty."

Studying Mengrire's dark gaze, trying to catch it and usually failing, Father Benedict again found himself wondering what the Indian really believed in. Mengrire, though professing to be a Christian, had many dark, sheltered corners, his eyes seeming to slip back into shadows that did not match his sly smile.

"All right," Father Benedict said, speaking directly to the other priest. "You go and start saying your farewells while I have words with Frank Poulson; if the walls come tumbling down around our heads you'll know our shouting has caused it."

The older priest chuckled, his ring of gray hair shivering slightly, then rubbed his nose with the palm of his hand and shook his head in bemusement. "As you wish," he said. "Pick your cause and go fight it. If the heavens split open above my head, I shall know what the matter is." He nodded at Mengrire, who nodded back, smiling slyly, then together they turned their backs on Father Benedict and walked off through the wet grass and mud, between the nearest thatched huts. Father Benedict watched them go, the sunlight stinging his eyes. He sighed and headed across the square toward Frank Poulson's house.

Tendrils of steam, dissipated in the returning heat, drifted about him. The earth beneath the grass was wet and muddy, making soft squelching sounds. He felt tension in his stomach, a quickening of his heartbeat, and was confused between embarrassment and rage, not knowing which he felt most. The master's house was raised on stilts, making it look larger than it actually was, and behind it, some distance away, was virgin jungle, the trees dense and enormous. He normally hated the sight of it, but now he wanted to get lost in it, and realized, as he tried to formulate what to say to Frank Poulson, that the possibility that young Alex might be present was disturbing him further. He didn't want that to be so—indeed the possibility was abhorrent to him—and he knew that if he found young Alex with his father, he would not, out of respect for the boy's feelings (which were, he was convinced, of a very rare and sensitive kind), be able to mention the death of the Indian. It was with some relief, then, that when he walked up the steps of the house onto the verandah, he was greeted by the plantation overseer, the amiable Antonio Bozzano who, to his instant inquiry if Alex was inside, shook his head in a negative gesture and said, "No. I think he is in old Peruche's hut, learning God knows what else."

Antonio was a *caboclo*, his mother Indian, his father a white man, and though too generously endowed with *café*-colored flesh, had the cheerful, almost mischievous good looks of a great many of his kind. His hair was black and usually windblown, his eyes were rich and warm brown, and when he smiled, as he now did at Father Benedict, he radiated benevolence.

"Why?" he added. "Did you come to see Alex? Or talk with his father?"

"I came to talk with his father."

"The Indian?"

"Yes. He's dead."

"Ah!" Antonio exclaimed softly. "Just as I feared." He visibly winced, shook his head from side to side, stared glumly at his feet for a moment, and then looked up again, forcing out a sad smile. "That really upsets me," he said, "but I wasn't here when it happened."

"You mean the beating?"

"Yes, I mean the beating. Apparently Frank was very drunk and just couldn't be stopped."

"Being drunk," Father Benedict said, "does not excuse brutality— and that bastard has been brutal too many times."

"I know, I know," Antonio replied, "but I can't be here all the time."

"He's not your responsibility."

"I think he is."

"I think not. Frank Poulson is old enough to be responsible for his own bloody actions."

"He drinks too much, Father. That's the problem. And when he drinks, he gets violent."

"Why does he do it?" Father Benedict said. "What *drives* the bastard?"

Antonio sighed, then shook his head from side to side, raising both hands in a placating gesture and offering a weary smile. "He's not a bastard, Father. He's just tormented and filled with fear. He might soon have to close the plantation, and he can't face that fact."

"He's a bastard," Father Benedict said, "beyond hope or redemption. That's all there is to it."

"Surely you, a Christian priest, should not accuse anyone of being completely beyond redemption. Redemption, after all, is for the sinner, no matter how bad."

Antonio smiled more broadly, gentle mockery in his brown eyes, as he leaned against one of the wooden supports on the verandah, his belly hanging ever so slightly over the belt of his trousers. Father Benedict smiled back, acknowledging the Brazilian's wisdom, then he walked up the remaining steps onto the verandah and stood facing the front door.

"You're quite right," he said. "This priest fails in his duty. Nonetheless, I often find myself wondering how you can work for that swine."

Antonio shrugged and raised both hands, spreading his fingers in the air, then pointed across the grounds of the plantation, at the nearest thatched huts. "I was *born* there," he said. "Thirty-one years ago. I lived there as a child, then became a *seringueiro*, when the plantation was run by Frank's father and Frank himself was a child." He lowered his hands and turned back to face Father Benedict, shaking his head slowly from side to side as he remembered the past. "You have to understand, Father, that the man inside that house is not the boy I used to play with all those years ago. He wasn't vicious then—not like he is today—he was simply a young man given too much too soon, and at the same time, not offered the slightest moral guidance by his parents. So he developed certain indecent appetites—and, particularly in Manaus, found them easy to satisfy."

"In other words, he became a degenerate bastard."

"Yes, priest, you might say that."

"So why do you stay here, Antonio?"

"I was born and raised here, and at the moment I wouldn't know where to go if I left. Also, I have, like you, great affection for young Alex, and feel that I'd be deserting him if I left him alone here with his father."

"That's a rare kind of devotion, Antonio."

"We Brazilians are like that."

Father Benedict, looking at Antonio's plump, kindly face, knew that he was speaking the truth—a truth that made Benedict sense an even greater void in his own nature. He glanced around the plantation grounds, at the linear roads and rotting shacks, saw the sunlight beating down on the thatched roofs and wooden steps, the grass long beneath the raised floors, swaying gently in the shadows, the inhabitants lazing on the small verandahs—rocking back and forth in hammocks, playing checkers with bottle tops, smoking or sniffing *epena* or snoring softly, their dark heads hanging over their chests like the fruit of the cannonball trees—and then he felt the weight of the silence, the pervasive silence of the surrounding jungle, and turned his gaze back upon Antonio Bozzano, relieved to see his humane smile.

"And Frank is, I take it, inside the house?"

"Yes," Antonio replied. "I've just left him. He's just finished his breakfast and is starting on his first bottle of beer."

"A late breakfast and early beer."

"He considers it lunchtime."

"Are you hinting that I shouldn't go in there?"

"You could have picked a better day for it, but do what you have to do."

"Is he alone?"

"No. He's with that bloated imposter, Rollie Thatcher, and they're drinking the beer to recover."

"You mean they've been together all night?"

"That's what I mean."

Father Benedict still felt his anger, but around it was depression, a gray, amorphous cloud of bad feeling that suffocated his spirit. Bad enough to face Frank Poulson regarding the death of the Indian, but much worse to have to do it in front of Rollie Thatcher, a failed plantationer who now lived off his friends—or what few he had left. Still, he felt a certain relief that young Alex would not be present, and knew that he would not feel too much concern for the finer feelings, if such existed, of the revolting and parasitical Rollie Thatcher. Feeling better than before, but a little bit unreal, Father Benedict grinned at Antonio. Trying to lighten matters, he jabbed him lightly in the belly, where his abundant flesh hung over his leather belt and threatened to burst from his shirt.

"You could do with going on a diet, my friend," he said.

"The ladies like me this way."

Antonio smiled, spots of sunlight in his brown eyes, nodded in a debonair manner, and jumped nimbly down the steps. Father Benedict watched him cut across the road, raised his eyes to survey the sky above a green swathe of rubber trees, and reluctantly turned around. He took a deep breath and knocked on the solid wood door with his large, sweat-slicked fist.

There was no immediate reply and he impulsively turned away, but then, regaining his courage, he knocked again, this time harder and longer. He heard Frank Poulson bawling something—a curse or angry instruction—then footsteps sounded within, the door opened a little, the withered face of an Indian servant peered out and then vanished as the woman stepped back to open the door fully and let him walk in. As he moved forward into gloom, the servant quietly closed the door behind him and waved him into the main room.

The room was like an empty bar, smelling of cigar smoke, yesterday's liquor, and stale sweat, and was illuminated, since its shutters were still closed, with some very dim oil lamps. There were carpets on the wooden floor, once luxurious, now fading; the curtains, a rich mauve to match the carpets, were covered in dust. If it seemed like an artist's nightmare, it was also an antique collector's dream, containing a wealth of expensive furniture, no piece matching the other, all of it obviously bought in a random, not to say haphazard, fashion, with market value, rather than aesthetics, being the only visible criterion, this being the only criterion to the overnight million-aires who had proliferated during the rubber boom at the end of the nineteenth century.

At this very moment, in the morbid gloom of the sunless room, Frank Poulson, slim, handsome, disheveled and clearly dissipated, was slouching in a seventeenth-century late baroque Venetian arm-chair with his booted feet resting on a velvet upholstered, gold-fringed, brass-stud-ornamented footrest, while facing him, over an English Palladian gilded console table, carved with large-scale mo-tifs and topped with Derbyshire marble, Rollie Thatcher, bloated, unshaven, wearing gray slacks and an unbuttoned striped pajama top, was squeezed into a carved giltwood French *bergère*, circa 1775, the patterned cushion almost flattened beneath him, the ornate arms squeaking dangerously. Indeed, the room looked like a museum, or some mad collector's warehouse—a Louis XV commode, a Flor-entine Pietra Dura cabinet, Chinese vases from the reign of the emperor K'ang-hsi resting grotesquely on sixteenth-century South German chests or French rococo cabinets replete with tortoiseshell-and-brass marquetry—and even in that dim light, through the blue cigar smoke haze, could be discerned the reflective glitter of glass and silver, of sculpture and bronzes. Father Benedict was impressed—his disgust was touched with wonder—and he quickly drank in the treasures of this seedy mausoleum before returning his slightly stunned gaze to the one who was, in a very real sense, incarcerated in here. Frank Poulson was staring at him, wiping his lips with the back of one hand, looking upward and offering a grin in which no warmth was manifest.

"God has arrived," he said, "in the shape of his servant, wearing a white shirt, floppy pants, and a funny felt hat. Indeed, God looks hot and bothered at this moment. Could I offer a cooling beer?"

"I can do without the beer," Father Benedict replied, "and would thank you to speak no more blasphemy, at least not until I leave."

"Since you've just arrived, priest, it would be impolite to ask when that might be." Poulson glanced at Rollie Thatcher, giving him a humorless smirk, then turned his bloodshot eyes up again, staring over his beer glass. "And so," he continued, "since you are here in my house, and more specifically, since you have not been invited, may I take it that this isn't purely a social call?''

''I think you know damned well that I would not come to this place for pleasure.''

''And do you, Father, know what pleasure is?'' So saying, Poulson, with a jaundiced, lopsided grin, indicated with a nod of his head the Indian girl who was, as Father Benedict noticed with some embarrassment, sitting on an antique settee in the shadowy corner at the far side of Rollie Thatcher, wearing only a flowery dressing gown, her feet bare, her upraised legs exposed, her long black hair hanging down in an uncombed tangle, her young, spotted face expressing exhaustion and shamed resignation. She reminded Father Benedict of the other Indian girl by the river—she was certainly not much older—and he stared at her, dumbstruck, feeling almost contaminated, and then followed her fearful gaze back across to Rollie Thatcher, seeing his fat, unshaven face, his pursing lips, his evasive eyes, feeling revulsion at the sight of his unbuttoned pajama top and wobbling belly, and then practically in relief, the choice being between two evils, forced himself to return his gaze to Frank Poulson, a slimmer version of Thatcher. How could this man be Alex's father? He just couldn't imagine it.

''Don't talk to me of pleasure,'' he said, trying to keep his voice steady. ''I don't need to take my pleasure by snorting like a pig in a trough.''

''Are you calling me a pig, priest? Is that how you convert the sinners? Do you come here to call me insulting names because I won't join your church?''

''You know why I came here.''

''You came to make a nuisance of yourself with your pious concerns. Get out of here, priest. I'm not in the mood for you this morning. Go and whisper your deluded nonsense to my son and encourage his silliness further.''

''I think we should leave your son out of this.''

''Your concern deeply touches me.''

The sarcasm was brutal and made Father Benedict flinch, but he forced himself to keep his gaze steady on Poulson's lean, dissipated and once handsome face. *A Dorian Gray face,* he thought. *Eternally young—only the unshaven chin, the hollow cheeks, and the blood-shot eyes reveal that his soul is much older than the flesh which surrounds it.* Poulson's eyes were very brown, his hair black with grease, and when he looked up. holding the beer glass to his thin, shivering lips. he appeared to be perceptibly shrinking. his skin taut on the bone. Father Benedict took another deep breath.

"I came about that Indian you recently mistreated," he said. "I went to see him this morning. but could do little for him—and he died just over an hour ago."

"Which particular Indian are we discussing, Father?"

"You know damned well which Indian: Sirire—the one you beat recently."

"Ah, *that* one." Poulson said. "I remember him, the lazy bastard. He'd do anything. that one. to get out of doing his work. and was always complaining that he was sick to excuse the fact that he hadn't tapped his required quota of trees. Of *course* I beat him, priest—the lying bastard deserved it—but that beating, if leaving a few bruises, would not have killed anyone."

"The Indian *was* ill. He was starving because you gave him no food, suffering from malaria because you gave him no quinine. If the beating did not kill him—and he shouldn't have been beaten anyway—it certainly broke the last of his resistance and hastened his death."

"Don't worry about it," Rollie Thatcher said. "There's plenty more where he came from."

The fat Englishman chuckled indecently at his own remark, keeping his eyes fixed on Frank Poulson and slapping his belly with one hand. Father Benedict, glancing across at the Indian girl in the corner, knew how completely disposable she must be feeling and felt shame for his own kind.

"As far as I'm concerned," he said. pointedly ignoring Rollie Thatcher and returning his gaze to Frank Poulson, "you are solely responsible for the Indian's death."

"You heard my friend." Poulson replied, nodding his head at Rollie Thatcher. "There's no need to worry about the Indian; there's plenty more where he came from."

This time, delighted at the repetition of his own tasteless remark, Rollie Thatcher laughed aloud, his fat belly quivering and encouraging the pajama top to open wider, revealing an unsightly mass of white flesh and sweat-dampened black hairs.

"Hear. hear!" he chortled. "Dispensable labor is the great advantage of this hellhole—more so when dispensed with."

Father Benedict was filled with revulsion but forced his attention back to Frank Poulson. Having just drunk some more beer, Poulson was wiping his lips with the back of one hand; an oddly defiant sneer exposed his tobacco-stained front teeth.

"You're contemptible," Father Benedict said, trying to stare Poulson down, but unnerved by the sight of that bloodshot gaze, the watery pupils malicious. "Do you really feel nothing at all? Or are you hiding your shame?"

"Shame, priest? Did you say *shame*? Because some damned Indian's died?" Poulson snorted with mirthless glee, throwing his hair back from his forehead, letting the lamplight fall on his dark eyes and his small, brown-stained teeth. "No, priest, I don't feel any shame. The more of these damned Indians we get rid of, the better off we'll all be." Father Benedict stared at him, fascinated by his moving lips, remembering when he had last seen teeth like those: in the mouth of a Japanese soldier, his lips frozen in death's grin, where he lay, in flattened foliage and mud, in a blood-soaked glade somewhere along the Kokoda Trail during the war in New Guinea. Poulson glanced past Rollie Thatcher, at the unfortunate girl in the far corner, and smirked when he saw her lowered head, his eyes devouring her body. "Bloody Indians!" he continued, returning his gaze to Father Benedict. "Lazy, mindless bastards, the lot of them; as worthless as pigshit. No wonder we're in such a bad state: you can't *work* with these animals."

"They are *not* animals, Poulson—they're human beings—and apart from the fact that they truly own the rubber trees, they cannot be blamed for the collapse of what you think were the good old days."

"*They* own the rubber trees? What on earth are you talking about? They didn't know what a rubber tree *was* until we came here and showed them."

"The Indians—"

"A bunch of bloody barbarians! As primitive as the cavemen! We British came here, and we organized the bastards, and instead of painting our bloody faces and practicing witchcraft and slaughtering each other, we made use of what the jungle had to offer and earned every last penny. We didn't steal a thing from these primitive bastards! What's latex to *them*?"

"I hardly think that justifies—"

"What you think, Father, concerns me not in the slightest. I have been here all my life, I know the Indians inside out, and I don't need some priest with pious notions to tell me what I can and cannot do. What do you *want* in this place, priest? Why do you people insist on coming here? If, as you suggest, I am exploiting these poor Indians, is it not also true that the Church, in its own way, is also stealing from them—taking away their history and culture, and replacing it, for its own selfish reasons, with its suppressive religion?''

"Christianity is not suppressive. Nor, if I may say so, is the preaching of Christianity to be compared to the physical exploitation which you so blatantly practice.''

"A bloody good whipping.'' Rollie Thatcher said, burping, "is something these ignorant blighters understand much better than the Bible.''

"Isn't it?'' Poulson said, now also ignoring his fellow plantationer. "Does the Church really think that stealing their souls is less disgusting than my very human abuses? Surely, Father, my exploitation is of a relatively minor nature when set beside the Church's systematic obliteration of the Indians' whole way of life.''

"Semantics,'' Father Benedict said.

"The truth,'' Poulson replied. "You bastards also have your greed—you want to strengthen your own Church—and so, no matter how you otherwise describe it, you grow stronger by devouring foreign cultures. Don't worry about *my* crimes, preacher. Go and wash your *own* hands!''

The words had a crude, primitive force. Father Benedict felt trapped, and this, combined with anger and shame, led him into confusion. He glanced desperately around the room, again aware of its seedy elegance, noting the shadows from the oil lamps flickering erratically on drapes and paintings, the pale yellow light on antiques purchased during the rubber boom—then saw that other acquisition, the shadowed and silent Indian girl, observing her disheveled clothes and long uncombed black hair, her almost naked brown limbs, the shame and defeat in her lowered face with its deprived, and already fading, pockmarked beauty. Just to be here made him shiver, thinking too much of decay and rot, and he glanced at Rollie Thatcher, a bloated buffoon in merciful shadows, and then reluctantly forced his gaze back to Frank Poulson, who was staring straight at him. Poulson was licking his lips, somehow gloating as he did so, and his eyes, peering out of his sallow and unshaven face, made him seem, in their vague and bloodshot weariness, twice as old as he was.

"No answer?'' he sneered. "Of *course* you've no answer! You're

just a priest—a man deprived of normal pleasures and satisfactions—
and so, in your frustration, and trying to prove your moral superiority,
you whine about your concern for the bloody Indians and my
unchristian behavior. Well, don't talk to me about the Indians. You
save their souls and I'll use their bodies, and between us we should
make a dirty progress while they gradually disappear. Go and talk to
my son, Father. You seem to have a rapport with him. After all, the
boy behaves like an Indian, so you should be simpatico."

"I am not frustrated and don't need to prove my moral superiority—
which, in any case, I do not believe in. As for your son behaving
like an Indian, that is quite understandable since, not having a father
he can depend upon, he has to turn to the Indians for emotional
support."

"And what do your precious Indians teach him, Father? Witchcraft!
Magic! Their idiotic hocus-pocus! None of which helps him to be a
Christian, nor makes him better than I."

"You talk about him as if he's not even your son."

"The seed of my loins, Father. I can state that without blushing.
Flesh of my flesh that boy is, if too much like his mother."

"Not a bad thing," Father Benedict said.

"He's effeminate," Poulson replied. "He's as sensitive as a
woman, shows no signs of actually desiring one, and believes in,
and dabbles with, magic—just like a woman would. And indeed,
just as the Indians do, the primitive bastards."

"It's that Peruche," Rollie Thatcher said, scratching his belly and
belching. "You ought to throw him off the plantation before he does
too much damage."

Father Benedict sighed, understanding that he was getting nowhere,
but compelled, like a dog with a bone, to gnaw at it some more. "I
didn't come here to discuss Alex," he said. "You're just trying to
change the subject. I came to tell you that I've had enough of your
brutality, and that this time I'm going to report you to the proper
authorities."

"Because of the death of the Indian?"

"Yes."

"Don't waste your time, Father," Thatcher said. "They'll just
give him a medal."

He grinned at Poulson and then stood up, rising heavily and very
slowly, his great bulk pouring sweat through his pajama top and
rumpled gray slacks. Standing there, in the flickering shadows, he

seemed enormous yet insubstantial, as if that inner light which gives
a man his character had been completely extinguished. If large, he
was also grotesque, the folds of his belly white and damp, his jowls
matching the bags under his eyes which, buried deep beneath bushy
eyebrows, were almost invisible. He belched and then farted, briefly
bending his massive legs, then turned around, holding his empty
glass, and walked like a wounded rhinoceros toward the girl in the
corner. The girl looked up, dismayed, when he stopped just in front
of her, his pajama top hanging open and his enormous belly, with its
overlapping folds of white flesh and hints of pubic hair, hanging
down just above her upturned face. Father Benedict was shocked,
his own imagination shaming him, helplessly visualizing the night
that this poor girl had just been through, either with Thatcher or
Frank Poulson, perhaps with them both, and half expecting, with
dizzying dread, the shadows flickering across his vision, that a
repeat of that performance was about to be enacted right there in
front of him. In the event he was proved wrong—though an eternity
passed before he knew it—and he glanced wildly at Frank Poulson,
still slouched low in his Venetian armchair, his booted feet still on
the footrest, still slim and disheveled and too young to be so
dissipated, and saw the beer glass moving away from his thin,
grinning lips, his sleepless, bloodshot eyes rising lazily to clearly
mock him; only then, looking away, staring across the flickering
dimness, did he see the enormous Rollie Thatcher crooking the
index finger of his right hand, hooking it under the girl's chin to pull
her dark face up, then grinning down at her, contemptuously and
insultingly, before turning away and pouring himself another beer
and walking back to his chair.

Father Benedict, shaking a little, turned away from the massive
bulk of the slowly subsiding and grinning Thatcher, and became
aware that Frank Poulson was staring at him with unusual intensity.
He thought of the girl by the river, of another girl, long ago, and
then his heart, impelled by memories of brown flesh curving down
to nothing, raced faster and made his breath catch in his tightening
throat. Perhaps Frank Poulson noticed it, or at least sensed it somehow,
for he now leaned forward further, his grin widening triumphantly,
and then looked across at the Indian girl, her bare thighs in light and
shadow, flicked his eyes to Father Benedict, to the girl and back
again, and then suddenly jumped up, his agility quite surprising, and
hurried across to the girl, put his glass on the table beside her, and

almost viciously, with a sharp flick of his wrist, before Father Benedict could protest, ripped the loosely wrapped dressing gown from her body, leaving her naked.

"Is that it?" he sneered. "Is *that* your guilt? That you should want her as we do?"

The girl had shrieked instantly, trying to hold on to the dressing gown, and was still shrieking when Poulson laughed, Rollie Thatcher his bellowing chorus, and Father Benedict, his heart pounding, shame and revulsion whipping through him, choked back his nausea and dread and fled that dimly lit, awful room—not only thwarted, but defeated, his resolution destroyed.

5

Still badly shaken, but trying to compose himself, Father Benedict hurried across the handsome lawn that bordered Frank Poulson's house, passing out of the blinding sunlight and into the cooler shadowed areas where the humble shacks of the *seringueiros* were nestled beneath the sheltering trees leading down to the river. The earth, already dried, felt warm through his thin shoes; sweat dribbled down his face and formed under his armpits. He swatted the buzzing flies away, avoided a cloud of mosquitoes, cut across a road, and went between some more houses, noting the crudely patched thatched roofs, the dark and tiny rooms inside, the adults and children on the verandahs, none of them wildly active, their silence pitched in despair, the children's bellies bloated with hunger, the women old before their time, the men playing checkers with Coca-Cola or Fanta tops, or forgetting their troubles by rocking in their hammocks and sniffing *epena*. None of this improved his mood, nor helped him lose the sour taste of defeat, and for once he appreciated, when he moved out of the forest gloom, the explosion of bright light and space above the wide, muddy Amazon.

He walked along the river bank, keeping well away from the edge, his burning face cooled by the breeze that came off the murmuring water and gently shook the foliage on his right where the forest began. From here the river seemed vast, more an ocean than a mere river, and across the other side, about five miles away, the forest was a solid thin green line dividing black water from blue sky, curving from the east to the west with incomparable grace. At once beautiful and repellent, slightly intimidating in its grandeur, it had often forced him deeper into himself, trying to trace his own boundaries. Now he knew that same sensation—the need to shelter within himself—and he gratefully reached the crudely hacked trail that led him back through the trees.

The gloom cooled his burning cheeks, settled the fires of his shame, but he still felt, as he walked through the forest's embracing silence, the full weight of the guilt and buried sorrow which Frank Poulson, with his ignorant venom, had dragged up from the depths. He passed a jacaranda tree, all alone in its sea of forest, heard the musical cry of a *seringueiro* bird, saw Venetian lace leaves, tangled liana, buttressed trees, and then emerged to a *verzea* lake, bright light pouring down through the clearing, and saw Father Symonds, Antonio Bozzano, Mengrire, and young Alex, all kneeling in front of a very small thatched hut, clearly in conversation with Peruche, the much revered, ancient Indian.

"The drums tell us that something of great importance is on its way." The voice of old Peruche was a dying croak, borne on the listless breeze. "And its coming is soon."

Father Benedict heard no more, since Antonio Bozzano, hearing the snapping twigs, turned around and saw him approaching, and immediately, doubtless trying to protect young Alex, stood up and walked away from the kneeling group and stopped by the lake. Father Benedict followed him over, pleased and touched by his sensitivity, noticing the slight smile on Antonio's face, a gentle mockery that soothed the soul.

"How did it go?" Antonio asked.

"They had a girl there," Father Benedict replied. "You didn't warn me about that."

Antonio sighed and shrugged. "It just slipped my mind," he said. "He has so many girls in that place, they've begun to look like the furniture."

"That girl was no prostitute."

"No, she was not. She's just the daughter of a *seringueiro* who couldn't pay his debts, and when that happens, as it so often does, Frank takes the daughter instead."

"He takes the daughter as *payment*?"

"Yes."

"That's obscene!"

"I agree."

Too shocked to reply immediately, Father Benedict glanced down at the hyacinths and tropical lilies in the limpid lake. Slowly, with great reluctance, he looked back at Antonio.

"Has he been doing this for long?"

"No," Antonio replied. "It's a recent, and very disturbing, innovation. But the Indians can't argue."

"He uses these girls and then casts them out?"

"Yes, I'm afraid so."

"So his nightly debauches are not even conducted with prostitutes but with innocent girls whose only sin is that their fathers are in debt to Frank Poulson for food they cannot afford."

"They used to live off the jungle, but now they depend on Frank, and since he always pays them less than what they need, he ensures that they will always be in debt to him. Once he merely used it to keep them under his wing, but now, no doubt encouraged by Rollie Thatcher, he has taken it further. Yes, he takes their daughters in lieu of latex—ostensibly as servants in his house, but truly as mistresses."

"And when he's finished with them?"

"He sends them back to their parents—and then lets them all starve."

Father Benedict closed his eyes and took a deep breath. He let it out very slowly and opened his eyes again, now staring across at those kneeling in front of the thatched hut. He saw Alex in front of Peruche, close beside the squatting Mengrire, and again could not believe that the boy had sprung from the seed of his father.

"When I told him that I was going to report him to the authorities," he said, returning his gaze to Antonio, "that bastard Thatcher said that if I did they'd probably give him a medal. Given that the revolting creature was being sarcastic, do you think there's some truth in it?"

"Oh, yes, Thatcher knows what he's talking about. The authorities—those that count—are in the pockets of the white men and have never shown much concern for the Indians. Frank knows damned well that even if you got him to court in Manaus, he would only have to swear that the Indian's death was an accident and they'd let him walk out of there without a murmur. What's another impoverished Indian to the authorities? They just won't want to know."

"I can't bear the thought of it," Father Benedict said, feeling the anger and frustration boiling up through his insides. "Not only does it enrage me that he can do what he wants and get away with it, but it appalls me to think that Alex, at his age, should have to stay in the same house with that man and hear his nightly debaucheries. The situation is extremely sick on both counts, and I feel so damned helpless."

"Well," Antonio replied, "on the one hand, I'm half Indian and can't stand to see them abused; on the other, I'm Frank's oldest friend and feel the need to protect him. I'll admit that I feel guilty—because I won't leave the plantation—and also because I'm worried that Frank's abuses could lead to something more serious."

"What, pray, could be more serious than the abuses that Frank practices on the Indians?"

"Indian vengeance." Antonio shrugged again, a forlorn, uneasy gesture. Across the lake some herons flew up from a tree and scattered into the dazzling sky. "Sooner or later," he continued, "some Indian, or Indians, might revolt—and then we'd *really* have trouble."

"What kind of trouble?"

"A reversion to past customs: physical violence or witchcraft, either of which could start by being aimed only at Frank, but could then go out of control and affect us all."

"I hardly think witchcraft—"

"Don't discount it. Let's go join the others."

The abruptness with which Antonio terminated the conversation left Father Benedict in no doubt that he had a reason for rejoining the group around old Peruche's hut. Confused, but not annoyed, he followed Antonio across the clearing, his eyes dazzled by the striations of sunlight that poured down over the hut while the jungle surrounding the lake in the clearing seemed laced with swathes of pure blackness. Mengrire glanced up and nodded, his face solemn, his eyes hooded, and Father Symonds, his bald head poking through his ring of gray hair, waved his right hand and smiled brightly, his cherubic face flushed. Father Benedict sat between them, the grass warm beneath his backside; he crossed his legs and nodded at old Peruche, who nodded lazily back.

The ancient Indian was almost naked, his loins covered in a modest *tanga* made from monkey skin and *arara* feathers, his wrinkled forehead encased in a headpiece of white-boned armadillo disks. His legs were crossed, his elbows rested on his knees, and his body, the skin wrinkled like that of a prune, was bent slightly forward, his face a parchment of age and experience. He was smiling, his mouth toothless; he spoke in a low voice, his rheumy eyes focused mostly on Alex.

"What comes is not written in the skies, but is in the voice of the wind. The drums announce its arrival."

"What arrival?" Alex asked, brushing the blond hair from his blue eyes, his youthful voice gentle. "What form will it take?"

Old Peruche closed his eyes, pursed his lips, and raised his face to the sky, his ears tuned to the light breeze. "It comes in darkness," he croaked, "bringing violence and death, opening the gates that lead into the unknown and the source of all things." He lowered his head again, opened his eyes, and stared at Alex, his lips closing over his toothless gums before they opened to speak again. "You were called and have come," he said. "Past and future exist within you. The drums tell me that that which comes to pass will come soon, and that you are the instrument of those forces that elude us and bind us. It is you, my son, in innocence and grief, who will stand where the earth spins."

"This is nonsense," Father Benedict heard himself say, his own voice sounding strange to him. "You must not preach such nonsense to the boy; it is neither sensible nor Christian."

He had spoken to Peruche, but now Alex stared at him, drawing him into the depths of his azure eyes as if into an empty sky. Father Benedict was startled, certainly not for the first time, as Alex's strange, indefinable beauty briefly fractured reality. Yes, Alex was beautiful—it was the only word to use—his beauty residing in his serenity and almost impossible innocence. He was handsome and unblemished, lean and pale, his blue eyes brilliant, yet these pleasing attributes, particularly in one only seventeen, were not all that unusual. No, the beauty came from within, from his radiant innocence and faith, giving his blue eyes, beneath the blond hair, a happy child's luminosity. There was something extraordinary about him—a singular gentleness or passivity—as if in his acceptance of the Indians and their Oneness, he had found a remarkable sense of security well beyond the normal. Alex lived in a private world, a mysterious and mystical place in which, under the guidance of Peruche, he had developed uncommon powers. He could travel the forest blindfolded, draw dangerous animals to his bosom, and sometimes, if so far only slightly, have an effect on the elements: making water ripple, causing flowers to open or close, conjuring light out of the darkness and a breeze from a windless day. Such gifts were indeed uncommon, and to Father Benedict, frightening; yet from Alex he received only the glow of inviolate goodness. And this, in direct contrast to the degeneracy of his father—indeed, possibly even magnifying that degeneracy tenfold—was what made Father Benedict, with some confusion but no embarrassment, think of Alex as of a beautiful work of art: something rare and invaluable.

"Nothing can be nonsense," Alex said, "when all things are possible."

It was a striking thing for a boy his age to say, and now, looking at him, drawn into his open gaze, Father Benedict felt as if the ground on which he sat were slipping away from him.

"All things are *not* possible," he replied, "which is something you'll soon learn."

Alex didn't take offense but merely smiled in his dreamy fashion, his blue eyes unwavering and benevolent, filled with childish acceptance. "If God is possible," he said, "then all things are possible, and since you, Father, have taught me to believe in God, I must believe in His miracles."

Father Benedict had a great paternal love for Alex, but there were times, and this happened to be one of them, when the boy's peculiar mixture of bizarre innocence and ruthless intelligence made him feel threatened and morally confused. Now, as he stared at that delicately handsome face, at the almost golden blond hair and the gently smiling poet's lips, into the glistening blue eyes beneath the long blond eyelashes, he felt again that the earth was shifting beneath him and tilting him out of his orbit.

"You're a lovely lad," he said, "but right now you're playing with words, and since the subject is of such importance, I don't think you should do it."

"I'm sorry, Father," Alex replied. "I didn't mean to make you angry. It's just that I sense things—things I cannot quite grasp—and what Peruche has just told us strikes a chord somewhere deep down inside me."

"When the Yano beat their drums," old Peruche intervened, "this child sees and feels what you have lost, and becomes one of us. He is special. A chosen one."

"Chosen for *what*?" Father Benedict asked.

"To serve that which is coming."

Father Benedict glanced at Mengrire and saw the movement of his sly eyes, then turned his own gaze on Father Symonds, who sat at his left side. "You know this kind of talk is helpful to no one. Why tolerate it?"

"*Tolerate* it?" Father Symonds replied, smiling benignly and shrugging his shoulders. "How can I *not* tolerate it when I have no right to stop it? Peruche has his beliefs—and if not agreeing with them, we must respect them—and he has simply been telling us, since we asked about the Yano drums, why he thinks they have been beating all night long for the past three nights."

"That much I overheard," Father Benedict replied, rather testily.

"He believes that something important is on the way—and I believe that is nonsense."

"I do not necessarily approve of what he is saying," Father Symonds replied mildly, "but since I am here to make my farewells, I must wait till he finishes."

"Never before have the Yano drums been heard three nights in a row," Mengrire said, "so we know that something exceptional must be happening and that it relates to the strange lights."

"We do not even know that the Yano actually exist!" Father Benedict said irritably, feeling a tug of unexpected fear in the pit of his stomach. "They are probably no more than one of the many unnamed tribes who still roam wild in the jungle and avoid contact with white men."

"Then how do you explain the lights that rise and fall when the Yano drums beat? Can we call those lights natural?"

The questions had been asked by Antonio Bozzano who, smiling mischeviously, without malice, was nevertheless staring at Father Benedict as if he meant what he said. Father Benedict, feeling defeated, the fear tugging at his stomach again, glanced briefly at his fellow priest, saw him shrugging and lowering his head, then looked into the rheumy eyes of old Peruche and felt the weight of their gravity.

"You know what is believed," Peruche said, "and you cannot disprove it. If, as you insist, the Yano are normal beings, you still cannot explain the lights that rise and fall over the jungle's dark regions."

That was true, and Father Benedict felt chilled, well aware of how the mysterious lights had burned relentlessly into his consciousness. Beautiful, inexplicable, always accompanied by the beating drums, the lights would rise and fall in his dreams and then draw him from sleep; and indeed, though he went to great pains to deny their magical nature, it was true that if he was, during the day, perfectly at ease with the Yanoama Indians who lived on the outskirts of the rain forest and worked on the rubber plantations, he was secretly, if not uncommonly, both haunted and frightened by the thought of the more mysterious Yano Indians.

"You described Alex as a chosen one," Father Symonds said to old Peruche. "What did you mean by that?"

Startled that the older priest had even asked such a question, Father Benedict saw, with a shock, that his good friend, who had formerly advised him to ignore all inexplicable phenomena, was looking very intently at Peruche, as if, in the knowledge that he was leaving the Amazon forever, he wanted to confront all the issues he had formerly ignored.

Peruche, like a scorched tree, his body shriveled and nut-brown, studied Father Symonds for some time and then opened his toothless mouth, his words sibilant and strange. "I have taught him the basic mysteries of the most ancient of wisdoms, which were brought down to my hidden brothers of long ago, when we knew not ourselves."

He stopped and sniffed, as if trying to catch the breeze, put his head back, took a deep breath, and then looked at each of them in turn, his gaze steady but unseeing.

"There is light and darkness," he continued. "Good and evil coexisting. Somewhere, in that place where time and space do not have meaning, the forces of good and evil, of day and night, war eternally, fighting for the souls of all men through rare individuals. Those individuals are the chosen few, drawn from chaos to ordain order, their innocence representing the strength and weakness which divide every soul. Just as men become Man, as all souls are of the One, so, then, do the few who are chosen represent those not called."

He stopped and licked his dry lips. Taking a deep breath and holding his nose between his fingers, he blew snot out and flicked it down to the grass, after which he pursed his lips and exposed his naked gums. Then, with a dignified and judicious nod, he focused his gaze on young Alex.

"Yes," he said, "I have taught him—because I recognized him at birth—and now, though white-skinned, he has the soul of the forest which alone, unlike the mortal soul of men, is the mothering womb of the Otherworld. Alex more than knows the forest—he is part of it, and it of him—and the wild animals come to him, and the serpents take warmth from him, and all that lives in the water, or thrives in bark and soil, accepts him because he is pure and as open as air. It is he, this mere child, who is more child than most children, who will stand between day and night—light and darkness—to represent all his brothers."

Father Benedict was speechless, struck dumb by the Indian's words, some part of him, rising out of his shaken faith, exhaling fear and revulsion. He felt hot and claustrophobic, far removed from himself, and his skin seemed electric with raw nerves, all being whipped by the outer world. Flies and mosquitoes swarmed around him, small spiders crawled across his feet, and the ants, always

ferocious and active, etched black lines through the flattened grass.
He glanced at Alex's radiant beauty, at Peruche's brown, wrinkled
face, was vaguely aware of Antonio and Mengrire. Then he stared at
his fellow priest. What he saw terrified him. His dear friend, Father
Symonds, always optimistic and benignly cheerful, seemed to be
changing before his eyes. He looked older and much more frail. The
intensity of his gaze, fixed on Peruche, was now almost tortured.
Father Benedict stared at him, paralyzed. With a shudder, something
breaking apart inside him, he had a sudden conviction that his old
friend would not see dawn, let alone England's green shores.

"Enough!" he said. "I will hear no more of this! What you're
saying is blasphemous!"

They all stared at him, startled, sensing the fear in his voice, then
Father Symonds, shaking his head as if trying to waken himself from
a trance, reached out and gently squeezed his shoulder, as if comforting a child. "Fear not, Paul," he said, glancing around him, looking
vague. "Listening is not necessarily believing, and it helps us to
understand." So saying, he turned away to face Peruche once more,
staring at him with the intensity of a blind man praying for sight.
Father Benedict shivered, again touched by some presentiment.
Frightened, he avoided looking at his fellow priest and instead fixed
his attention on the ancient Peruche, speaking to him with anger.

"Alex is a normal child. He is not one of your chosen ones. You
must not fill his head with this dangerous nonsense—and nonsense it
is! He does *not* belong to the forest, nor to the womb of your
Otherworld, and the mysteries you have taught him are shallow
tricks of no particular importance." In desperation he turned to
Alex, saw blond hair and blue eyes, a slight smile either tender or
mocking, but strangely seductive. His thoughts scattered and spun,
the earth shook, but he managed to speak again. "You are normal,"
he said. "Do you understand, my son? You are as normal as the rest
of us here, and I'd like you to stay that way. Don't imagine you
have any special powers; they are merely tricks of the mind."

"You are arrogant," Peruche said, "and your arrogance has
blinded you. Like most white men, you have forsaken all those
instincts and feelings which help us to commune with the earth and
the sea and the sky. Yes, your eyes see little, and your ears refuse to
hear, and your flesh, which should respond to a mote of dust, can
only feel the extremes of heat and cold, the bite of pain, lust's sweet
sweat. Yet such things are superficial, drops of rain on the mighty
river, and by denying your own senses, refusing to accept your true

nature, you are cutting yourselves off from your true spirit and its boundless potential. Alex, this white child in an Indian's skin has gained all you have lost. He is *not* like the rest of you: having faith, he was chosen. Now behold how, with the wave of his hand, he separates himself from you.''

Father Benedict heard the words, but he was not looking at Peruche; instead, feeling almost paralyzed, he was focusing his gaze on Alex. The boy was staring straight back, his blue eyes large and brilliant, glittering with an intense inner light which could not have been natural. Those eyes hypnotized Father Benedict, drawing him forward out of himself, away from his love for Alex, a paternal love that had been frustrated, and sucking him into some place where fear lived like a dragon. The fear breathed all around him, a living thing, palpable, emanating from the black swathes of the jungle and taking the shape of a snake. It was a boa constrictor, very thick, terribly long, its enormous body wriggling out of the undergrowth and over Alex's crossed legs. Alex sat there, not moving, apparently unconcerned, while the snake, its scaled flesh glistening in the sunlight, coiled around his slim body. Father Benedict wanted to help him, tried to do so but could not move, felt a shiver of revulsion sliding through him and dragging him down through a nightmare. He loved Alex like his own son, wanting to protect him from his father, believing him too innocent for his own good, naïve, unprotected. Yet at times, in recent months, the boy had confounded him, staring out of some secret inner place that was beyond comprehension. Once confounded, he was now frightened, unable to grasp what was happening, not knowing if the enormous snake, coiling around Alex's body, was real or the product of an imagination somehow unleashed by Peruche—or by Alex himself.

The snake tightened around Alex, its body as thick as a rubber tire, and Father Benedict opened his mouth to scream but could utter no sound. He choked back a sob, closed his eyes, took a deep breath, felt something wet and cold slide across him and then move away. Opening his eyes he saw the snake slither lazily through the grass, move around Father Symonds, then Mengrire and Antonio, and finally coil over the knees of a chanting Peruche, and head straight for the lake. The lake rippled and parted, letting the snake nose down into it, and then the ripples spread out and started swirling rapidly, until the water formed a whirlpool into which the giant reptile, its tail waving in a languid, seductive manner, was inexorably sucked. It disappeared very quickly, swallowed noisily by the whirlpool's vortex, and then out of that swirling black hole, with a shocking, staccato crackling, shot a blinding bolt of lightning that clawed its way up to the darkening sky like the fingers of a giant, tortured skeleton. Thunder roared in reply, a great beast devouring the lightning, and black clouds, as heavy and dense as smoke, materialized high above.

Father Benedict looked up, wondering where the clouds had come from, waiting for the rain, surprised when it didn't come, and then watched, astonished, as the clouds broke apart and revealed, inside a great ring of blackness, a mass of glittering stars. Around the clouds was the daylight, within the clouds was the night sky, and Father Benedict, in a fear that now seemed to be suffocating him, looked across at the roaring vortex of the water in the *verzea* lake and saw, in that swirling black funnel, another mass of bright stars.

Had Alex merely waved his hand? Had he waved his hand at all? Father Benedict, with such questions splintering his head like ice picks, tore his stunned eyes away from the roaring lake and stared at those sitting by him. They were all in the same position, as if time itself had stopped, but all of them, with the exception of Alex, seemed hazy and unreal. Alex was very different, his boyish profile clear, the whole of him bathed in a halo of brilliant light that appeared to pulsate to the relentless rhythm of faraway drums.

"Now observe," Peruche said, his voice bizarrely amplified, reverberating in Father Benedict's head and defeating the noise all around him. "The child has the power—he touched the spirit of the forest—but he only has such power when the Yano beat their drums, because their drumming is a sign that the forces of good and evil are present, and his power, which derives from his faith, is a gift from the Good. When the drumming stops—when the opposites disengage—his power seriously diminishes."

Father Benedict hadn't heard the drums before, but now he heard them quite clearly, a bass rumbling that came from far away in the jungle's interior. He looked above Alex's head, the blond hair like shimmering gold, and saw the black clouds surrounding a mass of stars in a dazzling blue sky. There were no rising and falling lights—they could not be seen in the daytime—but the drumming, like some rumbling from the earth, could not be ignored.

He closed his eyes and covered his ears, trying to will himself into oblivion, saw the bleak town in Australia, his aboriginal mission station, a brown shoulder, sensual, the flesh curving down to nothing— and cried out his protestation (the exact words he would never know) and then saw Alex's hand raised on high, his fist clenched and surrounded by that mass of stars. Father Benedict tore his eyes away, still refusing to believe, and saw, in the roaring whirlpool of the lake, another mass of brilliant, blinking stars, the funnel of water a depthless void.

Good and evil coexisting: he felt the force of that truth. The fear rushed up and locked in his throat, and he leaned forward to gag. His eyes beheld that upraised fist, stars arched across the black knuckles, then the fist became a web of outstretched fingers and the stars abruptly winked out.

No stars. Just that black hole. Then the sunlight took command. The light blinded Father Benedict, the roaring ceased, the wind vanished, and he gasped and rubbed his eyes and looked around him, seeing nothing unusual.

The *verzea* lake was perfectly still, the sky was blue, the jungle silent, and no light shimmered around Alex's head to turn his blond hair to gold. Father Symonds was rising slowly, looking unusually weak and frail, nodding his thanks to Antonio Bozzano, who was helpfully holding his elbow. Antonio was smiling slightly, good-humored as always, thoughtfully assisting the older man. Mengrire, his gaze shifting restlessly about him, was also standing upright. Father Benedict licked his lips, rubbed his forehead, coughed into his hand, tried to still the frightened beating of his heart as he looked across at Peruche. The old Indian was still sitting, his legs crossed, his head bowed; but then his frail body shivered, he raised his head and seemed to awaken, and Father Benedict was forced to stare into those rheumy eyes. He did not look for long. Instead he turned to look at Alex, at the boy he treated like a son, and saw that adolescent face, its innocence beautiful, the blue eyes fixed upon him.

"She arrives today," Alex said. "The photographer from America. Since you're going to Manaus, can I go with you? I can't wait to meet her."

Father Benedict, hearing the words, did not really comprehend them; but the sound of Alex's voice, that shy whisper, seemed to toll like a distant bell.

"What happened?" he asked.

6

"Pardon?" Alex said.

"I thought—"

"You fell asleep," Father Symonds said, his voice strained and unnatural. "It's my fault, of course, for staying too long and talking too much. However, the boat clearly won't wait forever, so we better leave soon."

Father Symonds seemed strange, subtly altered, somehow older, his face not as cherubic as before, his smile tentative and nervous. Father Benedict tried not to stare, aware that he might be imagining things, still fighting, as he was, to regain his senses and let his racing heart slow down.

"I fell *asleep*?" he asked.

"I think so," his old friend replied, stumbling over the words as he rushed them out, skipping over the lie. "Very briefly, of course."

"So," Alex said. "Can I come? I want to meet the American."

Father Benedict stared at him, the words taking some time to register, at first wondering what the boy was talking about, and only slowly remembering: the New York photographer, a lady originally from Hollywood, arriving on the boat that would take Father Symonds away, and due to stay in the mission camp for a month, writing about and photographing their daily routine. Distaste filtered briefly through him, but his sense of unreality remained, not helped when he looked into Alex's eyes and saw the blue sky reflected. No black clouds, no stars, no thunder and lightning: just a clear afternoon sky.

"Why do you want to see the American woman?" he asked.

"She's a stranger," Antonio intervened, walking up to stand beside them, his face lowered, his good-humored eyes raised, a pleasing grin on his face. "More important," he continued, "she's an *American*; and even more important still, she once lived in Hollywood. Even Alex, who has seen so few movies, can't fail to know what they are."

Alex blushed and smiled broadly, lowering his eyes in embarrassment, instantly like a normal adolescent, emotionally awkward and charming. Father Benedict, without thinking, put his hand on the boy's shoulder, shaking him affectionately and then letting him go, touched by his shyness. Had it truly happened? Had this boy's raised hand moved the elements? Father Benedict, remembering vividly, again felt a stabbing fear, but when he looked at Alex, who was running his fingers abstractedly through his blond hair, he was convinced that whatever it had been, it could not have been bad.

"She's not a film star, Alex. She only *lived* in Hollywood. And of course she lives and works in New York, a much less exotic place."

"Not to Alex," Antonio said.

"And not to me," Father Symonds said. "To me, right now, *any* place beyond the Amazon sounds exotic, so let's start for the boat." He turned to say good-bye to Peruche, but did not shake his hand, since the wizened Indian, looking up with his rheumy eyes, merely smiled and waved languidly.

"So it is," Peruche wheezed. "The winds blow us here and there. All of us are one, as the whole earth is one, and so, wherever you may be, you will also be here with us. Have a good trip, my friend."

"Perhaps I'll return some day," Father Symonds said.

"Just to your grave," Peruche replied. "As we all must do sometime."

Father Symonds stepped back, very quickly, his body twitching, and then turned to stare directly at Father Benedict, his lined eyes imploring. Yes, he had changed, his cheerful face now like a death mask, fearful yet fighting to retain some dignity, his teeth biting his upper lip. Then Father Benedict felt it again, spiraling up to grip his heart: the conviction that Father Symonds was doomed and would never see England. This terrible belief, which had no rational basis, shook him body and soul.

"Yes," he heard his own voice saying, speaking as quickly as had Father Symonds, "it's time we were all leaving for Manaus, so let's set about it. And of course, Alex, if you wish, you can come with us and meet the newcomer." He returned Alex's smile of pleasure, but it took considerable effort, since what had just transpired—and he could not accept that he had merely been dreaming—had completely disoriented him, filling his head with old memories that had resurrected buried guilt, and making everything around him—the green walls of rubber trees, the teeming grass and shifting foliage, the black-surfaced, very still *verzea* lake, the snow-white clouds in the azure sky—seem unreal and yet strangely threatening, as if closing in on him. "So," he said, "do we go by boat or car? It's up to you, Father Symonds."

"I'd like to see it all from the river one last day," Father Symonds replied. "So if no one really minds, the boat is my choice."

"It's your day," Father Benedict said, then turning to Mengrire added, "perhaps you could drive on to Manaus, Mengrire, and wait for us down by the docks. Since it will be dark by the time Father Symonds's boat departs, you can drive us, and the American woman, back to the mission."

"As you wish, Father. But first I will put the suitcases on the boat, to be certain that they will arrive in Manaus with you."

"You think you might get lost, Mengrire?" Father Benedict said with gentle mockery.

"Not lost," Mengrire said, returning the smile but avoiding his eyes. "I only fear that the Jeep might break down, or that there might be another bad storm, and that because of these unexpected circumstances our good Father Symonds might have to leave for England without his possessions."

"Most considerate of you, Mengrire," Father Symonds said. "And the thought is appreciated."

The Indian smiled and, clearly relieved that he would not have to go with them, turned around and loped back through the forest toward the residential area of the plantation, while Father Symonds, merely nodding one last time at the old Indian who still squatted before his small thatched hut, finally managed to tear himself away and headed toward the small *porto* with Antonio Bozzano walking beside him. Alex likewise nodded at Peruche, but then held the old man's gaze, their eyes locked in some secret communication that again disturbed Father Benedict. He started to move off, then stopped, surprised by the intensity of Alex's gaze, remembering how Father Symonds had also stared at Peruche and seeing almost the same expression on Alex's face, as if he were reading Peruche's mind, and the old Indian, his.

"Follow your instincts, my son," Peruche said. "For what will come starts today."

"I just want to go to Manaus and meet the American woman."

"If your impulse is to do so, then do it. Trust your senses in everything."

The boy nodded and turned away, smiling casually at Father Benedict, and together they walked behind the other two, around the lake, through the trees. Father Symonds was talking to Antonio, their voices floating back on the breeze, and Father Benedict, noticing the slope to his old friend's shoulders, felt a terrible sadness. *Just to your grave,* Peruche had said. What had he meant by that? Whatever, it had frightened the older priest—and Father Benedict as well.

He tried to not think about it, convincing himself that he was imagining things, and was relieved when they emerged from the wooded area and were walking along the great river. The brilliant sunlight was fading gradually, giving way to a cloudy grayness, and the immense expanse of water, its far bank ribboned with green, temporarily overwhelmed his worst fears and soothed his quivering nerves.

They soon came to the jetty and found Mengrire waiting for them, having deposited the suitcases on the deck of the boat and wanting to ensure that they found them. Satisfied, he drove off, the Jeep rattling and banging dangerously. The rest of them crossed the plank onto the lower deck of the small and dilapidated paddle steamer, Father Benedict sharing a wooden seat with his perspiring fellow priest while Alex and Antonio Bozzano leaned against the rusty steel railing.

Father Benedict, staring past the heads of young Alex and Antonio at the well-spread huts of the plantation, remembered his confrontation with Alex's father, Frank Poulson, and felt, in the sudden rage that stabbed through him, a more cutting shame. Good and evil coexisting; past and future as one: he thought of his own secret guilt—which Frank Poulson had unwittingly resurrected—and a hot flush actually rose to his cheeks, making him lower his head. The boat's engine charged into life, its muffled roar filled with metallic bangings, and the wheels of the paddle steamer, the white paint flaking off them, churned up the water around the small jetty and pushed the boat, sluggishly but surely, out into the river. Father Benedict raised his head, saw that Alex and Antonio were engaged in friendly conversation, and turned his attention to his departing friend. Father Symonds was studying the river, the sun shining on his bald head, the silvery hair that surrounded his eggshell skull being blown by the wind. His cheerful face, which had always

seemed too small for his portly body, now seemed to have shrunk
even more, losing color and life. Father Benedict, seeing that appari-
tion before him, thought he was losing his senses.

"Are you all right?" he asked, trying to sound as casual as
possible, blinking his eyes against the sunlight that flashed off the
rippling water, and keeping his hands in his lap.

"Yes," his friend replied, not looking at him. "I'm fine. A bit
sad, perhaps."

"But are you sure you're all right?"

"Of *course* I'm all right. Why do you ask?" Father Symonds
turned toward him, shading his eyes with a cupped hand, tilting his
head slightly to the right and squinting out of upraised eyes. "Your
question didn't seem rhetorical," he continued. "Why the sudden
concern?"

Father Benedict, still feeling bewildered, did not know what to
say. "I'm not sure," he managed to blurt out. "You seem changed.
Not at all your old self."

"I haven't changed," his friend replied. "I'm just sad to be
leaving. After fifteen years in this place, I should think that is
natural."

"I think it's more than that."

"It's not."

"I think it is. Something happened back there with old Peruche,
and it affected you dramatically. You seemed shocked, perhaps even
frightened, and all the life left your face."

Father Symonds sighed, visibly shuddered, and then turned his
head away, his gaze focused on the distant bank of the river, that
green ribbon of jungle. "Yes," he said, "you're right. I feel
terrible. Is it really that noticeable?"

"*I* noticed it. I don't know that anyone else did."

"I feel old. Suddenly very old. As if my whole world is ending."

"Why? What happened back there?"

There was a fairly long silence while Father Symonds pondered
the question, his lips opening and closing, his gaze fixed on the far
bank. Father Benedict glanced over his shoulder, saw Alex and
Antonio by the railing, the humus in the river making a brown wake
in the glittering black water, the nearside bank curving away out of
sight around the overhanging branches of the trees and the bank's
tall, swaying rushes. Hearing Father Symonds sighing again, he
returned his gaze to his strained face.

"I can't clearly define what happened," Father Symonds said

quietly, "but I do know that when I looked at Peruche, I knew, I just *knew*, I actually *felt* that I would never see England."

Father Benedict, hearing those words, experienced a chill that almost numbed him to the point of paralysis. "Imagination," he said, trying to make himself sound soothing. "Probably the tension engendered by your imminent departure made—"

"No!" the older priest interrupted. "It definitely wasn't imagination. I had the feeling that I was hypnotized, that Peruche was inside my head, and that through him I was experiencing my own future, which did not include England. My future was right here, in the Amazon, and did not go beyond it. What else could this mean but that I would not be leaving here after all—that whatever amount of time I had left, it would terminate here? And understanding this— knowing it to be the only truth—I felt something breaking inside my spirit and draining my strength—or more precisely, my will to live. It ends today, Paul, and Peruche saw it . . . and now I must accept it."

He had finally turned around to reveal his fear and wonder; but Father Benedict, either unwilling or unable to accept the truth, retreated into a protective cloak of disbelief. Yet he knew it to be true—ice trickled through him to tell him so—and tears, which he saw in his friend's eyes, came also to his eyes. He covered his face with his right hand, hiding the crying of his wounded heart, then took a deep breath and put his head back against the hard wooden bench, his face turned toward the graying sky.

"We're both crazy," he said. "We're letting our imaginations run riot. We're letting ourselves succumb to all the nonsense that's preached by the Indians. You are sailing back to England tonight, dear Michael, and nothing will stop you."

"I won't see another dawn," Father Symonds replied, "and both of us know it." They glanced at one another, lowered their eyes, each afraid to look too deep. "Yes, Paul, you know it, because you, too, experienced something—something that frightened you severely and made you question your sanity."

"You said I'd just been sleeping."

"That's what it looked like. You were sitting in front of Peruche, your eyes closed, your head moving from left to right. When you woke up, you seemed completely dazed—and obviously were frightened. What happened to *you*, Paul?"

Father Benedict licked his dry lips, remembering, wondering if he were mad. "I saw things," he said. "Things the rest of you clearly didn't see: inexplicable and miraculous events which seemed vividly real. I was *not* sleeping, Michael. I *know* it. I was wide awake through it all.''

"And yet the rest of us experienced nothing—only the sight of you sitting there, sleeping, moving your head left and right.''

"I was moving my head left to right in order to see all that was happening. I saw Alex's right hand raised in the air—and when it dropped, it all stopped. Peruche had said that with a wave of his hand Alex would separate himself from us—and then Alex waved his hand and created a new world that I did *not* imagine.''

"A form of hypnosis,'' Father Symonds said. "That possibly explains it.''

"You think so?'' Father Benedict rejoined, feeling fear and frustration. "And do you even remember Peruche making his peculiar remark about Alex?''

"Yes, I do.''

"And what happened then?''

"Nothing.''

"Nothing? You mean Alex didn't even raise his hand?''

"No, I don't remember him doing so.''

"You mean he ignored Peruche's remark?''

"I'm not sure. I . . .''

"Alex wouldn't have *ignored* Peruche. And if he had—or hadn't heard him—Peruche would have followed his remark up with *something*. What happened after Peruche told us that Alex, with a wave of his hand, would separate himself from us?''

Father Symonds looked confused, his eyes moving left and right, his hands rising to his cheeks and falling again to lie like fish on his lap. "You know, I *can't* remember. . . . I remember Peruche making the remark. I remember that I turned to look at Alex. I remember that he *started* to raise his hand, and then . . . then I remember deciding to leave and standing up to do just that, feeling unusually weak, Antonio holding my elbow. . . . Nothing else! *Nothing!*''

"And did you hear the Yano drums?''

"No, I didn't. . . . Yes. . . . Yes, I might have. Come to think of it, I'm *certain* that I heard them—for how long, I don't know. Presumably a very short time.'' He glanced up, bewildered, then looked across at Alex and Antonio, both of whom were still leaning against the railing, talking casually and watching the wake of the paddle steamer. After a short while, shaking his head from side to side, he turned back to the front again. "It's a mystery,'' he said.

They said no more for a while, the weight of their words hanging upon them, each retreating into his own private place with its separate reality. Father Benedict fought with himself, trying to resist his churning emotions: a growing dread mixed with terrible wonder and grief, his mind refusing to grasp it. He stared over the mighty river, to that ribbon of forest five miles away, then fixed his attention on the bank close to the port side, sliding past the large, spinning wheels. The wheels made a lot of noise, churning up water, their loose slats clattering, but the forest that came right up to the sloping bank was gloomy and silent. The boat eventually passed the mission, the buildings desolate in the shadowed clearing, and some Indian children waved from the jetty while others waved from the sick bay. Father Symonds waved back, standing up as he did so, then went to the railing and stood there until the mission had disappeared. He returned to his seat, shaken, and sat down, sighing loudly, then wiped some more tears from his eyes and looked straight at the jungle. The trees, overhanging the river, seemed almost humanly mournful.

"It's all right," Father Benedict said again with exhausted, forlorn hope. "It's all superstition and nonsense, so there is nothing to worry about."

"I'm not worried," his friend replied. "I just feel a terrible sadness. There was so much I wanted to do and now so little accomplished. When I think of what might have been, I feel my loss most acutely. Of course this must be so—life is one desire after another; no individual in history has ever known complete satisfaction—but still, when I think of it, and wonder what lies on the other side, if one carries one's memories with one, I am stricken by the thought of what I am leaving: all my friends, the dawn light, the sun setting upon the water, the wondrous variety of the forest and its inhabitants, my mother's face, my first tears. No, Paul, I'm not worried; my earthly anxieties have departed from me. What I feel is terrible grief over all that I am leaving—and great wonder at that which is to come when the time itself comes. Peruche said that something was coming soon and what he meant was my death."

His words had a dreadful finality, writing the end to a life, bringing an invisible curtain down between them, dividing one from the other. Father Benedict looked away, feeling bereaved and shocked, his mind reeling from the impact of this one day which had not, as he realized with increased dread, yet run its full course. He watched the forest sliding past, the river lapping banks of clay, primitive jetties running back to the Indian shacks raised high on stilts, the odd Indian passing them by in his canoe, children pulling small nets in. *Rio Negro: Black River* . . . merely one stretch of the mighty Amazon, its vitreous surface limpid and quiet, reflecting forest and sky. What was he doing here? He did not belong here. This place only filled his head with old memories that made his skin burn.

Buried sin and mounting guilt: the accumulation of all the years. One sin above all others—the sin of lust—was what haunted him night and day. It takes a sensualist to know a sensualist, as Frank Poulson had recently proved, and Father Benedict (his mind filled with an image of brown flesh leading to nothing) understood that one minute of weakness could make a lifetime's remorse. It had happened in Australia, near a bleak, sunstruck town, when he, in his middle thirties, but still a virgin, had dreaded trying to sleep at night. Yet why that particular girl? Was it perversity or compassion? Had he thought to set her free from her own self-revulsion or to martyr himself in the flames? He now remembered her vividly, a half-caste, exceptionally beautiful, first seen at the far end of his desolate mission station in the primitive, sweltering outback of north Queensland. A brown flesh leading to nothing? Or to his own latent perversity? He had been drawn to the girl instantly, almost blinded by her beauty, and had followed her beckoning eyes, pretending to inspect his miserable domain, secretly burning up with lust and trembling shame, a priest surrendering all virtue. Celibacy: that curse. Could it ever be truly lived with? His eyes had ravished the smiling girl—her long black hair and inviting lips, her swaying hips and quivering breasts—and only later, in his room, during a rare thunderstorm, did he see clearly her bare shoulders, exquisitely rounded and delicate, the brown skin, which his lips yearned to caress, curving down to . . . nothing.

A cauterized stump for a left arm, the skin curled beneath the shoulder blade—and his heart, as his eyes fell on that terrible wound, had opened out to embrace her.

That memory could still scorch him, laying waste every defense, stripping away the pretense that he was a man of God, his virtue inviolate. Now he remembered vividly—as he had been doing all day—and his soul, which too often had huddled in doubt's grave shadow, seemed to drain out of him completely and leave him spiritually bankrupt. Oh, yes, he saw her vividly. And now wanted to confess to someone. *She dropped her dress and stood naked before me, her beauty making my senses reel.* That—and more. Not just lust, but a great compassion. *I saw the stump of her amputated arm and could not take my eyes off it.* Heat and sweat, the buzzing flies, thunder rumbling and lightning flashing, the shadows dancing over her naked skin and emphasizing her female curves. *I prayed to God in pious humility. The heat flooded my aching loins. When she stepped close, clasping her hands around my neck, my vows choked in my throat.* Lust—and compassion, her perfect beauty marred so hideously: that cauterized stump, brutally destroying her exquisite youth, stilled the last writhings of his guilt and led him into the flames. *Oh, God, and I a priest! And what did I do? Even now I cannot bear to think about it, nor let it out in confession.* He had wanted to dissolve into her, to make her whole by ingesting her, and his lips had found her throat, her exquisite shoulders, then that stitched, folded flesh. So his mouth and tongue had worshiped that terrible wound, his heart and soul pouring over her.

Why her? He would never know (he had soon fled to New Guinea), but he would, without a doubt, ponder the question all the rest of his days. A ravishing adolescent, one arm torn off at the shoulder, she had clearly suffered the conviction that her relationships could not be normal and, her spirit and pride crushed by that fact, was offering all she could give. Had she sensed his repressed desire? And did it matter what she had thought? He only knew that her armless shoulder, a shocking blasphemy against one so beautiful, had drawn out of him an overwhelming compassion and hatred of God. Before the lifetime, one moment: a blind and heedless decision, defying God and asserting human need—erasing that blasphemy with his tongue, denying the ugliness with his lips, and perhaps confirming, in that incandescent moment, that his pinioned spirit still lived.

Father Benedict covered his face, feeling the warmth of his cupped hands, bending forward in the hard wooden seat, the deck vibrating beneath him. He didn't want to think about it, tried to avoid it, failed dismally, remembering Frank Poulson's instinctive knowledge of what he had himself tried to deny against all of the facts.

He had taken his vows, but his vows had not protected him; if celibate, he had not wished to be so and failed to subdue his lust. The simple hungers of the flesh? Or the need to love and be loved? Doubtless both, which for others was quite normal, but for him was a sin. *Yet in the end I resisted, casting the unfortunate girl aside,* his desire and compassion, beating with great wings in that dark room, brutally destroyed by the intrusion of a spiritual training more remorseless than flesh. *God, no!* he had cried out—the words still rang in his head—*God forgive me, you poor child, please forgive me; get dressed and then leave here at once. . . .* And had knelt for hours that night, the sweat dripping from his naked body, the light from the oil lamp flickering over his shaking limbs as he gave God his thanks for his deliverance—and felt the self-contempt smothering him. For indeed, if he had learned to fear God, he had also come to fear women . . . or at least their power to destroy him.

"—dock is crowded," he heard Antonio saying. "The boat must have arrived."

Father Benedict looked up, squinting against the sky's glare, and saw Antonio and young Alex standing just in front of him, their heads lowered toward him. The paddle steamer was turning to port, moving past some shacks on stilts, and he saw, beyond the silhouetted outline of the Indian captain, the great floating docks of Manaus, clearly crowded with people. He rubbed his eyes and glanced around him, feeling confused and very shaken, saw Father Symonds dabbing at his sweating forehead with a crumpled white handkerchief.

"Did you say—?"

"The boat from Belém has arrived," Antonio replied immediately, "and the crowds are all out."

Antonio grinned and stepped aside, leaving Father Benedict's view unobstructed, and he saw the mass of people crowded along the floating docks, the brown turrets of the customs house thrusting up well behind them, and below them, supporting the enormous steel plates upon which they stood, the great drums upon which the docks floated, the water splashing around them. Alongside the nearest dock, white paint rotted with rust and peeling, was the Amazon River Steam Navigation Company two-decker boat that had brought passengers, livestock, and cargo nearly one thousand miles up the river from the great port of Belém. Most of the crowd were milling around that boat, and there was much noise and jostling.

"Looks like a carnival," Father Benedict said.

"A lot of buying and selling," Antonio replied. "It's a fairly big day for them."

Alex grinned and ran to the railing, his blond hair flopping in the wind, and Father Benedict, his nervous system in disarray, followed him and stood close beside him, his hands on the railing. The paddle steamer was pulling in, chugging past the larger boat, water cascading down its wheels and splashing over them, warm and wet and refreshing. Father Benedict heard Alex laughing and glanced down, examining his profile, noting the aristocratic forehead, the finely chiseled nose, the lips almost feminine and delicately sensual, the eyes, when they turned to glance up, an impossibly beautiful blue— all that, plus boyish candor and enthusiasm, and a complete absence of arrogance.

"Are you excited, Alex?"

"Yes, Father, I am. I really enjoy coming here. And it's even more exciting when a boat arrives—"

"And when it brings a newcomer."

The boy blushed a little, but nodded his head and smiled.

The paddle steamer's engine was turned off and its wheels stopped rotating. The boat bumped against the dock, making a metallic, grinding sound, and some Indians, wearing dirty white shirts and trousers, prepared to put out the steps. Father Benedict glanced left and right, surveying the crowds milling about on the dock, buying and selling fruit, a variety of fish and trashy trinkets, and then, remembering Father Symonds's words, returned his attention to Alex, who was still obviously excited.

"You seem particularly enthusiastic about meeting this American woman, Alex. One is driven to think, from the way you're behaving, that you've known her before."

"Yes, Father, you're right," Alex replied. "I can't wait to meet her. In fact, I feel as if I already know her—because the night before last I had a dream in which she appeared to me."

"The *American* woman appeared to you? What made you so sure it was the American woman, since you've never seen her before?"

"It was her. I knew it was her. I recognized her immediately."

"Really?" Father Symonds's voice said from behind their backs. "And what was this creature of your dreams like?"

"*Beautiful!*" Alex said.

Father Benedict turned with Alex to face the older priest and found him standing beside Antonio Bozzano, both of them framed by the broad expanse of the river. Here at Manaus the river was a hive of activity: floating houses and shops, floating fuel dumps and *restaurantes*, even a large floating ice factory, its chimneys belching black, oily smoke. Father Symonds, forcing a smile for Alex's benefit, nonetheless still looked terrible.

"Well," he said, "you might be right. The woman could indeed be beautiful. You *do* have a modest talent for precognition and telepathy, and if you're right in this case, it will not be the first time that one of your dreams has come true. Be prepared, however, for disappointment, since I think that in this case your dream is probably the product of wishful thinking of a most common kind.''

The priest's words were good humored, but his face showed a terrible strain, as if he were only managing to hold himself together with the greatest of wills. Father Benedict felt cold and frightened, remembering what his friend had said. The sun had started sinking in a surreal, kaleidoscopic sky, and he shivered, as if shaking off a ghost, and then turned back to Alex.

"He's right about that, Alex. You *do* have some strange gifts. I still remember that dream you had, just a month or so ago, when you saw—and I quote—*a great ball of fire in the heavens; an umbrella of light.* I remembered what you said because later I learned that that very same day—shortly after you had your dream— the Americans had dropped the atom bomb on Hiroshima.''

"A new and more terrible age,'' Father Symonds said. "Truly the end of man's innocence.''

An embarrassed silence fell between them—eased a little by the noisy crowd milling about on the dock above—and then, as if sensing that the silence had to be filled, Alex, watching the ladder being lowered down to the boat, said, "I told Peruche about that dream, and you know what he said? *It's a sign that someone is coming to point the way to your future*—by which he meant *my* future.''

"And you think that that someone might be this woman, my son?''

"Yes, Father Symonds.''

The old priest's smile crumbled, giving way to a trembling grimace, and he turned aside, shivering visibly, and then walked toward the ladder that led from the deck of the boat to the dock just above. Mengrire, who had arrived before them, simultaneously scurried down the ladder, nodding and murmuring his greetings to everyone and then heading straight for the suitcases at the far side of the deck. Father Symonds stepped onto the ladder, started climbing, missed his step, but was rescued by the alert Antonio Bozzano who helped him continue the short climb onto the floating dock. Alex was right behind him, and behind Alex, Father Benedict, and soon they were grouped together on the dock, being jostled by the milling townsfolk— Africans and Portuguese, European and Asian, *mesticos* and *caboclos* and *cafusos*—most of them shouting and gesticulating, swapping anecdotes and jokes, buying and selling and bartering with good-natured zeal.

They pushed their way through the crowd, heading toward the Belém steamer, Father Benedict walking beside Alex, Antonio holding Father Symonds's elbow and walking ahead of them, Mengrire trailing in their wake, carrying the suitcases. The dock was covered with small stands, all painted different colors, all stacked with flour and rice and *farinha*, with bright fresh fruit and fish, the combination of which filled the air with rich, pungent odors. The sun was setting quickly, sinking down behind the steamer, silhouetting the boat in a great fan of riotous colors which blended and changed to display the whole range of the spectrum and finally covered the market on the floating dock in a golden, unreal light.

Father Benedict, at that moment, hardly noticed all the excitement, his senses numbed to everything but sadness and a great wash of shame. The whole day had been very strange, a dream of magic darkly cast, filled with unpleasant confrontations and bizarre, haunting incidents. What a day to remember! First death, then departure; then a flood of memories leading back to the past and its severe accusations. And with the past, the future: the revelations of his old friend who now, walking two or three steps ahead, looked like the ghost of his former self. Dark omens, premonitions, sundry portents of doom—and magic, a blasphemous play with unknown forces, turning the world upside down. Father Benedict remembered his childhood, his strict religious upbringing, his years of solitude in the Australian outback, then temptation, the flesh weeping, a girl with one arm wanting attention; then his eager flight to New Guinea and the horrors of the war against the Japanese, along the Kokoda Trail. True anguish filled his heart, he felt an almost physical pain—and then he heard a sharp gasp, someone crying "Oh dear God!"

He stopped, dazed in the twilight. Blinking into a golden haze, he saw his old friend Father Symonds clutching his left arm and falling forward, his knees hitting the steel dock with a horrible, cracking sound as Antonio Bozzano, hissing something, leaned forward to pull him back, his hand missing and merely brushing the dying priest's shoulder as he fell down and rolled over.

Had he seen all this before? *It came true: he is dead.* Father Benedict moved forward quickly, dropping down beside Antonio, pushing the Brazilian back and grabbing his old friend by the shirt and shaking him violently while silently begging him to live. Too late: the priest was dead. His weary heart had given out. Grief and pain lanced Father Benedict, cutting through to his mortal soul, and then everything inside him, all the guilt and fear and love, burst forth and temporarily set him free, his tears finding a way out.

Alex stared at him in wonder, kneeling right there by his side, and then Father Benedict saw him looking up as a shadow fell over him. The crowd had gathered all around them, a ring of faces painted black, and Father Benedict, raising his head, feeling the tears on his cheeks, saw an extraordinary beauty, her red hair like flickering flames, and her eyes, large and frightened, opening and closing much too rapidly, as green as the grass of that England to which Father Symonds, his heart stilled for all time, would not, as Peruche had prophesied, ever return. The strange woman, floating magically in that golden haze above, her long, fiery hair hanging down around her tanned face, flicked her eyes from Alex to Antonio to Father Benedict, and then, her sigh as tremulous as the light breeze, spoke through bright, painted lips.

"I'm Laura Wellman," she said.

PART TWO:

THE PLANTATION

7

"That poor man," she said. "A heart attack! Oh, dear God, that poor man!"

Laura Wellman, sitting in the back of the Jeep between Antonio Bozzano and Alex, brushing her long hair from her face, let it blow out behind her in the wind, shook her head in a bewildered manner from side to side, and stared all around her. Alex watched her shyly and slyly, avoiding her gaze when she turned toward him, still shocked by the unexpected death of Father Symonds, but also, to his shame, helplessly dazzled by the creature sitting by his side, his senses reeling from the initial impact of her beauty. Night had taken command, plunging the surrounding forest into utter darkness, but Alex vividly remembered her fiery red hair, her brightly painted lips, and most of all, her incandescent green eyes with their long, fine eyelashes rising and falling in peculiar agitation. Father Benedict was in the front seat, sitting silently beside Mengrire, the slump to his shoulders telling all there was to know of his grief and shock—though he too (or so Alex imagined) had reacted in a startled manner to the first resplendent appearance of Laura Wellman—almost as if he had recognized her, or something strange in her.

"Oh, God, I still can't get over it! The way he just fell down in front of me. I saw him immediately—a priest amongst all those *natives*—and then, just when I raise my hand to wave, he falls dead with a heart attack. I mean, I feel that it's *my* fault."

"It wasn't your fault," Antonio said. "It was nobody's fault."

"Had he been ill? Do you think he was ill?"

"It was a heart attack," Antonio said. "At his age it's not all that uncommon, so please stop worrying, Miss Wellman."

Alex felt her eyes upon him, staring wildly out of the darkness, and something reached through to his heart and took a fierce hold on it. Mengrire mangled the Jeep's gears, making the vehicle shudder violently, and the warmth of Laura Wellman, when she fell against him, touched Alex with glory.

"Worry?" Laura said. "Of *course* I worry! When someone drops dead right in front of you, then naturally you *worry.*"

"*Please,* Miss Wellman," Antonio said, sounding to Alex not quite himself, and actually looking annoyed with the American woman, "I think it would be best if we could just drop the subject for now. Talking about it won't make us feel any better."

"Oh, dear, I've upset you."

"I assure you, I'm not upset at all; I just think it will do us no good to dwell on this matter. And I'm truly sorry, Miss Wellman, that you arrived to such a tragic event, which naturally has shaken you."

"Call me Laura. I don't like using surnames."

Antonio turned to stare at her, taking a deep breath as he did so, then slowly turned back to the front without saying a word. Alex felt very peculiar, too emotionally confused to think clearly, and he found himself glancing at Father Benedict as if for support. His good friend, the priest, a shadowy form in the forest's darkness, was sitting very quietly beside Mengrire, his shoulders still slumped.

"Where did they take the priest when they drove him away in that truck?"

"To a hospital in Manaus, Miss Wellman."

"Laura, Please call me—"

"Laura."

"And then? What happens then?"

Antonio sighed. "They will do what is necessary, and then, the day after tomorrow, he will be buried in a small graveyard outside the city—exactly as he would be buried in America or, in his case, England."

"Swell," Laura said. "Great." She put her hand up to her head, her elbow tapping Alex's temple, then lightly stroked her windblown, streaming hair and looked around at the forest. It was almost pitch-black in there, certainly too dark to see. In the cover of night the whole forest had come alive with alien sounds: bird calls and chattering monkeys, croaking bullfrogs and chirping crickets, the infrequent, muffled growling of a jaguar or puma, the constant rustling of the vegetation as giant rodents and anteaters and snakes traversed the forest floor, while that even more varied wildlife— macaws, cotingas, pigeons, honeycreepers, marmosets, toucans, spider monkeys, and every imaginable kind of spider—lived and died over a hundred feet above in the forest's dense canopy. Laura Wellman was obviously impressed—her tall and lean body shivered— then she turned to stare directly at Alex.

"Oh, dear," she said. "*What* did you say your name was?"

"Alex."

"Ah, yes, that's it. You must forgive me, Alex, for forgetting. But, you know, the priest dying and all—"

"Yes."

"—it sort of made me stop thinking. Anyway, Alex, you're a *very* handsome boy. What age are you?"

"Seventeen."

"God—excuse me, Father—what I'd give to be seventeen again! Unfortunately my youth has long gone, and the wear and tear shows."

"You're still attractive," Alex murmured shyly.

"You're extremely kind," she replied. "I'm feeling better already." A *seringueiro* bird called out, its cry jagged and metallic, and she twitched and put her hand on Alex's wrist, making his cheeks burn. "This jungle is spooky," she said. "Is it always this noisy?"

"Only at night. By day it's very quiet. Most of the animals stay hidden during the day and only come out at night."

"Thank God—thank heavens for that," she corrected herself, glancing nervously at Father Benedict's slumped shoulders, perhaps fearing his anger. "I mean, this noise, if it went on all the time, would drive you out of your mind. So how do you sleep at night?"

"You'll get to like it," Antonio said laconically. "And then, when you lie in your bed at night, you will never feel lonely."

Mengrire mangled the gears again and the Jeep almost stopped, then shuddered vigorously and lurched ahead, the beams of its headlights boring into the darkness over the crude, winding road while Antonio, Laura, and Alex were thrown into each other.

"I think this Jeep needs attention," Laura said. "Or perhaps the driver needs lessons."

Mengrire showed no sign of having heard the remark, but Father Benedict, sitting in the other front seat, coughed into his right fist.

"Father Benedict?"

"Yes, Miss Wellman."

"Can I take it that you're now in charge of the mission camp?"

"That is correct, Miss Wellman."

"I hope you don't resent me coming here for a month."

"Of course not, Miss Wellman. We're glad of the opportunity to let the world know what we're doing—and naturally the publicity will almost certainly bring in some of the funds we always seem to be needing."

"I'll try not to get in the way too much."

"I see no particular problems, Miss—"

"Wellman."

"—so there is no need to worry."

Clearly Miss Wellman was not ready to insist that the priest call her by her Christian name, and Alex wondered why. He felt strange sitting beside her, slyly examining her exquisite profile, unable to distract himself from the soft pressure of her hips and thighs which, pressed between himself and Antonio, gave life to his flesh. He had no experience of women and had thought little of sensual matters, but now, as if shedding his old skin, he felt his hidden self awakening.

And as if reading his thoughts, Laura Wellman turned toward him. "Seventeen, Alex? And you've lived here all your life? It must be a strange way to grow up. Do you like being here?"

"Yes, Laura, I like it."

"And do you go to school here?"

"Yes, I normally go to school in Manaus, but right now we're on holiday."

He hardly knew what to say to her, so dazzled by her was he, his heart seeming to beat much too fast, his senses scattering like pollen in the wind. He glanced up at the night sky, saw the ink-black jungle canopy, the odd patch of stars materializing above the trees and glittering with remarkable clarity from that vast, distant void. Everything seemed magical to him, incandescent, blindingly vivid, and when he turned his gaze back upon the woman her radiant presence poured over him.

"Is the mission camp very far away?" she asked of no one in particular.

"No," Antonio said, "we'll soon be there."

"I didn't quite get what you said when we met, Antonio. Do you work in the mission camp?"

"No, Miss Wellman, I work in the rubber plantation owned by Alex's father. I'm an overseer—a sort of foreman—in charge of the rubber gatherers: the *seringueiros*. To confuse you even further, that bird which you can hear right this minute, making that earsplitting metallic noise, is also called a *seringueiro*, or rubber gatherer's bird. So, when we talk of a *seringueiro*, we could be discussing either a bird or a rubber gatherer."

"Fascinating," Laura said, continuing to glance all around her. "I just wish I'd arrived in the daytime. It's so *frustrating* not seeing it all." Alex felt her hand squeezing his wrist as she turned toward him again. "And *you're* fascinating, Alex: living here all your life. Have you ever left this jungle at all or is that still to come?"

"No, I've never left—I've seen nothing beyond the Amazon—but at the end of next term my father is going to send me back to England to a school in London."

"You get driven to your school in Manaus every day?"

"No. I stay there five days a week and come back on the weekends."

"You like that?"

"No, I prefer it here in the forest."

"Why?"

"The Indians, the animals . . ." Alex didn't know what to say. How could he explain what he felt when the forest spoke to him? "I just like to visit Manaus," he continued lamely, "when a passenger pulls in. Like today, when you came."

A sliver of moonlight illuminated her painted smile, then disappeared, leaving darkness. "You make me feel welcome," she said. "You have a way with the ladies."

Her remark seemed charged with meaning, setting off a flare in his mind, and he felt her fingers squeezing his wrist again and then trailing off. The Jeep roared and raced ahead, bouncing over a mound of earth, and the wind, rushing through between Mengrire and Father Benedict, whipped at Alex's face. He reached up and touched his cheek, where her hair had lightly grazed it, and some part of him, the adult too long buried, leaped out of his center. The beams of the headlights slid off treetrunks, slashed across some hanging plants, then raced out to converge further ahead on a crude wooden post. Alex saw the huts of the mission, light pouring out through their various windows, and then noticed that Father Benedict was straightening his shoulders, as if coming alive again.

Mengrire forced the gear shift and pressed the footbrake too hard, and as the Jeep slowed down too fast and then leaped forward erratically, Alex reached out and gripped the back of Father Benedict's seat, thus ensuring that Laura Wellman was not flung into it, and felt the warmth and softness of her breasts against his outstretched, taut arm. At that, his cheeks burned and his heart beat too fast, but then the Jeep slowed down further and eventually ground to a rough halt, and the woman, offering a sigh (which made her breasts expand and press more urgently against his arm), sat upright beside him and, blinking rapidly, gazed curiously all around her, unaware of his embarrassment and desire and increasing confusion.

"You've reached your destination," Antonio said, his tone oddly sardonic.

"I don't believe it," Laura replied, glancing around at the jungle.

Alex climbed out first, more or less vaulting out, but by the time he turned around Antonio was helping Laura Wellman down, and Father Benedict, ostentatiously stretching himself, was staring at both of them. The woman was wearing a white cotton dress, not particularly attractive but practical, her feet in flat white shoes, her wonderfully long legs in stockings, and she stepped down to the ground with natural elegance, every movement a musical note. Alex was entranced, feeling as if he were in a theater, hypnotized by the woman as she curved her spine and pulled her shoulders back, letting her breasts, full and firm, fill out the simple dress.

Mengrire was unloading her suitcases and the leather case containing her cameras, but when she saw the latter she rushed over to take it from him, moving from the darkness into an oblique column of yellow light that beamed down through the mesh-wire window of the medical hut. Rescuing the bag, she slung it over her right shoulder, then, jerking her head for no reason, turned to face Father Benedict. The priest, running his fingers through his gray and black curly hair, seemed to be getting his spirits back and managed to give her a slight, tentative smile, his lined eyes, nonetheless, avoiding her face and focusing somewhere behind her.

"That bag looks heavy, Miss Wellman."

"It *is* heavy, Father Benedict, but since it contains my cameras and accessories, it just has to be carried."

"Well, you look like a strong and healthy young woman."

"Is that a compliment?"

"Certainly."

Alex saw her smiling, taking a deep breath, looking around her, her white clothes looking greenish in the yellow light from the medical hut. "So this is it," she said, holding her shoulderstrap with one hand, the other hand resting on the languid curve of her outthrust right hip. "A few buildings on the edge of the Amazon—and I'm here for a month." She offered a soft, throaty chuckle, fixing her smile on Father Benedict, then turned her profile to Alex as she looked across the wide, still, black river which, reflecting the moonlight, was striped with wavering striations that formed a great silvery fan which constantly rippled and swayed. The river, so dark and silent, its far bank lost in the night, had a mysterious and frightening quality that few could ignore; and Alex, looking from it to the American woman, saw her shivering as she turned back toward him, a nervous smile on her painted lips.

"Spooky," she said.

Mengrire, his gaze shifting around the woman's intimidating beauty, asked Father Benedict where he should take the suitcases, but before the weary priest could reply Miss Wellman spoke up.

"And you are—?" she asked the young Indian, and then added, before he could answer, "I'm *so* bad with names, particularly foreign ones."

"Mengrire," the Indian answered, deliberately affecting a look of stupidity. "My name is Mengrire. I am Christian and speak English. I work here—in the mission—as general help, and am always obliging."

"Your English is *very* good, Mengrire."

"You are most kind, Miss Wellman."

The Indian bowed his head very slightly, a sly grin on his face, which gesture was not lost on Father Benedict who, moving deliberately, stepped between them and addressed himself to the woman.

"So, Miss Wellman," he said, a gentle smile on his lips. "I suppose we should show you to your hut and let you get settled in."

"I'll leave, then," Antonio said, rather quickly, and turning his attention to Alex, added, "What about you? Are you coming with me?"

Why? To what? Alex found himself staring: unable to remove his eyes from the woman standing there in the yellow light. No, he didn't want to leave, could hardly bear the thought of doing so; he had no wish to return to his father's plantation, to that mausoleum of a house, to the giggling and shrieking that went on every other night when his father, more often than not with that swine Rollie Thatcher, forced some unfortunate Indian girl into his room for some drunken debauchery. No, not tonight; not with Laura Wellman here. He stared at her, almost speechless, remembering what Peruche had said—wondering if she was part of what the old Indian had prophesied would come very soon—and then managed to remove his eyes, his own beating heart astounding him, and briefly fix his attention on Antonio Bozzano, his very good friend. Antonio, normally smiling, was staring at him with his lips firmly shut.

"Well?"

"I think I'll stay here the night. If Father Benedict agrees."

He looked desperately at Father Benedict, silently begging him to agree, and the priest, smiling out of his slightly battered, handsome face, nodded his thick-curled head in agreement. "Presuming, of course," he added to his unspoken words, "that your father won't mind."

"My father won't even know that I'm not at home," Alex said, "so whether or not he minds doesn't come into it."

"Well, goodnight," Antonio said, hoping to change the conversation. "I am leaving you in very good hands, Miss Wellman, so I depart without guilt." He smiled charmingly, with a slight bow of his head, and then turned to Mengrire. "I'll wait for you in the Jeep until you've taken Miss Wellman's suitcases to her room. Try not to be too long."

The young Indian nodded, glanced briefly at Laura Wellman, and without a word picked up the suitcases and started off across the clearing, heading away from the medical hut to the buildings situated in a crude semicircle around the edge of the forest. They soon reached Father Symonds's hut, and Mengrire, moving athletically, kicked the door open with his bare foot and led them all in.

Father Benedict lit the oil lamps, one by one, saying nothing, and the flickering yellow light, growing stronger as each lamp was lit, soon illuminated the whole room and filled it with their elongated shadows.

Now Alex saw Laura Wellman clearly and was intoxicated by what he saw, her unusual beauty exciting his senses and confusing his thoughts. She looked around the Spartan room—at the hammock beneath the mosquito net, at the wooden table and hard chairs, at the empty, dusty shelves and the mesh-wire windows—and then, pointing down toward the floor, said with a slow sensual softness, "That's a pretty hard bed."

"Yes," Father Benedict replied, "my friend lived very simply."

"You mean," she murmured, "the priest who just died? You mean you've given me *his* room?"

"Yes," Father Benedict said. "He was due to leave today. You would have had this room anyway."

Alex met her wandering gaze and was startled by what he saw: a panic that made her eyes go out of focus as her hands rose and fell, the fingers curving as if in search of something solid and, failing to find it, contenting themselves with resting on her thighs and scratching distractedly.

"Why me?" she said intensely. "Why do these things *pursue* me? I feel so goddamned *haunted*!"

She looked at Alex again, her gaze drawing him toward her. He stepped forward, into her wavering black shadow, and stopped. He saw Mengrire looking confused, stepping sideways toward the door; then, as the Indian disappeared, he glanced across at Father Benedict, sensing that he, too, had been subtly altered by this woman's arrival.

"You don't want to stay here?" Father Benedict asked, raising his hands in a questioning manner.

"No, no, it's all right." She brushed her hair back from her face in an agitated manner, staring down at her suitcases on the floor and furrowing her brow; then, looking up at him and smiling, she added, "Of course I do. It's all right."

"I'm sorry, but there's no other place available, so—"

"It's fine, Father. No problem."

She nodded and offered a tremulous smile, instantly managing to look like a little girl, lost and uneasy. If before, to Alex, she had seemed very sophisticated, now, in that lamplit, Spartan room, she seemed at once aristocratic and genteel, her very presence a rebuke to the modesty of the former priest's life-style. "Well, well," she said, clapping her hands and then spreading them out to take in the room. "Home sweet home for a whole month. It should be an experience." Alex watched her turning slowly toward him, as she smiled and asked, perhaps embarrassed for the priest, "Would a lady be indelicate in asking where—?"

"I'll send one of our Indian assistants over straight away," Father Benedict said, stepping forward as if preparing to leave, his glance passing briefly over Alex. "She'll bring you some sheets and everything else you need—and show you where to go to wash up and—"

"That's swell, Father Benedict."

Alex stared at them both, very aware of the embarrassed silence, and was relieved when Father Benedict coughed into his fist and then cleared his throat. "In the Amazon we go to bed early and rise early," he said, "but of course if you would like some supper . . . or something to drink."

"I'd really love something to drink. Dare I ask for a beer?"

"I'll have the woman bring some bottles and some ice. Have a good sleep, Miss Wellman."

At that precise moment, just as Father Benedict was about to brush past her and walk out of the hut, what sounded like a great many drums started beating—suddenly, very loudly—and obviously very far away in the depths of the jungle. Laura Wellman jerked her head around, tilting it slightly, her eyes enlarged, first staring at Alex, then moving her gaze to Father Benedict, finally glancing beyond the motionless priest to the starry sky outside.

"What's *that*?" she asked.

Alex saw Father Benedict examining the floor at his feet and then, after what seemed like a long time, raising his head again.

"Indian drums," he said. "You hear them a lot around here. Don't worry: it doesn't mean they're going to war; they're just having some ceremony."

"What *kind* of ceremony?"

"We don't know, Miss Wellman." Father Benedict sighed, shrugging his shoulders, his face angled away from her. "Truth tell, we don't even know who those Indians really are. Those drums sound muffled because they're a tremendous distance away; somewhere very far north in the unexplored interior of the rain forest. The locals call them the Yano, but we can't be sure of that; what we *do* know is that they're clearly some undiscovered tribe—of which, in this vast region, there are many. So, Miss Wellman, whatever they're like, and no matter how loud their drums sound, they're too far away to do us harm—though they do make sleep difficult."

He was obviously trying to make light of it, but Laura Wellman was unimpressed, her ears cocked to that distant, frightening noise which actually made the floor shake.

"They're far away? Are you *sure* they're far away?"

"Yes, Miss Wellman. I'm sure. And I won't forget to send you that beer. It will help you to sleep."

Alex followed him through the door, giving Laura Wellman a smile, noticing, as he stepped out into the cold, dark night, that she was staring not at him but at the sky, her eyes drawn toward the source of that relentless drumming with its fast, mesmerizing rhythms. The drums called to him also, making him want to find Peruche, but he followed Father Benedict into the medical hut, where an Indian woman wearing a white smock, her weathered face clearly disturbed, was preparing to dim the oil lamps. Father Benedict told her about Laura Wellman and asked her to do the necessary. Seeing her nervousness and knowing what was causing it, he patted her reassuringly on the shoulder as he thanked her and said goodnight. Then he led Alex across the clearing to his own hut sheltering under the shivering trees.

The drumming had not abated; it indeed now seemed to be louder, and when they closed the door of the hut, though the noise was reduced somewhat, those pounding, relentless rhythms shook the walls and made Alex's heart race. Father Benedict, with a sigh, sat on a stool beneath his hammock, lit a cigarette, and inhaled with obvious relief before looking up again. His blue eyes, Alex noticed, were slightly bloodshot and a little unfocused.

"So," he said, "what did you think of the woman you so much wanted to meet?"

"She's beautiful," Alex replied.

"And?"

"I don't know. . . . She's different from anyone I've ever met before. Glamorous, sophisticated, and . . . a little bit strange."

"*Strange?* How do you mean?"

"I'm not sure. I mean, I'm not sure how to take her. I don't always know when she's serious and when she's joking. She has an odd way of talking, a sort of theatricality. . . . She laughs a lot, but seems a bit wound up, as if always performing. . . . I've never met anyone like her before—no one at all."

"And you find her attractive?"

"Yes. I've already answered that: she's beautiful—just *beautiful*."

"She's beautiful. And she's in her early thirties, which makes her too old for you, my son."

Alex blushed and lowered his head and then looked up again, touched by the priest's kindly smile and strange, painful sadness.

"I feel as if I know her," Alex said, "and have always done so."

"That feeling is one I share," Father Benedict replied, "but I'm inclined to put it down to the day's events and the way they've played on my mind. To put it mildly, my imagination has been stirred to the point of insanity."

"It's not just because she's beautiful," Alex heard himself saying, his voice emerging from some lost cell in himself and fighting its way to the surface. "It's also that she's different in a way I can't make out. There's a strangeness about her."

Father Benedict nodded judiciously, letting smoke out through his nostrils, then turned toward the table beside his stool and opened a bottle of beer. He asked Alex if he wanted a drink, received a negative reply, and then put the bottle to his lips and had a very long drink, after which, wiping his lips with the back of his hand, he inhaled on his cigarette again and blew out a thin stream of blue smoke.

"Different, indeed," he said. "*Very* different. I think she might be neurotic."

"Neurotic?"

"Never mind, my boy. I speak too much too soon. Now lie down on that bed and have some sleep, if those damned drums will let you. It's been a long day."

"I'll never sleep," Alex said.

He did not remove his clothes but lay down on the small camp bed, clasping his hands under his head and staring up at the ceiling. The wooden walls supported a thatched roof which, he knew, was festering with insects, but he contemplated that with equanimity. As he listened to the pounding drums, his thoughts spiraled back to Laura Wellman. Were the drums announcing her arrival? Did her presence here signal something? Had Mengrire in fact known that she was coming and why she would come? Alex pondered the questions, but was not disturbed by them, merely letting them fill the dark, most secret corners of his mind while the sound of the distant drums, repetitive, insistent, gradually encased him in a fine shell of sound and shut out the real world.

Had he slept? He wasn't sure. The Yano drums were still pounding. He heard a sigh and the sounds of movement, and turned his head toward Father Benedict, who was, at that very moment, rising slowly to his feet and shaking his thick-curled head from side to side as if trying to clear it. There was a cigarette butt in the ash tray, still smoldering but clearly finished; the bottle of beer, now back on the table, had also been finished. Father Benedict stared at him, grinned forlornly, and shrugged his shoulders. Without a word he crossed the room, opened the door, and walked out.

Alex followed him immediately, feeling as if he were dreaming, moving out of the hot room to the chill of the night where the beating drums, which had reached some sort of demented crescendo, made the hair stand up on his neck and drew his eyes to the sky. He glanced up beyond the trees and saw an irregular patch of stars, other lights, not the stars, rising and falling in silent splendor. He followed the starlight down, down through the various canopies of the forest, down past the writhing liana and the great tangled roots, back to the clearing just in front of Father Symonds's hut, where Laura Wellman was standing.

She was wearing flat slippers and an oversize blue dressing

gown, her long hair trailing down her curved spine as she stared up at the sky. The lights were extremely high, and obviously very far away, looking, from this vantage point, not much different from the stars—but considerably larger than the stars, and, more bizarrely, rising and falling in serene, stately grandeur.

She kept staring, hypnotized, unable to believe what she was seeing, while the sound of the beating drums, as far away as the magical lights, reached a pitch beyond pure noise, an almost deafening cacophony, causing the ground to tremble and the trees to shed their leaves. Alex covered his ears, watched Laura Wellman doing the same, and then saw Father Benedict, his hands already over his ears, walk toward the American woman and stop. He just stared until she, as if touched by some peculiar intuition, turned toward him and returned his frightened gaze, her eyes bright as the moon.

The drums abruptly stopped beating.

8

"I didn't sleep a *wink* all night," Laura said, raising the tin mug to her lips to sip some more coffee. "Not after that incredible drumming. I mean, I've never heard anything like *that* before. And then, when it stopped so suddenly, that shocked me as well: I've never known silence like that before. It was like a great scream." She sipped the coffee and winced, burning her lips on the hot metal, then put the mug back on the table and drummed her long fingers on the wooden top. "Really," she continued, "it was a very *frightening* sound, and I think you both know what I mean. You both seemed so odd when it was going on."

"Odd?" Father Benedict said carefully. "I don't know what you mean."

They were having breakfast in the dining hut, Alex sitting beside Laura Wellman, both of them facing Father Benedict across the long, narrow table. The air was already hot, flies and mosquitoes swarmed around them, and large black ants repeatedly appeared on the table, fearlessly wandering back and forth.

"I think you *do* know what I mean, Father Benedict," Laura replied, her brightly painted, sensual lips forming a smile touched with good-natured mockery. "*You* looked very badly shaken—exactly as I was—while young Alex here, lovely boy, was staring at me as if in a trance."

Father Benedict also smiled, but more tentatively, a watchful look in his eyes. "I think you're imagining things," he said. "I was merely surprised to see you standing there. And of course, I was still a little shocked by what occurred in Manaus. As for Alex, I think he's been staring at you from the moment he saw you—and if I may say so, given your beauty, it is quite understandable."

Alex felt his cheeks burning, but he didn't lower his gaze; instead, he glanced at each of them in turn, feeling good being with them. Perhaps *good* was the wrong word, for in truth he felt ecstatic, the very sight of Laura Wellman filling his soul with the light of enchantment. He, also, had not slept all night, though the cause was not the Yano drums; it was the image of Laura Wellman, floating teasingly behind his eyelids, that had made him toss and turn all night long on his uncomfortable camp bed.

Amused by his embarrassment, Laura placed her fingers around his wrist and shook it affectionately. "You flatter me," she said to the priest, "but I won't let you change the subject. I know why you were frightened—and why I was frightened. The drums were scary enough, but those lights in the sky! At first I thought they were stars; then I realized they were actually *rising and falling,* which no stars can do. And how did you explain it? That it was a kind of mirage? Really, Father, how can you, a priest, deliberately *lie* like that? Now I'd like the truth, please."

Father Benedict shrugged, took a cigarette from his shirt pocket, lit it, inhaled, and blew smoke out in a long and slow exhalation. "A little white lie," he said. "Even priests must weaken sometimes. I told you that because I didn't want you worrying about things you can't understand."

Laura smiled at Alex and squeezed his wrist. With her fingers lightly stroking his skin, she turned back to the priest.

"Things that *I* can't understand?"

"Things that *no one* can understand. Those lights have been seen for years—have always materialized when the drums beat—but no one knows for sure who's playing the drums or what those lights are."

"Why doesn't someone just go to that area and *look*?"

"More than one person has attempted to do that, but no one, not one single person, has ever returned. We don't know what happens to them and can only speculate: quicksands, wild animals, poisonous snakes, spiders . . . or, most favored theory of the locals, the elusive, apparently very barbaric Yano Indians, who may or may not exist."

"Who may or may *not* exist?"

"I'll let Alex explain to you."

Father Benedict sat back in his chair, inhaling contentedly on his first cigarette of the day, while Alex, now almost breathless under the full scrutiny of Laura Wellman, recounted the story of the Yano as passed on to him by his old mentor, Peruche.

"According to Peruche," Alex said, "who insists that he was once their prisoner, the Yano Indians were originally a group of

Yanoama who had to flee from their tribe and eventually settled in the unexplored region of Gatrimani, far north in the Amazon. Those runaway Indians are now barbaric and obsessed, perhaps even insane, and practitioners of their own bizarre religion in which God is reviled and the Dark One—the devil—is worshiped in strange, frightening rituals. As Peruche has also often explained, it is the belief of those outcast Indians—since simply called the Yano by the indigenous Yanoama—that the Dark One and his forces arrived on earth eons ago to create a Gateway to the Oneness, or the infinite, somewhere in the unexplored interior of the rain forest, and that his forces have, since then, returned frequently to earth, passing in and out of the Gateway, to and from the Oneness, or the Otherworld, of eternal life; and that during certain nights, when the Yano drums are beating, his dark forces are at war with the forces of Good.''

''And the lights?'' Laura asked, her voice hushed, her eyes as bright as the sun.

''The lights represent the Good. They war constantly with the forces of darkness. The Yano, though mortal, are the slaves of the dark forces and exist on the perimeter of the Gateway that leads to the infinite. The lights that we see rising and falling pass in and out of the Gateway, which separates this mortal world from that place where time and space have no meaning.''

''Why were the Yano chosen to serve the Dark One and his forces?''

''Long ago the Yanoama were innocent, living in a state of grace, naked and unafraid of the darkness, protected by faith. But then some of them were tempted, and succumbed to temptation, committing crimes against their Creator and their fellow men, their sins both sensual and violent. For this reason they were cast out, along with their women and children, and eventually, after traveling a long time, settled in that part of the rain forest believed to shelter strange gods—and considered by the Yanoama to be World's End, where the past meets the future. There, it was told, the forces of darkness claimed the outcast Yano who, once enslaved, became the practitioners of foul rites which invoke the powers of darkness within the Gateway.''

Laura's eyes were radiant, almost luminous, drawing Alex into their mysterious depths, and when her fingers stroked his arm, which they did more or less constantly, he felt all of his senses focusing on that as if nothing else existed. Yes, she touched him a lot, as she touched herself and all things near her, first stroking his arm, then scratching the table with her long, lacquered fingernails, then squeezing his knee gently, tapping her teeth with her index finger, running her thumb around the rim of her metal mug and then stroking his arm again. He hardly heard his own voice, aware only of her jittery movements, but when he finished she ran her fingers along his whole arm, visibly trembling as she glanced first at Father Benedict and then back at him, beads of sweat on her exquisite face.

"Is it true, as some of the Indians have told me, that the Yano hate women?" Laura asked, as if in a trance.

"Yes," Alex said, his heart racing.

"But why?"

"Women are of the earth, giving life to mortal flesh; thus, to the Yano, they represent God, who, having created the earth and mortal man, is the immortal enemy of those who came here from beyond time and space: the Dark One and his forces."

Laura's eyes, facing into the sun, had the brilliance of gemstones.

"And their own women? What about them?"

"Apparently they treat them horribly—as the lowest of the low— and frequently use them in ritual sacrifices. It is said that they are engaged in their rituals when we hear the drums beating."

"And usually that's when you see the lights?"

"Usually: not always."

Father Benedict sighed and stubbed out his cigarette. Placing his hands behind his thick neck, he stretched his broad body. "These are myths, no more, mostly spread by old Peruche. Alex, of course, tends to believe them, because he believes in Peruche. Isn't that right, my son?"

"Yes, Father, that's right. I believe the Yano exist. I also believe, like the Indians, that there is life beyond the visible, here, there, everywhere, existing around each and every one of us, at this moment, and all moments. And I believe, as Peruche says, that the forces of good and evil are in conflict where time and space have no meaning, which for us, whose vision is severely blinkered, is that area where the Yano are hidden and the lights rise and fall."

He kept his gaze on Father Benedict, aware that he might have angered him, and was relieved to see no more than a gentle smile and a laconic shake of his head; but then, when he returned his attention to Laura, he saw something much more disturbing: disbelief and gradually mounting fear, one at odds with the other. She raised her right hand to her mouth and pressed her long fingers to her trembling lips, as if she had been about to say something but had changed her mind. Father Benedict, after studying her carefully, lowered his eyes as if embarrassed. With an oddly hurried movement, he pushed his chair away from the table and stood up.

"You are here for a month, Miss Wellman, and can discuss this at your leisure; right now, I must be off about my daily business which is, I believe, what you want to see."

"Please call me Laura," she replied, obviously having gained courage. "I'll really feel terribly unwelcome if you continue calling me Miss Wellman."

Father Benedict smiled, unconcerned. "Laura it is. And what about you, Alex? What are your plans? Do you want to spend the day here or go home? The choice is all yours."

"Are you doing your rounds?"

"Yes, I'm doing my rounds."

"Then I'd like to come with you."

In truth, it would have made little difference to Alex what had been planned for the day, since his only interest was in being close to Laura. When they stood up, he quickly offered to carry her heavy camera bag, an offer she accepted gratefully, rewarding him with a dazzling smile. When he had hoisted the strap over his shoulder, she lightly ran her fingers through his hair and stroked his scalp, making him soar like an eagle.

"What *is* your daily routine?" Laura asked as they stepped out to the clearing.

"It varies," Father Benedict replied. "We are here not only to spread the gospel but to attend to the health and education of the Indians, with particular emphasis on educating the children. That's why we have a few small schools scattered about the area. Here on the mission we have a modest medical hut cum hospital for which, alas, we are constantly short of supplies. Much of my time is spent in knocking on a lot of doors in Manaus and begging for cash or—less humiliating but just as time-consuming—writing letters to charitable organizations in America and Europe. Naturally, when not thus engaged, I have to visit the various schools, Indian villages, *and* isolated families along the river, sometimes delivering medicine and other supplies, sometimes settling disputes—and always preaching the Scriptures."

"Sounds like a pretty busy life."

"It is."

"And when you talk about doing your rounds, presumably you mean you'll be making all those visits today?"

"Yes, Laura," Father Benedict replied. "So I hope you like boats."

The center of the clearing was filled with Indian children, some wearing shirts and shorts, some naked, all barefoot. Most of them were playing in the spiraling dust, chasing one another or the unfortunate chickens, or drawing with sticks in the dirt. Their parents were gathered in front of the medical hut, sitting on the steps or leaning against the tall stilts on which the large wooden hut had been raised. All looked undernourished and forlorn, their eyes as dead as their tongues. Father Benedict went up the steps, nodding and smiling at the numerous patients, but Alex turned back to watch Laura. As she photographed the children she begged them not to stare at her, but inevitably, after a few shots, they surrounded her.

"Gee," she said, smiling at Alex. "I wish I had something to give them."

"Don't give them anything," he replied. "You'll just set a precedent."

She wiped sweat from her high forehead, using her hand in lieu of a handkerchief, and then used that same hand as a fan. "Phew," she said with a low whistle, "it's so damned *hot* here. My throat's parched and I'm dying for a drink already." She stared steadily at him, her eyes bright and too intense. He offered to fetch her some water, but she chuckled throatily and said, "Thanks, Alex, but that's not what I had in mind. I better take some more pictures."

She pushed him aside gently, her fingers scratching at his chest. She smiled, raised her eyebrows, and with the smile still on her face started photographing the Indians in front of the medical hut. A few of them showed curiosity, some actually smiled, but most were apathetic. When she had finished, they both went inside.

The hut was long, narrow, and gloomy and divided into two sections. One was a square-shaped area used as a combined consultation room, first-aid room, and dispensary. The other, much larger, was used for inpatients. This area was divided, rather pitifully, with ceiling-high, woven-bamboo partitions, into numerous cramped, twin-bedded compartments, each bed covered with a mosquito net strung from the wooden-beamed, corrugated-iron ceiling. The patients—lying or sitting on the primitive beds because there were no chairs—were surrounded by cardboard boxes, woven baskets, and tin buckets. The whole place stank of urine and vomit and medicines. It was not an attractive place, and Alex, standing with Laura at the front door, felt strangely ashamed that it should be such a mess.

The reception area contained two hard wooden benches for the patients, a curtained-off corner which was clearly the doctor's consultation room, and, near Alex and Laura, a badly chipped trestle table at which, behind an untidy mound of papers, sat the middle-aged Indian nurse they had seen the night before. Father Benedict murmured a few words to her before disappearing behind the curtain of the consultation room.

"God," Laura murmured, glancing distastefully around her, "now I could *really* do with a drink!"

Alex looked away from her, humiliated by his burning cheeks. Father Benedict emerged from the consultation room, nodded at them both, and after lighting a cigarette, spoke directly to Laura.

"Well," he said, "what do you think?"

"I might have seen worse," Laura replied, "but only in bad dreams."

"We're very short of cash, that's the problem."

"You're not kidding!"

Father Benedict's smile was wintry, but his eyes, Alex noticed, contained an interest that had not been there yesterday. "That's why, as I said, I don't mind you being here. Your article could help us. We need all the donations we can get, which means we need some attention." He waved one hand toward the hospital ward. "Do you want to take any photographs?"

"Not now," Laura replied. "I've got four weeks. I can do all that later."

"And do you still want to see how I spend my day?"

"Yes," she said.

"Then let's go."

They left the hut, walking out onto the verandah and then down the steps, past the Indians waiting patiently to get in, and across the clearing, through the enormous shadows of the forest to the small jetty. Father Benedict's boat, actually a canoe with an outboard motor, was tied to the posts thrusting up from the calm, humus-blackened water. When they were all in the boat, Father Benedict tugged the cord of the outboard motor until it had coughed into life. He took the rudder and headed out into the river which, with its ribbon of jungle etching a green line far away, seemed to be curved under the sky like a great, rippling bowl.

He headed straight across the river toward the endless green line of jungle, and soon, caught in the river's gentle flow, they were cooled by a merciful breeze. The sky was an azure sheet, the sun high and fiercely hot, but dark clouds were coming over the horizon, threatening rain. Alex put his hand in the water and watched it arch up on both sides of his wrist, curving down toward the boat's wake. It was warm but refreshing, sending tingles up his arm. Feeling the length of Laura's thigh against his own, he turned and met her abstracted gaze.

"It's beautiful," she said.

"Yes," he replied. "But a lot of people find it as threatening as it is beautiful."

"I don't think I'm one of them. I think it's beautiful. That's all there is to it."

"I'm glad."

"Why?"

"Because I want you to like it."

"Oh, Alex, you're such a sweet boy: you make me feel so important."

Her pleasure seemed genuine, but that could not stop him from blushing, and he found himself staring at Father Benedict, who, handling the rudder with considerable skill, was staring thoughtfully at Laura. There was admiration in his glance but also a certain tension, and Alex found himself wondering uncomfortably what his good friend was thinking. Then the priest leaned forward a little, his left hand still on the rudder, his face casually composed, looking directly at Laura.

"Well, Laura," he said, "what's it like to be in the Amazon after New York?"

"Strange," she replied. "*Very* strange. More so because of last night. I don't know what I expected, but I certainly hadn't prepared myself for anything remotely like *that*. Now I'm not only tired, I also feel disoriented—and here, in this great silence, I feel as if I'm losing myself."

"Would that be good or bad?"

"That would be wonderful."

"Why?"

"Never mind." She reached into her bag for a pair of sunglasses, put them on, and looked around her. "Lord," she said, "but it's so damned *hot* here! I'm just *dying* of thirst."

"Would you like a beer?" Father Benedict asked.

"Are you kidding me, Father?"

"No, Laura, of course not. We all drink a lot of beer in the Amazon; this boat is kept well supplied." He reached down to the wet burlap bag at his feet, pulled out two small bottles of beer, opened them, and handed one to her.

"What about Alex?" she said.

"Alex doesn't drink beer—nor, indeed, any other kind of alcohol. Now, isn't that true, Alex?"

"Yes, Father."

"So young, Alex," Laura crooned teasingly. "So pure."

"Yes, Laura, he is that." Father Benedict raised his bottle and tapped it jokingly against Laura's, and they both drank. Father Benedict took a swallow and lowered the bottle, showing interest in the speed with which Laura managed to dispose of more than half of hers. When she finally stopped drinking, gasping with relief, Father Benedict coughed into his fist and gazed steadily at her. "I believe you don't actually come from New York," he said. "How long did you live there?"

"About four years," she said. "I first went there in 1941, just before Pearl Harbor. God—excuse me, Father—I still remember that terrible scene. I had nightmares for months after I saw it—and still have them occasionally."

She shuddered and drank some more beer.

"You were *there* when the Japanese bombed it?" Father Benedict asked.

"No," she replied. "I photographed the harbor a few days after the attack. I was working for a newspaper in New York, and Pearl Harbor was my first big assignment. They flew me out to Hawaii, and I'll never forget what I saw as long as I live." She shuddered again and had another drink of beer, taking a lot very fast; then, holding the bottle up and dangling it between her fingers, she let her face express her disappointment at finding it empty.

"Another one?" Father Benedict asked.

"Oh, yes," she said. "*Please.*"

Father Benedict, still only halfway through his own bottle, opened another and passed it to Laura, then moved the rudder a little and turned the boat toward the opposite bank. The dark clouds, which had been coming toward them from the hazy horizon, had been blown by the wind to the west and were moving away from them, leaving the sky a clear, burnished blue from which the sun cast down a fierce heat. The river, spread around them like a huge mirror, reflected the few drifting white clouds.

"And how long have you been with *National Geographic*?" Father Benedict asked casually.

"Only since August," she replied. "Shortly after we dropped the bomb on Hiroshima. Though I must confess, coming here has made it seem a lot longer."

She had another drink of beer while Alex stared at her, fascinated, thinking of the dream he had had the night before that bomb fell on Japan. He wanted to tell Laura about it, but couldn't, feeling strangely embarrassed.

"You appear to have a penchant," Father Benedict said, "for somehow linking yourself to momentous occasions. Is that what you meant yesterday when you said that you felt haunted, and that bad events seem to pursue you?"

"They do, Father! They *do*!" She nodded her head vigorously, then had another drink. She licked her lips and stared at him again, this time almost defiantly. "I mean, why *me*?" she said. "I had only *joined* that newspaper! And yet two days after I joined—you understand? *two days*!—the goddamned Japanese bombed Pearl Harbor and *I* got the job. That's more than a strange coincidence, Father; that's what I'd call *fate*!"

"I hardly think—"

"Yes, Father: *fate*! I was somehow tied to it! And then later, when we dropped the atom bomb, I just *knew* that . . ." Her words trailed off to nothing and she turned her gaze on Alex, her flickering smile not disguising that she was clearly disturbed. "Oh, Alex," she said, reaching out and stroking his cheek. "You're so beautiful because you're so completely innocent that you seem almost unreal."

There was silence for a moment, broken only by the boat's engine, Alex a little puzzled by what she meant and noticing, from the expression on his face, that the priest felt the same. The opposite bank had taken shape as a dense forest, and they were heading straight for it.

"The atom bomb?" Father Benedict queried quietly. "What had that to do with you?"

"Things like that . . . You don't understand." She gazed across the sullen river. "The dropping of that bomb meant something to me. . . . I remember . . . I *can't* explain!"

She shook her head in a frustrated manner, her hair whipping her face, tilted the bottle of beer to her lips, and finished it off in one gulp. Alex watched her, amazed, and saw the priest's face, also amazed; then Laura lowered her bottle, letting it rest on her lap, licked her lips, and stared across at the approaching bank of red mud and yellow rushes, her dark glasses making it difficult to gauge just what she was feeling. Alex heard someone humming—it was himself, displaying his nervousness—and then Laura, as if understanding what he felt, reached out to him, her thin, delicate fingers wavering blindly in the air before settling, as light as a purple orchid, on his trembling, virgin knee.

"That bomb meant something to you?"

"Yes, Alex, it did."

"It meant something to me as well," he said, "because I saw it exploding."

"You *saw* it exploding?"

"I dreamt about it the night before. I saw a great ball of fire in the heavens; an umbrella of light."

"A dream . . ." Laura murmured.

"But very accurate," Father Benedict said. "Alex told me about that dream the morning after he dreamt it—and later, that same day, the Americans dropped the bomb on Hiroshima."

Laura removed her sunglasses and stared at Alex like a large cat, hypnotizing him and rendering him helpless. "*A great ball of fire in the heavens; an umbrella of light.*" Her voice was as gentle as a raindrop on the river, rippling across the surface of his heart with beguiling humility. "I felt that I was meant to come here," she murmured dreamily, "and now you've confirmed it. That bomb made me flee America . . . and now it's brought me to you."

"What do you mean by that?" Father Benedict asked, startled.

"Never mind," she replied vaguely. "I meant nothing."

Father Benedict stopped the outboard motor, letting it whine down into silence, and the canoe drifted gently toward the sloping red bank that led up to the lush green rain forest. There was no Indian village in sight—just a tiny natural clearing—but a crude path could be seen winding away into the forest's deep gloom. Mosquitoes and flies buzzed in thick clusters, animal tracks led to the water, and not far away, as if noting their arrival, the tall rushes parted and fell back together in a wavering line as a caiman or some other unseen creature moved well away from them.

Laura shivered and looked up, her gaze following the soaring trees, then put her dark glasses on again, the bright light defeating her. Splashing through the shallow water after Father Benedict, she turned back to look directly at Alex as he carefully followed her. He smiled at her, confused, hating his own innocence. He bent his neck to let his cheek touch her hand when it slid onto his shoulder. He blushed again, his heart pounding, but did not move his head, letting the warmth of her hand burn through his skin and warm the blood in his veins. Then he saw Father Benedict, his face lowered in embarrassment; feeling guilty and afraid, he straightened up and stepped sideways.

"You want to see how we live?" Father Benedict said tonelessly. "Then get ready to do a lot of walking through this very hot forest."

"I need another beer," Laura replied. "Or preferably something much stronger."

Father Benedict stared at her for what seemed a long time, then, shrugging his shoulders, turned away and headed into the forest. Alex, not sure of what was happening, reached out blindly toward Laura, trying to touch her with his fingers, with his heart, before the dark forest swallowed them.

He did not in fact touch her but let his hand dangle in the air. In a trance, without saying another word, they both walked into the shadow of the trees and left the river behind them.

9

The moon was pale and pockmarked, beaming across the black river, its silvery striations spreading out through the darkness and forming an alluring chiaroscuro on the rippling water. Laura shivered and leaned forward, wrapping her raised knees in her arms, then rocked herself gently back and forth as she stared at the darkness.

"Are we all right here?" she said. "Is it safe? What about snakes and things?"

Alex, sitting beside her, was amused by her concern. "Yes," he said. "We're perfectly safe. Nothing will harm you."

"No snakes?"

"No snakes."

"No poisonous spiders?"

"No poisonous spiders. All the things you fear are in the forest and will not come out here." It was a lie, but a harmless one, designed to ease her mind: the odd snake or poisonous spider would certainly be found here, but usually would, if faced with a human presence, promptly move off elsewhere. As for the forest, it had come alive, chattering incessantly all around them, weird and ghostly sounds ricocheting back and forth, held bizarrely within an outer shell of silence composed of water and sky. The river itself was still and very quiet, a glittering quiltwork of shifting light.

"It frightens me," Laura said. "It has a strange, terrible beauty. When I look at it, I imagine how easy suicide could be. The river, in the moonlight, is almost hypnotizing; it tugs at your body."

She raised her glass to her lips and drank some more of her *caipirinha*, which was a very potent mixture of *cachaça*, cane alcohol, mixed liberally with lemon and ice. She appeared more sober now—she seemed to have drunk herself back to sobriety—and she offered him a self-deprecating smile as she said, "Was I really terrible this evening? I can't remember it all."

"No," he said, too embarrassed to tell the truth, "you were just a little bit drunk."

"More than a little bit, Alex . . . and Father Benedict was angry."

"Don't worry about it."

She did not reply immediately, and he glanced sideways at her, his emotions confused and spilling over into areas unknown to him. Father Benedict, if not angry, had certainly not been impressed, and had left them just a few minutes ago, immediately after the evening meal, claiming that he was simply too tired to stay awake any longer. Of course it had been a lie, a mere diplomatic ploy, and Alex, naïve though he was, knew that Laura had caused it.

Now, as he gazed at her, the long day unraveled itself: the arduous walk through the forest, following the narrow, winding tracks, stopping first at a tiny village, then at a small school just outside it, then the first of many isolated families living down by the river; then another boat journey, the noon sun blazing overhead, another village, more lonely families, another shabby school in the forest, then another boat journey, another landing, heat and sweat their reward.

At first Laura had been fascinated, her tongue tripping out endless questions, her different cameras (Alex had carried the heavy bag) being used almost constantly: photographing the shacks on stilts, the children playing in the dirt, the skinny fishermen with their nets drifting out around their canoes, the *seringueiros* tapping rubber trees on the land of dying plantations—and, of course, Father Benedict's flock, a few Christian, most not, many *Umbanda* or *Quimbanda* worshipers, their common denominator being poverty and hunger and sickness: malaria, dysentery, skin diseases, and sleeping sickness, some suffering from hernias and suppurating sores, others with elephantiasis or hideously deformed limbs.

Yes, she had been fascinated initially, her photographer's eye seeing all, bedazzled by the visual possibilities and using film extravagantly. But then it became too much—too much walking, too many boat rides, either scorched by the sun that blazed down on the open river or drained by the suffocating humidity of the gloomy forest's interior—and so she had asked for another beer, and then another, and another, until Father Benedict, his face composed in weary sufferance, informed her that his beer supply was finished and she would have to go thirsty. That had made her really angry, exploding with, "Dammit, this jungle stinks!" Then she had called defiantly to Alex, making him open her large camera bag, and had withdrawn from it the bottle of lethal *cachaça* from which she had, during the rest of that grueling day, sipped regularly and defiantly.

"He did it deliberately, didn't he?"

"Pardon?" Alex said.

"Father Benedict visited more places today than he would normally visit—and he did it deliberately."

"I admit, he did a lot."

"He did it deliberately," Laura insisted.

"I don't see why—"

"For some reason he feels threatened by me—that's why he did it."

"I don't think he would do that, Laura."

"He would and he did. He wanted to humiliate me. And now, just because I was so hot and drank too much, he has something to hold over my head if I step out of line. Oh, yes, I can see it!"

Alex, not knowing what to say, gazed across the dark river. The *cachaça*, following the beers, had certainly loosened her tongue, making her talk of black magic, of destiny and fate, filling her conversation with words such as *haunted* and *possessed*, and causing Father Benedict, for whatever reason, to become angry and frightened. Later, after sunset, right here in the mission, sitting down over dinner with the flies and mosquitoes buzzing, she had said to Father Benedict, as if speaking to herself, "I know what you think, but it's not true: I don't actually drink that much."

"I think you've drunk a bit too much today."

"I'm not a celibate, dear Father."

That was when Father Benedict had left them, walking away in quiet rage.

"Oh, God," Laura said. "I *do* drink too much. And here I am, after that goddamned, awful day, still sitting here drinking. Alex, my friend, my beautiful young man, you must think me a witch."

"I think you worry too much."

"You're so mature for your age."

"You're making fun of me, but that doesn't matter: you *still* worry too much."

"It's Father Benedict I'm worried about."

"He's a nice man. Stop worrying."

"God, Alex, you're really wonderful for your age. You're a strange, lovely boy."

For the first time in his life, he resented that form of address, suddenly preferring to think of himself as a man and desperately, his wounded heart bleeding, wanting her to acknowledge it. As if sensing this, her right hand, fingers outspread, lightly fell on his head.

"Do you think he's jealous, Alex?"

"Jealous?"

"You *sweet* boy! Never mind!" She had another sip of her *caipirinha*, lowered the glass, and licked her lips. "Let me tell you something," she said, her voice sounding peculiar, floating toward him on an almost imperceptible breeze, each word sounding a different note. "On my first birthday, May the seventh, nineteen fifteen, a German U-boat sank the liner *Lusitania*. My mother, carrying me in her arms, visited Aleister Crowley, the Satanist known as the Great Beast, who was then staying in New York at 40 West 36th Street—an address I can never forget. As the *Lusitania* sank off the coast of Ireland, drowning nearly two thousand passengers, my mother witnessed—and, I believe, took part in—the sexual magic practiced between the Great Beast and a black prostitute, Anna Gray. I have lived with that knowledge all my life, and it haunts me relentlessly."

He saw her face in the moonlight, the green eyes still intense, no trace of a smile on her lips. Was she joking? No: she was shivering with emotion. Her free hand, which had been resting so lightly on his head, slid sensually down the side of his face and came to rest on his shoulder. Her other hand was holding the glass of *caipirinha*, which she sipped quite methodically.

"Aleister Crowley! The Great Beast! The world's most wicked man! Drunkard, drug addict, mesmerist, sexual deviant, and the most infamous and sinister black magician of the twentieth century, endeavoring to become a god, ending up as a monster, and driving many of those he met along the way into every kind of degeneracy and insanity. And my mother, in the madness of her delusions, lay down with him and his whore!"

She stared at Alex, almost wildly, then reached out and grabbed his wrist, shaking it as fiercely as a dog would shake a bone, her luscious lips trembling.

"Yes, Alex, she did that—and never ceased to remind me of it, telling me that she had engaged in some ritual with that monster and his whore while I, a one-year-old baby, lay right there beside them in the room—insinuating that because of what went on that night I, her daughter, had been committed to the forces of evil and that they would come to claim me sooner or later. That's what she told me, Alex—and what she told my father. She hated him. In her hatred she wanted to hurt him by telling him that his only daughter had been cursed. Of course the plan didn't work: the only person damaged was *me*. My father didn't believe in black magic—he simply assumed that my mother was mad. But I grew up believing that I was possessed. By the time I was an adolescent I lived in quiet, endless torment, haunted by nightmares.''

Alex was perplexed, not understanding what he had heard. ''But I thought you came from Hollywood,'' he said lamely. ''How did you—?''

''Hollywood! Hollywood! Don't *mention* that awful place! Oh, Alex, my Alex, don't tell me you romance about *Hollywood*!'' She put her glass to her lips, had another sip of the *caipirinha*, and stared at him intensely. ''The story I told you is true, Alex. God's truth, no less. My mother never stopped telling me about that night of debauchery with the Great Beast and suggesting that I had, because of that, been possessed by the forces of evil. Hollywood? What *better* place than Hollywood? That's where dreams become real!''

''I still don't understand.'' Alex said. ''I'm not sure what you're—''

''Hollywood, dear Alex, is where dreams become real, but whether that's good or bad depends on the dreams. And mine were all bad.''

Her words trailed off weakly, dissolving into the night's darkness. The forest's chattering, which Alex had briefly forgotten, returned to assail him. He was used to it—normally liked it—but now found himself resenting it, wanting to hear nothing but her voice weaving a fine web around him. Her fingers tightened on his shoulder, shook him slightly, and fell away, making him feel quite bereaved. But then she leaned closer to him, her eyes reflecting the moonlight, her breath smelling of *cachaça*.

''Yes,'' she said, ''I was born and bred there—where they make all dreams real—where most people don't know the difference between fantasy and reality: between the lives they created on the screen and the lives broken around them. And did I know the difference? I'm not sure that I did. We lived in Windsor Square, surrounded by the major studios, and my playgrounds were the studio backlots where, usually alone, my head filled with my private scenarios, I acted out my fantasies in abandoned forts and castles, deserted western towns, realistic Roman galleys still afloat in enormous tanks, luxurious, three-walled penthouses on huge, silent stages, and artificial tropical gardens and forests. And of course, in our rambling house on Lorraine Boulevard all those movie stars about whom the world dreamed came and went, pretending to be what they were not, unable to distinguish between their real selves and their public image. Between those idols and my lonely hours in the studio backlots I grew up in a world of make believe. And suffered for it.''

She sipped her drink again, licked her lips, and stared across the dark river, her brow furrowed. When she looked once more at Alex, he melted.

''There I was, surrounded by wealth, having the famous as neighbors and friends, yet living in a terrible, crippling solitude with a mother going crazy and a father too involved in his own life to take any notice of me. You have to understand, Alex, that my mother's marriage to my father had been *arranged* by their families—very powerful families—to enhance the business merger of their studios. Already feeling bought and sold as part of a package, my mother was further humiliated because she truly loved another man—a studio grip in her husband's studio. She claimed he was intimidated into getting out of her life when my father found out about their affair and took immediate, brutal action: he sacked the grip, paid him to leave Hollywood and never return, and saw to it that my mother, then a successful actress, never obtained work again. Yes, he got rid of the only man she had ever loved, destroyed her career by simply making a few phone calls, and then made her pregnant to enslave her to a motherhood she hadn't wanted at all. And of course she grew to hate him. Not only him, but the daughter he had given her against her wishes. Namely me.''

She lowered her eyes, gave an audible sigh, shook her head disbelievingly from side to side, and shivered a little. When she next spoke, her voice was like a whisper carried home on the gentle breeze.

''It was a terrible situation, an emotionally destructive situation, and it only became worse when my father's successes multiplied. My mother, more frequently ignored, and her resentment toward him increasing, started slipping from theatrical eccentricity into genuine madness. Heavy drinking, promiscuity, an increasing fascination with black magic and the occult—a fascination that had, as far as I could tell, first started the night Aleister Crowley seduced her in God knows what repulsive and evil manner.''

She put her empty glass down, setting it gently on the grass between her crossed legs, and leaned forward a little. A light breeze, coming off the murmuring river, made the surrounding trees shiver.

"So there was my mother," she said, "growing crazier every day, her face garishly painted and her clothes wildly Gothic, looking like some grotesque imitation of Pola Negri, picking up and dropping lovers with the casual indifference of suppressed mania, and attending every seance and black magic ritual that she possibly could. And I, a mere child. As a blossoming fifteen-year-old I was exposed to my mother's lovers, forced to attend her seances and rituals, and constantly reminded of her brief flirtation with Aleister Crowley. I became convinced that I had indeed been cursed and that the forces of darkness would sooner or later come to claim me. I believed it then, Alex, and believe it now. I can't help myself. I still have the vivid dreams, all those nightmares of light and darkness: of black men coming at me out of featureless blackness and filling me with the seed of their unnatural being while the heavens split open. Where is this? I don't know! It is here and everywhere. But it haunts me night and day, every minute, every second, and I know that my destiny lies where good blends into evil."

Alex could scarcely credit what he was hearing, but her tale drew him in: colored with mystery and luminous with dread, conjuring up a world beyond the visible very much like his own. Was she mad or was she as sane as his old friend Peruche—he who saw the reality behind the illusions of the material world and was thought of by many, particularly white men, as either a madman or a charlatan?

"And now your mother's dead?"

"Yes, Alex, she's dead." Laura's head moved left and right as she scanned the dark river, then she sighed and lowered her face as if praying, her body curved like a bow. "I left home," she said. "I couldn't take it anymore. I went to New York, hung around there for a year, and then received an urgent cable from my father, telling me my mother had died of cancer and ordering me home. The next day, I was back in Los Angeles attending my mother's funeral. At my father's insistence I stayed on there, moving back in with him in that big, rococo house in Lorraine Boulevard, near most of the studios."

Her voice faded into a whisper as she glanced at the sky, where instead of rising and falling lights she saw commonplace stars.

"It just didn't work out, and I should have known it would not. Wearied by what he felt were my mother's—and presumably my own—neuroses, my father burst out into freedom by leading a hectic social life, bringing different women home every night and constantly criticizing *me* for remaining alone and rarely leaving the house. He was right, of course—I rarely left that house. Completely dependent on my mother for protection against the forces of darkness, and now left without her protection, I was terrified of the night but more terrified of going out. I became a recluse, taking tablets to keep me calm, sleeping all day and staying awake all night with all the lights in my room on. This drove my father crazy—and embarrassed him socially. Finally, when he threatened me with psychiatric treatment, I became really scared. So, Alex, can you see what had to happen? Unable to face my father's other women—mostly ambitious starlets—frightened that my mother's death had left me unprotected against the forces of evil to whom she had committed me, terrified of being alone in the darkness, and unnerved by the possibility that my father might commit me to a mental institution, I plunged headlong into a hopeless marriage.''

"You were . . . *married*?"

"Yes, Alex."

Alex was shocked, ridiculously so, not having even thought of this possibility and, being suddenly faced with it, feeling immeasurably betrayed. He didn't know why he felt this way—and had no reason to do so—but the pain, piercing through his jumbled emotions, was unfamiliar and terrible. He stared at her, feeling the pounding of his heart, and observed her lost in herself.

"It was 1936," she said, "when I was twenty-two years old. Robert, eleven years older than me and the son of one of my mother's friends, was a financially struggling atomic physicist, full of talk about the mysteries of atoms and other strange things, and working in a secret establishment in Los Alamos, near Las Vegas, Nevada. Naturally, we had little in common either socially or intellectually, but decent and dedicated, he was also understanding and patient, and soon—by which I mean after a few weeks—he managed to encourage me out of that big house and back into the world of real people. Did I love him? No, I don't think I *ever* loved him. But being lonely and frightened, almost pathologically so, and increasingly estranged from my bewildered and embarrassed father, I soon convinced myself that what I felt *was* love, and so, much too quickly after first meeting Robert, accepted his proposal and married him hurriedly in Las Vegas.''

Alex sat there, scarcely breathing, hearing the murmuring of the mighty river, the sighing of the breeze in the trees, the forest's incessant, dominating, chaotic chatter and (or so he imagined) his own beating heart. He wanted the darkness to ease his pain and desire—and wanted never to leave her.

"Of course," Laura continued, her voice adrift in its own drama, "I was still a virgin at the time—almost frigid in fact. From the first night of our marriage our physical relationship was a disaster. Convinced I was being haunted by the forces of darkness, I couldn't give myself over to the sexual experience. As I soon found out, all I really wanted was someone beside me in that frightening darkness. Oh, God, it was terrible! Even now it makes me blush! I made love with my body, but my mind was always elsewhere, my inner eye roaming constantly through the darkness in search of those demons. I still had the vivid dreams—so vivid they seemed real—and felt presences in the darkness, surrounding the bed while my husband slept, not real, incorporeal, sort of swimming around me, drawing me out of myself and somehow carrying me to that place where, while the darkness was divided by the light, my mortal body was desecrated in the most obscene fashion and made the repository for evil in its most vile manifestations. . . . Oh, God, how I suffered from those hauntings! And fought to cling to my sanity."

Her voice trailed off again, this time with a note of despair, and Alex, for the first time finding pain in his beloved darkness, wished that he could talk to Peruche and learn what he should know.

"Are you still married?" he asked, shocked to hear his voice trembling, equally shocked to find that he was frightened of what the answer might be.

"No," she said, "I'm not married anymore. I couldn't satisfy my husband in bed—because my nightmares were growing worse and because I couldn't stop talking—dear God, as I'm talking right now—about the subject that obsessed me and refused to leave me alone. So naturally this eventually convinced my husband and most of his pragmatic, scientist friends that I was either neurotic or completely insane. In the end Robert grew weary and frustrated. After about three years we both had enough sense to call it a day. In 1939 I returned to Hollywood. With the assistance of my forgiving and influential father, I became a portrait photographer for his studio—right back where I had started."

Her voice trailed off again and she looked appealingly at Alex, reaching out to stroke his bare arm with her fingers and fill him with warmth.

"What made you finally leave Hollywood?" he asked, wanting only to hear her voice.

"I hated Hollywood," she said, "and everything it stood for. Again through a friend of my father's, I obtained a job with a newspaper in New York, starting, when I was twenty-seven years old, two days before the Japanese bombed Pearl Harbor."

She shuddered visibly and straightened up, removing her hand from his wrist, then glanced up at the starry sky with a certain longing and took a deep breath.

"It doesn't look like we're going to see the lights tonight," she murmured.

"You're looking in the wrong direction," Alex replied. "The lights always materialize north, and you're looking south. But tonight I don't think you'll see anything: the Yano aren't playing their drums."

Laura smiled wanly, turning her empty glass between her fingers.

"In Hawaii," she said, almost as if speaking to herself, "shortly after that Japanese air raid, as I was photographing that terrible destruction, I was reminded of the sinking of the *Lusitania* on the day my mother took me to Aleister Crowley's apartment. The sinking of the *Lusitania* had encouraged American involvement in the First World War, and I was frightened to think that I had been given, as my very first newspaper assignment—and only because, quite remarkably, no more experienced photographer was available—the job of photographing the attack that would lead to American involvement in the *Second* World War. I also remembered that Aleister Crowley had himself sailed on the *Lusitania* just a few months before it was sunk, and that he had, according to what he told my mother, cursed it and all those who sailed on it."

"I don't see what all that has to do with you."

Laura didn't reply immediately but simply sighed and stood up, holding her empty glass in her right hand and turning away from the river to look up at the odd patches of nocturnal sky visible through the densely packed trees of the darkened rain forest. Satisfied that there were no lights rising and falling, she spread the fingers of her free hand and lightly stroked Alex's hair. He wanted her to do more—to touch him everywhere—but he just looked up, unable to respond, his heart beating too quickly.

"Because my mother told me that part of my curse was that wherever I went I would be connected, in some way or another, with destruction or death. So when, during the very first day on my new job, the Japanese bombed Pearl Harbor and led us into another world war, I felt that what my mother had said must be true, and that this was my curse.''

She removed her hand from his head, and he stood up. When he saw those eyes, staring straight at him, he felt his soul taking wing, rising up, rapturously and with ease, over a sea of confusion.

"You assume too much from too little," he said. "You may see what's not there."

He watched her expectantly, hardly aware of the chattering forest, his whole world contracted to the moonlight that shone in her green eyes. He was twice reflected there, miniaturized, adrift in space, and he traveled down through silence and time to where her soul joined with his. Then a sound, her voice, tumbling words, drew him back to the river bank, clasping one hand in the other, staring at her attentively.

"You think I'm not connected with destruction and death?" she said, as if having a perfectly normal conversation. "Well, in June 1945 I had a meeting in Los Angeles with my husband to discuss final settlement of our pending divorce. When I met him, he seemed terribly harassed and disturbed, and when I asked him what was wrong, he confided that his work in the secret establishment in Los Alamos had been taken over surreptitiously by the military and was at that stage virtually beyond the control of the original research group of which Robert, my very idealistic husband, had been a modest but fairly important member. The product of that new, military-dominated research, he informed me, would soon be terrifyingly evident for the whole world to see. I never saw my husband again—he committed suicide shortly after that meeting—but not before I realized what he had been talking about: on August sixth that same year the Americans dropped the atom bomb on Hiroshima. My husband, then, was one of the men who, without wanting to, contributed to the emergence of the atomic age and probably set the groundwork for doomsday."

Alex felt hypnotized, her presence permeating his whole being and rendering him helpless. Was she sane or insane? It didn't matter to him now. The only thing that mattered was to touch her—and be touched in return.

"And that's when you left the newspaper," he said, not knowing what else to say.

"Yep," she replied. "And got a job with *National Geographic* and was immediately sent here. And what do I find here, Alex? Tell me if it isn't true. A priest falls dead at my feet the minute I walk off the boat, and then I see brilliant lights, rising and falling impossibly, and am told that they represent the forces of good and evil in conflict at the gateway to eternity. Is that a coincidence, Alex? No, it is not! That bomb made me flee from America, and then it brought me to you—to you, Alex, who dreamed about that bomb the night before it was dropped, and who, like myself, have grown up without a mother—for believe me, Alex, I never really had a mother, only that spiteful and perfectly demented creature—and have had to endure the contempt of a father who doesn't know what love means. Oh, Alex, my Alex, we're so similar in so many ways, and I know—*I just know!*—that someone, or some power, has deliberately brought us together for some hidden reason. I was *destined* to come here!''

At that moment, for the first time, Alex truly felt very strange—uprooted and thrown into the web of a conspiracy that seemed to defy all reason. Indeed, as he stood there, he was willing to believe all she had told him, feeling a common bond in their similar problems with their parents and convinced that he had, in some secret part of him, known her before. Had he dreamed about her husband's bomb? The old Indian, Peruche, had had the very same dream and had told Alex that the dream was a sign that someone was coming to point the way to his, Alex's, future. Should he tell Laura about that? No, he didn't think so. It was true that when he had seen her he felt immediately that he had always known her, but something in her voice, in the words now filling his head, made him feel that to confess that her arrival had been anticipated would send her, unprepared and ill-informed, in pursuit of the Gateway. Thinking of that, and of the possibility of losing her, Alex was filled with love for her.

''God, I'm tired,'' she said, shaking her head from side to side. ''Walk me back to my humble shack, my handsome escort. I think I'll sleep well tonight.''

She wrapped her arm around his and held his hand in her own. Then, her hip rocking against him, she walked with him across the dark clearing toward the small hut on stilts. Most of the mission was, in darkness, the buildings illuminated in the moonlight, but light shone from Laura's hut—formerly Father Symonds's hut—and from the hut that Alex was sharing with Father Benedict. Alex thought of the priest fondly, knowing his anger would not last long, but soon forgot him when he glanced sideways at Laura. They stopped just in front of the hut, facing each other near the wooden steps. Alex, feeling feverish, his heart beating fit to burst, leaned forward and kissed her on the lips, very lightly and chastely. Embarrassed by his own action, hardly believing he had done it, he let go of her hand and stepped away. Then, to his horror, this time not believing his ears, he heard the sound of his own voice giving words to his feelings.

"I love you," he said. "I really love you. That's what my heart tells me."

She pressed her fingers to his lips, preventing him from saying more, her smile at once tender and gently mocking, her eyes reflecting the moon and stars.

"No, you don't," she said. "I'm too old for you, Alex. You may think you love me, but you don't—though what you think melts *my* heart."

She removed her fingers from his lips, blew him a kiss, and turned away. As she climbed up to the verandah and went inside, he stood there, the forest chattering all around him, joy and pain at war in his soul.

10

"So," Laura said, "this is it: your daddy's plantation." She smiled at him and squeezed his shoulder, then turned away from the Jeep and glanced around her, squinting into the noon sun. Mengrire watched her with hooded eyes, his shirtless body rippling with muscles. He glanced with a certain muted appeal to Alex and spread his hands in the air. "Yes, Mengrire," Alex said, reading the expression on the Indian's face. "You can go and see your friends. Come back here at two o'clock precisely, if we don't come for you first." Grinning and nodding, the Indian put his thumb up in the air and loped off across the road. Alex returned his attention to Laura, her profile framed by blue sky; his heart, turning over inside him, made the pain no less bearable.

"Is that where the workers live?" she asked, indicating the wooden shacks and houses that lined the intersecting roads at the far side of the lawns.

"Yes," Alex said.

"Not exactly palaces, are they?"

"No, I'm afraid not."

She smiled at him, obviously embarrassed by what she had said. "And are the other plantations pretty much the same?"

"Some are a lot better, some are worse, but most aren't doing well now. The end of the war has put an end to the rubber boom here. A lot of the plantations are falling apart and will probably soon close. Most of the rubber trade has reverted to Malaya, and we're feeling the pinch."

"Will you be sad to see it go?"

"It doesn't matter: I'll be returning to England anyway—to continue my education and learn good manners."

"The education won't do you any harm, and your manners are exquisite." She smiled at him and took his hand, holding it affectionately. Then she kissed him lightly on the forehead and raised her eyebrows. "So," she said, "shall we go for the quick tour or go see your father first?"

"Let's see my father first," Alex replied. "Let's get that over with."

He had spoken without thinking. Once the words were out, he realized what he had said by the look of surprise on Laura's face. Then he started to walk, his right hand entwined with hers, leading her across the mowed lawns toward his father's large house.

"Hot," she said. "Very, very hot. I've lost pounds already."

"Yes," he said. "Hot."

He didn't know what else to say, her presence turning him inside out, his power of reasoning, which only recently had been perfect, now swamped by emotional chaos. He had never known anyone like her—had never *imagined* anyone like her—and since first meeting her three weeks ago, when Father Symonds had dropped dead in front of her, he had repeatedly vowed his love to her as if in a trance. When he thought of it, he blushed (as even now he was blushing), but that impulse to express desire, which before had been dormant, continued to hammer relentlessly at his temples and burn in his racing heart.

Yet she had constantly rejected him—gently, often humorously—usually insisting that she was much too old for him and that his feelings, no matter how strong they were, would change soon enough. Was that true? He didn't think so—a part of him died with each gentle rejection—and he also felt, because of her warmth, because of how she touched and stroked him, that no matter what she claimed to the contrary, she felt deeply for him.

"You're not very keen on your father, are you?" Laura asked as they cut across the lawn, her index finger scratching the palm of his hand in a sensual manner.

"I don't see him that much," Alex replied, "so I can't really say."

The sun blazed down on the palm trees, on the forest of rubber trees beyond them, and on the river glittering black and silver beyond the workers' homes.

"Rubbish! We're talking about your *father*, Alex."

"He's all right. I just think he drinks too much. He says a lot of things that seem unpleasant, but it's just the drink talking."

"But it hurts you, doesn't it?"

"No. Really. It doesn't matter."

"It matters and it hurts. I sensed that my first night here. 'My father won't even know that I'm not at home,' you said. There was, as I recall, just the slightest touch of bitterness in your voice.''

''Maybe you're right,'' Alex said. ''It's just one of those things.''

But it did matter, and he knew it as he led Laura up the steps onto the verandah of the large house and saw his father stretched out on a low-slung hammock in the shade of the porch, some bottles on the table beside him well within arm's reach. He was wearing a crumpled white shirt and unwashed matching trousers, his sleeves rolled up, his feet bare; and although his bloodshot eyes widened in surprise when he saw them, he made no effort to sit up when they approached, but merely, with a lazy nod and a sardonic grin, acknowledged their presence.

''My God!'' he exclaimed. ''Visitors!''

His glance quickly passed over Alex in favor of Laura, at whom he stared, with an almost suggestive admiration, for a considerable time. Laura, simply elegant in sky-blue blouse, slacks, and flat shoes, stared back, her tall body straight.

''And I take it, Alex, that this wonderful creature you've brought to me is the American journalist?''

''Yes, father: Laura Wellman. Laura, this is my father.''

''Frank Poulson,'' his father said very quickly. ''Please call me Frank.'' He waved his hand languidly toward the table just below him on his left and added, ''Would you care for a thirst quencher? Or perhaps a medicinal?''

''You have Scotch?''

''We call it whiskey.''

''I'll have some.''

''It's right there on the table.''

He didn't move from where he lay but merely grinned up at Laura, cradling his own gin and tonic in his lap, his fingers stroking the glass. Laura stared steadily at him, making no move toward the table, and Alex, feeling angry and embarrassed, rushed to fix her the drink. His hand was shaking when he poured it, still shaking when he put the ice in, aware that the silence had only been broken by the sound of the tumbling cubes. He handed her the drink and received a nod and a sly smile. She looked back at his father and then glanced around her.

''You have a *chair* here?'' she asked.

''It's right behind you, Miss Wellman. Alex, don't stand there like a dummy: fetch the lady a chair.''

Alex hurriedly fetched the chair—a seventeenth-century hardbacked Chippendale, its woodwork damaged and bleached by the sun, its padded seat torn—and positioned it behind Laura, sliding it under her as she slowly sat down and crossed her elegant legs. His father's gaze roamed up and down her, as if inspecting merchandise, and eventually settled, with that same loathsome suggestiveness, on her slightly upraised face.

"Thanks for the drink," Laura said, tilting the glass to her mouth and having a sip with what to Alex appeared to be an unexpected and very exaggerated delicacy.

"My pleasure, Miss Wellman. It's always a treat to see a new face in this deplorable jungle."

"You don't like it here?"

"Most uncivilized—as I'm sure you already appreciate."

"I'm not sure what you mean by uncivilized."

"Rain and humidity, flies and mosquitoes, lack of proper sanitation and other basic amenities, ignorant bloody Indians and general Brazilian stupidity, little decent conversation, little money, no culture at all."

"It sounds like hell, Frank."

"It is, Laura."

"Then why do you stay here?"

Alex studied his father's face and saw the brief crack in his humor, the sardonic smile leaving his lips and then returning again, dominating his dissipated good looks in some indefinable manner.

"I stay here," he said, "because I've lived here all my life and because, as long as I remain here, I am king of my own domain."

"You mean this plantation?"

"This plantation—and everyone in it."

Still lying there in the hammock, his slim body slunk low, he raised his glass toward her in a mocking salute, which gesture she returned with a mockery that equaled his own. They both drank and then studied one another in a brief, strangely challenging silence which made Alex, whose throat was very dry, feel terribly uneasy.

"This plantation, if I may say so, doesn't look like much of a domain. In fact it looks about as dead as a doornail."

"We have fallen upon unfortunate times, my rich American friend, but brave the situation with fortitude, this being the English way."

"The American way would be to get off your backside and do something about it."

Alex felt a sort of shock, a sharp stabbing through his nervous system, as the smile on his father's face quivered and then came back to life again, the thin lips pulling reluctantly over teeth that had long required treatment.

"The American way," his father said, "may well work in America, but here, where the only thing worth having is the rubber, we are faced with the knowledge that our rubber is no longer required." He had another drink, wiped the back of his lips with one hand, then gazed at Laura with a sly, contemptuous smirk behind which, to Alex's consternation, was reluctant, and possibly base, admiration. "And so, Laura—may I call you that?—I simply accept my fate, looking after my ignorant, helpless workers and praying the tide will turn."

"Your workers don't seem that well looked after."

"These are hard times all round."

Laura made no immediate reply but simply raised her eyebrows and held her empty glass up in a questioning manner. Alex watched, fascinated, not understanding what was happening, as his father, taking note of Laura's empty glass, grinned and nodded his head. Laura leaned out of her chair, not quite standing but almost, poured a goodly portion of whiskey into her glass and then, sitting back in an upright position, again raised her glass in a mock salute and put the drink to her lips. She drank some of the whiskey—a considerable amount, Alex noticed—and then lowered the glass to her lap and smiled again at his father.

"Alex," his father said, "why don't you go off and read a good book? You look bored sitting there."

"No, Alex, it's all right." Laura glanced at him and smiled, then, turning back to his father, said, "Your son is my friend, and I really get lonely when he's not near."

"Ah, yes, my dear Laura, I've repeatedly asked Alex about you—but he's really been *extraordinarily* reluctant to discuss you, which makes me think, rightly or wrongly, that he cares *deeply* for you."

"We care deeply for one another," Laura said, "but in a way you might not understand."

"Friendship, Miss Wellman—Laura. A very wonderful thing."

"And do you have many friends around here?"

"Not many. I must confess to that. Not many at all."

"Why not?"

"I don't get out much anymore. The good days have all gone." He had another drink, crooked his lips in a sardonic grin, then ran his eyes up and down her body in a way that made Alex burn. His father? No, not his *father*! He could not bear to think of it. "Why ask? Are you concerned for my welfare? Do I look all that pitiful?"

"You could do with a shave."

"I will bear that in mind."

"You could also do with washing your clothes."

"I will bear *that* in mind."

Alex felt very confused, not knowing what was going on, watching first one, then the other, noticing the smiles on both their faces, each challenging in its own way, the antagonism almost palpable in the air, and yet . . . and yet, he felt uneasy, at once embarrassed and obscurely threatened, sensing that beneath the antagonism was a mutual attraction.

"I was going to show you the whole plantation," he said to Laura, "and there's a lot to be seen."

"What was that?" his father said sharply.

"I was talking to Laura," he replied. "I brought her to show her the plantation, and I thought—"

"I'm sure Laura could do with another drink, Alex, so kindly fill up her glass."

Alex took Laura's glass, saw her small, secret smile, poured the whiskey with a very shaky hand, and then handed the glass back. Laura thanked him, rather quickly sipped at the drink, and then turned back to his father.

"You have a lovely son here," she said.

"You think so?" his father replied. "Like father like son is the general supposition, though in this case I do have my doubts."

"What the hell does that mean?"

"That makes you sound so American."

"I want to know—"

"I wasn't insulting my own son; I merely suggest that we're different."

"A blessing?"

"Perhaps. Is that whiskey to your taste?"

"I'm enjoying the Scotch—and I *really* think you have a fine son."

"He's just like his mother. An equally fine woman. She died, alas, just after he was born, which has not made life easy."

Alex closed his eyes briefly, feeling the pain obliterating him, saw a blackness filled with stars, a swirling cosmos beyond time and space, entered into the past where his radiant mother smiled in welcome, and then, when he opened his eyes again, heard his father's malicious wit.

"Alex is much too private, too romantic and naïve, and spends far too much time with the Indians, learning all the wrong things. God, the ignorant, unclean savages! We should put them all in cages. Without them this would have been a better place—perhaps even civilized."

"You really seem to despise the Indians."

"I've lived with them all my life. And you, if I may say so, have already spent too much time in that ridiculous Christian mission, no doubt listening to Alex's other friend, Father Benedict, and being brainwashed accordingly. Believe me, my dear, God may side with the priests, but not, I am bound to say, with the Indians and their abominable ways."

He rolled over in the hammock, balancing precariously on his side, and reached down to the table just below him to fill his glass with gin. He then added the tonic, dropped some ice in and swirled it around, and rolled back to his original position without spilling a drop, his grin, oddly attractive in his dissipated handsomeness, also still challenging and indecently suggestive in a manner that still baffled Alex and made him uneasy.

"How long has it been, my dear Laura? I mean, how long have you been here?"

"Three weeks," Laura replied.

"Ah, yes, that's a long time—relatively speaking, of course; certainly long enough to be a little brainwashed by our good Father Benedict. Has he already turned you into an Indian lover, saying that all men are equal?"

"He didn't have to brainwash me into that: I already believed it."

"Really?"

"Yes, really,"

"I am always so touched by American democracy, by an image of the huddled masses in the boats that pass the Statue of Liberty—"

"Sarcasm is cheap."

"—but I remain an Englishman, take great pride in the concept of empire, and believe that the white man's mission is to educate, by bribery, blackmail, or deceit, our generally primitive brothers. Or, failing to do so, to keep them firmly in place. Alas, Alex, my only child, strongly disagrees with this, having been influenced by that miserable priest and, even worse, by that old rogue of an Indian,

Peruche, who, were he not so damned old, would feel my whip on his back.''

"I believe *that*," Laura said. "The tales of your mistreatment of the Indians are, to say the least, legion.''

"And who told you such tales? My loving son? Or Father Paul Benedict?''

"Neither. It's the Indians who gossip. The very mention of your name is enough to make them angry or fearful, when they're not actually spitting on the ground. Naturally, as I'm sure you must know, most of the gossip concerns the *seringueiro* who died, reportedly after being badly mistreated by you. It is said that you—and apparently your only friend, Rollie Thatcher—work your rubber gatherers half to death, give them only a quarter of the legal minimum daily food allowance, fail to pass on to them their necessary antimalaria tablets and instead sell them to the burgeoning pharmaceutical shops in Manaus for extra cash, and finally, perhaps most disgustingly, exploit your position as *fazendeiro* by making use of your workers' women in ways which are best not mentioned here.''

"Most delicate of you, I'm sure—but really, you're repeating nonsense: the Indians have always been notorious whiners, and that clearly hasn't changed. Who's to say I work them too hard? Who's to say I feed them too little? Such judgments are surely subjective and should be ignored. As for the sale of quinine tablets, I doubt that the law would let me get away with it; and in this place, where everyone knows everyone, they would find out soon enough if I were really doing it.''

"It's the fact that everyone knows everyone in this place that makes them turn a blind eye to you.''

"Pure hypothesis, my dear. And regarding the so-called exploitation of the Indian women, let me just say—and I'll phrase this as delicately as I can—that I don't have to succumb to the use of physical force in order to obtain gratification of the kind you suggest. That I may enjoy a certain popularity among the ladies is hardly *my* fault—and jealousy, as both of us know, always speaks with a forked tongue. Your glass is empty, my dear.''

Watching Laura as she leaned forward in her chair to pour herself another drink from the depleted bottle of whiskey, Alex felt shame and despair, the former because of his father's tasteless and slyly suggestive performance, the latter because Laura, while superficially antagonistic, appeared to be responding to his father with poorly disguised pleasure. Did she despise his father? Alex wasn't sure what she felt.

"And does your good friend Rollie Thatcher visit you often to share in your excitements?"

"He comes to visit me, Miss Wellman, to share drinks and conversation, most of which revolves around our business with its manifest problems. As for the *excitements* you mention—well, what can I say?—I shall leave those to your imagination which, I've no doubt, is considerably more colorful than mine. I reiterate, dear Miss Wellman, that we mostly drink and discuss business, most of which concerns how to deal with our thick-headed and indescribably useless Indian workers. In fact, even as of this minute, Rollie—who more than anyone else understands my particular problems—is helping me out by collecting from the family of that halfwit Indian who died compensation for all the unpaid debts that now lie on my desk."

"*What* unpaid debts?"

"Food, drink, rent for, naturally, the accommodation used while working on the plantation—"

"You mean one of your own shacks."

"Correct. And of course, since the food and drink is bought on credit from my own company stores—a system first devised, dear Laura, in the coal fields of your own excellent democratic country—and since, but naturally, I am the owner of the rented accommodation, the Indian owed more than he had earned on the day that he died. So compensation is required from the family."

"You bastard."

"Just call it democracy."

"And what sort of compensation do you hope to get?"

"Alas, the man's family can supply little. All the Indian's relatives were totally dependent upon him, and his wife is unfortunately much too old to be of any use to me. However, he does have a daughter who is healthy and strong enough to do some kind of work here on the plantation; ergo, she will be brought here to work in a certain capacity until such times as her father's debt has been paid off."

"And of course, since she has to eat and drink and sleep while she is working off that debt, she will have to get credit from your company store and abide by your self-serving rental arrangements, which means she may in fact be here forever as, more or less, unpaid labor."

"That is the unfortunate truth of the matter."

"And what, precisely, will be required of her here?"

"That has not yet been decided—though I'm sure I'll manage to come up with something. Perhaps some other evening, when I'm having a drink with my good friend Rollie, you could return here and spend a quiet evening with us, during which you could pursue this matter to its final conclusion."

"I don't think so."

"You might enjoy it."

"What makes you say that?"

"You strike me as a lady who has learned to appreciate—and might appreciate still—the new and unexpected."

"Go to hell, Mr. Poulson."

Laura finished off her drink and put the glass on the table. Ignoring the smirk that creased the face of Alex's father, she turned to Alex and said, "I think it's time we left for the rest of the tour." Glowing, Alex jumped forward to pull her chair out of her way as she moved toward the steps. His father still lay in the hammock, his body curved like an inverted bow, tapping his finger against the glass on his chest, his grin crooked and fixed.

"A pleasure to have met you," he said to Laura's departing back. "I trust this will be but the first of many more such encounters."

Laura stopped. Her spine visibly stiffening, she took a deep breath and turned around, that secretive smile on her face.

"Of course," she said. "That would be nice. Thanks a lot for the drinks."

Alex stared at her, bewildered, as she walked toward the steps, her tall body moving sinuously in the sky-blue slacks and blouse, her hips swaying in a manner that made his father's eyes widen. Alex felt, for the very first time, a stab of pure hatred.

Stunned, feeling his innocence collapsing, he turned away and followed Laura down the steps to the flat lawn surrounding the house. Laura smiled and took his hand reassuringly as they walked together across the road. When they reached the huts of the *seringueiros*, they stopped, both looking back at the big house, their attention drawn by the Jeep that had coughed its way around the curved drive and was now braking to a stop. Rollie Thatcher got out of the back, snapped his fingers at the girl who had been sitting beside him, and stood back while she climbed down. She was about sixteen or seventeen, and beside the bloated Rollie Thatcher she appeared too fragile and graceful to be real. The sky was cloudy, bending the rays of the sun, and the wavering light dissolved the house in a silvery haze. Rollie Thatcher grabbed the girl's shoulder and shook her rudely. She bowed her head demurely, and he dragged her, none too gently, up the steps of the verandah. Like figures in a bad dream they dissolved in the shadows.

Alex felt close to breaking, his throat dry, his heart beating, and he dug his fingers into Laura's palm and glanced desperately at her. She returned his stare, blindly, as if not really seeing him, and then, before he could question her, before he could work out what she felt, he saw her green eyes widening and slipping away to glance over his shoulder.

Following her gaze, he saw Mengrire, standing a short distance away, his chest heaving as he breathed in painful spasms, his hands opening and closing in frustrated, violent motions, and his eyes, usually sly or completely unreadable, focused with glittering intensity on the verandah of the house into which, like a slave from the auction block, the Indian girl had been taken.

Mengrire was weeping.

11

Embarrassed, Alex led Laura away from the weeping Indian, something inside him dying a little at what had transpired. Laura obviously understood this: she gently squeezed his hand. He glanced up, squinting against the sun, to see her flickering smile. Mengrire was trying to control himself, his sobs sounding like choking sounds; before they managed to get out of hearing range, they heard him hissing, repeatedly and brokenly, "*Bastardo! Bastardo!*" Alex stared straight ahead, too mortified to look at Laura, his shame and disgust almost too much to bear, laying waste to his senses. They crossed the first road and reached the *seringueiros'* shacks, and he saw the Indians on their cramped verandahs, the small dark rooms behind them, and knew that he no longer had the enthusiasm to show Laura around the place.

"Let's go and see Peruche," he said. "I think I'd rather do that."

"Okay," Laura said. "Fine."

She squeezed his hand again, clearly trying to reassure him, but instead unwittingly resurrecting his blindingly helpless love. He needed her desperately, as the night needs the moon, and was sure that if she disappeared from his life the light within him would burn out.

"Was that big fat brute Rollie Thatcher?" Laura asked.

"Yes."

"And the Indian girl was the one whose father died? Mengrire's girl?"

"Yes, I'm afraid so."

"Does it hurt you to talk about it?"

"No," he said. "No, it's all right."

He saw her glancing at the verandah of the small house they were passing, where two very weathered rubber gatherers were playing checkers with Coca-Cola and Fanta caps. Laura smiled, but uneasily, as if unsure of her own reactions, her eyes scanning the other verandahs and the people grouped upon them—aged women in hardbacked chairs, old men rocking in hammocks, children hanging over wooden railings or playing with the chickens and dogs around the supports of the shacks. She shook her head sadly, her hair swinging across her face, and glanced over the stone wall that led down to the plantation's *porto* at the vast, rippling surface of the Rio Negro and its solid green far bank.

"It's *so* wide," she said, "and so *quiet*. . . . It always gives me the shivers." Then she did in fact shiver, and chuckled deliciously. Giving his hand another squeeze, she said, "Oh, Alex, this plantation is *diseased* . . . and so is your father."

"I thought you liked him," Alex said, feeling guilty as soon as he spoke. "I mean, I got the impression that although you didn't like what he said, you had a kind of sneaking fondness for him."

"He has a certain appeal," Laura replied, unconcerned, "and once, before the drink took command, must have been pretty attractive. What led to the drinking and cynicism? The death of your mother?"

They had turned right in front of the *porto* and were now walking along the river, cooled by the river breeze and by the shadows of the trees. At Laura's question, Alex felt some grief that had too long been buried squeezing the life from his heart.

"I don't think so," he said. "It might have been, but I doubt it. I was too young to remember. My mother was visiting here with her family when my father met her and swept her off her feet; they married and in a very short time realized they weren't compatible. According to Antonio Bozzano, my mother was a quiet woman, very loyal and romantic, but my father was an inveterate womanizer. This sickened my mother to her soul, though she remained loyal to him. They were estranged before I was born, and I honestly don't think that her death concerned him all that much."

"God, you must hate him for that."

"No, not really. At least I didn't at the time. I believe that most people are basically good and then somehow get warped."

"You mean even the sinners are victims?"

"Yes, perhaps I do."

Laura chuckled at that, her head shaking, her throat curved and inviting. "Oh, boy," she said, "have *you* a lot to learn! You're so pure, you're like Adam in the Garden of Eden—and like him, doomed to grief." She gave him a hug. "Well, maybe not," she said. "I hope not. Let's get back to your father."

"There's nothing more to add," Alex said. "My father is what he is. He once had a lot of money, but he squandered it as fast as he made it. Then the rubber boom died out. He was temporarily saved by the war, but he can't keep this place going much longer, and he is making the most of it.''

"He's trying to make as much money as quickly as possible before he has to close up.''

"That's right. And he's doing it on the backs of the Indians, which I think is hideous.''

"But you still don't hate him?''

"I don't think so—at least I didn't until this morning.''

"Why this morning?''

"Never mind.''

How could he tell her what he had felt when his father leered at her—or what he had felt when she smiled at him? No words could describe the hurt. As he turned away from the vast, dark river and led her into the gloom of the small stretch of forest, he knew he was changing. His calm acceptance of life, the harmony of his life, was surrendering to chaos.

He had wanted to talk to someone older who could guide him, but even Father Benedict seemed to suddenly have become unapproachable. He knew that the priest did not approve of his feelings for Laura and in fact had virtually told him so. He knew he was beginning to resent the priest for the very first time. There were many first times now—suppressed anger, desire, hatred, and fear— and as the trees opened out, revealing the *verzea* lake and Peruche's hut, he prayed that he would find peace in the old Indian's presence.

Laura stopped and put her two hands to her mouth, her eyes widening as she took in the unexpected beauty of the clearing. Peruche's hut was right in front of them, a miniature version of the enormous *malocos,* and the still lake was close behind it, shaped like a painter's palette. Water hyacinths and tropical lilies created pink, purple, and white patterns, the trunks of the trees were decorated with climbing plants and leaf mosaics of peperomia, and countless lianas, using the treetrunks for support, writhed upward in bizarre green coils and loops into the downpouring sunlight. The pale flowers of the cauliflorous trees wafted down from the forest canopy high above like a magical rain in a child's dream. The whole clearing looked magical and dreamlike in its exotic perfection.

"It's fantastic,'' Laura murmured.

"Yes,'' Alex said. "It is.''

"I feel like I'm on another planet.''

"Maybe you are."

"Is that where Peruche lives? That thatched hut?"

"Yes."

"This is wonderful."

She shook her head in bemusement, then moved toward the hut, walking as if in a trance, a touching smile on her face. Alex hurried to catch up with her, then passed her and reached the hut first. Indicating that she should wait, he knelt down and called to Peruche through the motionless cotton curtain that covered the entrance. Peruche's voice came back immediately, a cracked, sepulchral sound, and Alex, signaling to Laura to follow, pulled the curtain aside and went in, practically down on his knees. Peruche was squatting on the mud floor, one hand resting on each knee, the brown withered skin on both hands and knees webbed with blue veins. Laura came in after Alex, crawling in on knees and elbows, and sat beside him. She glanced at him automatically, then fixed her gaze on Peruche. The old Indian's head was bowed over a bowl placed just in front of him; his hammock, stretched between two tall poles, hung not far above him. He sniffed, raised his face, sniffed again, and opened his eyes; he smiled gently at Alex and then fixed his gaze on Laura, his rheumy eyes hardly blinking.

"Ah," he said, "the American woman."

"Yes," Laura said. "Laura Wellman."

"I know your name. Alex has told me much about you. He thinks highly of you."

"And of *you*," Laura said.

The old Indian smiled, very slightly but warmly, leaned far forward over the bowl, sniffed deeply, and then sat up again, fixing his gaze once more on Laura.

"You have come to the Amazon to take photographs?"

"I was given the opportunity of coming here to take photographs, but I wanted to come to the Amazon anyway, and now that I'm here I feel that I was destined to come here."

"Why?"

"I think Alex has already told you."

"Alex has told me that you think yourself possessed because of your mother's relationship with a man of evil. This may or may not be true—if you believe it enough, you will make it real—but why did you want to come here and now feel it was destined?"

"I have suffered since I was a child—terrible nightmares and waking dreams—and believing myself to be possessed, I was look-

ing for escape. I thought that I might find, in this untouched,
primeval forest, another kind of reality, through which, if I embraced it wholeheartedly, I might lose my old self.''

"And you thought that by losing your old self you would also lose
the demons that you think are possessing you?''

"Yes."

"And?"

"I believe there is another world—the world of the spirit or
soul—and that that world, which so-called civilized men have lost
touch with, is a very real and accessible world to those peoples who
have remained more close to nature than the people I come from.''

"You mean more primitive people, such as the Indians."

"If you care to put it that way."

Peruche nodded, not offended, then glanced across at Alex, fixing
his eyes on the tiny stone amulet around Alex's neck. Satisfied that
the amulet was still there, he returned his attention to Laura.

"And you felt that by finding this other world you would set
yourself free?''

"Yes, Peruche, I did—and still do. I feel that if what I believe to
be true *is* true—that indeed I have been possessed by the devil or the
powers of darkness—then I can only free myself from that evil by
finding out what it is.''

"You wish to know the *nature* of the evil?"

"And then cast it out."

There was silence for a moment, distant thunder, more silence;
Peruche bowed his head and breathed deeply and looked up again.

"And why, when you arrived here, did you feel that you had been
destined to come here?''

"Wherever I go, I touch destruction or death—"

"Alex told me."

"—and when I walked off the boat onto Manaus, a priest fell
dead at my feet.''

"You give importance to a natural event."

"Maybe, maybe not. But then I heard the Yano drums, saw the
lights that rise and fall, and was told of the Gateway over which the
Yano Indians stand guard: that place where time and space have no
meaning and good battles with evil. When I discovered I had come
to such a place as this—apparently by accident—I knew I had
actually been *drawn* here for some undefined purpose.''

"To discover the nature of evil?"

"That is part of it, certainly. As far as I'm concerned, the forces of darkness possessed me, and now, thousands of miles from my home, I am close to their source. I don't think that's an accident."

"Have you thought to question your sanity?"

"I have questioned it. I simply can't find an answer."

Laura's voice was very steady, matching her unwavering gaze, and Peruche, after studying her for some time, nodded judiciously.

"There might be a purpose," he said. "What it might be, I cannot say. But we dreamed of a ball of fire in the heavens, an umbrella of light . . . and then you, who felt haunted by that bomb, arrived here as expected."

"*Expected* . . ." Laura's lips sought more words, but eventually settled for silence.

"We expected something," Peruche said. "We thought it might be an event. It was not an event but a person—and you are that person. Why you are here, I cannot say. It is for you to discover."

"How will I discover it?"

"You will do so. One way or another."

"I'm afraid."

"Fear, also, is natural. It is there to be conquered."

He raised his right hand in the air, fingers outstretched like a fan, then waved it very gently to and fro and lowered it back to his lap. Alex studied Laura's face, saw her eyes turning downward, widening in horror as they focused on her own left foot, and then saw the enormous, hairy, bird-eating spider. It had been hidden beneath the fern leaves but was now rising groggily, its long legs spread very widely around its dark-furred body, bending in and out with scissor-like movements as it shook the leaves off. Laura stared at it, drawing her breath in, too terrified to move, then stopped breathing as the leaves fell off its back and it advanced on her exposed foot.

"Fear is natural," Peruche reminded her. "It is there to be conquered. Now face it and conquer it."

The spider straddled Laura's foot, its silken belly grazing her bare skin, its legs jerking in irregular, hypnotic movements until it settled upon her. She bit her lip, let her breath out, stared mesmerized at the spider's eight eyes—then flicked her own eyes to her other foot and saw the thick, nine-foot snake. The snake's jaws opened and closed, its tongue tentatively explored her foot, and then its slime-covered, thick, pulsating body coiled over her legs. Alex watched, undisturbed— or at least disturbed only for Laura—as the giant anaconda slid over her right leg, curved under her left, then arched back to slide over her trembling thighs and then leave the hut, passing between him and Laura to slip under the curtain. When he returned his gaze to Laura's other foot, the spider, also, had vanished.

Laura heaved a great sigh and wiped the sweat from her forehead. Her whole body still trembling, she stared right at Peruche.

"I didn't conquer my fear," she said. "I was practically paralyzed."

"No. You did well."

Laura smiled nervously at Alex, let her trembling body settle down, and returned her gaze to Peruche. Her voice, when she finally managed to speak, sounded firmer than usual.

"How do I find the Yano?"

"That is not for me to say."

"Am I *supposed* to go and find the Yano?"

"Only you can decide that."

"Can you tell me about them?"

"What do you wish to know?"

"I'm told you were their prisoner long ago. I'd like to know about that."

"There is little to tell. As you say, it was long ago. I was then but a child, a member of the Yanoama tribe, and I was taken by my father on a hunting expedition very far north in the rain forest, where no Yanoama Indian had ever been before. It was the forbidden territory of the Yano—those who had been cast out of our tribe and had, since their exile, become slaves to the forces of darkness and seduced into the most barbaric and corrupt activities, which had eventually rendered them helpless slaves of their evil masters. The Yano captured our hunting party and had much pleasure with them, killing some immediately, torturing others for days after, until finally only my father and I were left, I being the only child captured.

"They had left us to the end for that very reason, and now, with the others gone, they wanted the finest sport of all: to skin my father alive, taking three days to do so, removing his flesh from his bones in countless thin strips. I, his ten-year-old son, was forced to pull those strips off, my ears filled with his terrible screaming, my hands soaked in his blood. Ah, yes, three days and nights, and the Yano greatly enjoyed my tears, and then later, when I was starving, they gave me his cooked flesh to eat, and then there were many months— how many I cannot remember—when I lived in a world of nightmares and insanity, wanting only to die.

"The Yano gave me *epena*, the drug I keep in this bowl, and under its influence my mind expanded and beheld wondrous things. I saw heaven and hell, the faces of Good and Evil, that place where space curves down into a funnel and opens out into the Otherworld. There I saw beauty and horror, knew exultation and terror. When I lost my old self, when the child in me had died, I was drawn back through the funnel on wings of song and returned to the Yano camp. Drums played and voices shrieked, lights rose and fell in the sky, there was sacrifice and mass fornication where the stars filled the earth. I witnessed and survived, hearing the bedlam give way to silence, watching as the lights that rose and fell disappeared, and the dawnlight, giving shape back to the jungle, wiped the stars from the sky.

"After that I became their slave, to be used as they saw fit, as labor, as sport, as a suppository for their seed; and yet I never became one of them—what they had made me do had been too much—and so, when I was full grown, and had learned much of their magic, I escaped and made my way back here to await my time of returning."

"You mean you intend going back?"

"My heart tells me I must."

"When?"

"Before I die."

"And when is that?"

"When my dreams give me warning."

So saying, he leaned forward and sniffed very deeply of the hallucinogenic drug in the bowl, the *epena*, then sat upright again, closed his hands, and started to take very deep, rhythmic breaths as if exercising. Alex nodded at Laura, indicating that they should leave, and as she rose onto her haunches and began inching backward, Peruche started rocking to and fro and making a weird humming sound. He was clearly in a trance, exploring his liberated mind, and Laura stopped, fascinated. She might have remained that way for hours but was encouraged by Alex, by means of pushing and prodding, to turn away, brush the curtain aside, and leave the hut.

The sun, which had been sinking, was now completely hidden behind black clouds which, low and boiling, seemed to be touching the forest canopy and had made the gray air sultry and humid. Thunder rumbled in spasms as the first of the raindrops fell, making remarkably loud splashing sounds on the languid papaya leaves. Laura shivered and glanced around her, obviously looking for the snake and spider. Seeing nothing, she shook her head and took hold of Alex's hand.

"God," she said, "it's a lot later than I thought. How long were we in there?"

"A long time," Alex said.

"Did I fall asleep?"

"No."

"What about the snake and the enormous spider?"

"They came and went through our minds."

"They were real!"

"What we perceive through our senses we tend to call real. I saw them, you saw them, Peruche saw them—so they must have been real."

"Was I drunk? Did I drink too much Scotch? No, I don't think so. I know what I saw and felt in there: they were real, and they *touched* me."

"Then of course they were real."

Thunder rumbled again and the rain suddenly fell heavier, so Alex, entwining his fingers with Laura's, walked her away, back into the darkness of the forest, which already, with the falling of the rain, was dripping constantly and noisily. Laura kept gazing around her, rubbing her eyes and blinking repeatedly, but they soon emerged from the forest into the graying afternoon light and headed in the opposite direction from the small *porto* toward the shacks of the workers. By the time they had passed the houses and reached the Jeep in the parking lot, both of them were reasonably wet and feeling the cold.

Mengrire was in the Jeep, his forehead resting on the steering wheel, but he sat up when they approached and he stared at them, his brown eyes filled with grief. Alex blushed and avoided his gaze, turning aside to face Laura, his shame over his father eased only by the love he felt for her. Something broke in him that instant: the last of his pride or inhibitions. He wanted to tell her again and again how much he needed her with him, but with Mengrire's wounded eyes fixed upon him, he could only squeeze her hand harder.

"I'll go straight back," she said. "Right now I couldn't face your father. I think dinner with Father Benedict, if more sober, will be easier to handle."

"Give him my regards."

"I'll do that. Now look after yourself."

She climbed into the Jeep, resting her hand on his shoulder; when she sat down, she slid her hand lightly along his body to take hold of his wrist. He stared at her, drowning in her, filled with love and despair, actually jealous that his good friend Father Benedict would later be sharing his table with her while he, Alex, spent another night listening to the drunken revels of his father and, no doubt, Rollie Thatcher. The thunder rumbled again, the rain suddenly became ferocious, and Laura, with the raindrops exploding in silvery spray off her body, making the darkness bright around her curved, sensuous form, reached out and took hold of the small stone amulet around Alex's neck.

"What is it?" she asked him.

"It's just an amulet," he replied.

"No," she said. "You're lying. It's much more than that. Peruche kept staring at it."

"It's a magic amulet," Alex confessed. "He told me to wear it always. He said that as long as I wore it, no harm would befall me. Here"—he did it impulsively, out of love and concern, his beating heart making him remove it from his neck and press it into her hands—"take it. It's yours. Other than this, I have nothing of value to give you; more than anything else in the world, I want you to have it."

"No, Alex, no!" She opened the fist he had clenched, her upturned palm framing the black stone amulet, the rain, as if being forced down by the rolling thunder, pouring into her quivering fingers and spraying up around the amulet in a miniature fountain that splashed Alex's face. "I can't. . . . Really, I can't. . . . I don't think I should. . . ."

"Take it, Laura! Please take it! For me! It's all I can give you!"

He closed her hand again, held it tightly and shook it vigorously, then waved to Mengrire to start the car. Raindrops glistened on Mengrire's brown face and rolled around his bright brown eyes; he nodded, hiding every thought and feeling, and turned back toward the wheel. Hearing the thunder and the hissing rain, Alex held Laura's hand as the Jeep roared into life, churning mud around him, dragging her hand out of his, and carrying her away into the semidarkness of ferocious rain and gray light.

The thunder roared and the lightning flashed as he walked back across the broad lawn and up the steps to the verandah of his father's large house. He felt bereaved and lost, his heart bursting. The world, which before had been God's gift, now seemed infinitely threatening. The rain fell in a torrent, drumming relentlessly on the verandah floor as he opened the mesh-wire door and entered the house, the gloom further depressing him. *I love her*, he thought. *I love her and feel anguished. If love is good, where is the joy that this goodness should bring?* The question was like a bell, tolling sepulchrally in his mind, making its pronouncements with arrogant gravity but offering no answers. He clenched his fists and kept walking, passing the rooms of this long, dark corridor, keeping his eyes fixed on the floor and praying for privacy. Thankfully no one interrupted him—he swallowed dryly with relief—and when he entered his own room, closing the door behind him with excessive care, he lay down on the bed, closed his eyes, and fell asleep almost instantly.

Had he slept? He wasn't sure. The rain was hammering on the roof. The thunder rumbled and the room was illuminated by flickering mosaics of lightning. He saw Laura hovering above him, her green eyes enigmatic, her red hair falling down around him as her voluptuous lips opened. He reached up to her, yearningly, in his mind if not his flesh, and then heard his father's laughter, at first ghostly, then more clear, emanating from the main lounge just along the central corridor and entering his hearing with the brutality of a knife slicing through his heart.

The main lounge was not far away, just three doors down from his room, and he heard, through the rumbling thunder, through the crackling sound made by the lightning, someone weeping—a girl weeping—other laughter, raucous and crude, then the weeping again, this time a little louder, and then his father's laughter once more, clearly drunken and salacious, mingling with the other laughter to form a joyless, mocking, ghostly chorus. It was his father and Rollie Thatcher. They were both enjoying themselves. The person weeping, being the object of their sport, was obviously the Indian girl.

Alex didn't know what to do. He was a child and felt afraid. The thunder roared, the lightning flashed, his ears were stung by that awful revelry, and then he also wept, crying aloud in helpless anguish, and rolled over on the bed, burying his face in the feathered pillow, his heart breaking as he surrendered completely to the image of Laura, spending himself in the stormy night.

12

She broke his heart because she drank too much, favoring the deadly *cachaça* cane alcohol, usually taking the first one just before noon and then continuing with shameless regularity until she went to bed, regardless of how early or late that might be. Her drunkenness never showed except in her lovely eyes, which gradually developed a mild pink hue, and in her conversation, which as the day wore on became quicker and more compulsive, invariably wrapped possessively around her past with its demons, imaginary or otherwise, and mostly tragic events.

Fact or fabrication? Possibly a little of each? Alex spent much time wondering (and lost a lot of sleeping doing so) but could neither find a comprehensible answer nor subdue his increasing love and fascination. He knew she was drunk when she talked too much, and at such times he felt pain, but he also felt seduced and rendered helpless by what she was saying: her words conjured up another world, a world totally alien to him, peopled with the rich and the powerful, with the rare and exotic. Hollywood, Los Angeles, with its film studios and famous stars, its exclusive clubs and magnificent hotels, with its cinemas and restaurants and swimming pools and automobiles, and all the other luxuries of civilization: he heard about them from her ruby lips, constantly thought of them with wonder, and gradually, though her drinking broke his heart, sensed the sly growth of corruption in himself, wanting to fly back there with her.

"Of *course* I'd take you back!" she said. "You're my treasure and delight. And also because, dear Alex, your purity might help me to defeat the demons trying to possess me."

"Stop talking about that," he said.

"I *have* to talk about it," she replied. "I can never let my guard down for a minute. I must constantly remind myself."

"Don't have another drink."

"Stop hectoring me. You sound just like St. Paul."

St. Paul was Father Benedict, who also disapproved, his brow wrinkling as he narrowed his eyes to watch her downing a fresh glass. Laura rarely missed such glances and appeared to take pleasure from them, almost defiantly drinking even more in his presence and, as far as Alex could see, deliberately exaggerating the degree of her inebriation. They clearly liked one another and were in constant conflict for that very reason, Father Benedict concerned that Laura was ruining herself with her drinking, Laura resenting his repeated insinuations that she could not look after herself.

"God, you're well named," she said to him. "Paul Benedict! St. Paul! A puritan who drinks a fair bit himself but tries to stop others doing it."

"Don't blaspheme," he replied. "And I only drink beer. I don't drink *cachaça* all day and night, and retire to bed in a stupor."

"A *stupor*? When have you ever seen *me* in a stupor? I've never been in a *stupor* in my life, so your remark is insulting. And even if it *was* true, you should, as a priest, have some respect for the fact that I'm a lady and keep your mouth shut."

The arguments, which were frequent, sometimes good-natured, sometimes not, took place all over the mission at any time of the day—over the breakfast table, in the crowded medical hut, in the small school at the end of the clearing, in the Jeep on the road to Manaus, but most often over the dinner table in the evenings—usually when Laura was moving around with her cameras, following the priest as he engaged in his numerous activities and was under some pressure. They also occurred in the small boat, during those long stretches on the river, when the jungle was sliding past as a solid wall of tangled greenery and the sky above was dark with low, black storm clouds, about to unleash another rainfall and send the humidity soaring.

"Please, Laura, not another one."

"Dammit, Father, it's so hot."

"That rain is going to fall any minute, and it's more cooling than alcohol."

"Very funny, I'm sure."

"All that drinking won't help you."

"It does. It helps me to sleep at night. It keeps the nightmares away."

"Did you ever stop to think that it might be the other way around: that it's the drink that might be *causing* the nightmares?"

"Nonsense."

"Then prove it. Stop drinking for a few days. I'm sure that if you do you'll actually get a few nights' good sleep. That drink has your head spinning."

Alex bore witness to it, but through love's dazzling prism, every gesture and inflection colored dramatically by his inflamed and untrustworthy senses. His mind was a hall of mirrors, his perceptions distorted, turning his former grasp on reality into something more dangerous: shadows, reflections, odd words becoming echoes which, reverberating through his emotions, rebounded as something else.

"You're pretty cute when you furrow your brow in that ferocious manner, Father Benedict. You are, in fact, fairly attractive in a primitive way."

"Stop talking like that."

"Why?"

"You'll embarrass Alex."

"No, Father Benedict—not Alex—it's *you* I embarrass!"

When they scowled at one another, he sometimes felt that they were actually smiling; when they smiled, he was sure he saw great tension hiding deep in their eyes. Laura mocked and teased the priest, sometimes shocked and outraged him, and the priest, in his turn, would be slyly mocking or brutally frank, either parrying her words or beating them back with no attempt at mercy. He sometimes felt that the priest detested her, other times that he was fond of her, and occasionally, with a guilt that made him writhe, that the priest, like his father, was actually attracted to her. The jealousy, which was for him a totally new emotion, quietly stripped him of dignity and pride and made him squirm with self-hatred.

"You embarrass me, Laura, only because of your intemperance."

"Say no more, Father Benedict."

They traversed the river a lot, using canoes or paddle steamers, visiting riverbank shacks, floating villages, jungle *portos,* where Laura took countless photographs, frequently changing cameras, and filled one small notebook after another with her urgent, almost frantically scribbled thoughts, usually biting her lower lip as she did so. The floating villages were on great platforms—wooden shacks on enormous rafts, the esoteric foliage of the jungle actually grazing the thatched roofs—and Laura climbed up the ladders and wandered among the impoverished tenants with an enthusiasm that melted all resistance and opened all doors. The Indians thought her a glorious alien—her long red hair fascinated them—and they often, when she

raised her camera, reached out tentatively to touch her, then giggled
like children when they did so, and then touched her again. She
responded with similar wonder, apparently touching them with her
spirit, and at such moments even Father Benedict could find little to
criticize.

Alex always carried her camera case, only too pleased to assist
her, glad to be away from the plantation, from the debaucheries of
his father, and more comfortable under the oppressive sky above the
wide, sullen river.

The river was a world apart, supporting a floating population, its
immensely wide, calm surface either black or mud brown, bending
and curving around the forest that came right to the water's edge,
then lapping and splashing against the wooden struts of small one-
family jetties or the much higher and imposingly large floating
villages which thrust out from green inlets, the forest foliage forming umbrellas over the clutter of shacks, shops, and cafés, dropping
white flowers and fern leaves over the numerous small boats that
bobbed together all around the great platforms. The floating villages
were near Manaus, not too far from its many *portos*, and the
villages, like the *portos*, were a hive of activity, the Indians buying
and selling, or bartering, their wares: *assai* berries, plantains, mangoes and papaya, cashew nuts and pineapples, *jenipapo* and *maracuja*,
the fruit piled high on the stalls that swayed rhythmically on the
floating platform while from other stalls the varied fish—*pirarucu*,
jaraqui, *tambaqui*, *tucunare*, and even the dreaded piranha—filled
the air with a nostril-tuning smell that encouraged either nausea or
delicious hunger.

If Laura enjoyed the floating villages, she enjoyed the many
portos even more, almost laughing with delight as she and Alex—
usually dropped off by Father Benedict—wandered along the narrow,
sloping streets that led straight down to the river, past the open-
fronted shops stacked ceiling-high with boxes, past the children and
dogs playing around the stalls soaked with wet fish, right past the
raised shacks that opened out to frame the *porto*, where, between the
battered boats, bobbing up and down in the splashing brown water,
rotten fruit and dead fish formed large carpets of brightly colored
and foul-smelling detritus. The boats themselves were a gift to
photography, mostly old and incredibly battered, many used as
permanent homes as well as floating warehouses, these packed with
large families, most of which could hardly move, the cabins decorated with Virgin Marys and photographs of various popes, or with

Umbanda and *Quimbanda* statues and trinkets, or with what seemed like hundreds of well-used votive candles of countless bright colors. Here, also, in the *portos*, were a wide variety of nationalities—Argentinians and Venezuelans, Peruvians and Bolivians, Malays and Chinese and West Indians and Europeans, Jews and Syrians and Lybians—and in the melting pot of the bars and cafés, surrounded by noise and stench, Laura drank her *cachaça* and stroked Alex's hand and talked to him, her voice musical and seductive, about all that she saw.

"It's so *real* to me, Alex! So elemental and natural. It's so different, it completely overwhelms me at times—and yet I also feel I've known it all my life, as if born and raised here. I think I was meant to come here, Alex. Not *think* it: I *know* it! I felt it from the moment I set foot on the floating dock, and I've been more convinced of it every day, as I see more and more. I was here in another time—maybe the past, perhaps the future—but somehow, although I can't quite explain it, I have had a separate existence here. I *belong* to this place; I'm part of it. I'm the river and sky."

She was *Alex's* river and sky, completely permeating his consciousness, flowing endlessly like a river through his thoughts, her face the ravishing sky of his erotic dreams. He wanted her—and her world—he wanted all that she represented, and ironically, the more she romanced about the Amazon, the more he romanced about America and the glamorous world she had sprung from. He had formerly loved the mighty river and felt at home in the endless forest, but now, as Laura explored it and let it weave its spell around her, he found himself drawing further away from it and wanting what she had left.

"You'll soon be going back," he said.

"Don't count on it," she replied. "The fact that I've only another week left in the mission doesn't necessarily mean I'm going home."

"You might stay?"

"I think I will. I can't bear the thought of leaving. And more important, I can't leave until I've been to that place where the lights rise and fall at night."

"You must never go there, Laura. You'd get lost or the Yano would kill you. And even if neither of those happened, we don't know what you'd find there."

"I'd find release, Alex. I know it. I'd find the forces of light and darkness. When I heard about that Gateway, about what the Yano are guarding, I knew that I'd been destined to come here and find what my fate is.''

"Promise me you won't go into the forest, that you'll never do that.''

"I can't promise you anything.''

"Your love?''

"Not the kind that you mean.''

"I want everything. *All of it!*''

His own intensity could sometimes shock him—he was still getting used to it—and much of it sprang from his inability to gauge what she felt for him. His declarations of love amused her, but also clearly touched her, and when she wasn't trying to let him down gently, she was actively flirting with him. He had previously noticed her need to touch—to touch objects and people—but with him, the touching seemed to be tied to her need to repeatedly excite him and then cool him down again. She would run her fingers along his bare arm, press his hand to her lips, abstractedly scratch the back of his neck, stroke the blade of his sweating spine. If she did this with affection, she also did it to arouse him, after which she would mock his burning cheeks and ask him, with whole armies of innuendo in her tone, what it was in his thoughts that had made him blush. He didn't know what to think, felt despair and glory at once, and in the end was convinced that she loved him, but didn't dare show it.

"Of course I love you, Alex, but not like that. I'm too *old* for you, dearest!''

"It doesn't matter. I love you.''

"You don't know what love is. You love the idea of *being* in love, which is something much different. Oh, God, Alex, don't talk of love. Love's the dream that destroys us all. It's an impulse that makes mockery of intelligence and renders pride obsolete. I had enough of it when I was young—in your beloved Hollywood, during my adolescence—because at that time, right up to when I got married at twenty-two, I really was an extraordinary young beauty and looked more mature than I actually was. Men didn't just think me attractive—they went a bit crazy over me—and although *they* all called it love, they turned my life into hell.''

For Alex it was hell to listen—or heaven and hell at once—one part of him in despair at the rejection of his love, the other part of him dissolving into ecstasy just because he was near her. He saw the river dividing the jungle, over four miles from bank to bank, the dense forest hanging over the muddy water as if trying to claim it. They were on a boat south of Manaus, near the meeting of the waters, where the humus-blackened Rio Negro met the mud-brown Rio Solimões and both flowed side by side without blending, as if a thin line divided them. The effect was surrealistic, as if nature had been defeated, making one river of two distinct colors, flowing in parallel streams. Like the river, so his mind: his dark and light visions of Laura, one vision offering the promise of pleasure everlasting, the other offering a glimpse into the hell of bottomless anguish.

"That was during the early thirties, during the heyday of the movies, when my father was filthy rich and too powerful to talk to mortals, and I was just about your age—if built a bit differently. God, yes, the men wanted me—one after another fell in love with me—but all I ever felt was their sweaty hands, all I saw was their greed. Was it love or just lust? I don't remember if I thought about it. But I know that the only reason I went out with those men was that I couldn't sleep at nights for my nightmares and wanted some company. I actually thought that love might save me—that's why I later rushed into my marriage—but then, when I was much in demand, I knew what they were after: a piece of prime steak beneath them."

Alex studied the river, staring along the Rio Negro, seeing that limpid black surface ending sharply at a thin white beach that seemed to run for miles in either direction. A beach? No: as the boat moved nearer, he saw the Solimões, the striking sun making its brown surface gray where it ran, side by side, without mingling, with the vitreous water through which the boat was moving. It was like the end of the world—the Rio Negro marked World's End—and there, where the black water appeared to abruptly end, the gray water, sometimes almost silvery, resembled the empty, sunbright haze over the mouth of a canyon—nothing but space beyond. The effect was weird, disorienting, like an optical illusion; it reflected, with terrible irony and accuracy, what he was feeling.

"And so, Alex, I never knew love—or at least not your concept of love—and instead buried my fears in various affairs which brought me, if not tender feelings, a temporary oblivion. And when I eventually married—a good man, a *decent* man—my fear of the darkness, my recurrent nightmares and premonitions, refused to let me lose myself in his embrace, and so even that ended. Love? Oh, yes, Alex, I love you—but not in that way!''

His need for her increased, making his nights long and sleepless, forcing him to writhe alone in bed and drain himself in heavy silence. The shame of this was overwhelming, laying siege to his breaking heart, and he wondered how men lived with themselves when this dark desire tortured them. He wanted to talk to someone about it, most particularly to Father Benedict, but the priest, in the wisdom of his age, already knew what was happening.

"It's madness, Alex. Madness! You must try to understand what's happening. Laura Wellman is attractive, but she's also twice your age—and if I may say so without malice, she may not be all there. You understand what I'm saying, Alex? In every way your romance is pointless. The woman is twice your age, she is unhappy and drinks too much, she will be leaving sooner or later to return to America, and—no matter what you may think to the contrary—she will be returning alone. You're not a man yet, Alex—a young man, but not a man—and at your age, particularly in a place like this, your passion is dangerous. Forget it, Alex. Don't be hurt later. Accept the truth of this now."

But Alex could not accept it; his desire for her blinded him to everything except the need to possess her. He thought about her day and night, his mind inflamed, his body burning, losing his old self in the corruption of his lust and tormented constantly by his new, adult yearnings. He tried to explain such yearnings to her, with a naïve, impulsive frankness, shamelessly employing every form of emotional blackmail to break down her resistance; yet resist she did, stroking his cheek but shaking her head, kissing him lightly but then laughing at him, embracing him but pushing him away when his body responded.

"Oh, God, Alex, you're really *so* attractive . . . but you're just too *young* for me."

What was he to think? He had no way of knowing. Had she led him on? Embraced him just to push him away again? She said "No, Alex! *No!*" again and again, but what did she mean? He was bewildered and wounded, now hopeful, now crushed, bouncing from the very heights to the depths and then back up again. Yet his pride knew no depths: he would sink as low as need be; he closed his eyes to the possibility that he was shaming himself and only opened them long enough to shed the tears that she could drink from his glowing cheeks. Yes, she kissed his tears away, murmuring "Alex! Oh, Alex!" her voice tremulous with compassion and despair at the extent of his need for her.

"Don't think me a child," he said. "I'm nearly eighteen years old. I may not be very experienced, but I know what I feel, and my feeling for you is a pain that only you can ease. I want to hold you and touch you, to know you in every way, and I can't stop myself from thinking about it nor from wanting it desperately. You're all I care about, Laura. There's no one else. You've become my whole world."

"You'll find someone else, Alex. Someone much more suitable. Next year, when you go to England, you'll meet people your own age, and when you do, you'll probably find some young lady for whom you will feel as you feel now, but even more so. What you feel for me can't possibly last. You need someone your own age."

"Stop talking about my age all the time. Age has nothing to do with it."

"Age is everything, Alex. I know—because I was once your age."

And she told him more about her past, about her numerous loveless affairs, wounding him deeply with each fresh revelation, and bewildering him further. She had had so many affairs, and yet had never been in love, claiming to have remained virtually untouched in that particular manner. He could not understand that—not in someone so emotional—and her claims about her fear of the darkness struck him as facile. No, there had to be another reason, something more directly personal, and Alex, in the pain of his own unrequited love, stumbled like a drunkard in the darkness, trying to fathom the answers.

"I always felt like a whore," she said. "I couldn't give myself to it. I always felt that it was basically disgusting, and not romantic at all. In fact I thought it was not only disgusting but pretty ridiculous: two sweaty bodies heaving at one another in that singularly undignified manner, as mindless as two dogs in heat, and certainly not much more graceful. Was that love? Not for me. I wanted something more pure and gentle—something that no man has so far been able to give me."

He studied the jungle for consolation, staring across the enormous river, his spirit sinking into the oppressive humidity and sullen gray sky. The Amazon was too quiet, its silence praying on the mind, drawing out of it buried doubts and fears, draining strength and volition. He reached out to Laura, taking her hand in his own, and then pressed his lips yearningly to her wrist, trying to suck up her tender skin.

"*I* can give it," he said.

13

"I can give you that," he said. "All that and much more. My love is pure and gentle—it's real—and it will last all our lives."

They were on a raft in a large lake, not too far from the mission, and the sun, sinking down behind some clouds, turned the sky into drifting pools of flame, with multicolored grottoes and arches drifting over the burnished trees.

"Oh, my Alex," Laura said. "How beautiful you make it sound. You speak from the heart—I know you do—but that isn't enough."

"Why?"

"Because age separates us . . . and so does experience."

She stared at him very sadly and he reached out for her hand, raising it to his lips as he had done before on the river, and sucking very tenderly at her skin, as if wanting to eat her. She sighed—a despairing sound—and he felt her hand on his lowered head, the fingers first stroking, then scratching and taking hold, tugging at his hair and pulling his head back, making him look at her. She was beautiful and forlorn, the jungle framing her long red hair, and he sensed, as the raft turned beneath him, that she was trying to help him.

"A pure and gentle love," he said quietly, "is what I'm trying to give you."

She closed her eyes and nodded. "Yes, Alex. But what will it lead to?"

He didn't quite understand, but felt the lurching of his heart, then glanced around the lake, at the crimson light filtering through the jungle, his spirit sinking with the sun, his hope fading into the dusk, his pain rising with the first sounds of the forest as night started to take command.

"A pure and tender love?" Laura murmured. "Oh, yes, Alex, I know of that." Her voice trailed off weakly, as if swallowed by her painful thoughts. Then she opened her eyes again and stared at him, shaking her head in despair. "I'll have to tell you," she continued. "I once had such an experience. It was as pure and tender as the moon, and I'll never forget it." Now she returned his gesture, holding his hand up to her mouth, pressing her lips down on his naked wrist and letting her tongue set his blood on fire. "It was in 1930," she said, "when I was sixteen years old. I looked like a woman, not a girl, and many mature men wanted me, pursued me. My mother encouraged such attentions—it was her ticket to those same men—but I always felt that I was being used and retreated accordingly. So, if I was attractive to them, doubtless I was even more so because I was so hard to move, either emotionally or sexually. Am I shocking you, Alex?"

Yes, he was shocked, his cup of pain running over, but he shook his head in denial and avoided her gaze.

"Of all the Hollywood friends of my parents, the one I most liked was an actress who shall go unnamed, but who, at that time, had acquired a fame of almost legendary proportions; that actress—then twenty-five years old and at the pinnacle of her success—visited our home regularly for years and gave me a lot of badly needed attention."

She stared steadily at him, not blinking for once, and he found himself looking down at the raft to avoid returning her gaze. The raft swayed very slightly, turned a little, trying to drift from the taut rope. He took a deep breath, drawing in the warm air, feeling as if he were choking in the oppressive humidity.

"Yes, Alex, she was twenty-five, and I was sixteen, a disturbed and lonely girl who desperately needed the attention that I received from her as she insinuated herself into the void left by my self-centered parents. Already, by then, I was suffering my nightmares and found the desires of men gross; I desperately needed someone to lean upon, and in my friend I found that person—the first one I had so far found—and so over a period of years our relationship changed subtly: at first she was a surrogate parent, then a friend and confidante, and finally, when I was eighteen years old, she became . . . my lover."

The shock was considerable, almost making Alex's heart leap, briefly stopping the breath in his throat while his burning skin froze. A tremor of revulsion shook him, passed away, leaving a numbness, a great void into which his mind was dropping as he silently screamed. Then he saw her long, fine fingers, curving gently around his wrist, shaking it lightly and then lifting it up until his hand grazed her cheek.

"Oh, God," Alex muttered, "I can't stand this. You're not . . . ?"

"No, Alex, I'm not. Believe me, I'm not. If my friend lived with that secret, I myself had no such secret; I did not surrender to her out of sexual desire, but out of the need to take comfort from the only human being who had, up to that point, understood me and tried to comfort me. She didn't believe in black magic, didn't believe that I was possessed, but feared that *my* belief in those things would do me great damage; and so she supported me, and encouraged me to ignore my mother, and eventually taught me that love—yes, Alex, love—could, no matter how it was expressed, help us to transcend our deepest fears and make life seem worth living. She might have saved me, Alex. I thought she would . . . but it wasn't to be."

She finished off her *cachaça* and put the empty glass down, then took hold of his other wrist with her free hand and pulled him slightly toward her.

"No, Alex, it was not to be; the forces of darkness would have their way; I sometimes think that they actually used her in an attempt to destroy me. She taught me love—a love that briefly changed my life—but then, over a period, the pleasure we had gained turned to guilt—my natural adolescent guilt; her guilt at having seduced me—and a feeling of shame which, because she was basically a puritan, my friend could not bear for long."

As she stared intensely at him, he felt his hands being pressed down on her thighs, and her warmth, coursing up between his fingers, soon flooded his loins. His senses began to scatter, his will dissolved, and he started losing himself.

"Am I tied to destructive events? Yes, Alex, I think I am. I was sure of it from a tender age, and was even more sure of it when, during one of my parents' famous all-night parties, my mother found my friend and me in bed together. We hadn't meant to do it, we hadn't planned it at all, but something took hold of us, desperation mixed with excitement, the knowledge that all those people at that party would have reviled *us* for our pure, selfless love—and so, in that atmosphere, and knowing that we soon must part, we convinced ourselves that it would be perfectly safe and crept into my room. Then my mother came in and found us. She was drunk and became hysterical, and soon half of the guests were crowding around her, staring down at the pair of us. . . . My friend knew what that town was like; she knew she could never survive the scandal. The very next day, when in defiance of my parents I went to console her, I found her lying in a pool of blood on her bed. She had slit her own wrists.''

Alex looked down at his hands and saw them, fingers outspread, one resting on each of Laura's thighs, her own hands pressing on top of them. He felt cold and then hot, his fear consumed by his desire, and he couldn't prevent his fingers from curling down and digging, very softly but demandingly, into her flesh. Startled, he looked up, and saw the tears in her eyes, glistening as they rolled down her high cheekbones and made spots on her blouse. She lifted her hands from his, slid them up his bare arms, grabbed hold of the sleeves of his shirt, and whispered her words with great passion.

"It's true, Alex! It's all true! And I can never forget it! I still dream about her body in that pool of blood, and I wake up screaming. Do you understand what I've told you? Do you think I'm just drunk? She was dead, and I was sick for years after and still haven't recovered. I need magic in my life—the sort of magic you possess—and I look for some such magic to rescue me from the nightmare I live in. Is it you, Alex? *Show me!*"

Alex stared at her wild eyes, at her quivering, sensual lips, then dropped his gaze to stare at the amulet that lay on her beating throat. Peruche's gift, a black stone, imbued with magical and protective properties, it drew him toward it and then into it, his lips tasting the skin around it while Laura, her hands pressed to the nape of his neck, repeatedly kissed the top of his head, her lips pliant and wet. He felt the power coursing through him, as if coming from her body, then heard himself groaning when her tongue slid around his earlobe and down his neck until, with her wet, burning lips, she sucked up his skin.

Something snapped and whipped through the air, making him jerk his head up. Following Laura's gaze, he saw the retaining rope of the raft, obviously broken for no good reason, flying mysteriously above their heads and splashing into the water.

"Magic!" Laura hissed. "*Magic!*"

He drew the power from her body, through the amulet and into himself, calling upon it as Peruche had taught him and letting it live by his faith. He was shaking, bathed in heat, saw the yellow-streamed crimson sky, the sun an enormous circle of flame that set fire to the drifting clouds. Magic: all magic. The whole of the natural world was magical. He breathed deeply as Laura's hands trailed over his body and then tugged his shirt. He closed his eyes and opened them again, fixing his gaze on the distant shore. The whole lake started moving, the water swirling around the raft, until eventually the raft itself started turning in slow, languid circles.

Laura stared around, gasping. The great lake had become a whirlpool. The black water was swirling around them in a gentle but regular manner, sinking down a little in the middle and making the wooden raft turn as if on a revolving base that was invisibly supporting them.

"Oh, my God!" Laura murmured.

Alex pulled his shirt off, hardly knowing what he was doing, then lay down on his back on the raft and felt himself turning round and round. He glanced up and saw the spinning sky, streams of color, a kaleidoscope, until Laura's face, her red hair falling down around him, filled his whole vision. Her eyes were like the forest, green and impenetrable, and then he felt her breast grazing his bare chest as she lowered herself on her bent arms.

"Oh, my Alex," she crooned. "My strange, magical Alex. I can't let you make love to me. It just wouldn't be right. Oh, you poor boy, I know how you feel, but I can't let you do that."

"*Please*, Laura . . ." He heard his own voice far away. "Don't leave me like this."

"Oh, my Alex. Poor Alex . . ."

He closed his eyes as she undressed him, ashamed, terrified, his heart pounding and his body ethereal as the lake, now a great, lazy whirlpool, made the raft slowly spin. There was noise—the rushing water, branches and rushes breaking free—but it seemed very distant and unreal, muffled behind his own breathing. He was naked and erect, his quivering loins the center of being, his every nerve and sensation concentrated on that member being stroked and massaged by her light fingers. He opened his eyes and saw the sky, a kaleidoscope spinning above him, then her unraveled hair fell over him, covering his eyes and nose, while her tongue, sliding between his burning lips, explored the roof of his mouth.

He sucked her tongue, trying to swallow it, feeling her nipples against his chest, first grazing it, then pressing firmly into it as her breasts flattened on top of him. Heat. Sublime softness. Silken skin against his own, first warm, then hot, then sweat-slicked as breasts and thighs permeated him. He wanted to cleave to her being, to enter her and become her, but when he tried to roll over she pressed him back with the delicious weight of her body. His own body was all sensation, rivulets and streams of feeling, the pores of his skin like grains of sand blowing over each other. The raft was hard beneath his spine, but still turning, and turning him, and he felt that he was drifting in space with heat and light passing through him.

He just drifted there, imprisoned, turning constantly in the sun, his fingers pressing and probing, relaying messages from her flesh, as if her blood, pouring out of her veins, were racing up through his own. The lake swirled with a soft rushing sound, their bodies turning as they intertwined, and that sound, which matched the rhythm of their beating hearts, became a strange, distant symphony. He went with the music, following its primal, hypnotic beat, its melody, *mezzo forte* all around him, raising his spirit on high. Laura's tongue was on his neck, licking his throat, sliding lower, her lips pressing upon and sucking at his chest and belly as his quivering spine arched. He shrank down to his own center, his whole being that aching member which, a pulsating shaft that defined his being, was thrusting up through her fingers. All that was, was in her fingers, being rhythmically squeezed and stroked, and then her soft hair fell upon him, covering his loins like a silken sheet, and her lips, following a lightly flicking tongue, drew him out of her fingers.

"Oh, God," he said, "*please!*"

She drew him into her scalding breath, into the juices of her mouth, her tongue light as a feather as it licked him, her contracting lips making soft sounds. She was swallowing him, all of him, ingesting him deliciously, melting his very marrow and bone and making him part of her substance: softness and heat, flowing blood, pounding heart, pores of flesh lapping in gentle waves over all that he was—pure feeling, sensation, chaotic impulses drifting, the raft turning beneath him, the sky spinning above, all quivering, breaking apart, his center exploding out into her, an almost painfully intense excitation and pleasure, a jolting discharge of recurrent spasms— then he cried out—something meaningless—his voice reverberating within him, and reached down to clasp her rocking head in his hands, imprisoning her face at his groin while she drained him completely, rendering him, in that moment of anguished ecstasy, a slave to her fantasy.

14

"Oh, God!" Laura cried. "What have I done? *What have I done?*"

She had rolled away from Alex and was propped up on one elbow, tugging the tangled hair out of her eyes and blinking repeatedly. The enormous lake was still swirling magically, forming a whirlpool around them, but the rate of flow was slowing down, with the rushes and broken branches that had been torn free by the water now drifting freely around the raft. Alex was still flat on his back, not believing what had occurred, his body glowing in ecstatic renewal, a great dread and wonder in his soul. He flicked his eyes toward Laura, saw the curves of her reclining form, the dying rays of the sun casting black and crimson patterns on her white shirt and slacks and golden skin. She was not staring at him but at the lake's circular motion, and she kept her gaze fixed on that miracle until the water had ceased to flow. Only then, when the lake was still and the black water was reflecting the moonlight, did she turn her face back toward him, her expression revealing bewilderment, her limbs visibly shaking.

"I love you," Alex said.

"Oh, God," she replied, "*what happened?*"

"Did you hear me, Laura? I said I loved you. I love you, I need you, I want you, and I can't let you go."

"Was it a dream? Did it really happen? Did *you* make it happen, Alex? Oh, Alex, what I did . . . I didn't mean to . . . It was the way the lake was moving—I couldn't believe what was happening—and then, you seemed so unhappy, so much in need of me, and I really felt compelled—yes, a *compulsion*—to make you feel better." She glanced around her again, visibly distraught, her hands fluttering in the air like wounded birds, the darkness deepening about her. "But what a terrible, *terrible* thing! And with someone *your* age! Oh, God, I don't know what got into me. *I don't know what I'm saying!*"

Her speech was indeed hysterical, springing randomly from her scattered thoughts; listening to her, Alex felt love and pain in equal measures, the latter coiling tightly around the former like thorns strangling an orchid.

"Please, Laura, calm down. What I did was nothing special. All of nature is magical—all of it—and I simply use nature. Such powers are not unusual, but in fact are within us all; but most men, through lack of faith, have lost their power and cut themselves off from nature. What I showed you was nothing special; what you showed me was: I can still feel and smell you all over me, and my body is singing."

"Please, Alex, don't talk like that. It was madness! *Madness!* Oh, God, I can't bear to talk about it! What must you think of me?"

"I've already told you what I think. I love you, Laura, and always will. And now *I* want to make love to *you*. I'm not a child: I'm a man."

"No, Alex, you don't love me. You *can't possibly* love me. You're confusing sex with love, physical desire with emotion, and if you didn't live here, isolated from those your own age, you would soon know the difference between the two and love me a lot less."

"You're insulting me by saying that."

"I'm not insulting you: I'm trying to help you. Oh, Alex, my Alex, please forget what we did here today and don't mention it to anyone."

He felt betrayed when she said that, his love turning to ashes, but then, when she sat upright and covered her lowered face with her hands, he felt his heart going out to her again in compassion and love. Still lying there, he reached up through the darkness and stroked her bare arm.

"It's our secret," he said. "I promise you, I won't tell anyone—but I can't promise that I'll ever forget it. And I want you to know that if I loved you before, I love you even more after this."

She picked his shirt off the raft, which had stopped turning in circles, and handed it to him in an abrupt manner. "Let's go," she said. "I'm scared in this place. I don't like it in darkness."

The lake did look mysterious, its black surface reflecting the moonlight, the trees surrounding it a deeper darkness than the night and, in its macabre fashion, gradually letting its nocturnal silence surrender to the varied and exotic clamor of its hidden inhabitants: the twanging sound of *seringueiro* birds, the chattering of monkeys, a mass rustling as the branches came alive with things that slithered and crawled. Laura shivered and stared at him, offering a nervous smile, then gently placed her fingers on his hand and pushed it away from her arm. Her face, framed by her long hair, was also framed by the stars, and he felt the pain of sorrow and love as he sat up beside her.

"Kiss me," he said.

He was kneeling right in front of her, actually feeling her breath on his face as she stared back intently. She seemed hesitant and very sober, lost in some private domain, but eventually she smiled—not too confidently, her lips shivering—and leaned forward and pressed her lips to his in a very light, deliberately nonprovocative manner. Nonetheless, the kiss aroused him, instantly filling his loins with heat, and he wanted to press her back onto the raft and then sink down on top of her. Doubtless she sensed his mood, because she suddenly stood up, running her fingers lightly through his hair, and then stepped back, the starbright sky streaming over her.

"Please, Alex, let's go. I'm really quite frightened. After what I've seen, I don't want to be on this raft in the darkness. That water now scares me."

"Of course," Alex said.

Since the retaining rope had been snapped, the raft was drifting freely, but Alex took hold of Laura's hand and helped her off, then guided her up the short, sloping bank to the Jeep parked under the trees.

They drove off immediately, following the crude, narrow track, ducking as foliage materialized out of the darkness and whipped over their heads. Laura was really nervous now—she was frightened of spiders or snakes falling on top of her—but the track soon opened out into a minor road where the cool air, making a low, moaning sound, rushed all around them. The road, which ran parallel with the river, would lead them back to the mission, and Alex, handling the Jeep with practiced ease, had only to keep his eyes peeled for straying animals, since no humans, either Indian or otherwise, would be likely to be out walking at night. He did not speak to Laura, hardly knowing what he could say, but was relieved when he heard her voice after a very long silence.

"Alex, it was madness. Really, it was just *madness*. I feel so depraved, so . . . *ashamed*—and can't believe that I did it."

"It was wonderful."

"*Please*, Alex!"

"It was beautiful. I won't ever forget it."

Laura sighed and shook her head, then placed her hand on his shoulder, digging her fingers lightly into his skin and letting the hand slide away again. "Oh, dear God," she exclaimed, "you're impossible! I just can't believe this!" She sighed again, looking left and right as the jungle slid past them. "I was frightened back there," she said. "It was really terrifying. I was drunk at first—when I asked you to give me magic—but then, when that lake actually turned into a whirlpool, when I felt us sinking down into the vortex of that swirling water, the fear sobered me up and then dissolved my senses in another way, making me feel part of the lake, of the raft, part of you—I mean *part* of you, Alex: flesh, blood, and spirit. I felt that we were one, and as one were part of the elements, part of the water and the forest and the sky and the moon and stars, part of the whole. And only when it was over—when the swirling water was slowing down again—did I realize just what I had been doing and come back down to earth. God, it was frightening!" She stared intently at him. "Tell me, Alex . . . *how did you do that?*"

"I willed it," he replied. "That's all. I simply willed it to happen."

"And did it happen? Did it *actually* happen?"

"What do you think?"

"It happened."

"You've just answered your own question."

He kept looking straight ahead, feeling secretive and vain, both of which vices were very unexpected and slightly tainted the purity of his love. The forest road was incredibly dark, illuminated only by his headlights, the tops of the trees forming a narrow, star-studded avenue that appeared to run through the night sky, curving away and vanishing not far ahead, approximately over the mission camp.

"You learned that magic from the Indians?" Laura asked him.

"Yes. From Peruche."

"Was he *really* a prisoner of the Yano?"

"Yes. An awfully long time ago."

"And no one else has ever escaped from them?"

"Not as far as we know."

"Peruche must have been incredibly lucky."

"Or incredibly smart."

He ducked to avoid some branches, saw Laura leaning forward, her hands crossed on the back of her head to form modest protection from the spiders, snakes, or insects that could, she imagined, fall out of the trees. He smiled to see that, watched the road where it curved right, then saw the black, linear shapes of the mission buildings at the end of the straight stretch.

"How much power do you really have?" Laura asked him. "A lot? Or a little?"

"It's not *power*," he replied. "It's merely the faith that human beings had long ago, and have long since deserted."

"Faith?"

"Faith in oneself as part of nature, able to make nature do our bidding like our very own limbs."

"But just how much can you work what we call miracles? I repeat: a lot or a little?"

"A little," he replied. "At least compared to Peruche. What you saw me do tonight was about as much as I can do—and even that, I hadn't planned at all; I didn't know what would happen."

"But you said you *willed* it to happen."

"I willed *something* to happen—I didn't know what it would be. I just love you so much, and wanted you so desperately, that I tried to impress myself upon you with all of my being. If I moved you, I also moved the water—but I hadn't expected that."

"And that was the first time you ever managed something like that?"

"Yes. Normally my ability is quite modest: I can make flowers open their petals, make inanimate objects move, let poisonous snakes and spiders rest upon me without fear that they'll poison me. According to Peruche, what I'm actually doing is hypnotizing them."

"The snakes and spiders?"

"Yes."

Laura visibly shivered as he drove into the mission camp, passing the medical building and Father Benedict's living quarters, and braking right in front of Laura's hut. He turned the lights and ignition off, then moved to climb down, but Laura's hand fell on his wrist and held on to it tightly.

"*Please*, Alex," she said, when he had turned back to face her, "no matter what happens, don't tell anyone what went on today. I didn't want it to happen, I didn't plan for it to happen, and when it happened I was just as surprised as you. And today of all days, please believe me, I didn't want that of all things. So, Alex, *please* don't say anything to anyone. It's your secret—and mine."

He stared at her a long time, wondering just what she was saying, unable to turn away from her and actually wanting to grab her. He felt her fingers around his wrist, her grip tightening and relaxing repeatedly, skin against skin, bone on bone, her blood warming his blood.

"God, I love you," he whispered.

She immediately let his wrist go and pressed her fingers to his lips, smiling at him with what seemed to be her former assurance and then letting the hand fall. He reached out to pull her to him, feeling dizzy from her proximity, but she very quickly and gracefully slid away from him and swung her legs out of the Jeep and raced for her hut. She climbed up the few steps, blew him a kiss, and stepped inside, letting the door slam behind her. Alex looked at the closed door for a long time before he sighed and climbed down.

The night was blessedly cool, the stars gloriously abundant. As he walked toward Father Benedict's hut the pockmarked moon was like a single eye following his movement, and he felt its mysterious, magnetic pull on his body and mind. Nature was magical, both without and within, and within him he was reaching out for Laura and her transcendent presence. She was doubtful, afraid, constantly anxious about her age. He knew that without the years between them she would have had no such doubts, that she would have accepted that he knew she must surely feel for him. No, he was not a child—he was a man and knew himself—and now, when he lowered his gaze, blinking into the light of Father Benedict's hut, he let his spirit soar to the stars on the wings of his faith.

The priest was sitting behind a small desk at the far side of his bed, a cigarette in one hand, a bottle of beer at the other, a pair of spectacles balanced precariously on his nose, scribbling some notes. He glanced up when Alex walked in, dropped his pen and gave a grin, then clasped his hands high above his head and gave a loud sigh.

"Ah," he said, "Miss Wellman's guide has returned. Did you have a good day?"

"Yes."

"And Laura?"

"I think she enjoyed herself."

Father Benedict lowered his hands back to the desk and picked up his beer glass. "Well," he said, holding the glass up, "here's to you. And I bless you for this wonderful excuse to stop doing my homework."

"What are you writing?"

"More begging letters. It's how the mission survives." He took a sip of beer, inhaled on his cigarette, blew a cloud of smoke, and settled back in his chair. "You're looking fairly somber," he said. "Do you wish to confess?"

"Pardon?"

"Only *joking*, my son! Only *joking*! You just didn't seem your normal calm self, so I made a small joke. Don't look so startled, my young friend: I know you've no sins to worry about." He stubbed his cigarette out in an earthen ashtray and then settled back again. "On the other hand," he continued, "I can see there's little doubt that once more the close proximity of Laura Wellman has caused you great pain. You haven't listened to a word I've said, have you? You still pine for that woman, no matter how much older than you she is; you still hope to win her."

"I love her, Father Benedict." Alex couldn't say much more. Everyone knew what he felt for Laura—Father Benedict, Antonio Bozzano, even, God help him, his father—and there was very little point in hiding it now; yet what had happened earlier, that delirious dalliance on the raft, was something he had promised not to mention, though he was bursting to shout it out. "You all think it will pass, but that's just because you're older. You can't understand what I'm feeling—and what I'm feeling simply can't be false. I will love her forever."

"I repeat: you're too young to fully understand yourself; and your feelings for Laura, no matter how intense, will fade when she leaves here."

"She isn't leaving yet. We already know that. She sent her resignation to that magazine she works for, and is going to stay on here indefinitely."

"Indefinite, my son, is not forever—and sooner or later, when she is rid of her foolish notions about the jungle, she will pack her bags and return to America where she truly belongs."

"By that time she'll understand that she also loves me."

"I would seriously doubt that." The priest shook his head sadly from side to side and then sipped some more beer. "She *does* love you in a certain way, Alex. It's known as affection. It is *not*—do you hear me?—it is emphatically *not* the kind of love you so vividly imagine."

"You're making fun of me."

"No, Alex, I'm not. I'm trying to save you from future pain."

Alex realized that he was still standing, and so sat down on the canvas camp bed, clasping his hands and sliding them down through his knees to rest on the floor. He felt hot and flustered, his mind reeling from the day's events, all the pain and glory of love churning ceaselessly inside him and making him suffer like a condemned man repeatedly offered the hope of life.

"I can never work out what you really think of her," he said. "Sometimes you seem so considerate and helpful, other times you become rather distant and even, unusually, downright rude."

"I don't approve of her constant drinking," Father Benedict replied, "and of course it gets my blood boiling."

"It's her business if she drinks."

"We are all one another's business—besides which, when Laura drinks too much she tends to be far too *risqué.*"

"You mean all that talk about Hollywood?"

"Yes, I suppose I do. I'm not at all sure that I approve of you listening to her countless tales of promiscuity in the Hollywood hills. Nor, come to think of it, do I care for her belief that she is possessed by evil and requires her own peculiar form of exorcism—namely, since she is here via the intervention of the possibly mythical Yano Indians."

"The Yano Indians are not mythical, and it's possible that Laura has been sent here to find them."

"For what purpose?"

"I don't know."

"No, my son, you don't know. And neither does old Peruche. And I really do think that to suggest such an idea to Laura—who is possibly already unstable—is to run the risk of incalculable damage—certainly to her, and possibly in other ways that we cannot yet understand."

"I love her. That's all that matters to me. The rest doesn't interest me."

Father Benedict lit another cigarette. "Thank God," he said, "you will soon be going to England in order to further your sadly lacking education. You might also learn something of the real world and meet ladies your own age."

"I'm hoping to persuade her to come with me. And I'm sure she will come."

"You're daydreaming, Alex. This love has surely turned your head. She wouldn't even consider it, because she's knows you are too young—and besides, your father would never permit it, which means it won't happen."

"You're all against me," Alex said.

"We are not. As you will learn in due course."

Alex shifted uncomfortably, feeling horribly guilty, realizing he had changed during the past few weeks, and probably not for the better. Jealousy, suspicion, resentment, and rage—all of these had manifested themselves at one time or another, and all of them, prior to the arrival of Laura, had been totally alien to him. Now, studying Father Benedict, his guilt increased tenfold, because he knew that the priest, his good friend, was only concerned for his future.

Yet what did the priest, a celibate, know of passionate love? And was not Antonio Bozzano too old to still believe in it? And how could his own father, with his degenerate ways, have the nerve to make suggestive remarks, as he had done so often recently, intimating that Laura was a woman of exotic tastes and rather dubious morals?

Indeed, his father was the worst offender, mocking Alex with relentless zeal, either embarrassing him or inciting him to rage with his acidulous humor. Alex had hated him for it when he did it at home—usually in the presence of Rollie Thatcher and the unfortunate Indian girl—but he hated him even more when he did it in Manaus or here at the mission in the presence of Laura herself. At such moments Alex's hatred was considerably more complex, arising not only from his father's sarcasm but from Laura's own sardonic wit, which was also rather flirtatious. The thought that Laura found his father attractive made him writhe in sheer torment.

"You all criticize her," he said, fixing his gaze on Father Benedict, hating himself even as he said it, but needing to strike out. "You complain about her drinking, and about the way that she talks, but really you're just jealous that she gives me so much attention. I hate to say that, Father, but it's true—and it applies even to you."

He expected the priest to explode, but instead he just smiled gently, raising his glass in a mock toast before taking a sip.

"Well, Alex," he said, "if you believe it, I won't deny it; but you should be comforted by the fact—at least regarding myself— that the new priest arrives in two days' time, after which Laura will take leave of the mission and my unworthy presence."

"Good," Alex replied, feeling ashamed of his own vindictiveness. "I can see her all alone in her hotel, away from your prying eyes."

Father Benedict looked startled and jerked upright, his sunburnt brow furrowing.

"Good God, Alex," he said, "do you mean you haven't heard? Are you saying that Laura hasn't told you yet?"

"Told me what?" Alex said, now sitting upright himself, clenching his fists and feeling his heart race. "*Told me what?*"

"Laura's *not* going to a hotel in Manaus. She decided she didn't want to be alone. She spoke to your father and he's agreed to let her stay in the plantation. He's offered her a room in your *fazendeiro*, and that's where she'll be staying."

"In my *father's* house? She'll be staying with *us*?"

"That's what was arranged, my son."

Alex recoiled with shock, some part of him disbelieving. The shock changed to joy and returned to shock; he kept bouncing from one feeling to the other. He went outside and remained there for a long time, gazing up through the towering trees to the pale moon and stars, letting the chattering of the forest fill his ears and distract his mind from its torments.

She had surprised him again.

15

Something had changed in Laura after the incident on the raft, and the change became even more apparent when she moved into the plantation, staying in a room in the modest guest wing and otherwise having the run of the house. She seemed more intense, more distracted and remote; and to Alex's dismay she drank even more than usual, encouraged in this activity by his father. She spent many evenings with Alex and his father—and other evenings with his father and Rollie Thatcher, though not with the unfortunate Indian girl. And now when Laura drank, during those evenings in that decaying lounge, she became more visibly drunk, her speech slurred and repetitive, her eyes blinking repeatedly, and her hands weaving arabesques in the dimly lit, yellowish, smoke-filled air.

Nevertheless, her daily presence had a dramatic effect on him, laying waste to his senses, further inflaming his imagination, and forcing him to lie on a bed of nails during his long, anguished nights. She had not touched him seriously since that evening on the raft, and his hurt at this neglect, and his confusion about what that incident meant to her, made him leap back and forth between the belief that she secretly loved him and the conviction that in truth she was playing with him and quietly mocking his love.

He knew he had lost some part of her, but he convinced himself that she might have returned his love had it not been for the fear that was making her keep him at arm's length by spending most of her evenings with his father, drinking heavily in that dim room, trading anecdotes, reminiscences, and *bons mots* with an ambiguous flirtatiousness. She talked far too much, recounting the history she had given Alex, making Alex feel oddly betrayed and painfully wounded, his heart breaking when his father responded to Laura's anxieties with his customary sarcasm.

"So you think you're possessed, Laura? And can't sleep nights? Might I offer the suggestion that you might in fact be suffering from that perfectly commonplace itch which, in all of us pitiful mortals, occasionally needs to be scratched?''

"May *I* suggest, Frank, that that sounds like wishful thinking? I can't sleep because of my bad dreams—and I *know* what is causing them.''

"You're simply a dissatisfied woman. Your whole history attests to that. You had an unhappy childhood, you matured far too early, you received too many unwanted attentions from too many older men, and this, alas, made you suspicious of the whole rotten male sex.''

"No, Frank, it was really much more than that. It was—''

"Then, of course, there was your father, who should have loved you and cherished you, but instead methodically drove your mother crazy and then, when she died, brought his various mistresses back home and thus increased your already well entrenched antagonism toward all base men. After that, in a kind of panic, perhaps to prove to yourself that you were normal, you married a man you didn't love. And naturally, when the marriage collapsed, you had to find an excuse for it, doing so by retreating further behind your colorful story of demonic possession, escaping into this elaborate fantasy like a nun entering a convent.''

"I was not entering *anything*. I was trying to escape from the demons possessing me. I was trying to find protection from my fear of what the darkness might bring to me.''

"An elaborate fantasy, Laura—but a fantasy all the same. What you suffer from, my dear, is not fear of the forces of darkness but fear of your own helpless dependency upon the sex you despise. The devil you fear is within yourself—and I could help you get rid of it.''

Alex sat with them too often, hardly knowing what he was doing there, enduring pain and confusion as he glanced from one to the other and tried to work out what was going on between them, his speculations destroying him. His father sneered constantly at Laura, poured relentless sarcasm upon her—mocking her "spoiled" Hollywood childhood, her "pitiful belief in the occult," her failed marriage and various love affairs and "demented retreat" to the Amazon—and Laura took it all from him, sparring with him, but not seriously, actually responding to him with what seemed, at least to Alex's tortured perceptions, helpless admiration and even affection, her smile coming alive.

"So, Laura my dear, let me get the picture straight. You got divorced from your husband, you moved back to Hollywood, and then, still convinced that you had been possessed by the forces of darkness, you started sliding into promiscuity, started drinking too much—as both of us are doing right now, God help us—and then you went to work for a New York paper, photographed the aftermath of Pearl Harbor, and after that, being finally convinced that, as your mother had formerly intimated, you were in some way connected to destructive events, you became even more neurotic and drifted into a life of depressing degeneracy, by which I mean, of course, alcohol and sex.''

"Yes, Frank, that's right. By that time I had come to understand that I had only married my husband in hopes of escaping my fear of the darkness, and that I would only know genuine love when I had been exorcised of the demons that had been possessing me.''

"This is truly the most wonderfully ludicrous story. You should put it in writing.''

If Alex had previously forgiven his father for his distasteful and vicious activities, he could not, in those obliquely squalid hours, forgive him for anything. In fact he came to despise his father—sensing in every word, in every smirk and innuendo, a contempt that Laura either was blind to or simply ignored. Their rapport bewildered him, cutting the ground from beneath his feet, making him feel immature and insecure, his former levelheadedness deserting him and leaving him dizzy with rage.

"I doubt that you'll understand this, Frank, but my promiscuity—which is clearly what thrills you—was not for sexual satisfaction. It was a means of avoiding having to spend my nights alone—''

"You were frightened of the bogey men.''

"—and of finding, if not sexual satisfaction, at least a temporary oblivion. Naturally, this didn't work—you don't find oblivion in loveless sex—and I started suffering a great deal of self-disgust as I became less choosy about my men friends and increasingly indiscriminate in the way I went about picking them up. Emotionally anesthetized with alcohol, I woke up once too often in a strange bed with a stranger beside me, hardly knowing how I had gotten there or what we had done. I rarely went after decent men—I didn't want a lasting relationship—and so I found myself with selfish, self-centered men, some of whom were quite dangerous.''

"And that's why you came to the Amazon? To get away from your sordid self?''

"Yes, Frank, I suppose so. In fact, shortly after we dropped the atom bomb on Hiroshima—and, incidentally, shortly after my divorce finally came through—one of my casual pickups beat me so badly that I had to be hospitalized for a few days. That was when, to put it mildly, I knew it was time for a change, so when my father visited me in the hospital and chastised me quite brutally for the social embarrassment my activities were causing him, I told him that I wanted to leave the country and go very far away—far away from him, from America, from civilization in general. Subsequently, through a friend of his, he got me the assignment with *National Geographic*—the assignment that brought me, at thirty-one years of age, to the Amazon and those strange lights in the sky. Now you know all there is to know.''

Drunk, they forgot Alex, talking as if he weren't there, unaware of the pain they were causing him as Laura's life was unraveled. Laura talked as if in a dream, sparred enthusiastically with Alex's father, and often drank until she could hardly stand up, her eyes becoming bloodshot and vague, her movements erratic. Alex listened and watched, in despair at what was said, understanding that his father was physically attracted to Laura and sometimes believing, if reluctantly, that she was attracted in return. This realization tainted his image of her, throwing a different kind of light on the stories she had told him. In his bewilderment there were times when his love turned to hatred.

''Do you *have* to drink so much?'' he said to her. ''And especially with *him*?''

''I *like* to drink,'' she replied. ''And now you're sounding like Father Benedict. And further, young man, since I'm actually living in your house, I can't possibly see how I could *not* talk to your father. You think I should spend every evening in my goddamned bedroom?''

''He makes fun of you. He sneers at you. He insults you and you just take it. And not only do you take it, but you actually seem to *enjoy* his abuse. It's embarrassing just being there.''

''It's not as bad as you make it sound. And you shouldn't talk that way about your father. I know he drinks too much and can be cruel and sarcastic, but it's possible that he's that way because he's lonely and misunderstood, hiding behind his cruelties because he doesn't know how to express himself. It's just possible, Alex.''

''That's ridiculous and you know it!''

''Stop shouting at me, Alex!''

"The very fact that you're making stupid excuses for him just proves that you like him!"

"I just think he needs some sympathy."

"That's nonsense! Pure *rubbish*! The ones who need sympathy are those poor Indians who have to endure his constant abuses."

"Alex! He's your father!"

"I don't want reminding of it! And I don't want to see you ending up like him, which you will if you stay here."

"You exaggerate, Alex! He's not that bad! And he *doesn't* despise me!"

"Of course he does! Are you deaf and blind?"

Was she indeed deaf and blind? He sometimes thought she must be. Clearly she did not see the same sneers that he saw, the same cynical raising of eyebrows, the same sidelong glances at Rollie Thatcher when that specimen was present. And how could he tell her what was said behind her back? What his father said to him or to Rollie Thatcher when she walked out of the room? Sarcasm, innuendo, and blunt character assassination. Alex was tortured by all of it.

"For such a spiritual lady," his father once said, "she appears to have had a certain flair for debauchery. I think she's worth looking into."

"A neurotic," Rollie Thatcher replied, lolling phlegmatically on a settee, his piggish eyes fixed on the Indian girl who was cowering on the floor at his feet, her eyes as dead as the moon. "All that talk of possession and black magic and dark forces is only an excuse to hide the fact that she can't do without it. Alcohol and sex, first in Hollywood and then New York—so much so that she had to flee to the Amazon to get away from the scandals. I bet you that bitch has had more than we could count, and now, with the lines beginning to show, she's going a little bit potty. Pass the brandy, old boy."

Alex hated that room anyway, too aware of its fading elegance and its smell of damp rot, stale beer, and cigarette ash. He avoided it during the day—that musky gloom was too depressing—but at night, after dinner, which was eaten in an adjoining room, there was little choice, as Laura had noted, but to while away the time in there. He would do it with heavy heart, as he had done for years, sitting in a chair near the magnificent baroque fireplace, watching the large, bizarre shadows on the walls which, in the flickering yellow light of the oil lamps, seemed to be in constant, shivery motion.

That room, he knew, would live forever in his mind. It was a refuge for his mother's ghost, her ethereal, ageless beauty. But he would never see it without his vision of his father, slim, handsome, dissipated, and disheveled, slouching in his Venetian armchair with his booted feet on his velvet upholstered footrest; and of Rollie Thatcher—bloated, bleary-eyed, drinking, and farting; and of the Indian girl whose father had died and who was now paying her father's debts with her body.

Alex learned to despise it and was glad to be out of it, always sighing with relief when he opened the door and stepped outside, either into the enlivening light of day or the night's soothing freshness, usually to rush straight to old Peruche and seek comfort from him.

The old Indian was growing more frail and very rarely left his clearing, spending most of his time in meditation and prayer, physically surviving on the food and drink brought to him by the other Indians, and sniffing *epena* at frequent intervals throughout the day. He was usually outside his hut, sitting cross-legged on the grass, his head bowed as he ventured down through his inner self, the lake glittering behind him, the white flowers of the cauliflorous trees falling gently about him. Always, when Alex arrived, he would raise his nodding head, work his lips experimentally, and stare at Alex out of his rheumy eyes, a small smile on his lips.

"I cannot help you," Peruche said on one such occasion. "This is something between you and her. Either your love was written or it was not, and only time can reveal that. You must not let this obsess you, but accept it with dignity, showing your faith in Him who guides our fate and suppressing resentment and anger."

"But I feel resentment and anger. I can't help it. It eats me up night and day."

"You never felt such emotions before. Not until this woman arrived. You were innocent and lived in the purity of one newly born. Yet I sense a purpose to this: I have dreamed and seen strange things. You may have to lose your innocence, to suffer guilt and shame, to endure the fires of penance and know redemption for some much larger purpose. There is something in you, and in this woman, that is one and the same."

The old Indian leaned closer, trying to focus his almost blind eyes, then reached out and scraped at Alex's bare chest with his long fingernails. Finding nothing, he sighed and straightened up, his rib cage clearly visible.

"Where is the magic amulet?" he asked.

Now it was Alex's turn to lower his head, trying to hide his embarrassment.

"I gave it to the American woman," he said. "I'm not really sure why."

The old Indian sighed and nodded in a judicious manner, showing no anger at all, just a sad understanding.

"You wanted to show how much you loved her?"

"Yes, I suppose so."

"You may have sacrificed a lot in doing so—much more than you realize. Yet now, more than ever, I feel there may be a purpose to it: the amulet was your protection against the forces of darkness, those forces which, because of your powers, might specifically seek you out to destroy you. You, my child, have always been a representative of the Good, and now, without the amulet, and with your protective innocence already degenerating, you may be reaching that stage where you will be forced to suffer hell in order to regain your faith and become a light through life's darkness."

Alex always left regretfully and often took himself down to the jetty to sit and stare at the river. Still and silent, vast and dark, it curved away into the distance, through the impenetrable, mysterious jungle. He often saw Mengrire at the jetty, fishing from one of the small boats, his net stretched out like a fan on the water, his muscles tightening to pull it in. He felt too shy to approach the Indian, his cheeks burning at the memory of the day that poor girl was brought to his father's house. It had killed something inside Mengrire.

"He worries me," Antonio said. "Mengrire's not the Indian we knew. He wanted that girl very much—I'm convinced he was going to marry her—and since the day your father took her, Mengrire's not been the same. He's polite but not friendly, obedient but sullen. He's nurturing a hatred that's growing each day. I'm worried about it, Alex—and not just about Mengrire. There's talk among the Indians. Your father and Rollie Thatcher have gone too far. I know what Mengrire's suffering—I'm part Indian. And if our feelings are shared by the rest of the Indians we could *all* be in trouble."

"I feel so helpless, Antonio. What can I do? If I say anything to my father, he'll just laugh me out of the house. Already he calls me an Indian lover, and despises me for it."

"You *are* an Indian lover, my young friend. That's why I love *you*."

The plantation was no longer somnolent—it was tense to the point of bursting. Alex walked beneath its trees, between its shabby shacks and huts, convinced that evil was brewing. He spent much time thinking about what Peruche had said and wondering what it all meant. All things were the one thing, all events the one event—the death of the *seringueiro*, the death of Father Symonds, the arrival of Laura, the beating drums, and the wondrous lights—and he sensed that they were all coming together to explode in some manner he could not define.

"Fear," he said to Father Benedict. "I live with fear night and day, and I can't shake it off. Is it all to do with Laura? Do I love her too much? Am I simply letting my own doubts rise up and take me over completely?"

"Your doubts about your love?"

"About *her* love, Father Benedict. I love her more than anything in the world, and I want it returned."

"You feel rejected?"

"Yes."

"If she rejects you, it's out of kindness."

"I simply can't accept that."

"Unfortunately Laura does."

"I'm not interested in what she *thinks* she feels; it's something else that I'm frightened of."

"What?"

"The Yano. She's becoming obsessed with them. Every time she hears the drums and sees the lights her obsession grows stronger."

"She won't be able to do anything about it because no one will take her. And I doubt that even Laura would be mad enough to go in there alone."

"I'm not so sure about that."

If, as Peruche said, there was a time of penance coming, the mysterious lights and the drums of the elusive Yano seemed to be part of it. They now materialized with disturbing frequency, the lights illuminating the sky above the jungle's distant interior and the drums louder and more frantic than ever.

At such times the world changed. The sky darkened, the air became sultry, the relentless drumming made the head reel and distorted reality. For Indian plantation workers the effects were dramatic: hysteria and convulsions, religious ecstasy and violence, wild dancing, loud sobbing, and shrieking; they foamed at the mouth, their bodies jerking in violent, epileptic movements, their eyes closed in a trance.

It was terrifying. If it affected the Indians dramatically, it also affected those with white skins, stretching their nerves to the breaking point, putting their tempers on a short fuse, forcing them out of the *fazendeiro* to the long, narrow verandah where they would stare at either the hysterical workers or at the lights that rose and fell like silent flares high above the black jungle.

"I have to find them!" Laura said. "I have to go into that jungle and face them! When I hear those drums and look at those lights I know they're trying to call me. I have to find them! *I have to!*"

Her determination frightened Alex and preyed constantly on his mind. He had no way of knowing what she might do and was increasingly losing touch with her. She was dividing her time equally between the plantation and the mission, taking photographs and notes, talking a lot to the Indians, and even, on occasion, venturing alone into Manaus where, after too much to drink, she would spend the night in some shabby hotel.

Alex hated it when she did that, thinking it stupid and dangerous, and bluntly informed her, more than once and apparently in vain, that she was solving none of her problems with such behavior, but was instead merely making the local people think her crazy or shameless.

"Oh, I know, Alex! I know! But I just can't help myself: I get depressed and drink a bit too much and then have to sleep. Nothing ever happens, Alex. I just drink myself to sleep. I always know when I'm going to have one of my bad nightmares, and because I don't want you or your father to hear me screaming, I book myself into a hotel in town and then drink myself into oblivion. I *know* it looks bad, Alex, but I simply can't help that: if I must scream in the night, I like to do it alone, and if that means spending the night in Manaus, then so be it."

She was growing more distant. Alex knew she was drinking harder every day and no longer working.

She often drove herself to the mission, staying away for days, and returning only to hide out in that awful room with his father and Rollie Thatcher, the sound of their drunken laughter reverberating along the corridor and entering Alex's room with hideous clarity, making him toss in his tortured bed.

Did she not care about the Indian girl? Did she simply ignore all the others? Could she not hear, even from the guest wing, the girl sobbing and the men laughing, the music from the phonograph blaring loudly to hide the sounds of debauchery? Of *course* she knew—there was no way she couldn't know.

Alex wanted her to revile his father, to pack her suitcase and walk out—and yet, because he loved her, because his love was fierce and greedy, he also dreaded that she might actually do that—perhaps to disappear into the jungle in search of the Yano. That fear, more than anything else, broke the last of his will and pride.

Nothing was normal, nor ever would be again.

16

The day was approaching when Alex would have to return to the school in Manaus for his last three months before flying to England for his further education. He became increasingly fixated on Laura and was constantly trying to keep his eyes on her.

Inflamed by desire for her, he was blinded to everything but the need to possess her. There was no end to this yearning, no respite from his burning loins, and he suffered both his body's betrayals and his heart's beating anguish.

"It is madness," Father Benedict said. "You are making a spectacle of yourself. Everyone is talking about how you moon after an older woman, no longer taking an interest in anything, and simply following her about all day. You must stop it, Alex. It will serve no good purpose. You are causing yourself more pain, causing Laura embarrassment, and letting people like your father and Rollie Thatcher have a good laugh at you. Accept the fact, Alex, that you're much too young for her, and that sooner or later she will leave and never return."

"I won't accept anything. If she leaves I'll go with her. And if I can't persuade my father to let me stay here, I'll persuade Laura to come with me."

"What are you talking about, Alex? What new insanity is this? You'll soon be going back to school in Manaus and then on to England: you simply can't take her with you."

"Why not, Father Benedict? What makes you so sure? She already spends lots of nights in Manaus, staying in sleazy hotels. All I want is for her to move into somewhere more decent, somewhere in one of the better areas close to the school."

"You mean you want her available."

"I just—"

"Don't bother answering, Alex. Clearly you are almost deranged about Laura Wellman and are now fantasizing. Miss Wellman would never be a party to such an arrangement—and your father will not, as you might be hoping, let you forget school and remain here in the plantation. Your father wants you to go back to England, and that's all there is to it.''

''I love her. I can't live without her.''

''You'll recover in England.''

''You're beginning to sound as if you want me to leave as well.''

''Maybe I do. Your fixation on Miss Wellman is extremely unhealthy. It is obviously hopeless; it might be that the only way to cure you is to send you away.''

''I'd rather kill myself,'' Alex said.

If Laura was putting a distance between herself and Alex, there was also an increasing distance between himself and Father Benedict, most of which was caused, he assumed, by his helpless fixation on Laura and his increasing inability to communicate with anything remotely resembling his former lightheartedness. This knowledge truly pained him, since the priest had been like a father to him, but think about it as he might, he could do little about it. Some part of him seemed bent on destroying his former self, filling him with almost pathological insecurity and fear.

''I can't help it,'' he told Peruche. ''I love her and want her. No matter what she is—sane or insane, one of the wise or a fool—no matter, I can't help longing for her night and day.''

''You have lost faith in yourself. You gave your amulet away. When you did that, you threw away your protection against those who would prey on you. Now you are like other men, your will weak, your thoughts disordered, and you leave your childhood innocence behind and give yourself to corrupt ways. This woman has been sent here. I think she truly is possessed. And if this be the case, then you surely must be in great danger, which in itself must have purpose. For this reason I cannot guide you. All decisions are now your own. Whether you turn toward the darkness or the light, I cannot hold you back.''

''You think she is corrupting me.''

''Yes, this is corruption. She asks you to perform miracles—to demonstrate your powers and you, in your vanity, in your need to impress her, perform what should only be performed in silence and secrecy. The powers are not to be revealed to those uninitiated, and by weakening before the attractions of this woman, you have opened your arms to the powers of darkness and invited them in.''

He knew that Peruche spoke the truth—that he was inviting his own ruination—and yet he could not stop himself from lusting for Laura and trying to buy her with miracles. He would take her into the forest, usually to some *verzea* lake, close his eyes, and raise his hand above the still, black water and will it to move. The silent forest would start rustling, shedding its leaves in a sudden breeze; the clouds would gather above, turning the gray light darker, the grass around them would bend, and the flowers open their petals and bow. Then, while Alex sweated, his brow furrowed in concentration, the water would bubble or swirl, become a cauldron or a whirlpool, and a snake might emerge, a giant and dangerous anaconda, and curl itself around his legs and body with the most gentle, loving care. Minor miracles, but impressive, making Laura stare in awe: he could lure the birds out of the trees, have them flapping their wings upon him, sitting side by side on his bare skin with the bird-eating spiders which, enormous and normally savage, would be remarkably passive; he could stroke the deadly alligators, wade through shoals of piranha, make rain fall out of the trees on a sunny day, their branches bending down toward him as if alive, trying to stroke his blond hair. Yes, he showed her his powers, wanting to impress her and succeeding—but what he could not succeed in doing was having his love returned.

"No, Alex, I won't. I don't care how much it hurts you. What happened on the raft should never have happened, and certainly will not be repeated, no matter how much you talk of it. It was a moment of madness—I hardly knew what I was doing—and I've felt ashamed of myself ever since for what I seem to have started. Believe me, Alex, I love you, but I'm not *in* love with you, and I'd rather hurt you now than make it worse later by leading you on. So please don't remind me of that particular day, because that's not being fair to me."

"Fair? What's *fair*? To do it once and never again? Yes, Laura, you started it—you encouraged me to love you—and now, when I'm helpless without you, you pretend not to care."

"I *don't* pretend not to care. That's a crude exaggeration. I'm simply saying that I care for you, but not in that particular way. I'm simply too old for you, Alex; it would never work out."

"Age has nothing to do with feelings."

"Feelings change as we get older. And at your age, young man, your feelings will change quicker than mine."

"What I feel for you won't change."

"Yes, Alex, it will. When you meet a girl your own age in England, you'll soon forget me."

But he didn't believe her. How could he? He hurt too much. He brooded with growing bitterness over the amount of time she spent away from him, at the mission, in Manaus, in the main room of the *fazendeiro*, getting drunk with his father and Rollie Thatcher. He more than once found himself the focal point for his father's sarcasm and contempt.

"You want to find the Yano, Laura? Then get Alex to take you to them. My good son, if not too bright, has great empathy with the Indians, and might possibly lead you through that miserable jungle without getting you lost. Then, when you find the Yano—if indeed the bastards exist—you will have someone who understands not only their language but their obscene hocus-pocus."

The nights often went on a long time, continuing after Alex had left, the drunken laughter echoing in the hall and breaking his heart. He didn't understand how she could be comfortable with them, was encouraging them to think of her as cheap.

"My son's in love with her," his father once said to the chortling Rollie Thatcher. "She behaves like a whore with us gentlemen—but still, he's in love with her."

"Such is youth," Rollie Thatcher replied. "All sweetness and light. You get a woman like that—quite clearly a shop-soiled creature—but youth can only view her in virgin white, wanting to hold her nimble, expert fingers, not guessing at what they've been up to."

Alex found their talk revolting, their attitudes and actions base, and failed to understand how Laura could ignore it, more so because during those evenings when she wasn't present (though she certainly knew it was happening) the Indian girl would be sent for and the sounds of revelry would change, becoming humorless and obscene, first his father laughing, then the revolting Rollie Thatcher, his contemptuous mirth sometimes broken up with periods of disturbing silence, occasionally with the sounds of weeping, the latter making Alex bury his head beneath his soft, sweat-stained pillow until, in blessed silence, he would drift into his troubled sleep.

He would dream about Laura, about drums beating in fury, about lights rising and falling out of a large jungle clearing and illuminating the naked, brown-skinned men who committed terrible blasphemies. The lights rose up from the ground—or from a swirling black hole in the ground—and he saw Laura's face, her red hair streaming across her closed eyes, superimposed upon the vortex of the whirlpool and the stars in its awesome depths. Yes, the whirlpool's vortex formed a tunnel, boring down through time and space, revealing the stars frozen in eternity, down there, in those dizzying depths, beneath Laura's enormous, transparent face, her red hair, streaming across her closed eyes, forming a river of flames. Around the stars, which were benevolent, was the darkness, which was malignant, and Laura was sucked down, shrinking rapidly as she sank, and then went spinning into the faucet of eternity to be torn between good and evil. The lights rose and fell, the drums pounded, the Yano danced, there was laughter and screaming, pain and joy, a tremendous tumult and chaos. Alex dreamed it with a startling immediacy, tossed and turned and cried out, then woke to the pearly light of morning with his skin bathed in sweat and his heart beating rapidly.

He was building up to violence, to a blind and destructive rage, now feeling that he had, as Peruche had said, damned himself and let the bad consume his soul. Yes, slowly but surely his innocence had collapsed before the realization that love, which could ennoble, could also wound and even destroy, and so, ignorant about such violent and uncontrollable emotions, completely at the mercy of his suddenly released sexual desires, his passion for Laura was overwhelming him, his sense of futility enraging him, and he floundered like a fish on the riverbank, out of breath and defeated.

When did his world explode? He would never forget as long as he lived. It began when Father Benedict, after complaining to Alex's father about his abuse of the Indian girl, left the house in a rage and found Alex on the verandah where he was sitting in a chair, his legs outstretched, watching the sun sinking over the river. Alex was steeped in gloom, his self-pity swamping his sense, and the priest, already enraged by his fight with Alex's father, exploded in the face of this fresh misery and made clear his disgust.

"What is it?" he said harshly. "Are you going mad as well? Do I have to deal with your father, who exploits and degrades unfortunate Indian girls, and then deal with your increasingly senseless obsession with a much older woman? Is it living in this jungle? Is it this damned plantation? Can you really not see that your passion will fade, and that sooner or later you'll feel the same for someone more suitable? Well, whatever, I won't stand for it! I'm fed up watching you brood like this. Either get control of yourself, stop your moping and complaining, or I'll tell your father to send you to England on the very next boat. Do you understand what I'm saying, Alex?

Either get that woman out of your system or get ready to pack your bags. I won't let you make a fool of yourself any longer!''

Alex listened to no more, but simply stood up, brushed past the angry priest, and feeling sick to his stomach, hurried into the house. He walked past the main room, knowing that Laura wasn't there, and went along the gloomy corridor past his own room, turning right at the end and passing through the door that led into the modest guest wing. He was quivering with rage, with despair and a kind of madness, convinced that everything was collapsing, his friendships, his former peace of mind, perhaps even his sanity, and wanting to sort it out once and for all, no matter what the results might be. He hammered on Laura's door with his tightly clenched fist and heard his own voice calling her name as if from far away. The door opened, and Laura was there before him, holding a dressing gown around her, her face sleepy and sensual.

''Alex!''

''I love you. I came here to say I love you. Tomorrow I have to go back to school in Manaus, and I want you to come with me—you can stay in a hotel.''

''Sorry, Alex, *what* was that?''

''You heard me, Laura, you know you did. I want you to either come to Manaus or say you don't love me.''

''Alex, this is ridiculous.''

''Dammit, Laura, I'm serious. I won't leave unless you come with me or tell me you love me.''

''You *know* I love you, Alex.''

''I don't mean it in that way.''

''No, Alex, I won't lie about the other—and I won't go to Manaus. Are you crazy? Do you know what you're suggesting? You *know* it's not possible!''

''You could come if you wanted to!''

''I won't—and that's final! Now leave me alone, Alex. This is silly. We'll talk it over tomorrow.''

''It's my *father*, isn't it?''

''Pardon? What are you—?''

''You're rejecting me because of my father. You spend all your evenings in there, getting drunk with him and Rollie Thatcher. You pretend to despise him, but actually you find him attractive. He insults you and humiliates you and makes suggestive remarks to you—and all the time, no matter what you say, you're actually enjoying it. You know what? I think my father's right: *you behave like a whore!*''

Laura slapped his face.

Startled, hardly believing it, Alex touched his cheek tentatively, then stepped back and stared at her for some time, trying to hold back his tears. He was speechless, deeply wounded, both by what she had done and his shame because he knew he deserved it.

The silence between them was terrible, but then the Yano drums started beating and Laura jerked her head around, staring back across her room to the window and, obviously, the sky beyond.

''Oh, God,'' she murmured, ''it's starting again. And there they are: those damned lights!''

Alex started to cry. She had forgotten him already. The tears rolled down his cheeks as he turned away from her and walked out of the house. The sun was just sinking and the sky was turning dark, great pillars and streams of gold and crimson being swallowed by blackness. He hurried across the verandah, down the steps onto the grass, and saw Father Benedict standing at the far side of the lawn, a cigarette in one hand, his head raised to look at a patch of sky far beyond the big house. Alex turned away immediately, now sobbing uncontrollably, and walked along the front of the house, past the tall struts of the verandah, and across the open space at the end, heading straight for the forest. He glanced north as he crossed the clearing, toward the direction of the pounding drums, and saw the lights rising and falling in gentle splendor, making a beautiful tapestry. He stared at them, fascinated, his tears making them seem hazy; then, when he heard Father Benedict calling out to him, he wiped his eyes dry with one hand and hurried into the forest.

He soon found old Peruche, squatting in front of his hut, swaying back and forth like a reed and chanting a bizarre, high-pitched litany. Alex sat down in front of him, hearing the drums, almost *feeling* them, the humid air seeming to press in upon him as if trying to smother him. The old Indian stopped chanting and opened his eyes. He stared at Alex for a time before recognizing him. He told Alex he could speak, and Alex did so, pouring his heart out about Laura and the pain she was causing him, saying he felt like killing himself.

He could hardly hear himself speaking, his words getting lost in the sound of drumming which, though coming from far away, seemed to be all around them. That noise was louder than ever before, seeming to hammer on his very head, but Peruche, nodding his head in a gentle manner, had clearly heard every word. He replied with soft-voiced brutality.

"Why do you tell me this?" he said. "What do you think I can do? When you gave the amulet away, you renounced your faith and lost your innocence—and threw away the protection you once had. The drums sound, the lights live, and you come here in tears, claiming you wish to kill yourself because of love's wounding passions. Well, my child, why tell me? Do you wish me to talk you out of it? Though pained, as I am, by your behavior, I cannot interfere. Whatever will be, will be. What is written will be done. Therefore what now happens, while the drums sound and the lights live, will happen no matter what I say or might foolishly attempt to do. I *cannot* interfere. I myself will soon be gone. My child, the time of which I spoke—the time of penance—has come, and the form of the suffering, which you will choose, will give shape to the manner in which you change, for better or worse. I have my own penance to bear. And so, my child, whatever you decide, please decide it elsewhere. Now I must be alone."

Alex stood up, choking back his anguished sobs, and walked away from the old Indian, back through the forest, crying more than before. His pain was unendurable, like a blade scraping bare nerves, and the forest, now in black and chattering night, suddenly seemed threatening to him. He walked faster, feeling afraid, wanting to reach the clearing quickly. When he reached it, he looked up to see the lights, far away and spectacular.

They were like Catherine wheels, ascending and spinning rapidly, their brilliant outer rings swirling around a darker core, their silvery striations shooting out for miles and turning into great cobwebs. There were a great many of them, forming kaleidoscopes in the starry sky, shooting up from the jungle depths, far north, in the interior; and equally mysteriously, exploding out of the sky itself, first as pinpricks of light, then as dazzling, fluorescent flares that descended in slow, elegant arcs and disappeared in the jungle.

He stared at them, fascinated, knowing that Laura was staring at them too. Seeing that Father Benedict had disappeared, he walked furtively around the back of the house to tap on Laura's window.

The light in her room was still on, beaming out through the protective mesh wire, and he saw Laura framed by the window, wearing only an elegant dressing gown, her beautiful hair hanging down to the base of her spine, a drink in her hand. He walked toward the window, raising his hand and preparing to call her, but then she threw her head back and laughed, and his father stepped into the window frame, reaching out to put one hand on her shoulder and run it down to her breast. Laura chuckled in a throaty manner, then placed her hand on his father's. Alex, his world collapsing, became a cauldron of pain and suffering. He stifled an anguished sob and headed straight for the river.

At that moment he hated them all and wanted to use his powers to damage them. Remembering what Peruche had said, hating him more for having said it, he determined to test his powers to the limit and use them for vengeance. The drums were pounding relentlessly, in aggressive, hypnotic rhythms, and the Indian workers, drawn out of their humble shacks, were all dancing and shrieking on the roads beneath the papaya trees. Alex hurried through them, feeling as if he were dreaming, his head reeling from the insistent, almost violent rhythms of the drums, his body pummeled by those jerking epileptically around him, some staring wildly at the mysterious lights, some with heads back and eyes closed, some foaming at the mouth and wriggling on the ground, their shrieks demented and piercing.

He had seen all this before, but it had never been so hysterical, and he sensed that the distant drumming, which seemed to come from directly around him, was not only louder but more deliberate, inciting the violence. Dazed, his heart pounding, he leaped over the low wall onto the steps that led down to the *porto*, turning right at the bottom and following a narrow path along the river bank.

The pounding drums were like his feelings, tumultuous and chaotic, driving him forward into the darkness of the forest and deeper into his blinding rage. He was momentarily insane, his senses swirling outside himself, and when he came to a muddy inlet and saw a large family of alligators, he waded into the inky black water without hesitation. The water rippled and parted, forming silvery tapestries in the moonlight as the alligators, sensing his presence, glided silently toward him. He shuddered, knowing fear, the pounding drums making his head tight as the reptiles, like wet, rough-barked logs, started drifting around him. He just stared at them, wondering— would he live or die painfully? —but the alligators simply examined him, their hideous jaws opening and closing, and then, as if finding him distasteful, gradually glided away.

He sobbed with relief and then heard himself muttering—demented, senseless words—and waded across the inlet, following the rippling wake of the *caimans*, and saw them turning away and nosing out towards the river's dark center. Sobbing, shivering with cold, he saw the rise and fall of beautiful, mysterious lights and heard the loud, violent drumming. He slashed his arm on a sharp stone and kept close to the bank, letting the blood drip through the swaying rushes and into the water.

The water bubbled and swirled. The piranha were beneath the bank. They came out in a large gray shoal, following the smell of his dripping blood, and churned the water up all around him as they surrendered to frenzy. He sank down, defying death, feeling the water boiling around him, his skin grazed by the rough bodies of the flesh-eating fish but otherwise remaining untouched in that seething, gray mass. The fish were crazed with blood lust, but miraculously did not touch him, instead turning against one another and tearing each other to pieces. The water around him was exploding, turning into a cauldron of blood, spitting dead fish and pieces of bloody meat into the dark air around him. He could not credit what was happening—those razor teeth never touched him—and finally, when the water had settled down, when the dead fish were floating around him in the streaming, crimson water, he felt a mixture of triumph and despair, and climbed up to the bank.

He was dripping water and blood, shivering with cold and shock, and as he headed into the dark forest he glanced up through the trees and saw, in a patch of brilliant stars, the rise and fall of the other lights. The drums were pounding, filling his head, seeming to hammer at his racing heart, drawing him deeper into the forest—and into his madness—in search of further proof that he was inviolable and could turn those same powers against them all.

He saw the bush he had been seeking, the two enormous poisonous spiders, and he shoved his bloody arms through the foliage and let them pounce on him. This they did, very quickly, their revolting feelers probing his skin, but then they wandered up and down, from his wrists to his shoulders, their hairs tickling his hairs, their feelers pinching his skin; like the alligators, they refused to attack him. In a rage such as he had never before known, he smacked the hideous spiders off their branch and stumbled on through the forest.

He no longer knew what he wanted, feeling only the shame of his hatred, realizing that no matter what Peruche had said, the forces of good were still protecting him. He heard the drums and saw the lights; he was convinced that they were part of it: that he was tied to that distant place and was in fact being controlled by it. He sobbed, feeling wretched, hearing someone calling his name. He ignored the distant voice and continued onward. He reached a black, still *verzea* lake.

Not quite still: the water was rippling, the ripples forming large triangles, each containing wavering lines of silvery moonlight. Then he saw the giant snakes, each thirty feet long. He stepped forward, hardly knowing what he was doing, and stood at the water's edge.

The drumming was getting louder, reaching a deafening crescendo, pounding relentlessly at his head, at his racing heart, and destroying the last of his senses. He saw the giant snakes coming toward him, flat snouts parting the moonlit water, moving up to his feet and moving away again, as if undecided. If they touched him, he would die—they would coil around him and crush his bones—but he sensed, in defiant rage and shameful pride, that they were not going to do so. He stood there, his tears flowing, his body shaking with cold and shock—and then the drumming stopped abruptly, the silence cut like a knife, and the giant snakes, as if sensing his sudden loss of power, shot through the water toward him.

"*Alex!*"

Father Benedict grabbed his shoulders, pulled him away from the lake, jerked him around, and slapped him across the face. Then, as he heard the snakes hissing and slithering up out of the water, he grabbed his wrist, ordered him to run, and dragged him into the forest. Alex did as he was told, still sobbing, feeling drained of life, and ran away from the giant snakes as quickly as he could, crashing through the undergrowth as leaves and flowers rained down. When he stopped, gasping for breath, his head lowered in shame, he found himself close to the road that encircled the plantation.

No drumming. No strange lights. The forest chattered in an outer silence. Father Benedict shook him vigorously, almost brutally, then pushed him against the trunk of a rubber tree and forced his chin up. He couldn't stop sobbing. Mortified, he looked through a film of tears at his good friend's perspiring face.

"They've gone!" he cried. "My magical powers have gone! I wanted to use them in hatred—for revenge—and now they're all gone!"

"*No more!*" Father Benedict roared. "There has been enough of this! Give her up, Alex! Go away! Set yourself free from this madness and get your sanity back. Go back to school tomorrow. Take the first boat to Manaus. Stay there until your father can arrange to have you shipped out to England. Are you listening to me, Alex? Will you do that? *Will you leave here tomorrow?*"

Alex's spirit broke completely, making him sob even louder, somehow managing to shake his head in a gesture of consent, falling forward into the arms of the priest and burying his face in his shoulder.

"Yes!" he cried. "*Yes!*"

They held one another tightly, rocking back and forth together, the forest chattering all around them, ignoring their mutual grief, while high above their heads, above the canopy of the towering trees, the stars, multitudinous and bright, shone in cold, lifeless beauty.

17

It was hard to believe that it had only been six weeks. As the two-decked paddle steamer inched slowly through the black water toward the modest *porto* of the plantation, Alex, standing on the upper deck with his hands on the steel railing, stared through the gray light of the early afternoon at the steps leading up to his father's plantation. He saw Antonio on the top step, looking just as he remembered him, but he still felt that he had been away for six years instead of six weeks.

His father was dead. That much he knew. The headmaster had given him that somber news, saying he had no more specific information but that his presence was required back on the plantation immediately. Alex had responded strangely, not too sure of his own feelings, still hating his father for his relationship with Laura, still thinking too much of Laura to get a proper grip on any form of reality outside her. So there had been shock, a quietly numbing blow to his system, but overall a constant, nagging pain and helpless bewilderment.

The paddle steamer bumped gently against the rubber tires protecting the wooden jetty, and the steps upon which Antonio was standing shook visibly, making the overseer and the Indian bearers standing with him hold on to each other. When the jetty steadied, Antonio waved, a sad smile on his kindly face, and Alex waved back automatically, hardly aware of his action. As the deck crew shouted and threw out the restraining ropes, he glanced beyond the *porto* to the distant shacks of the *seringueiros*, saw the roof of the main house beyond them, then green jungle and gray sky. The plantation did indeed look desolate, merely deepening his depression, and he clenched his fists tighter on the steel railing, ashamed of what he was thinking.

The six weeks in the boarding school had been miserable. He still felt the shame of what he had attempted, and every night was filled with thoughts of Laura and how she had betrayed him. He felt years older, and when the news of his father's death came, he felt no grief, only bewilderment and curiosity about what had happened.

Above his shock was his bitterness and the love he felt for Laura—and, worse, the realization that he was more concerned with seeing her again than with the loss of his father. This more than anything else made him feel old and empty. Much as he wanted to see Laura, he picked up his suitcase with reluctance, feeling he was in a bad dream from which he might never wake up.

He walked across the empty deck, took the steps down to the lower deck, then made his way through the milling bearers to the gangplank that sloped gently across the black water to the small wooden jetty. Some bearers moved out ahead of him, carrying sacks and boxes on their stooped backs, and he followed them down the narrow, swaying gangplank to the sun-bleached stone steps that led up from the jetty. Antonio was waiting there for him, wearing a white shirt and slacks, his smile sad, his brown eyes wet and welcoming. He stepped forward and embraced Alex, holding him for some time, then moved back a little and stared at him, his gaze open and warm.

"So," he said, "you don't look too bad. How are you feeling?"

"I'm all right, Antonio. Not too happy, but otherwise fine. You won't have to use kid gloves."

"You seem older."

"I *feel* a lot older. I'm not a child anymore."

Antonio grinned and nodded. "No, indeed you're not. Come on, let's get you into the *fazendeiro*. I'll fill you in then."

The Jeep was parked at the other side of the low wall bordering the *porto*, a new Indian driver, not Mengrire, sitting in the driver's seat. Alex wondered why Mengrire wasn't driving but decided to wait until they reached the main house before asking. He threw his small suitcase in the front seat, beside the new driver, then climbed into the back beside Antonio, starting to feel nervous and disappointed. He was nervous because he didn't know what he was about to hear, and disappointed because neither Father Benedict nor Laura had turned up to greet him.

"Okay," Antonio said to the driver, speaking in Portuguese. "Take us to the back of the *fazendeiro:* to the door of the guest wing."

"*Sim, Senhor.*"

Alex stared at Antonio as the Jeep growled into life and lurched along the tarmac road between the papaya and palmetto trees. He saw that his Brazilian friend was uneasy, though offering a forced smile.

"You'll be staying in the guest wing," he said. "I'll explain all when we get there."

"Explain it now, Antonio. Why the guest wing? It really doesn't bother me that my father's lying at rest in the main house."

"It's not that," Antonio said. "Your father's body isn't here at all. Your father's lying at rest in the morgue of the hospital in Manaus."

"The morgue? What are you talking about? He should be lying at rest in his own house. That's the custom, Antonio."

"I know, I know," Antonio said, waving one hand in an agitated fashion. "I'll explain all when we're inside."

The drive only took a minute and soon they were outside the window in which Alex had seen Laura with his father. He glanced at the window quickly as he got out of the Jeep but just as quickly looked away, his heart beating fast. The new Indian drove off, the Jeep banging and coughing, and Antonio, carrying the suitcase, led the way up the wooden steps and through the mesh-wire door into the guest wing. It was gloomy inside, and remarkably silent, chilling Alex to the depths of his soul. He knew, then, on the instant, that the house was completely empty, and that something was therefore terribly wrong. Antonio led him to the room beside Laura's room and opened the door.

"In here," he said.

Alex stepped into the small but comfortable room and glanced around at the antique furniture. Through the window he could see the lawns running to the thatched shacks of the *seringueiros*. Over them, low and foreboding, were dark, stormy clouds. He shivered and turned away, a part of him quietly retreating. Antonio set his suitcase on a rack in the mahogany wardrobe, after which he lit a cigarette, sat down on the edge of the bed, and balanced an ashtray precariously on one knee.

"Sit down," he said.

Alex did so, taking a wooden chair near the window, still aware of the awful silence of the house and wondering what was to come. Antonio inhaled nervously on his cigarette and blew the smoke out.

"This is not going to be pleasant," he said. "Would you care for a drink?"

"No."

"Fine," Antonio said. "If you can do without one, then so can I." He inhaled again, blew the smoke out, and tapped the ash into the small ashtray on his knee. Looking directly at Alex, he said, "Your father didn't die of natural causes, Alex. He was murdered."

Alex stared at him steadily, not too sure of what he was hearing, certainly not too sure of what he was feeling, though his heart seemed unsteady. *The silence,* he thought. *The empty house. Now I know why it's empty.* . . . He kept staring at Antonio's gentle brown eyes, knowing how he was suffering, noticing that the hand holding the cigarette was shaking.

"Go on," he said. "I'm all right."

Antonio sighed. "That's why the house is empty, and why I haven't put you in there, near the main room. You see . . . that's where he was murdered." He inhaled on his cigarette, blew a smoke ring, and watched it drifting away from him. "I'm sorry, Alex, but you might as well have it straight: it was a regular slaughter. Both your father and Rollie Thatcher were killed with machetes. The whole room was covered with their blood . . . and was, apart from that, in a terrible mess."

"It was vandalized?"

"Yes, you might say that. As if done in a frenzy."

Alex leaned forward in the chair and covered his face with his hands. He sat like that for some time, drifting down through that terrible silence. With a shudder he straightened up and stared at Antonio.

"Do you know who did it?"

"We *think* it was the Indian girl, but we can't be too sure, because she disappeared, with Mengrire, the night it happened and has not been seen since. Certainly she had a motive: it was your father's mistreatment that led to her father's death, and of course, as we all know, your father was making her pay off her father's debts by being his whore. I think you would agree she had good reason to hate him."

"And Mengrire disappeared with her?"

"Yes."

"That figures: he wanted her." Alex found himself staring out the window, yearning for fresh air; there was no hope of having it right now, so he returned his gaze to Antonio. "I think I'll have that drink now," he said.

Antonio nodded, set the ashtray on the bed, stood up, and poured some of the *caipirinha* he had brought over for Alex's arrival. After handing the glass to Alex he sat on the edge of the bed again, balanced the ashtray on his knee, and continued his story.

"Anyway, we think it was the Indian girl—or at least something to do with the Indian girl. As I said, she disappeared with Mengrire the same night it happened; and since old Peruche also disappeared that same night, we're inclined to think it was some kind of ritualized vengeance. Yes, Alex—don't look at me that way—your friend Peruche has gone."

Alex drank his *caipirinha*, feeling it burn down to his stomach, subtly expanding his awareness of himself while easing the shock and pain of Antonio's gently spoken but very brutal revelations. He had already imagined that his whole world had collapsed (the night he lost his magical powers) but now, as he stood up and replenished his empty glass, he understood that the real, complete collapse was occuring this moment. He felt hot and then cold, hot again, cold again, and as he sat back in his chair and sipped his drink, the horror quietly crept over him.

"God," he said. "I can't get to grips with this. I think I must be imagining it." Then another thought came to him, more horrible than all the others, and he looked up at Antonio, feeling a tremor running through him, and said, "Laura! What about Laura? Was she here when it happened?"

"We're not sure, Alex. We—"

"What do you mean, you're *not sure*? Where *is* she? Oh, God, of course, *she's not here!*" Alex stared wildly about him, as if expecting her to materialize, his heart racing wildly as he looked back at Antonio, his voice, reverberating in his own ears, sounding shrill and demented. "*Dammit, where is she?*"

"Calm down! Calm down!" Antonio was waving his hand placatingly. "She wasn't killed as well—we *do* know that much— but she *did* vanish with all of the others—and, like them, hasn't been seen or heard from since."

"She vanished the *same night*?"

"Yes."

"Oh, Christ! Oh, my God!" Alex leaned forward again and covered his face with his left hand, dropping down through some dark hole in himself and hoping to find there oblivion. Instead he found only memories, vivid images of them all: the Indian girl in his

father's room, her face lowered in shame; Mengrire watching her
from the lawn, his tears silently filling his eyes; Rollie Thatcher on
the settee, belching and farting and laughing scornfully; old Peruche
in front of his hut, by the lovely *verzea* lake, rocking back and forth
and meditating, his mind alight with *epena;* and finally, but most
vivid of all, like a glowing flame in a dark cave, Laura's beautiful
face.

"Oh, Christ!" he said."No!"

He felt a hand on his head, pressing lightly, stroking gently, and
he looked up at Antonio's brown eyes and saw his kind smile. "It's
all right. You're all right." Antonio nodded and stepped away, then
sat down on the bed again, stubbed his cigarette out, and set the
ashtray back on the walnut cabinet beside the bed. Alex straightened
up and drank some more *caipirinha*. He took a deep breath and fixed
his gaze on Antonio. He wasn't too sure what he wanted to say, but
the words came out anyway.

"All right," he said, "why do you think she's vanished?"

Antonio shrugged. "Who knows? We have two or three theories.
We certainly know she was on the plantation the night of the
killings, and unless she happened to be with Peruche, she had to be
in the building. One way or the other, she had to know it was
happening."

"That doesn't necessarily mean she was involved."

"No, Alex, it doesn't. She spent nearly every evening in that
room with those two men, so it's possible she was there when the
killings occurred and that she, also, was killed and her body carried
away for some reason—possibly to complete some ritual—or that
she *wasn't* killed, but that she was abducted either to prevent her
from reporting the crime or, I fear, to be killed later for the reasons
already mentioned."

"But you don't believe either of those possibilities?"

"No, Alex, I'm afraid I don't. If they had killed her they couldn't
have gotten her body out of the camp without being seen—and if
they had abducted her, it would have been even more difficult."

"So she wasn't killed and she wasn't abducted, which means she
was part of it."

"Well, it certainly seems that she knew about it and that she left
of her own free will. What we think is that Laura, if not directly
involved in the killings, certainly knew they had happened and left
the plantation willingly with the perpetrators—presumably Mengrire,

the Indian girl, and Peruche. She was, you will agree, totally obsessed with the Yano, and since both Peruche and Mengrire both believed in their existence, *I* believe that the killings were done in a ritualistic manner, that the murderers then fled north in search of the Yano, and that Laura, who had been searching for someone to guide her to the Yano, saw her golden opportunity and went with them.''

"Oh, God," Alex murmured.

"Exactly," Antonio said. "Right now they're probably heading toward where those lights rise and fall—and if they actually manage to get there, God help them. Particularly Laura.''

Alex shuddered. He walked to the window and looked down on the lawn. It was empty and silent, bathed in a sullen gray light. Shuddering again, he closed his eyes and thought of the Yano. His dreams about them had been so vivid they were almost real—and now, as he remembered the shocking contents of those dreams, he felt himself trembling uncontrollably with fear and revulsion. Laura, whether sane or insane, might indeed soon find herself face to face with the forces of darkness—and what they might then inflict upon her was too unbearable to think about.

"So," he said, hoping to distract himself. "What happens now?"

"It's all over," Antonio said. "We have to close up the plantation. Your father left you money in England, but you have to go there to claim it; apart from that, he left nothing here but debts and a bad reputation. We'll sell the *fazendeiro* and everything it contains, use the proceeds to pay off his local debts, pay off the workers, close the plantation down, and send you back to England to be educated in a civilized place."

"How long will all that take?"

"About a month."

"Then it's all really over?"

"Yes, Alex, it is."

"And Laura?"

"You know about Laura: we can't do a damned thing. If my theory is wrong she'll turn up sooner or later; but if my theory is correct—if she's gone with them to find the Yano—there's no way on earth we'll ever find her, and it's certainly the end of her. She's not in the vicinity, Alex. We've already looked everywhere possible. That means they've gone north toward the unexplored regions. If that is so, they won't be coming back. I'm sorry, Alex. It's finished."

Alex stayed at the window, keeping his back to Antonio, not wanting his friend to see the shock and pain in his face.

"Yes," he said, sighing, "I know. I'm sure you've done all you can."

"And can I go ahead with the sale of the *fazendeiro*?"

"Yes, Antonio, of course."

"And you'll go and live in England as planned?"

"I see no point in staying."

He heard Antonio sighing, a very sad, weary sound, followed by the sound of glass against wood as Antonio put his drink down.

"Do you want something to eat?" Antonio asked him.

"Not yet," Alex replied. "I think I'll lie down and try to sleep. All of this has exhausted me."

"It's all closed here," Antonio said. "I've already let the house staff go. When you've slept, come to see me in my house and I'll cook you a meal—a real Antonio Bozzano special. You know where I live."

"Yes, Antonio, I'll do that."

Antonio sighed again, the door opened and closed quickly, and Alex was alone in the small room, staring out through the window. The afternoon was fading, the gray light turning darker, and he looked down and imagined each one of them in turn, all wandering through that unreal pearly haze in a parade of the lost: the Indian girl, Mengrire, old Peruche, Rollie Thatcher, his father, and finally Laura Wellman, his true love and catalyst. He kept staring, in a trance, seeing ghosts on the lawn, and then blinked and saw his friend, Antonio Bozzano, walking toward the thatched shacks. Antonio lived just beyond them, in a halfway decent house, and Alex, feeling desolate, watched him crossing the road, then turned away from the window and lay down, fully dressed, on the bed. He stared up at the ceiling for some time, and then closed his eyes.

It was quiet . . . too quiet. He saw the damned parading past him. The silence of the house was like a ringing that was pitched beyond sound. He kept his eyes closed, feeling lonely and terrified, aware that the silence, like a physical presence, was slowly pressing in on him. It was quiet . . . too quiet. He could hear his own heart beating—and then his heart almost missed a beat when he heard a noise in the main house.

He opened his eyes immediately, startled, concentrating, straining as he listened to the silence and heard . . . another noise. The soft squeak of wood on wood—a piece of furniture being moved—then silence, then a distant, indecipherable sound, then the squeaking of wood against wood again, then silence once more. After that, there was nothing—no, a muffled sobbing—but very brief, and then it trailed off into the silence that permeated the main house. Yes, it was definitely in the house . . . and the noise had come from the main room.

Alex shivered and sat upright, his imagination running riot. He reached out for the glass of *caipirinha*, drank it down and let it burn away his fear, and then quietly stood up. He heard the noise again, a distant sobbing or choking, and immediately opened the door and stepped out into the gloomy, uninviting, dusty corridor. Laura's room was just behind him, empty, stirring memories, but he went through the door on his left and entered the main house. The long corridor stretched before him, high-ceilinged, semidark, and he walked along it, passing his former bedroom, until he came to the main lounge. He heard the sobbing clearly now. He thought of the killings and shivered. Then, taking a deep breath, he stepped inside and stopped almost immediately.

It was truly a shocking sight—all the carpets and curtains slashed, the antique furniture smashed to pieces, the floor covered in broken vases and glassware and other ornaments, the walls and floor desecrated with large splashes of dried blood—and there, in the middle, sitting in one of the antique chairs, bent forward and sniffing back his tears, was Father Paul Benedict.

He looked up when Alex walked in, almost as startled as Alex, then wiped the tears away from his eyes and sniffed again—not in the least embarrassed, but clearly anguished, his eyes bloodshot and stricken.

"Oh, Alex, my son," he said, "you've returned. How awful. How terrible!" He shook his head from side to side, as if wanting to deny reality, then took a handkerchief out of his pocket and blew his nose and looked up again. "Antonio told you?"

"Yes."

"A truly terrible thing."

"Yes."

"You must try to be brave about it, Alex. You must try to forget it."

"I won't *ever* forget it." Alex stared around the room, suddenly remembering his dead mother, imagining her ghost, her angelic presence, being forced to look with horrified eyes upon what had transpired here. A bloodbath: a punishment and hideous desecration, one due to, the other wrought by, his father and his rank, indecent ways. Alex shivered with rage and grief and a malignant, lurking horror, then walked across the room to the priest and sat down beside him. He was shocked when he saw his handsome friend up close; the priest had aged overnight.

"My father deserved it," he said.

"Don't say that!" the priest replied.

"I'm saying it: My father deserved it. He only got what was coming to him."

"No, Alex! Please stop it! You mustn't say any more! No matter how you feel now, you'll regret it later, so please say no more."

"He deserved it, Father Benedict. He degraded everything he touched. He broke my mother's heart and drove her into an early grave, he treated his workers like slaves and their wives like common whores, he tried humiliating me to excuse his own failures, and finally—and I'll never forgive him for this—he stole Laura from me and seduced her. He caused her to be in this house and get involved in this mess. Yes, Father, he deserved all he got—but not Laura. *Not Laura!*"

His own vehemence shocked him, and he turned away from the priest, his eyes roaming around that awful, blood-stained room and coming to rest on his feet. A shiver of revulsion passed through him, nausea ravaged his stomach, and then, even as he heard the priest sniffing back more tears, a choked sob broke out of his own throat as his true rage found its target.

"She left with them!" he cried. "She went willingly! How could she? *How could she?*"

He buried his face in his hands, feeling choked with grief and bitterness, then raised his head to stare wildly at Father Benedict, vividly aware that his good friend had aged terribly and was likewise grief-stricken.

"I can't answer your question, Alex. Only God can answer that question. What happened that night remains unknown, and will always remain so. Get out of here, my son. Out of this house and out of this country. Go to England, to civilized society, and never come back. You have nothing left here, and there'll be nothing here in the future. As for now, let us get out of this room and all of its memories."

He reached out for Alex's shoulder, gripped it lightly, and shook him gently. Together they stood up, took one last look at the room—at the seventeenth-century Venetian armchair in which Alex's father had often reclined, at the now upended French *bergère* into which Rollie Thatcher had often been squeezed, at the slashed curtains and carpets and trampled paintings and broken antiques—and then, without a word, turned away and walked out.

The afternoon had grown darker, the cloudy sky threatening a rainstorm, and they stood together on the verandah, looking across the plantation, at the thatched shacks, the intersecting roads, the extraordinary variety of trees that lined the roads and formed the forest, and beyond, flowing with the silent majesty of its agelessness, the flat and enormously wide Rio Negro, that mere part of the Amazon. Alex stared at it, shocked to realize that he would hate it forever.

"We don't really know," he said, speaking to himself. "I refuse to believe that we can't find her. *There must be a way!*"

He saw horror on the priest's ravaged face: horror that he, Alex, not yet eighteen years of age, was more concerned about the loss of the American woman than he was about the death of his own father. The priest stared at him a long time, hardly moving; then, as if putting Alex's attitude down to grief, he took hold of his elbow and guided him down the steps to the lawn. Then, turning around until they were facing the house, he waved in the direction of the sky in the far north, the clouds drifting like sludge over that unexplored jungle where the lights rose and fell, and within which were the dreaded Yano Indians and the hell they were reported to represent.

"We tried repeatedly to find her," Father Benedict said, lowering his bloodshot eyes and looking distraught, "but she had just disappeared. Nor did we find the Yano. We sometimes heard them, but we never saw them. We saw the lights in the sky, but no matter how methodically we marched toward them, they always seemed to be in a different direction, and slightly farther away. Believe me, this is true. Out there the senses deceive one. North suddenly becomes south, east suddenly becomes west, and fairly soon you think you're walking in circles, doubling back on your own tracks. And as it was with the lights, so it was with the drums: we would head for the beating drums, always thinking we were getting closer, but once we got there, where the drumming had seemed to come from, they seemed to come from elsewhere again—usually spread all around us—and no matter which direction we went, it was always the wrong one: go one way and the drums would be directly behind you; turn around and they were behind you again—or perhaps off to the side—but never, *never* in front of you once you got close to them. No, we never found the Yano. We never caught a glimpse of them. I'm convinced that they were there, and that they knew *we* were there, but I'm also sure that they simply had no interest in us, one way or the other. So it was useless. We just walked in endless circles. We tramped around there for a great many days, but we didn't see anything. We think the Yano found the others—or that the others found the Yano—since Peruche, who was probably one of them, doubtless knew what the secret was. And so, if this is true, the Yano certainly got Laura and if they got her, they almost just as certainly killed her. We think it, but there's no way of proving it, and never will be. There's only one thing to know, Alex. One thing! *Laura Wellman has gone!*''

The priest suddenly walked away, stifling another sob, hurrying across the darkening lawn toward the concrete car port while Alex simply stood there, too shaken to move, staring over the *fazendeiro*, now empty and haunted, silent with the voices of the dead and the damned—his mother and father, the Indian girl and Mengrire, Rollie Thatcher and Laura Wellman, and yes, even himself, at least the child that he had been. He looked at the sky above the jungle where the Yano played their drums, that unexplored, frightening territory to which Laura might have fled, and then he suddenly turned away—turned away as fast as the priest had done—and looked across the thatched shacks at the mighty river succumbing to darkness. He finally accepted that he would soon be on his way to England.

A month later he was on a boat, the sun sinking behind the forest, turning the sky to blood, making the river seem like lava. He gripped the railing tightly, looking down at the swaying jetty, his head filled with thoughts of the thirty days that had just passed—of his father's funeral in Manaus, of the furniture being auctioned, of the Indians, paid off, filing sadly out of the plantation, of solicitors and surveyers and contracts and deeds, of the keys being turned in the numerous doors of the *fazendeiro* and the silence of desolation coming down—everything coming down, drawing inexorably to a close, his own eyes looking down at his two friends on the jetty: Antonio, trying to smile, his brown eyes filled with sadness, and Father Benedict, his once handsome face now grim and much older.

Alex held the railing tightly, the deck vibrating beneath his feet, watching his friends grow smaller, the jetty seeming to shrink with them, the plantation moving back to let the jungle move in around it while the sinking sun sent rivers of fire across the forest, turning green into yellow, the yellow into gold, the gold into a deep, pulsating crimson that devoured all it touched. And then it was gone, and only the mighty river remained, and Alex leaned forward, placing his forehead against the railing, looking down at the black river which now boiled in black night, and he wept, his body quivering with loss and grief. He turned his face to the wind.

THE RIVER

18

A Cidade Maravilhosa: the Marvelous City. As the aircraft began its descent toward the Aeroporto Santos Dumont, Avril, even though she had never been here before, instantly recognized the ravishing blue sweep of Guanabara Bay, the long, thin white ribbon of Flamengo Beach, and the great rock of Pão de Açúcar, or Sugarloaf Mountain, towering high in the gold-streaked, azure sky. She looked quickly at Alex, sitting beside her in the aisle seat, but he had his head back against the cushion, his eyes closed, his lips tight. Momentarily concerned, she reached out to touch him, changed her mind, and looked again through the window. Now she saw the marvelous city, the fabled Rio de Janeiro, its tall gray buildings embraced by the encircling mountains, its thousands of lights starting to wink on as the sun sank in splendor. Avril gave herself up to childish wonder as the sea filled her vision.

"It's beautiful," she said. "It's everything they say it is. Everything I've heard and read about it is perfectly true. It's just wonderful. Glorious!"

Alex opened his eyes, turning his head to stare at her, and again, when he smiled gently, she noticed how drained he was, how much older than his nineteen years he appeared to be, his face pale, his cheeks hollow.

"Yes," he said, "it's beautiful—like you. But just a little bit older."

She smiled, pleased by the compliment, knowing that he meant it, but more pleased that he was trying to keep his sense of humor at this particular moment. She knew how painful it must be for him, how he had dreaded this return, as she knew, when she studied him, how truly ill he was, the dark bags under his eyes revealing the sleepless nights that had preceded this trip.

"Thank you, kind sir, for comparing me to Rio, but I don't think I'm quite in the same class when it comes to either beauty or age."

He smiled, but his eyes were still lusterless, as if focused inward upon himself yet fearing what he might find there. He had aged a lot during his one year in London—the nightmares making him frightened to go to bed, his appetite failing along with his nerves, his health breaking down to the point where he could hardly make love to her—and so, even though they were here at her insistence, she wasn't at all sure that it would cure him, and actually feared it might make him worse.

"Are you all right?" she asked him.

"Yes, Avril, I'm fine."

"You're too quiet."

"I'm just tired—really tired. I just need a good sleep."

"Are you nervous?"

"Yes, a little bit. I don't know what I'll find back here."

The aircraft shuddered briefly, its engines roaring and subsiding again, then turned and headed down toward the parallel lines of lights that marked out the runway of Santos Dumont. The lights swung into view, then disappeared as the aircraft faced them, and Avril found herself looking at alluvial mountains and a bright blue, white-flecked, rippling sea. She felt tired but exhilarated, scarcely believing they were here at last, thinking back on the many days spent in many different planes—from war-torn London to sunny Lisbon, from there on to the Canary Islands, spending a few days exploring the mountains, boating from one island to the next, drinking sweet wine in a waterfront bar in Santa Cruz de Tenerife, then on to Accra on the West African Gold Coast, entertained by her father's friends at Achimota College, a few more days adjusting to the tropical monsoon climate (constant rain, sweltering heat), then across the South Atlantic, staying over on Ascension Island, volcanic rock and sea turtles, and then, the next day, this very day, the last leg of the journey to the Tropic of Capricorn and the view now below her—and realizing that already the journey seemed completely unreal, something she had simply dreamed about but not really experienced.

"We're coming in to land," she said. "I caught a glimpse of the airport. It looks dangerously narrow—just a strip of land stuck out there in the sea."

"That's exactly what it is," Alex replied. "In fact you're going to land on the very soil were Rio de Janeiro was born. The birth of the city dates from the founding of a settlement—on *Morro do Castelo*, or Castle Hill—by the Portugese in 1565, after they had driven out the French. A few years back that hill was demolished and poured into the harbor to form the promontory on which the airport was constructed.''

Avril laughed softly. ''They tore a historic hill down and poured it into the sea?''

''That's right,'' Alex said. ''The Cariocas, always enthusiastic for change, are not concerned for their history, and the flattened remains of Castle Hill, which you may have seen a few minutes ago, are now covered with the skyscrapers of the city's business area.''

''Oh, my!'' Avril exclaimed softly.

The plane was still descending, the graceful mountains growing larger, and Avril kept her eyes glued to the window, watching the sea race by below, and then the runway was there, a blur of distant hangars and hills, and then the plane bounced a little, gradually slowed down, taxied along the runway and finally stopped.

''Well, Alex, we made it,'' Avril said. ''And we're still in one piece.''

The aircraft's engines whined into silence, but the passengers were highly voluble, their uninhibited conversation again reminding Avril that she was a very long way from England's green shores and restrained social habits. She stared at Alex, an old man with a boy's face, and felt a little uneasy.

''Well,'' she said, ''do you think we can disembark?''

''Yes,'' he said. ''Let's get to it.''

It did not take very long, and soon they were on the tarmac, walking through the early evening darkness toward the great linear block of the Panair building, its numerous windows casting beams of light over them as they reached the broad entrance. The heat surprised Avril. It was less humid than she had imagined, but she was still glad to get inside the building where the air was much cooler. There were very few passengers, and they were processed quickly and amiably. The customs men and passport control were unexpectedly casual, if not actually flirtatious. Alex didn't appear to mind, clearly accepting it as natural, but when they finally walked out, a *bagageiro* carrying their luggage, she could see that he was truly very nervous to be back on home grounds.

Antonio Bozzano was waiting for them, stepping forward with both arms raised, his brown eyes as warm as his smile, his slightly plump, *café-au-lait* face strikingly handsome, his well-fed stomach quivering over his trouser belt. Avril knew it was Antonio (Alex had described him very accurately and had told her he would be meeting them) and, also knowing how fond he and Alex were of each other, discreetly stepped back while they embraced. This done, Antonio straightened up and offered a broad grin.

"*Tudo bem?*" he asked, his voice low and melodious.

"*Tudo bem!*" Alex replied, jabbing his thumb in the air, trying to affect an ebullience that just wasn't there. "And in English: 'All's well!' "

"Ah, yes, your young lady!" Antonio stepped up to Avril, took hold of her right hand, turned it over as he raised it to his lips, and planted a kiss on her wrist. When he lowered her hand, he kept holding it lightly—not in a remotely suggestive manner, but in genuine friendliness. "*Muito prazer em conhece-lo,*" he said. "And now for you I will speak only English: I am very pleased to meet you." He nodded and smiled, instantly making her feel good. He stepped back and offered another broad grin, his eyes fixed directly upon her. "Avril," he said. "A nice name. . . . And the lady is beautiful."

Above the grin, Avril noticed, Antonio's brown eyes were perceptive, only a slight wrinkling of his brow indicating to her that he had not failed to notice Alex's drawn appearance. He led them across the pavement to the car and, raising the lid of the trunk and jabbing his finger at it, indicated to the *bagageiro* that he should put the suitcase in there.

"So, my young friend," he said to Alex, "how was your brief time in England?"

"I would hardly call a year a brief time, Antonio."

"Well, Alex, you were supposed to be staying for good—so, given the fact that you're back already, the year seems fairly brief. Anyway, how did it go?"

"Not bad."

"By which you mean not good."

"That's right, Antonio."

The Brazilian grinned and nodded. He paid off the *bagageiro*, walked around the car, and opened a rear door. "Well at least," he said, "you found a most attractive young lady, so the year over there has done you *some* good." He smiled at Avril, his brown eyes filled with warmth, and then looked back at Alex. "I assume you'll want to point out the sights to Avril, so you'll both have to sit in the back. Now get in and we'll go."

"Where are we staying?" Alex asked him.

"In a suite on the top floor of the Copacabaña Palace. With what your father left you in England, and the remaining money from the sale of the plantation, I figured you could afford a good hotel instead of a shack in a *favela*. I hope you agree.''

"I agree," Alex said.

Avril slid into the back seat, followed by Alex, and then Antonio closed the door behind them and climbed into the driver's seat. He drove off immediately, bypassing the business area, then driving around smooth green lawns and what appeared to be a marina (Avril could see lights beaming down from numerous masts) and finally along an imperceptibly curving boulevard which divided central Rio from Flamengo Beach and its now jet-black, curvaceous rock formations. The boulevard was very long, passing various residential areas, and as Alex pointed out the sights to her, his voice low and oddly flat, she felt increasingly confused: on the one hand enamored by what he was showing her, on the other disturbed to be reminded once more that he was, for all she might love him, very far removed from her, locked inside that nightmare of his past and being slowly destroyed by it.

"I have once been in London," Antonio suddenly said, obviously wanting to lighten the conversation, "but that was a long time ago, before the war started. I loved it then, but it must have changed a lot during that war. Did they damage it badly?"

"Yes," Avril said, "they damaged it badly, but you would still recognize it. It's surprising, really, how much is still standing, when you think of how many raids there were."

"It must have been rough during the war. I think you all had a bad time."

A bad time? Avril glanced out the window of the speeding car and saw, as Antonio weaved around the buses, streetcars, private cars, and taxis, the dark sea on one side of her, the lights of apartment houses on the other, the colorful streets of Botafogo rising up toward the candle-lit hills, and realized, even as she thought of the difference between here and London, that the worst experience she had had in her home city was dealing with Alex. So she told Antonio about the Blitz, answering his many questions; as she talked (the car emerging from a noisy tunnel and turning right into the beautiful boulevard of Copacabaña Beach, the Atlantic on one side, its waves crashing down on the sand, ten-story apartment houses rising up on the other side), she thought of how she had first met Alex, of being struck by his extraordinary gentleness, of falling hopelessly in love with him and learning of his strangeness: his nightmares and visions and obsession with the Amazon which, he claimed, was haunting him because of a woman who had disappeared after capturing his soul. Yes, Avril loved him, but that love was under siege: threatened by the ghost of a woman whom Alex claimed to love no longer, but who obviously, in some way or another, still had him enslaved. It was in the hopes of learning the nature of that enslavement that Avril had come to Brazil with him.

"Well," Antonio said, "after the blackout and the Blitz, perhaps you will enjoy it in Brazil."

"Yes, perhaps," Avril said.

The car turned right again, crossing the broad boulevard, and drove up to the front of the elegant hotel. A uniformed doorman opened the rear door, letting Alex and Avril step out, and Avril glanced up the towering building at the canopied windows and railed-in balconies, then lowered her eyes to meet Alex's gaze. He was staring steadily at her, his eyes weary yet loving, a gentle smile on his lips as he took hold of her arm.

"So," he said, "we're actually here. You must be awfully persuasive."

"I'm persuasive because I love you," she replied, "and I know I'll have to fight for you."

Antonio arranged their signing in, took them up in the elevator, personally showed them around the enormous suite with its large rooms and tasteful décor, poured Alex a beer and Avril a chilled white wine, then sent them both out to the balcony while he oversaw the delivery of their luggage. They were six stories up, overlooking Copacabaña Beach, and they stood at the wrought-iron railing, leaning lightly against one another, sipping their drinks and gazing down at the sea and the dark, crowded beach. The beach was actually filling up all the time, and hundreds of candles were burning, making a smaller sea of yellow flames that moved back and forth restlessly.

"What's going on down there?" Avril asked.

"New Year's Eve," Alex replied. "At midnight it will be 1947, and they're all there to celebrate."

"I'll take you down later to see it," Antonio said, stepping out onto the balcony with a drink in his hand. "It's really quite an experience if you haven't seen it before. Every New Year's Eve here in Rio, thousands of *Umbanda* and *Quimbanda* believers gather together on all the major beaches—Copacabaña, Leblon, Ipanema, Flamengo—and pay homage to Yemanja, goddess of the sea. People of all ages, sexes, and colors come, and what you are seeing down there, right now, are the first of these many thousands of believers bringing their candles, fresh flowers, portable altars, *cachaça* alcohol, and various gifts for the goddess. Soon they will be drawing numerous mystic signs on the sand, indulging in various black and white magic rituals—*Umbanda* is white magic and *Quimbanda* is black—and then, a little later, white-costumed drummers will start playing, a lot of believers will go into trances, and at midnight they will all rush into the sea to worship Yemanja."

"It certainly seems worth seeing," Avril said.

"It is," Antonio replied.

Alex finished off his glass of beer, set the glass down on the small table on the balcony, and then gave a weary, nervous smile that failed to brighten his eyes which, very blue beneath the blond hair, were blinking repeatedly. Avril, studying him closely, was again struck by his extraordinary appearance, by the fact that his face was beautiful—not merely handsome, but strangely beautiful—and that his beauty was so strong that it could not be destroyed, even though physical and mental strain had hollowed out his cheeks, put bags under his eyes, turned his skin sallow, and generally worn him away. What it *had* done, she thought, was make him look young and old at the same time. Ageless.

"So," Antonio said, aware that silence was no blessing, "I want to know all about you two. Where and how did you meet?"

"At school," Avril said.

"That sounds very unromantic."

Avril smiled. "My father is the head of the private school Alex was attending. As an old friend of Alex's mother, he invited Alex home for Sunday roast."

"Home, of course, being a wing of the school."

"That's right, Antonio."

"And your eyes met across the roast beef in that discreet English manner?"

"That was it," Avril said.

Antonio smiled with delight, making Avril feel good again, but behind her feeling of goodness was fear—a fear that was almost a part of her love for Alex. She had not fallen in love that first day, but very slowly, with reluctance, first intrigued by his odd beauty, his romantic air of introspection, then moved by his silence—a silence resonant with unstated pain—and finally, after months of seeing him, of wandering the streets of London with him, of sitting with him in pubs or cinemas or theaters, often after an exhausting day with the Women's Voluntary Service, in love with his remarkable sensitivity and almost feminine tenderness.

Yet it hadn't been easy, had in all truth been hell, because as romantic yearning turned to desire, as she had drawn closer to him, she had learned about his nightmares, about the extraordinary events he had fled from, and worst of all, although they finally made love, always in his rented apartment and not often, she had learned that he was not only very inexperienced but also frequently impotent because of fear and ill health. His nightmares, which were killing his spirit, were also destroying his body.

She shivered just to think of it as she sipped her white wine. She glanced over the balcony at the people on the beach below, then looked back at Alex as he smiled in that nervous manner at Antonio.

"You're being very polite, Antonio," he said, "but you know why I'm back."

Antonio sighed. "Yes, I know. You have a mystery to solve."

"She never came back?"

"No, Alex. Laura never returned."

Just hearing that name made Avril experience a hurt that rose from the fragile web of the past year. She glanced again at the people on the beach below, trying to distract herself from the doubts that constantly gnawed at her. Did Alex really love her? Or did he still love Laura Wellman? Those questions had haunted Avril for most of the past year, scrawled on her mind by an unsteady, ghostly hand—as ghostly and yet as potent as that women who had disappeared into the jungle. Now Avril felt like crying—for Alex's pain, for her own doubts—and actually rubbed her eyes, observing the beach through a slight haze, the thousands of flickering candles moving back and forth like waves on a fiery sea.

"Forget it, Alex," Antonio said. "It's in the past and should be buried. You have a lovely lady here, you have money in the bank, you stand the chance of a good life in England—so don't keep looking back at the past and tormenting yourself."

"You don't understand, Antonio: it's not a matter of choice. Whether I want it or not, those nightmares *make* me look back."

"You won't stop the nightmares by returning here. In fact, as far as the nightmares go, the further you are from the Amazon the better."

"I *had* to come back. The nightmares brought me back. If there's a cure, it's right here."

"You mean the Amazon?"

"Yes."

Antonio sighed with gentle despair and then went into the suite, returning with a fresh *caipirinha;* he swirled the drink lightly in the glass, glanced at Avril, and then turned his gaze on Alex. Down below, on the dark, crowded beach, the first of the Indian drummers had started playing.

"Okay," he said, "I'll ask the dreaded question: Do you *really* intend going into that jungle to find Laura Wellman?"

"Yes."

There was a brief silence, disturbed only by the drums below, and Avril felt an almost palpable tension quivering around her. Her wine was finished and she wanted some more, but she didn't dare move.

"Laura's dead, Alex," Antonio said eventually. "I'm sorry, but you'll have to face that fact. She either died in the jungle or was killed by the Yano; no way could she have managed to survive both of them."

"That may or may not be true," Alex replied, "but in this case it hasn't any relevance. It's not really Laura I'm looking for, but what *she* was looking for."

"You mean the Yano?"

"Yes, I mean the Yano."

"You haven't a hope in hell of finding the Yano, Alex. Or at least you won't find those lunatics and come back alive. In fact, as you damned well know, you won't come back at all."

"I don't think it's true that I won't be able to find the Yano. I think quite a few people have found the Yano—or the Yano have found them. What is true, of course, is that those unfortunates are never seen again."

"Correct. And now you want to be one of them?"

"I think that it may be different in my case: that I was *meant* to find the Yano—as Laura was meant to go to them—and that there's some kind of meaning to all this."

"I should never have let you listen to old Peruche."

"No, maybe not."

The drumming on the beach had become much louder, and Avril leaned over the railing to gaze down at that mass of flickering candles. There were thousands of people now, packed along the enormous length of the beach, and when she looked left, at Leme, she saw even more candles, surging toward the sea and returning in that warm, cloudy darkness. She straightened up when she heard Alex's voice, speaking quietly but firmly.

"And what about Father Benedict? Have you heard any more about him?"

Turning around, Avril saw that Alex was staring at Antonio, but almost leaning toward the wrought-iron railing, as if drawn by the beating drums, tightly controlled tension in his face, beads of sweat on his forehead.

"Please, Alex," Antonio said, "leave this alone. Leave the past to itself."

"I *can't* leave the past to itself; I'm *part* of that past. Now what about Father Benedict?"

"What I wrote you in my letter still stands: Father Benedict has gone. He disappeared four weeks ago and hasn't been seen since."

Alex stared hard at Antonio, his eyes blinking and unfocused; then he wiped the sweat off his furrowed brow with a shaky right hand.

"It gets worse," he said. "Worse!"

He turned away, gripped the wrought-iron railing of the balcony, and stared down at the beach. Avril followed his gaze and saw the thousands massed below, all obviously agitated, moving back and forth in waves, the countless burning candles forming an alluvial sea of yellow flame which illuminated wildly shaking heads, waving hands and kicking legs, white robes and feathered headbands and fluttering banners and glowing altars, and the drummers who were making an ear-splitting racket of mesmeric ferocity. Then Antonio walked up to the railing and stood beside Alex, resting one hand gently on his shoulder and, likewise staring at the teeming beach, spoke quietly to him.

"Listen to me," he said. "Try to put this thing into perspective. To be suffering from nightmares is not particularly odd after what you've been through. You were completely inexperienced with women, Laura Wellman drove you almost crazy, you almost got yourself killed, your father was savagely murdered, and Laura Wellman, along with his probable murderers, disappeared without a trace. *Of course* you're suffering from nightmares, Alex—you had a series of terrible shocks—but you're not going to cure yourself by returning to the scene of all that unhappiness."

"I'm sorry, Antonio," Alex replied, "but you're wrong: I *have* to return there. You don't understand: these nightmares aren't ordinary; they began that first night on the boat to Belém, they got worse

during the few days I spent here in Rio, and by the time I actually
reached England they were a living part of me. No, they're not
ordinary nightmares: they're the same nightmares that Laura had: I
dream about dark barbarians, about lights rising and falling, about a
conflict between good and evil, with myself, and sometimes Laura,
in the middle. It was destiny, Antonio! Peruche said so and he was
right. There's some sort of purpose to everything that happened, and
since leaving the Amazon I've felt that my nightmares have been
designed to force me to return. I feel *haunted*, Antonio—just as
Laura felt haunted—and like Laura, I now have to go to the jungle
to find out what the cause is.''

Antonio sighed again. "I simply can't believe it," he said.
"However, let's not waste Avril's first night in Rio with this glum
conversation. Come on: let's go down to the beach for a real
Brazilian New Year's Eve."

Avril appreciated what he was doing and smiled at him. She put
down her glass and took hold of Alex's hand.

"A wonderful idea," she said. "I want to feel like a tourist."

"Right," he said. "Naturally."

Alex smiled at her, with love, but also with infinite weariness, as
if some part of him, his life-giving center, had died long ago. Once
more she felt crushed, defeated by his crumbling spirit, but she
squeezed his hand tighter and walked with him across the suite,
curtsying to Antonio when he opened the door and waved them both
out. They took the elevator down, crossed the lobby, and left the
hotel. The noise from the beach, like an unexpected clap of thunder,
suddenly exploded out of the silence and made Avril's heart leap.

The boulevard was crowded, people dancing to the pounding
drums, men smoking cigars, women gyrating sensually. Avril held
on to Alex, her blood stirred by the beating drums, her nose filled
with the smells of incense and tobacco, her eyes bedazzled by the
myriad candles and blazing torches and wavering torchlights. She
felt unreal as she crossed the road and found herself standing on the
sand, hemmed in on all sides by the thousands she had seen from her
balcony.

From above they had been no more than a sea of yellow flames
and gyrating limbs; up close they were a multitude of contrasting
faces: a blend of Portuguese and African and Moor, European and
Indian, pure Tupi-Guarani and light-skinned mulatto, *mestizos* and
caboclos and *cafusos*, excited *mestizo* children and simply curious
Caraibas, all generating an exotic scent of garlic, cloves, and cinna-

mon enriched with incense, cigars, and *cachaça*. The polyrhythms
of the many drummers and chanting groups made her head reel. She
watched, dismayed, the *Umbanda* and *Quimbanda* believers, the
witch doctors and the mediums, gyrating and wailing, prostrating
themselves or dancing crazily, their gymnastics quite incredible,
kissing the forked tongues of snakes, extending their hands over the
sea, falling down in what appeared to be epileptic fits, foaming at
the mouth and shrieking wildly and plunging their limbs into blazing
fires.

She squeezed Alex's hand tighter, glanced at him, saw his tension,
turned the other way and saw Antonio smiling at her, his head
framed by a patch of sky. There were a few stars in that sky, framed
by drifting, black clouds, and the light of the candles burning all
around her lent a glow to the darkness.

"Is this the sort of magic that Alex practiced?" she asked Antonio.

"No," he said. "Everything here relates to black and white
magic—to *Umbanda* and *Quimbanda*, both deriving from African
practices, but one, *Umbanda*, standing for Jesus and Christianity,
the other, *Quimbanda*, standing for the *Exus*—those spirits considered to be lowest on the astral ladder and therefore used by the
worshipers to do evil."

"And does that relate to what Alex told me about the Yano?"

"No. As I said, both *Umbanda* and *Quimbanda* are African-
based. The Yano, springing from pure Tupi-Guarani Indians, have a
religion that is uniquely their own."

"A religion that originates with the forces of darkness," Alex
said. "Those forces that are now haunting me—and once haunted
Laura."

Avril looked at him, feeling angry, hardly realizing what was
causing it, but then he suddenly cried out—a breathless, anguished
sound—and clasped his hands over his head and fell to his knees.
Avril looked down, startled, her senses numbed by the relentless
drumming, as he rocked back and forth on the sand, still holding his
head in his hands. She glanced at Antonio, saw his brown eyes
growing larger, then dropped to her knees, slid her arms around
Alex, and drew him to her as the sand swirled around her.

"What's wrong, Alex? Why—?"

He turned his head to look at her, but the swirling sand obscured
his face, and the wind, which had built up with a startling, unnatural
speed, suddenly howled and raced across the beach like a minor
tornado. There were shouts and screams, tumbling bodies and flying

debris, and Avril found herself rolling like a log across the beach, pummeled by similarly rolling bodies and numerous hard objects—smashed altars and broken chairs, candle holders and bottles—before coming to rest in a tangle of kicking limbs, her dazed eyes trying to focus on the sky above the thick, sweeping sand. She twisted around, gasping for breath, hearing howling wind and screaming, saw Alex on hands and knees, the sand sweeping fiercely across him as he struggled forward and reached out for her hand and then pulled her toward him. They fell against one another, spitting sand out, gasping for breath, and then managed to climb to their feet with the wind hammering at them.

The wind howled, the sand hissed, people shouted and screamed in panic, and Avril caught a glimpse of sky, a few stars, obscured cloud, and then raced, or was pulled forward by Alex, toward the broad boulevard. More debris flew past her—lots of candles and pieces of plaster—and then a human torch crossed her path, screaming hideously, shuddering and jerking, fell down and rolled wildly away, the flames leaping off arms and legs to curl through the acrid smoke. Avril stopped, wanting to help, momentarily thinking she was back in London—during an air raid, the bombs falling about her, smoke and flame everywhere—but she was tugged forward instantly, saw Alex, then Antonio, and followed them across the boulevard toward the lights of the hotel.

More screams, more burning bodies, noisy wind and biting sand, shadowy forms racing back and forth, others rolling across the pavement, the air filled with flapping hats and fluttering flags and extinguished candles, with plaster torn off portable altars and feathers swept off countless heads, with bits of clothing and cigars and spinning bottles—and then Avril saw the light, a blinding radiance in that howling darkness, and stumbled forward, or was pulled, to fall through the opening doors, and then into the arms of Alex and Antonio in the hotel's brightly lit lobby.

She choked, almost vomiting, her throat filled with sand and dust, and looked up, first at Antonio, his brown eyes filled with concern, then at Alex, his blue eyes wide and luminous, filled with wonder and fear.

"What's happening?" Alex said to Antonio. "*What kind of storm is this?*"

And then it suddenly died away, fading as fast as it had come, and they turned around and looked back out, across the boulevard, to the beach, and saw the stars in the sky, the clouds drifting languidly

across them, letting them shine their benevolent light on the gently
curving waves, on the sand as it settled down—on the people who
were staggering to and fro in a daze or sitting with heads bowed, or
stretched out as if unconscious—on the debris that covered every
visible stretch of beach as if, with the wanton rage of a petulant
child, some god had scattered his toys.

"I believe you," Antonio said.

19

"It was a warning!" Alex said passionately, sitting beside Avril in the rear of the car as they drove along the Avenida Rio Branco. "That storm wasn't natural—not at this time of the year nor any other—it must have been a warning to us."

"A *warning*?" Avril said, exasperated. "What *kind* of a warning?"

"A warning that we shouldn't interfere with the forces of darkness by going in search of the Yano," said Antonio.

"Oh, God," Avril said, lighting a cigarette and inhaling deeply, hoping to steady her shaky nerves. "I just can't believe that you two are discussing this so seriously: demonic possession, powers of darkness, a violent storm as the manifestation of the forces of evil—forces that are watching us right now. I'm an educated, middle-class English girl, and I find it ridiculous."

She blew a cloud of cigarette smoke, watched it drifting in front of her, then rolled the window down to let fresh air in. The car was passing through the business area of the city. At this early hour of the morning it was almost deserted, the windows of the buildings reflecting the street lights and the darkness surrounding them.

She suddenly felt desolated, aware of how far from home she was, no longer excited but faintly frightened by the thought of what she might have let herself in for. Contrary to what she said, that unnatural storm had shaken her badly, emerging, as it had, out of a perfectly clear sky and then fading away as quickly as it had come. No, not a natural storm, and one that had affected her strangely, setting her imagination free and arousing fear in her heart.

"If you think it's ridiculous," Antonio said over his shoulder, "then why have you made this journey with Alex?"

"Because I love him," Avril replied. "Because I'm worried about his mental health. Because I believe that he has to face up to his past, no matter how unpleasant, before he can even hope to be cured of his nightmares."

"And do you think those nightmares are natural, Avril?"

"I certainly don't think they're supernatural. I think they're caused by something Alex has refused to face, and that sooner or later he'll have to face whatever it is or break down completely."

"*Please*, Avril," Alex said. "I can do without that kind of talk—particularly when I'm sitting here right beside you."

"You'd rather I said it behind your back?"

"No, but—"

"You're a very levelheaded young lady," Antonio said, still speaking over his shoulder as he drove, keeping his eyes on the road. "So tell me: what do you think it is that Alex has refused to face? Do you mean something concerning Laura Wellman or the death of his father?"

"One or the other," Avril replied, looking out at the dark sky, seeing fireworks exploding under the stars as the celebrations optimistically started up again. "And then, again, maybe both. Alex is being haunted by something in his own mind: something he deliberately buried because it was too much to bear. And until he finds out what it is—and then faces it fully—he's going to continue having his nightmares."

"I'm hiding nothing," Alex said firmly. "What I told you is what I know. I can only know what I experienced personally . . . and none of that's been forgotten. No, I'm not hiding anything, nor being driven mad with guilt: my nightmares are exactly the same ones Laura had, and they've driven me back here for some purpose. I dream about the Yano, about the lights that rise and fall, about a conflict between good and evil where time and space have no meaning. I'm caught up in that conflict—I'm at the center—but I don't quite know how."

"No," Avril said. "I can't accept that at all. I believe in flesh and blood, in what I can see and touch; I do *not* believe in forces of good or evil, nor in life after death. We *create* good and evil by the manner in which we live; we create them by the things that we do. You are *not* being haunted, Alex: you're just tormenting yourself. You're having the same dreams as Laura Wellman because you're still obsessed with her."

There was a brief, uneasy silence as Alex digested her statement, but eventually he managed to stare at her, his gaze candid with hurt.

"You think I still love Laura?" he asked her gently.

His gaze filled her with guilt, making her spin within herself, thinking back to the streets of London, the gaunt ruins around them both, her love breaking out of the prison of childhood and changing her whole life. She had been drawn to his remoteness, his air of weary maturity, to the realization that he was open to tenderness and love's delicate nuances. Now she recognized all that again, in the muted anguish of his crystal gaze, and she wanted to fall into his arms and set him free with her body.

"Yes," she heard her own voice say reluctantly, "I think that might be the case."

"That's not true, Avril. You *know* what I feel. I've loved you from the moment I met you—and I love you right now."

"And Laura Wellman? What about your love for her? Didn't you love her in the same way as you now love me?"

"No, Avril, I didn't. I thought I did, but it wasn't true. I was totally innocent when I met Laura—more innocent than you can imagine—and so, when she entered my life, the most glamorous creature I had ever seen, I made a fool of myself. It wasn't real love, Avril: it was romantic obsession. It was very different from what I feel for you, and couldn't possibly have lasted. What I felt for her was painful and confusing and tormenting—but loving you isn't a torment: it's my one hope for peace."

It was a beautiful thing to say and it made Avril feel even more guilty, bringing a blush to her cheeks and quickening her heart. She glanced out of the car, saw the dark and grim dock area, wondered what Antonio was taking them to see, and then glanced back at Alex. He seemed frail and exhausted, slumped weakly beside her, his eyes scanning the shabby structures of Praça Maua as they slid past in silence. Why had she said that to Alex? Was she really that jealous of Laura Wellman? Did the ghost of that woman now haunt her as it clearly did Alex? She reached out, suddenly shaken by emotion, to take hold of his hand. He quivered when she touched him, as if shocked by human contact, but then, obviously gratified to have it, took hold of her fingers.

"Believe me," he said, "I love you."

"I know," she said. "I believe it. It's just that sometimes I feel as if that woman is breathing over my shoulder."

"Perhaps she is."

Antonio was slowing down, the car passing warehouses, the lights of the boats in the bay twinkling brightly between them. This was a different Rio, neither beautiful nor friendly, the streets dilapidated and desolate, lamps beaming over the *churrascarias*, music filtering out of the rough bars, sailors moving in and out of the shadows in which their women were standing. *Prostitutes*, Avril thought, and was slightly shocked at the idea, even though she had seen it all in the streets of London during the war. She kept looking, fascinated, feeling very far from home, and then Antonio braked to a halt, in front of an enormous warehouse.

"Okay," he said. "This is where I wanted to take you. I'm still not sure that I'm doing the right thing, but I have to take the chance. We're going into that warehouse. Once inside, you must stick close to my side, and speak to no one and touch nothing. What you will see are forbidden practices, so strangers aren't normally welcome, but they know me and won't bother you two as long as you're with me."

"Voodoo practices?"

"Yes, Alex, that's right."

"Why are you showing us voodoo, Antonio? It has no relevance to what happened in the Amazon."

"No more questions, my young friend. Just let me show you. First you will see what you will see, and then you can do what you want. Now, come on, let's go inside."

Antonio got out of the car and opened the rear door for Avril. As she stepped out into the dark street, she heard music and shouting emanating in a ghostly manner from inside the enormous warehouse. The road was dark and empty, devoid of any kind of lighting, containing nothing but other warehouses and derelict buildings. She shivered, feeling nervous and despising herself for it. Alex took hold of her hand.

"Are you all right?" he asked.

"Yes," she replied. "I'm fine."

"You're in for a bit of an experience, but don't worry about it."

There was a harsh, metallic squeaking as Antonio opened the large steel door. He stepped inside, indicating that they should follow. Avril stepped in first, feeling Alex's hands on her waist; the music and shouting exploded from the interior of the warehouse and beat all around her. Smoke and incense stung her eyes, making her blink and rub at them; she began looking around her, as Alex's hands pushed her forward.

She saw the back of Antonio's head moving through a sea of faces, smoke from joss sticks and burning torches swirling above the milling people, brown, black, and mulatto, their eyes dazed or closed in ecstasy, the whole mass forming a circle around the cleared central area toward which Antonio, occasionally glancing over his shoulder, was making slow progress. The drumming was demonic, polyrhythms of hypnotic intensity. The people, men and women of all ages, some wearing ordinary clothing, others in flowing white robes, were swaying back and forth and gyrating wildly and shaking their limbs, leaning toward the drummers and the voodoo "mediums" in a smoke-wreathed clearing in the middle of the building.

Antonio broke through to the clearing, pushing the onlookers aside, tugging Avril forward even as Alex pushed her from behind, and then, when he had reached his chosen position, stopping beside her. Avril rubbed her eyes again, wiping her stinging tears away, and stared through the blue smoke at the central cleared area in front of which the drummers were playing in a frenzy, the mediums were chanting their invocations, and the acolytes, some foaming at the mouth, were writhing like epileptics on the stone floor. One of the men, dancing dramatically, was burning himself with a flaming torch, while another, barefoot, was dancing on broken glass, and a third, his head back as he shrieked loudly, was slicing himself with a glittering knife, the blood flowing freely down his chest and soaking his trousers.

"Are they drugged?" Avril asked.

"Some of them," Antonio replied. "Most of them are simply in a self-induced trance, but some are on a hallucinogenic drug called *epena*."

"Why did you bring us here?" Alex asked stubbornly.

"Here he comes," Antonio said.

The crowd roared and parted, forming a pathway to the cleared area, and into it came two bare-chested mulatto mediums, each holding the elbow of a man who was half-walking, half-staggering between them, his eyes closed, his head hung low. Obviously heavily drugged, barely conscious, he was practically dragged toward the center of the clearing and placed without ceremony on a rickety, hardback, wooden chair. He was wearing a white shirt and gray slacks, his bare feet in leather thongs, and he just slumped there, his head hanging, his chin resting on his chest, while the mediums set a table in front of him and then, all the time dancing ecstatically, placed a long wooden box on the table and opened its lid.

The frenzied drumming continued, blue smoke swirled through the air, people swayed to and fro, back and forth, and clapped their hands to the rhythm of the drums, and babbled and cried out. The noise and movement hurt Avril's head, making her heart quicken, and she held Alex's hand even tighter, as if frightened of losing him. He was staring straight ahead, squinting into the smoke, his brow furrowed as he concentrated on the man who was slumped in the chair. The man was still at the table, behind the coffin-shaped box. Avril shivered as she saw the emerging heads of two large, swaying snakes. The man raised his head, his shock of white hair jumping electrically, and seemed to stare directly at her through that streaming blue haze.

She was shocked to see that he was a European, once handsome, now old and ill. His untidy white hair fell over his wrinkled forehead, his eyes were bloodshot and dazed with dark bags under them and numerous lines around them, his cheeks were sunken, his skin deathly pale, and his lips, which once might have been sensual, now trembled helplessly.

"Oh, my God!" she heard Alex exclaiming beside her. "*That's Father Benedict!*"

Even as Alex uttered those words, his voice strangled with shock, the two giant pythons, which had been emerging from the long box on the table, rose higher and swayed to and fro in front of the priest's glazed, haunted eyes and prematurely white hair. They curled over his shoulders and wrapped themselves around his shivering body as he merely shook his head from side to side while tears rolled down his cheeks. Yes, an old man—not the man she had been told about—and when she turned away, horrified (as much by the sight of him as by the snakes coiling around him), she saw that Alex was close to tears.

"Father Benedict!" he murmured in a daze. "Oh, dear God, *it can't be!*"

At that moment, as the snakes were tightening dangerously around him, the priest opened his eyes wide, stared up at the warehouse ceiling, and in a manner reminiscent of the excited voodoo mediums at both sides of him, let out a high, demented wail. He then shook his head wildly, beads of sweat flicking off him, his whole body shivering in the deadly grip of the tightening snakes as the drummers behind him became frantic, the smoke swirled more densely around him, and the onlookers whooped and shrieked and let out strident lamentations, their hands raised above their heads, their bodies jerking. Then the mediums beside the priest, as if sensing that he was on the verge of death, spat out a stream of gibberish, grabbed the snakes with their bare hands and pulled them, unresisting, from their shuddering victim. As he sobbed and slumped forward in his chair, the snakes coiled around the sweating arms of the Indians who placed them back in the oblong box.

Alex suddenly rushed forward, letting an anguished sob break loose, pushing the Indians aside and grabbing hold of Father Benedict while Antonio, shouting over the bedlam, rushed up to help him. There was a brief and noisy commotion, lots of tugging and pushing, but then Antonio shouted again, directing his words at the excited Indians, and they reluctantly moved away, letting Alex break free with the babbling priest and, supporting his old friend, with Antonio pushing them from behind, awkwardly weave his way back to Avril.

"Let's get out of here!" Antonio said.

The priest looked up in a daze, murmuring something incoherent, and Avril was again shocked at how old he looked. More than old: wrecked, his blinking eyes filled with despair, moving left to right in pitiful confusion, his tongue licking his lips, his frail body trembling. This was not the Father Benedict about whom Avril had heard so much—handsome man with silver-streaked black hair and a robust physique—but another, much older and broken man. As he moved his weeping eyes all about him, he finally managed to focus upon her and offer a humorless smile.

"A testing," he said, slurring. "To challenge death and survive it. To be embraced by the symbol of the powers of darkness and not feel their crushing strength." His voice trailed off as he nodded, his head rising and falling sleepily, before his eyes opened fully again and focused upon her. "*In the end it will bite like a snake,*" he croaked hoarsely, "*and will spread abroad poison like a basilisk. Thine eyes shall behold strange women, and thine heart shall utter perverse things. And thou shalt be as one sleepless in the midst of the sea, and as a pilot fast asleep when the stern is lost.*"

Avril thought of the snakes and shivered, trying to still her beating heart as Antonio, helping Alex to support the muttering priest, led them all back through the clamorous crowd, through the swirling smoke and the sweet smell of incense and *epena*, away from the ferocious polyrhythms of the drums and out of the warehouse. The slamming door cut off the music, or at least muffled its demonic clamor, and the fresh air, wafting in from the bay, was cool and refreshing. Father Benedict was still muttering, hanging between Alex and Antonio, the former wiping tears from his eyes with his free hand, the latter using his own free hand to open the car's rear door. He eased the priest into the back seat.

"I thought you should see for yourself," Antonio said, "but perhaps I was wrong."

"No," Alex replied, "you were right. But what *happened* to him?"

Antonio raised both his hands in a familiar gesture of defeat, his smile touched with sadness. "As you know," he said, "Father Benedict was extremely disturbed by the murder of your father and the disappearance of Laura Wellman. He was, I think, particularly shaken by his own conviction that he, as the local priest, should have been able to do something to prevent that situation exploding as it did—that he should have taken firmer action when that *seringueiro* died because of your father's mistreatment—and that he should definitely have taken action when your father took the Indian girl into his house as repayment for the so-called debts of her own dead father. He felt very, very guilty over what had occurred."

Avril glanced into the car and saw the priest in the back seat, his shoulders slumped, his chin on his chest as he slept off his stupor. *It will bite like a snake. . . . Thine eyes shall behold strange women.* She thought of the snakes around the priest, of that strange creature Laura Wellman, and wondered yet again just what she had let herself in for when she had encouraged Alex to make this return trip and agreed to come with him. Right now Alex was leaning against the car, giving his attention to Antonio, both of them painted in black shadow and pale lines of moonlight.

"Anyway," Antonio continued, "from the day of the murders and the American woman's disappearance, Father Benedict became a changed man—drinking a lot, it was said, and also studying the magic practices of the Indians—and after we closed down the plantation he was extremely depressed, usually drunk, and gradually became something of a recluse, ignoring even his work with the mission and the local Indians, and often disappearing for days, returning from Manaus reeking of drink. Of course the locals talked—you know how news travels here—and it was said that the priest was taking an interest in Indian magic, that he was sniffing *epena*, that he had been seen in certain villages which he did not normally attend to, and that he was, in general, very much a changed man. A month ago he disappeared completely, leaving the mission unattended and offering no clue to his whereabouts—and only yesterday, when I came to Rio to prepare for your arrival, did I learn that he had moved into a *favela*, that he was either drunk or drugged most of the time, and that he had started involving himself in dangerous black magic practices of the kind you witnessed here tonight.''

"But *why*?" Alex asked. "What *happened* to him?"

"Father Benedict, your Christian friend, is destroying himself by flirting with a particular form of Indian witchcraft far beyond anything known to *Umbanda* or *Quimbanda*; it is very close to the most dangerous forms of black magic—the kind that was once practiced by the Yanoama Indians and is now, reportedly, the sole province of their outcast relatives, the Yano. Whether or not this has something to do with your father's murder and Laura Wellman's disappearance is for you to decide, but right now I think we should take him home and put him to bed.''

"You mean the mission?"

"No, I mean the nearby *favela*. I don't think he would want to wake up anywhere else—and, sad to say, after he had disappeared for a month, his superiors in Australia decided to close the mission down. The mission—and in a sense Father Benedict's whole life—has gone for all time.''

"Not his life," Alex said fervently. "We can give him that back.''

"Maybe you can," Antonio said, "and then again, maybe not. For now, let's get him back to his new home.''

The journey back through the city seemed unreal to Avril, the darkness, the silence, the stars glittering above the black hills, all combining to make her feel that she was dreaming and losing touch with herself. The dream was couched in fear, but that fear was colored by magic: the clouds crossing a pale moon, Pão de Açúcar glimpsed fitfully, Christ the Redeemer, arms outstretched, surveying the city from Corcovado, lamplight and starlight on his head, a crimson glow bleeding over him. Avril shivered, feeling cold—or convinced herself that the shivering came from coldness—and turned her head to look at the priest slumped between her and Alex.

She still could not imagine him as the man Alex had told her about. Only four years ago, in 1943, Father Benedict had been in New Guinea, serving with the Australian Army, moving with the troops along the bloody Kokoda Trail and, according to Alex, witnessing some appalling atrocities. His faith in God, never strong, had apparently wavered badly then, bending before the realization that man's worst actions could be part of God's great plan. Nothing had been secure after that—the scales had tilted against his faith—

but at least he had been a handsome, well-built man of considerable charm; not this man, this beaten thing, this frail, snoring creature, now held between herself and Alex as the deserted streets slid past.

She looked at Alex, also haunted, also frail from the lack of peace, and her pragmatism, drilled into her from childhood, dissolved and drained out of her. Her own father had been an agnostic, a good-humored, sardonic realist, teaching her that man had come from dust and to dust would return. Yes, she had believed that, and had lived contentedly with it, but now, looking out, seeing the hilly streets of Botafogo, she realized that her own belief in the material world was likewise starting to waver before unnatural and supernatural events, buffeted in the winds of experiences that had no rational explanations. She shivered, feeling cold again—or again pretending that she was cold—and was glad when the bricabrac streets of Botafogo gave way to the shacks of the enormous *favela* she had seen earlier as a sea of soothing yellow lights on a sweeping black hill.

"He lives *here*?" Alex asked.

"Yes," Antonio said. "He could not have picked a worse place if he had tried—but he found what he wanted."

"Penance?"

"Yes, a form of penance—but not that alone. This *favela* is renowned not only for its poverty but for its very large proportion of pure Indians and black-magic worshipers. Why black magic instead of white I don't know—but that's why he's here."

Avril looked out and was appalled. What she saw was poverty exemplified, shacks numbering in the thousands, raised on stilts on the steep earth, rising up in long tiers and sloping over one another, and disappearing over the crest of the enormous hill to run on down the other side. She stared at the roofs of cardboard and corrugated iron, holes stuffed up with newspapers and other debris, the surrounding ground made of hard earth and strewn with much litter. Candles still burned on the verandahs, in the tiny rooms inside, and a surprising number of the inhabitants, most dark-skinned, all wearing rags, were still awake and either resting on their porches or idling between the leaning shacks. A bleak, depressing sight, it was also quite frightening, and Avril, when the car braked to a halt, stepped out feeling nervous.

"You're having a night of rare experiences," Antonio said, smiling reassuringly at her. "Very few visitors to the city see what you have seen—and certainly very few could come here and go back in one piece.''

"You're known here?"

"Yes, I'm known here . . . and so is the priest. They let him live here because he is a priest—and because they think he is crazy.''

"Maybe they're right,'' Avril said.

"We're *all* crazy,'' Antonio replied.

Alex had climbed out the other side of the car and was walking around it to help pull Father Benedict out. He glanced at Avril and smiled, but seemed a million miles away. His return to Brazil, to the events that had broken his spirit, seemed to have driven him deeper into himself and even further away from her. He tugged repeatedly at the priest's sleeve, and eventually, after considerable difficulty, awakened him. The priest swayed groggily, placed one hand on Alex's shoulder, stared at him as if not recognizing him, and then glanced vaguely around him.

"What?" he said. "Where?" He was obviously still dazed, shaking his head from side to side and rubbing his eyes. "God," he said. "Need a drink."

"Father Benedict—" Alex began.

"*What*?" the priest said irritably, his voice hoarse and tremulous, and then, pushing Alex aside, took a tentative step forward. "Throat's dry as a rasp," he said.

Alex, near to tears, stepped away to let the priest pass, watching him as he walked forward a few paces and then stopped again, coughing into his fist, shaking his head, and glancing around him once more. The *favela* was quiet and eerie, lit mainly by flickering oil lamps or candles, and some of the residents had come up to stare at them with curious, unfriendly eyes. Antonio approached the priest and gently took hold of his elbow, coaxing him toward the shack straight ahead and murmuring soothing words to him. Together they walked up the wooden steps, the priest mumbling incoherently. Avril and Alex followed them inside.

It was a small, one-room shack, the wooden floor covered in dust, the one table littered with empty bottles and opened tins and dirty dishes, unwashed clothing scattered haphazardly on hardback chairs and bare floorboards, the whole place smelling of *cachaça*, incense, and foul cigar smoke. The priest already was at the table, irritably scattering the empty bottles, cursing because he couldn't find something to drink and rubbing his eyes repeatedly even though the room was only lit by the light of a very weak oil lamp. He finally found a half-full bottle of beer and slumped into a chair. He had a drink, rested the bottle on one leg, and stared blearily at each of them.

He looked at Avril first, his brow furrowed in puzzlement, then nodded his head in a dreamy manner and offered a slight smile, obviously vaguely remembering her from the warehouse. He had another drink of his beer, wiped his lips with a shaky hand, then opened his eyes wider in surprised recognition.

"Antonio!" he exclaimed.

"Yes, Father Benedict."

"Oh, Antonio, Antonio, my old friend, what brings you here?"

"I brought Alex," Antonio said.

There was a very long silence as the priest took in this news, first staring at Antonio with an air of complete bewilderment, then letting his weary gaze roam across to Avril, and finally, with great reluctance, a fresh alertness riding on pain, looking through the flickering pale light and shadow at the silent, obviously shocked Alex.

"Oh, my God," he murmured.

Avril reached out and took hold of Alex's hand, squeezing it reassuringly as the priest, staring at him, shook his head from side to side and started to weep.

"No," he murmured. "No! Oh, Antonio, why did you do this?" He stared again at Alex, as if to confirm what he was seeing, and then, as if a blade had been driven through his heart, shivered violently, sat up in his chair, and tried to sniff his tears back. "Alex!" he said. "My young friend! Oh, dear God, why come back here?"

"To find Laura Wellman," Alex said.

The priest shuddered to hear her name, drank some beer and licked his lips, sniffed and wiped his weeping eyes dry, and then shook his head again.

"How foolish," he said. "How very foolish to come back here for that. That unfortunate woman, as we all know, was seduced by old Peruche's magic, led by him into the jungle, and there was captured, and doubtless killed, by the barbaric Yano Indians. Laura Wellman is dead, my son."

"She isn't necessarily dead," Alex replied.

"She is *dead*!" the priest said.

He had said it with such vehemence that Avril was startled. She held Alex's hand tighter, feeling the shock jolting through him. She turned her head and saw his face, his extraordinary abstract beauty, the blond hair flopping over his clear blue eyes and hiding his pain.

He was staring down at the sitting priest as if seeing him for the first time. Then he, too, shuddered visibly and let go of Avril's hand, moving away from her to get down on one knee, just in front of the priest.

The priest refused to meet his gaze, but Alex reached up with his left hand, cupped it under his old friend's unshaven chin, and very gently turned that wasted face toward him, almost like a father with his son, reversing their original roles. The priest, his chin resting in Alex's hand, stared down at him, fearfully.

"What happened to you, Father Benedict?" Alex asked. "And what are you doing here?"

The priest kept staring fearfully, then with flickerings of pain, until eventually the tears rolled down his cheeks and settled on Alex's hand.

"Your father is dead," he said. "And Laura Wellman is doubtless dead. And I hold myself responsible for what happened."

"It wasn't your fault," Alex said.

"It was," the priest replied. "I let the situation build up until it exploded. I should never have let your father get away with what he was doing, but I did—doubtless out of cowardice—and look what it led to. Yes, it was my responsibility, and that's why I'm here."

"And what do you hope to do here?"

"Find oblivion."

"Not quite true, priest," Antonio said. He had stepped out of the shadows near the flickering oil lamp and now stared very levelly at the priest, his hands on his fleshy hips. "Is it not in fact true, Father Benedict, that you are also involving yourself regularly in the kind of practices we all witnessed tonight? And that you are, in truth, growing obsessed with Indian witchcraft?"

The priest immediately looked defensive, huddling up into himself. "No!" he exclaimed. "No! That's not true! Tonight was just"—he drank some beer and wiped his lips with a trembling hand—"just something that happened. A stupid accident of drunkenness."

"An *accident*, Father Benedict? Mere *drunkenness*, you call it? No mere drunkard could walk accidentally into such an event, let alone take part in it. No, my good friend, you weren't drunk: you have been practicing voodoo."

"No! That's not true!" The panic-stricken priest jerked his chin out of Alex's hand to drink more of his beer. "No!" he repeated, wiping his lips with that shaky hand. "What you say is all nonsense!"

"No, priest, not nonsense! You know damned well what you're

doing! This is the shack of a *Quimbanda*—a black magic medium—
and what we see here on the walls and on that table are the tools of
his trade: that small altar, those effigies, the incense, this bowl of
epena, and the various statuettes and amulets. Admit it, Father
Benedict: you're flirting with voodoo of the most dangerous kind!''

''No! *Oh, God, no!*'' The priest almost shrieked the words as he
twisted away from them, bending forward and covering his face with
his hands, his body shaking as he sobbed uncontrollably, with a
wounded child's passion.

He looked lost and pitiful, the yellow light flickering over him,
and Avril, awash in an equally uninhibited pity, could bear to look
at him no longer and instead found herself staring down at the table
beside her, her vision gradually focusing on a stone amulet that lay
covered in dust.

Alex, it said to her.

Blinking, shaking her head, wondering if she was hearing things,
she impulsively picked up the amulet and examined it closely. It was
the size of a penny, made of black stone, perfectly featureless—and
yet, as she examined it, as she concentrated on it, the priest's
sobbing faded away, the surrounding walls fled from her consciousness, her thoughts seemed to congeal into a single burning moment,
and she felt the power entering her—unrecognizable yet strangely
familiar—a power that flowed like an electric current directly from
Alex and poured into her quivering body to make her skin burn.

Dazed, slightly dizzy, losing touch with her sense of reality, she
tied the string of the amulet around her neck and let it rest on her
throat. Then Alex was there in front of her, staring at her with
unusual intensity. He reached out and took the amulet in his right
hand and studied it closely. Apparently satisfied, if slightly shaken,
he let it slip back through his fingers and rest, with the coolness of
frozen glass, once more on her warm skin.

''What is it?'' she asked him, feeling as if she were dreaming, her
own voice echoing ethereally in her head and fading away into
silence.

''It's mine,'' Alex replied. ''Old Peruche gave it to me. It was
supposed to be a magical amulet that would ward off evil spirits and
endow me with strange powers. I gave it to Laura shortly before all
the troubles began.'' He turned back to face the priest, who was
staring up at the pair of them, his bleary, bloodshot eyes filled with
guilt and unstated denials. ''I gave that amulet to Laura Wellman,''
Alex said sternly. ''How did you get it?''

"I didn't steal it!" the priest exclaimed. "I swear to you, I didn't steal it! I found it in your father's room, just before the plantation was closed down. It was lying there, in all that dust and rubbish, so I decided to take it. I swear to you, Alex, that's true! *I did not steal the amulet!*"

He stared at each of them in turn, his eyes wide and glazed, and then buried his face in his hands. Resting his elbows on his knees, he started sobbing again, his frail body wracked by recurrent spasms and uncontrollable shivering. He was close to a breakdown, his despair too much to bear. Alex again dropped to one knee, grabbed him by both shoulders, and shook him vigorously.

"You're coming with us," he said. "You can't stay here, Father Benedict. I won't let you destroy yourself in this manner. This has gone on long enough. I won't let it continue. You'll come back to our hotel and spend the night with us, and then, tomorrow morning, when you've had a good sleep, we'll decide what to do about all this business. Do you understand, Father Benedict? *Do you hear what I'm saying?*"

"Yes, yes, I'm listening! But I can't do it, Alex! Why did you come back to torment me with this? I can't do it! *I can't!*"

Avril found herself stepping forward, moved by a mysterious impulse, and then was pushing Alex aside and standing over the quivering priest, bending slightly toward him. She felt that strange power—Alex's power: a mesmeric force—flowing out of him and leaving him drained as it charged her with new life. Her own arrogance shocked her, her self-awareness overwhelming her, but she reached down, placed her hands on the priest's shoulders, and squeezed him gently.

"Please, Father Benedict," she said, "do as Alex asks of you."

The priest stared at her, startled, his eyes wild with grief and fear, and then fixed his gaze on the amulet that lay on her beating throat. He kept staring at the black stone, drawn to it and into it, his tongue slowly licking his lips as his shivering body went still. Avril squeezed his shoulders again, letting her essence pour down into him, a great compassion, perhaps, Alex's abiding love, giving back to the emptied cavern of the priest's spirit a certain measure of strength. She hardly knew what she was doing, but felt quietly, supremely confident, and as she gazed down at him and saw his pain in that flickering pale light, she felt bound to him by love and understanding, her new faith like a rock.

The priest ceased his violent trembling, and for a moment stopped breathing. He removed his gaze from the amulet, stared more boldly at her, and then, in that squalid shack, in the silence of his inner struggle, his frail form a patchwork of shifting light and shadow, he managed to drag up from his tortured depths a faint trace of his former will.

"All right," he whispered, "I'll come with you . . . *and God help us all!*"

20

"We haven't slept since we arrived in Rio," Avril said. "No wonder we're tired."

Alex nodded and smiled weakly, sitting across the table from her, sipped his coffee and glanced over the railing at the deserted Copacabaña Beach, six stories below them. It was just before dawn and the boulevard was deserted, a great moon gliding behind heavy clouds, the stars bright and plentiful. There were three cups of steaming coffee on the table, one of them untouched, because Antonio, at that moment, was putting Father Benedict to bed in the spare room of the large and elegant hotel suite. Avril sipped her own coffee, let it burn down inside her, placed the cup back in its saucer, and studied Alex. If still drawn and pale, he seemed more alive than before, a fresh brightness in his formerly dull eyes, his posture a little more positive. He was staring at her and smiling affectionately, itself an improvement.

"You've seen an awful lot in one night," he said to her, "and, I think, stood up to it very well. You give me courage and strength."

He smiled when he said it, but she was pleased to know that he meant it. She was also pleased that his sense of humor was still quietly alive.

"Do you think your priest will actually sleep without another drink—or another sniff of *epena*?"

"*Epena* doesn't put one to sleep: it induces extraordinary hallucinations, hallucinations that the Indians are convinced are the only true reality: that other world beyond time and space which, according to the Indians, exists within us all. So if Father Benedict was sniffing *epena*, it certainly wasn't to find sleep."

"Then why *was* he taking it?"

"I've just told you: Father Benedict, a Christian, has become involved in Indian magic, and I think it all relates to Laura Wellman. The stealing of the amulet, the taking of *epena*, and that ritual with the snakes are all ways of trying to obtain extra powers, notably magical powers, of the kind that I had in very minor ways, old Peruche had in quite spectacular ways, and Laura Wellman, in her obsession with the forces of darkness, very much wanted to obtain. Now, it seems, Father Benedict is also in search of those powers, perhaps because, in his guilt at not preventing the tragic events of two years ago, he hopes to make amends by pitting himself against those very forces which Laura insisted had possessed her.''

"*To challenge death and survive it,*" Avril quoted the priest. "*To be embraced by the symbol of the powers of darkness and not feel its crushing strength.*"

"Yes," Alex said. "The priest knew what he was doing. One way of obtaining the power, as Peruche taught me, is to directly challenge death—particularly death in the form of one of the symbols of the powers of darkness, the major one of which is the serpent.''

"And you once practiced that?"

"Yes, Avril. Peruche taught me that all forms of life are part of the one life, that good and evil are two sides of the same coin, and that the way to purity, and thus power over normal things, is in the testing of one's faith and courage by facing evil or death. For that reason I would, under his supervision, let myself be embraced with snakes—the biblical symbols of evil and death—and covered in poisonous spiders and other insects. So, by overcoming my natural revulsion and fear of such creatures, I actually became one with them, making them indifferent to my presence and ensuring my safety. So, also, I strengthened my faith in the good and gained the first of the latent powers which all men possess, though most are unable to call upon. Those powers, which include what you would call telepathy and precognition, are the ones that Laura Wellman hoped she would find where the good fights with evil: in the jungle where the Yano, enslaved to Satan, guard the Gateway that leads to eternity and the light of redemption. To reach eternity and the light of redemption, one has to brave those dark forces, this being the test all men must take one way or another.''

"And in attempting to find those same powers, Father Benedict is unwittingly destroying himself?"

"He doesn't know the way. He's fumbling in the darkness. He's a priest, a Christian, whose faith has never been strong, and who now, feeling that his lack of faith contributed to those terrible events, is flirting with very dangerous forces and losing his soul.''

"That, of course, is only your theory."

"Yes, Avril, it's only my theory . . . and of course it could be wildly off the mark. Who knows, after all, what really goes on in the priest's mind? Only him. Perhaps God."

Avril sipped her coffee, trying to keep herself awake, aware that her eyes were very tired and that the darkness was comforting. She studied Alex over her cup, captivated by his expressive face, but shivered when she thought of him in the jungle with snakes and spiders all over him.

Was all this really happening? Was she living some kind of dream? Was she really starting to believe that she was hearing about other worlds and strange powers? Yes, in truth she was—the evidence seemed to be overwhelming—and she felt that from the moment she had placed the amulet around her neck she had herself taken on certain powers that she had not known before.

"And what about this amulet?" she asked, lifting it up in her hand. "Do you really think the priest stole it in the hope of obtaining such powers from it?"

"I really don't know. He possibly told us the truth. I did give it to Laura, and maybe she later gave it to him, though somehow I doubt it. Then again, she spent most of her evenings on the plantation in that awful room with my father and Rollie Thatcher where, according to Father Benedict, he found the amulet—so possibly it was Laura who actually lost it, most likely during the night of the murders. So, either Laura actually gave the priest the amulet—which I doubt, since she was so obsessed with magical powers—or, more likely, he found it where she had lost it during the events of that horrible night."

"Do *you* think the amulet has magical powers?"

"Yes. Everything bad that happened to me happened after I gave the amulet to Laura. Shortly after that, I tried to test the limit of my powers—and did so, against Peruche's warnings, for negative reasons—only to find, when the snakes actually turned on me, that my powers had gone. They disappeared not only because I gave away the amulet but because I then gave vent to anger and hatred. So, as Peruche had told me, I lost my innocence and faith and, because of that, also lost all the advantages he had given me. Yes, the amulet certainly has magical powers, both negative and positive."

"Now that I have the amulet, will that same magic work for me?"

"I don't know. It probably depends on your own nature. It might well have worked for the priest, but in a negative manner, destroying his badly needed faith and plunging him into despair. Doubtless it worked for me because I believed in it; whether or not it works for you only time will tell—and even then, it could actually work against you, and actually endanger you. I'd rather you got rid of it immediately but can see that you won't.''

"What makes you so sure of that?"

"Your eyes. They turn strange when you look at it."

Avril did just that, almost challenging him to try to stop her, looking down at the blackstone amulet that lay in her palm, featureless and strangely opaque, as if hollow and depthless. She blinked and looked again, sensing herself drifting away, then saw black night, dark clouds, wheeling stars: the impenetrable cosmos. There were murmurings, ghostly whisperings, all around her, inside her, and a light seemed to blossom up through her to warm her whole being.

She dissolved into herself, passing down through her essence, entered a curving tunnel of light and darkness and emerged to the infinite. Here past and future merged, time and space became one, all that had been and would be pulsated beyond color and sound. There were stars in all directions, some exploding gently into fountains of light, others moving back and forth in glistening clusters of no known dimension. Then sound: a rising clamor, whisperings forming a wall of noise, voices separate, then as one, all around like the streaming light, above and below like the stars: a single great sound that filled the void and gave it life everlasting.

One voice: a million voices. One sound: a rising tide. The boundless, anguished cry of human history echoing far in the future. She was shaken and then sundered, her soul scattering through time and space, then returned, trying to gather herself together, through that tunnel to tangibles: lights rising and falling, drums beating in cacophony, sweat gleaming on black skin, faces painted and scarred, a slit throat pouring blood on gleaming steel as flames flickered and scorched.

She recognized her immediately—how often had she been described? —that red hair long and windblown, cheekbones classical, lips thin yet sensual, the emerald eyes large and demented as she cried out for help . . . *Laura Wellman!* Was it she? What was happening in that fearful darkness? Yellow flames flickered on and off her body as she writhed in the mud.

Fire in darkness, trees dripping, the stars above, the mud below.

Fierce, barbaric men, skin black, faces painted, inflamed by the drums and the hallucinogenic *epena*, were dancing around her, holding her down, kneeling over her heaving form. Was it she? Who else? Horribly abused but at least alive, her long hair falling over her stricken face and trailing into the mud. Yes, it was Laura—sobbing brokenly and calling for help—and Avril retreated from her, shrinking back into herself, shaking her head vigorously in protestation and then opening her eyes again.

She saw it all high above her: black night, dark clouds, wheeling stars: the impenetrable cosmos around the earth—as it always had been. She was on the balcony of the Copacabaña Palace Hotel, staring up at the sky.

What had happened? Had she imagined it? Was the amulet some kind of mirror? Had she really heard the voice of Laura Wellman crying out in despair? Avril shivered and stared at Alex, saw his steady, gentle gaze, shivered again, and let the amulet fall from her hand and rest on her throat.

"Are you all right?" Alex asked. "You look strange."

"I'm all right. I'm just tired."

It was a necessary lie and she averted her gaze, feeling oddly ashamed of herself, perhaps even cowardly. She was considerably relieved when she heard footsteps in the apartment and Antonio walked out onto the balcony, smiling in his warm and relaxing manner and reaching down for his cup of coffee. He sipped it, winced, and put the cup back on the table, then shook his head sadly from side to side, his face a picture of tragedy. "It's almost cold already," he said, "but I'll have to live with it. Better cold than no coffee at all at this time of the morning." He pulled his chair out and sat down between Avril and Alex, rubbed his eyes and stifled a yawn and glanced from one to the other. "The priest is sleeping," he said. "He's not happy, but he's unconscious. He hasn't stopped talking since he closed his eyes, but at least he's not drinking."

"What do you think he'll feel like when he wakes up?"

"Terrible, my beautiful English rose. Quite simply awful."

"*I* feel awful right now."

"You've been through a lot in a short time. You traveled a tremendous distance, arrived in a strange city, and then had some extremely strange experiences, most naturally disturbing. You are, like the priest, paying the price for being close to our Alex here."

He gave Alex his warmest smile, easing the cutting edge of his joke, and Alex responded by nodding his head in obvious agreement.

"Avril's been paying that price for a long time now," he said, "and I'm not at all sure that I'm worth it."

"Do *you* think he's worth it, Avril?"

"Yes, Antonio, I think he's worth it. And so, as far as I can judge, is his good friend, Father Benedict."

"Ah, yes," Antonio said, "Father Benedict . . . who needs the sleep he's now getting."

"Father Benedict isn't the only one who needs sleep," Alex said. "I can't keep my eyes open a minute longer, so I think I'll creep off to bed."

"I'll join you in a minute," Avril said, "when I've finished my coffee. And I want to spend a minute or two with this handsome Brazilian."

"Fine," Alex replied, unconcerned. "Antonio, I'll see you in the morning, when we'll decide what to do."

"So be it, my friend."

Antonio waved his left hand lazily as Alex stood up, nodded, smiled at each of them in turn, and then walked, almost drunkenly, into the suite. For a moment there was silence, broken only by the lapping sea, and Avril, seeing Antonio's gentle smile, knew why Alex was fond of him.

"I'm very pleased you're here, Antonio," she said. "I'm not sure I could handle all of this without your support. Alex is terribly fond of you and now I can see why, and I'm glad not only for him but also for me, since I need the reassurance of someone sane."

"You think Alex and Father Benedict are insane?"

"No, Antonio, I don't. But I *do* think they're both very disturbed, and that I, given the events of this extraordinary night, might be going the same way."

Antonio smiled even more broadly. "I don't think so," he said. "I said it before and I stand by it: you're a very levelheaded English girl who can do nothing but good here."

"I think my level head is increasingly disoriented. What's happening, Antonio? What have I let myself in for? There are things happening here that I don't understand, things that are changing my way of thinking and making me fearful. Once I was pragmatic, but I'm not any longer: I feel that I'm slipping into a dream from which I might never wake up. I might have been good for Alex back in England; I'm not sure about here. I feel as if I'm losing control, being taken over by something: this place, this whole situation, perhaps that damned woman, Laura Wellman. Will you tell me the truth, Antonio? Does Alex still love her? His obsession is so strong, I think he must, but I can't be too sure.''

She hadn't wanted to ask that question but now it was out, lying in the silence between them like a stone on the riverbed. She felt Antonio's gaze upon her (she had lowered her own eyes in embarrassment) and understood that he was weighing his words. When she looked up, she saw dark sky and pale moon, the stars beginning to fade before morning, Antonio's *café-au-lait* face framed by the distant hills. He smiled and shrugged, then raised both hands in the air—an oddly bemused gesture that touched her with its gentle sincerity.

''Of course he loved her,'' he said. ''It was the first such love of his life. He wanted her with the kind of innocent passion that simply can't last. She was twice his age, Avril—his love was hopeless from the start—but she entered his life as his first great temptation, and exploded his quite remarkable innocence. Yes, it was love, but not the kind you have for one another: it was the sort of romantic obsession—a violent, insane obsession—for which he was totally unprepared.''

''But he's *still* obsessed with her, Antonio—more than with me.''

''No, Avril, I think you're wrong. It is of course true that he's obsessed with her in one way, but that doesn't necessarily mean that he still loves her. You must accept, for a start, that Indian magic may in fact work, and that Alex's nightmares, which are the same as those suffered by Laura, could in truth be the products of witchcraft or voodoo, rather than just Alex's subconscious way of identifying with the woman he once loved. However, assuming that this isn't the case—which I think we must for now—my own view is that Alex is obsessed with Laura Wellman not only because of his similar nightmares, but because of her brief relationship with his father.''

''That's true,'' Avril said. ''That discovery still haunts him. He's talked about it a lot—and feels that they both betrayed him and therefore didn't give a damn about his feelings.''

''Exactly. No matter how good or bad Frank Poulson was—and in my opinion he had degenerated to the degree where such terms were almost an irrelevancy to him—he was still Alex's father; and Alex, who had a surprisingly clear-eyed view of his father's nature, was still in no way prepared for the discovery that his father and Laura were having an affair behind his back.''

''And you think that's all there is to it?''

''No, I don't think that's all there is to it—but I think that if he hadn't found out about Laura and his father, he would have been able to face up to the rest of it.''

"His father's murder and Laura's disappearance?"

"Yes. Make no mistake about it: Alex really does believe that those terrible events were preordained for some purpose or other—believes it because Peruche suggested it—and so, until he can discover that purpose, he won't find the peace he sorely needs."

"And you think he can only discover that purpose by first finding the Yano and even, possibly, Laura Wellman?"

"You're a very bright girl."

"And what about Laura, Antonio? Do you think she was simply living in a world of fantasy—all those strange stories about her background—or that she might have been quite mad, as Alex sometimes believed?"

"Who knows? Certainly she was a peculiar one. From the moment I met her, I felt there was something odd about her—something distracted, erratic and potentially destructive. Her eyes, which were quite lovely, never fixed directly upon you, but usually seemed focused inward to some dark, hidden corner of herself. Likewise, when she talked, she seemed to be talking to herself, and she often behaved like someone sleepwalking—and drank far too much. Her mad mother? The Great Beast? Her conviction that she was possessed? Even if all those were simply the products of her imagination, they still might have been as real as life to Laura."

"Where I come from," Avril said, "we would call that madness."

"You would," Antonio replied, "but the Indians would not. The Indians believe in a universal consciousness—that all minds are part of the one mind—and that the instant something is imagined, or simply *thought* into being, it becomes as real as anything else held in that mind, past, present, or future. Thus, by Indian terms, everything that Laura believed had happened to her in the past, had in fact been willed into being by that very belief, and was therefore as real as any other part of her consciousness. In other words, if Laura believed herself to be possessed, then she *was* possessed."

Avril thought of that and shivered, automatically touching the amulet, remembering what she had experienced when she looked at it with too much concentration. She had felt mesmerized, lost in some other world, her spirit roaming freely through time and space to survey infinity's gateway. *What's happening to me?* she thought. *Can I really believe what I seemed to experience? Did I actually hear the voice of Laura Wellman when she cried out in torment?*

And then she dropped her hand, suddenly frightened of touching the amulet, and realizing that the last of her old beliefs were quickly turning to dust.

"This is all too much for me," she said. "I can't handle it right now."

"Understandably," Antonio replied. "Right now you are very, very tired and should be in your bed."

"I am on my way, *Senhor*."

Antonio smiled and pulled her chair back as she moved away from the table. She leaned on the balcony railing, looking down at the dark beach, still unable to grasp what had happened. The city of Rio was sleeping, the sea murmured, the hills were black-faced. She turned away from it, feeling unreal, and saw Antonio's thoughtful face.

"What about you?" she asked. "Are you going to bed?"

"I don't need sleep as much as you two," he replied, "so I'll stay out here a little bit longer and make sure that Father Benedict doesn't play up again."

"You're a very good friend to both of them, Antonio."

"It's just the Brazilian way."

Avril smiled and nodded, then walked into the apartment, going directly to Alex's room and opening the door. He was stretched out on his bed, his hands folded behind his head, his eyes wide and focused on the ceiling as if trying to stare through it. She closed the door quietly, then walked toward him, aware that back in England, even during the war, she would not have been so casual about staying under the same roof with a man, let alone sleeping with him. She and Alex had certainly shared a bed together occasionally (a lot of old rules had been quietly broken during that heady year), but they had never so overtly shared accommodation nor made so clear their relationship; it had always happened in Alex's flat during the early hours of the evening; not once had she stayed overnight or even left after midnight. *Respectability*, she thought. *So necessary to us English. I'm a very long way from that now—and from all I believed in.* . . . She stopped and smiled at him, saw him looking back up, his exceptionally blue eyes illuminated in the circle of light from the lamp by the bed. Yes, they had made love often, but never very successfully, and now, behind the gentleness of his smile, she saw the pain of that knowledge.

"Can't you sleep?"

"I've been waiting for you."

"That's nice," she said.

She sat on the edge of the bed, let him take hold of her hand, turning it over to kiss the back of her wrist and pressing her palm to his cheek. He held her hand there for some time, a mute gesture of affection, then lowered it to his side but kept holding on to it.

"I'm so glad you came back with me," he said. "I couldn't face this alone."

"Is it that painful to be back?"

"Yes," he said. "And right now we're just in Rio. If it's this bad simply being back in Brazil, it'll be much worse in the Amazon."

"Why are you so upset at being in Rio? Nothing happened in Rio."

"I'm upset because Father Benedict's here—and in such a bad way. You can't imagine how much he's changed; how much he's deteriorated. And of course, if he's deteriorated in a physical sense, he's deteriorated in other ways as well. To see someone you remember as being exceptionally sane and bright taking part in one of those rituals . . . well, there isn't much I can say except that it shocked me. No, it was more than merely shocking: it was actually frightening."

"And seeing him must have brought you closer to Laura."

"Yes," he said. "That's true."

Jealousy, Avril thought. *I am jealous. Oh, dear God, how pathetic . . .* and refused to flinch from her own conclusion, despising herself for the truth in it, understanding that no matter the circumstances, human frailty would always win.

"But it's not just Laura," Alex continued. "It's the whole of that horrible time: just being back in this country has reminded me of everything, particularly the slaughter of my father and that pig Rollie Thatcher. Natural justice? Perhaps. They died at the end of their era. They were obliterated by the Indians they had themselves tried to obliterate, and now the mission and the plantation are closed and only the mystery remains. I was a child then, Avril, viewing it through a child's perceptions, most of it heightened and dramatically colored to the stage where it blinded me. And now, no longer a child, I still can't feel like an adult, instead feeling crippled, emotionally and physically, by all that occurred."

Avril knew what he was thinking and understood his pain: they had lain together infrequently, on the narrow bed in his modest room, touching one another like children at play in the darkness. They had wanted to make love, to find fulfillment, but each time he tried to enter her body, his fears had forced him away from her. Inexperience? No, more than that; it was all part of his suffering: he had shivered in the fevers of the fear that had been wrecking him, body and soul. Asleep, he had suffered nightmares—about the Yano Indians and the jungle, about the lights rising and falling over some unseen horror that involved Laura Wellman—but even awake, in Avril's arms, he had suffered from a fear that had no cause but made his shaking limbs ice cold. Now, looking down at his upturned face, Avril shared in his anguish.

"What happens when we make love?" he asked her. "Why can we *not* make love? God knows, I want you so much that my heart races just thinking of it. And yet we can't get satisfaction; we both flounder in pain afterward. When I lie with you, the images fill my head and paralyze me completely: my father and Laura together, silhouetted in that well-lit window; my deliberate brushes with death and the one that nearly killed me; that terrible month in the school in Manaus, my body burning, my mind in turmoil; my return to that awful desolation and the news of the slaughter; and finally, perhaps most crippling of all, the knowledge that Laura's disappearance had seared me more than my father's death. That, more than anything else, seems to haunt me relentlessly."

He had spoken desperately, clearly frightened by his past. She stood up, unable to say a word, and deliberately started to undress. Her blouse fell to the floor, then her skirt, then her underclothes, and eventually she stood naked before him, her vision hazed by the bedside lamp. He stared up at her, almost breathless, and then pulled the bedclothes back, and she crawled into that warm space beside him and let his thin arms enfold her.

She felt ruthless, in command, determined to break down all his fears, not caring that she also felt wanton as her tongue licked his dry lips. His mouth opened to accept her and she pressed her lips on his, twisting her body until her breasts flattened against him and his warmth filtered through to her. She felt his belly, his long legs, a shoulder bone against her own, the slow slide of his tongue down her cheek and around the lobe of her ear. Then she pushed him away, forced him down, and rolled over on top of him.

"Keep your eyes closed," she whispered to him, "and don't say a word."

He did as he was told and then she closed her own eyes, letting her instincts guide her over his body and its lean, trembling hardness. She had never felt him like this before—not this close, not this *real*—and she sensed every nerve in her body coming alive to receive him. There was light behind her closed eyelids, diminishing circles of brightness, receding to become pores in the skin that she could see in her mind. Her fingertips touched him—his heat, his racing heart—and then she traced the rise and fall of his ribcage and pressed her hands on his belly. Yes, his stomach—a man's stomach, unlike a woman's—and she, a mere girl, still struggling to be a woman, explored that alien flesh with tentative fingers, sliding them down through his pubic hair. He responded with a gasp, a light convulsion of his groin, and then she touched him and felt him growing between her fingers as he moved closer to her.

It was darkness and heat, the gradual melting of the self, the sound of quickening breath and beating hearts, of hands sliding on sweating skin. She had started by dominating him, by commanding him to obedience, hoping to break down his fears by stealing his will; but the girl had done that, not the woman she wanted to be, and now, blossoming into that new woman, she felt her own will surrendering. His tongue was licking her aching breasts, his lips sucking her burning nipples, and she found, with dismay, with uncontrollable pleasure, that she wanted to give herself up to whatever he willed for her. He was molding her with his hands, turning her flesh to flowing clay, stroking and squeezing her into something she had not been before: a passive creature, acquiescent, spreading herself in complete surrender, awaiting obliteration or renewal to some new sphere of being.

"Yes!" Alex said. "*Yes!*"

She slowly opened her eyes and saw him staring down at her, his body half leaning across her, propped up on one elbow. His blue eyes, unusually intense, gleamed in the moonlit darkness, and when his face, pale and thoughtful, came down toward her, she closed her own eyes again.

Darkness and heat. His weight flattening her burning breasts. She felt herself opening out to receive him, her lips rising to find him. Something hot and hard touched her, withdrew, returned again, and her body, rising and falling in convulsive spasms, became a pool of sensation; then it slid into her, dividing her and warming her, making her melt and pour all around it while it moved in her hidden depths. Everything that she had been, all her separate parts, became the one, extraordinary, pulsating well of pleasure, raising her up through various levels of passion to pure, limitless feeling. There was sound—her own groan of greed—and only that clung to memory.

"Alex, don't stop!" she begged. "*Never!*"

Her voice humanized her, his name reminding her of herself, returning her to a vague, shifting awareness of their separate bodies. She was lying on her back, legs outspread, knees raised, her arms stretched out languidly behind her head as he fondled her breasts. He was lying between her legs, his full weight pressed upon her, his belly sliding slowly along her belly as he moved in and out of her. She was responding in kind, remotely shocked by her own wantonness, her spine arching involuntarily, her groin shaking and thrusting upward, her legs bending farther back to lock across the blade of his spine. She moved against him and with him, trying to hold on to her senses, losing them and getting them back again and finally losing them totally. She tried telling him—babbling something—lost the power of speech and groaned, felt him very deep inside her, then something pouring up from her center, flooding across her every nerve, that astonishing multitude of sensations, making her soul grieve and sing for joy as the woman emerged in her.

"Yes!" she groaned. "*Yes!*"

And then she felt it in him, also, as he poured himself into her, as the groaning accompanied the spasms that whipped through his body: felt his grief and exultation, his stunned awareness of freedom's slavery, his escape from the prison of childhood to the bonds of commitment. He was leaping out of his fear, vaulting away from his constricting past, joining with her, not only in body but in mind, to find the courage that would help him face the dangers that she sensed were to come. And then he shuddered one last time, his wet lips groaning into her breast, his hands gripping her hip bones as she spasmed and finally settled beneath him.

They lay together in the darkness, one on top of the other, letting the night surround them with the song of its silence, until he, his tears of gratitude on her shoulder, pulled his head back and studied her.

"I love you," he said. "Not Laura: *you*. I know it, but now I'll have to prove it—not only to you, but to myself. So, I'm going all the way: I'm going to follow Laura's footsteps. I'll make Father Benedict come with me and then see what transpires. It's not love that motivates me—it's the nature of my dreams—because until I find out what those dreams mean, I can't be a whole person. I'm going to go deep into the jungle until I find the Yano Indians; once I find them, I'll set myself free once and for all. It's dangerous, but I want you to come with me, because I think you're part of it."

He rolled off her and lay beside her, clasping her fingers in his hand, his face turned to the side to stare at her as she made her decision. She returned his gaze calmly—or at least feigning a certain calmness—trying to accept that she had changed for all time and could never turn back again. She could still feel him inside her, every nerve recording his presence, and her flesh, once a mere shell for her spirit, now thrived on itself. She was glowing inside, almost exalted to be alive, but as she looked directly at him, seeing the radiance of his fresh courage, she instinctively reached up, touched the amulet at her throat, suddenly remembered that dream of Laura, again heard her cries for help, and even as the fear returned, wrapping her tingling skin in ice, she knew that she could not stay here in Rio while he, who had helped her become a woman, ventured into the unknown.

"I'll come with you," she said.

21

Avril first viewed Belém from the window of the airplane, a cluster of white buildings in a great jigsaw puzzle of flat green islets and dense jungle. It was a small city of considerable charm and much humidity sitting on the delta of the Amazon River, its streets, long and straight, all lined with mango trees, forming elegant corridors along which the cooling breezes brought the perfumed fragrances of the nearby tropical forest.

"Now you're in the real Brazil," Alex told her. "The Brazil of forest and river. From here on, we can only travel farther from civilization."

They had arrived directly from Rio that morning, but had only one day to spend here. Now they were having a late breakfast at the Bar da Parque, sitting in the open air on the raised platform that overlooked the Praça da Republica and the busy main road that led down to the dock area. Father Benedict was sipping coffee, his face screwed up in distaste, and Antonio and Alex were sitting on either side of him, with Avril opposite.

She glanced along the tree-lined boulevard, then across the triangular park, observing the shoeshine boys, the pagoda-shaped bandstand, the wooden food stalls that lined the handsome mosaic pavements, the beautifully slim mulatto girls who walked with an open sensuality unknown in staid England—and realized that if Rio had made her feel far from home, this city, with its heat and constant rain and humidity, with its exotic mingling of races and its tropical languor, was truly uprooting her from her past and casting her free from her old self.

"We're meeting him in thirty minutes," Antonio said, "so let's pay up and go."

"Where are we meeting him?" Alex asked.

"At Castle Fort in Ver o Peso. We're having drinks overlooking the market to give Avril a thrill."

He said it jokingly, and Avril appreciated the gesture, but she still felt a little on edge to think of whom they were meeting: a gentleman named John Nicholson, the old friend of Laura's father who had been instrumental in getting her the job with *National Geographic* and was presently working right here in Belém. The meeting had been arranged by Antonio, who had written to Nicholson in New York and had been surprised to get a reply from Brazil. He had written about Laura's disappearance, but had also asked Nicholson to confirm the bizarre background details given by Laura to Alex; Nicholson, in his reply from the offices of the Central Press Agencia, had suggested that they meet him for drinks on their way to Manaus. Now, as Antonio was putting cruzeiros into the waiter's hand, Avril, standing up with the others, could not ignore her own nervousness and realized that what she most feared was the effect that Nicholson's revelations about Laura might have on Alex.

"Right," Antonio said, "let's go. We've still got thirty minutes to spare, so we might as well walk."

Alex reached out to Avril as they walked away from the tables, holding her hand as they went down the steps and stood on the pavement. Father Benedict came down behind them, helped by Antonio, and stood beside them very unsteadily, his bleary eyes squinting into the sunlight, looking across the busy road at the Praça da Republica with its ornate bandstand, grassy mounds, and leafy trees. He shivered, as if shaking off a ghost, and reluctantly crossed the road with them.

"This is senseless," he said, repeating a complaint he had made all morning, rubbing his nose and sniffing repeatedly like an old man with asthma. "Why did I let you talk me into this journey? We're all behaving as if we're mad. We can only find out what we already know: that Laura is dead, that she was killed by the Yano Indians—and we're putting ourselves in danger for no more than that."

"Laura isn't necessarily dead," Alex replied. "And I don't know what kind of danger you're talking about."

"You know *exactly* what I'm talking about. I'm talking about the Yano Indians. The powers of those Indians are far-reaching, and have already affected us. They caused your storm on the beach— they were giving you fair warning—but they'll doubtless manage something much worse if you continue this madness."

"The storm might have been natural," Alex said without anger.

"But even if it *had* been caused by the Yano, I wouldn't turn back."

"And Avril? You will put her in danger, also, by dragging her with us?"

"Alex gave me the choice," Avril said, "and I decided to come. I have my own reasons."

The priest made no reply, but he glanced left and right, and then, with a furtive, greedy expression, at the amulet lying on Avril's throat. She put her hand up to touch it, automatically protecting it, feeling that the priest was about to grab it and run away with it. He didn't, but he stared at it and shivered.

"It's all madness," he muttered.

They were walking along the main road, heading down toward the dock area, the park on one side of them, food stalls on the other, the air smelling of fish, vegetables, and stewing meat, barefoot children and shoeshine boys playing and working around them. Avril kept touching the amulet, remembering the visions it had given her, and suddenly wondering just how far the priest had gone into the depths of its mysteries.

"Why this Nicholson fellow?" the priest asked irritably. "We already know about Laura's past. I seriously doubt that he can add anything new to the subject."

"We don't know that," Alex replied, his voice reflecting his freshly energized appearance. "We don't know if *anything* Laura told us was true, or if she was quite simply mad. Also, according to his letter, John Nicholson was sent by his employers to Belém because they were concerned with Laura's still unexplained disappearance and wanted him to investigate the matter further and submit a report. So he probably knows more than we do about what actually happened during the night of the murders. Anyway, what have we to lose except an hour of our time?"

The priest didn't reply but merely sniffed and glanced around him, as if constantly searching for something that only he knew about. In the daylight he looked frightful, extremely ill and very old, as if the tragedy of what had happened on the plantation had crushed him completely.

Avril stared at him, mystified, unable to understand his anguish, refusing to believe that his guilt over the events that had led up to the murders could account for all that *Angst* and failing health. More baffling, when she could bear to think of it, was the fact that the priest's symptoms were uncomfortably similar to those suffered by

Alex in England—and if Avril could blame Alex's suffering on his former passion for Laura Wellman, she could find no particularly cogent reason for the priest's singular downfall.

"Are you all right?" she asked Alex, feeling a rush of concern for him. "Are you sure you can sit there and listen while that man talks about Laura?"

Alex squeezed her hand and smiled cheerfully at her. "Oh, yes," he said. "After last night, the best night of my life, I can face up to anything."

"You were wonderful last night," she replied. "I can still feel you inside me."

It was true, but that was not enough: there were shadows still remaining: she could not shake off the feeling that Laura Wellman was a threat to them both. Alex had found release last night, making love with a new confidence, and she had responded (and the memory made her blush) by surrendering completely. The experience had exalted her, and she had known, in an almost holy ecstasy, that Alex had felt that also. It had changed him—she could see that: he had the glow of renewed faith—but she still felt endangered by the ghost that had called out of his past.

Antonio shouted and waved at them to follow him and Father Benedict across the wide, busy road. This they did, dodging the traffic, and continued walking toward the docks. They turned left into Rua Alfredo, a long, narrow street filled with open-front shops of all kinds, the buyers and sellers representing many races and creeds, the men in shorts and vests, rubber thongs on their bare feet, the women with loose dresses and turbans, pouring sweat from abundant flesh. It was a noisy, colorful street, but blessed with a cooling breeze, and it eventually led them into the linear Praça Relogio and the port of Ver o Peso on the Bay of Guajara.

Sunlight flashed off the water, numerous boats jostled the wooden jetties, and the fruits of the many market stalls spilled onto the ground, adding a multitude of colors to the already colorful Portuguese mosaic stones: Brazil nuts and berries and mangoes and peaches, pineapples and short, fat bananas, and exotic fruits whose names she did not know—all piled up on the stalls or forming large mounds on the pavements and roads beside the enormous fish that were stacked in soaking heaps, their silvery-gray bodies gleaming wetly in the brilliant noon sun.

Antonio led them around the square, past the stalls, through the hawkers, in the general direction of the raised Castle Fort. Here, in the older part of town, the buildings gave the impression that they were rotting from those relentless alternatives of tropical heat: daily afternoon rain and subsequent humidity. Everywhere on the walls of the baroque and splendid Portuguese architecture posters were peeling, plaster was crumbling, and jagged holes let light shine through the brick, the buildings in general being in an advanced state of decrepitude and disrepair, yet still retaining a seedy elegance with a charm all its own. Antonio led them up some steps to the top of the famous hill; out of breath and beginning to sweat, they arrived at the old gun emplacements on Forte da Castilo, overlooking the full sweep of the bay and the market immediately below.

Behind a rusty iron railing, in an area bounded by the large black guns, was an open-air bar with simple tables and metal chairs. Only about a quarter of the tables were occupied, and at one of them, near the railing, a man stood up and waved to them, obviously recognizing them from the description he had been given: three men and an English girl. When introductions had been made and they all sat down, John Nicholson ordered drinks—Chopp beer for Father Benedict and Antonio, white wine for Avril, Alex, and himself—after which he clasped his hands under his chin with a pleasant smile. He was a tall, slim man, rather elegant, with silvery hair and a well-tanned traveler's face, immaculate in striped shirt and tie, white slacks, and dark blazer.

"It's a humble bar," he said, "but the view is the best in town, and I thought it might make a more pleasant hour than one spent in my office."

"Avril is a stranger to Brazil," Antonio said. "Your choice was excellent."

John Nicholson chuckled and laid his hands on the table, sitting back and looking at everyone in turn, finally letting his gaze rest on Alex, who stared back with calm interest.

"So," Nicholson said, "you're the young man whose father was murdered."

"Yes," Alex said.

There was a very brief silence, during which Alex was almost expressionless. Avril, knowing what he must be feeling, squeezed his hand under the table. He glanced at her and smiled.

"A terrible business," John Nicholson said. "I truly sympathize with you. Terrible, and yet quite aboveboard—or, rather, relatively normal given the area and circumstances."

"Normal?" Avril said, feeling shocked. "Did you say *normal*?"

"I said normal given the area and circumstances. Bear in mind where you are, Avril: this isn't London, it's the Amazon—and the laws here are different, based not on white man's logic but on religion and old tribal customs." The waiter brought the drinks, set them on the table, and departed. "As you know," Nicholson continued, now directing his attention mainly at Alex and Antonio while Father Benedict opened a hip flask and poured something stronger into his beer, "I was sent here by my employers to find out what happened to Laura Wellman. My brief was twofold: one, to find out exactly what had happened to her and, two, to see if there was a usable story behind all this."

"Such being modern publishing," Father Benedict said, his eyes bloodshot but intense, the glass of laced beer hovering in front of his lips, held in a shaky hand. "And . . . ?"

Nicholson shrugged. "I wasn't particularly successful," he said. "I know where Laura went, but don't know whether she's alive or dead. As for the murders, they were vengeance killings, no more and no less, executed in accordance with old Yanoama rituals." He glanced with genuine concern at Alex and asked, "Can you listen to this?"

"Yes," Alex said, but squeezed Avril's hand, his tension rippling up through her veins.

"Okay," Nicholson said, obviously relieved. "As I've already pointed out, the murders were quite normal given the particular area and circumstances. The evidence indicated that the killings had been committed by one person wielding a machete, that person clearly being the young Indian, Mengrire, who disappeared with the girl and Laura Wellman that same night. Your father and Rollie Thatcher had been in the main lounge with the Indian girl, and Mengrire had simply let himself in—as you know, the front door was never locked—and killed first your father and then Rollie Thatcher. The position of the bodies indicated that your father was killed immediately while sitting in his Venetian armchair in the middle of the room; Rollie Thatcher almost immediately after that, doubtless as he attempted to flee from where he had been stretched out on the sofa near the windows. The bodies were then mutilated with a hand knife—we can ignore the precise details—in this case, the weapon being a knife rather than a machete, probably wielded by the Indian girl, the particular form of mutilation showing that it was ritualized vengeance."

"By which you mean," Antonio said, "vengeance for the death of the girl's father and her subsequent sexual exploitation."

"Correct." Nicholson turned to Alex again. "I take it you already know, Alex, that these particular cases were not the first as far as your father was concerned."

"My father's abuse of the Indians was widely known and couldn't be ignored—not even by me."

Nicholson looked relieved, sighing loudly and nodding. Then, with a hesitant smile, he had a sip of wine. He was obviously a decent man, trying to lighten Alex's burden, and Avril felt a certain affection for him.

"It is not very likely," he continued, "that Laura was directly involved in the killings. How she came to go with the fleeing Indians remains a mystery, but it *is* our belief that it was not a case of abduction—they could not have taken her away from the plantation by force. For whatever bizarre reason, she must have gone voluntarily."

"Where?" Father Benedict said, wiping his lips with one hand, and staring at Nicholson over his hip flask with watery, challenging eyes.

"Investigation of the terrain surrounding the plantation reveals that three people—presumably Mengrire, the Indian girl, and Laura Wellman—took a boat along the Rio Negro, discarded it about fifty miles upriver, and then marched north into the jungle toward Catrimani, just south of which is reported to be the province of the Yano. If, as your letter indicated, Laura was obsessed with finding those Indians, it would seem that that's where she went with Mengrire and the girl, both of whom might have hoped to find protection there. In any event, only one person fled with those two—and it had to be Laura."

"What about Peruche?" Alex asked. "Didn't he go with them?"

"No," Nicholson replied emphatically. "That was naturally the immediate assumption, but it proved to be wrong. Every *seringueiro* we talked to confirmed that Peruche had vanished, for reasons unknown, three days before the murders were committed. Nobody saw him go and nobody knows where he went—though the assumption is that he, also, went into the rain forest to return to the Yano as he had, reportedly, said he would do some day."

"That's absolutely true," Alex said. "He told me that he had once been a prisoner of the Yano, that he had escaped, but that he would have to return to them in the future. He didn't say why."

Nicholson nodded. "Anyway, no matter his reasons or ultimate destination, Peruche had nothing whatsoever to do with the murders— and at his age it is unlikely that he would have gotten very far into the jungle at all. We have therefore assumed that he died somewhere deep in the rain forest."

There was silence for a moment, and Avril looked over the railing at the picturesque market scene below. The bay was attractive with the sun beating off it and the fishermen spreading their nets from small, bobbing boats. The confluence of the Guama and Para rivers created a mixture of muddy brown and humus-blackened water. This was the beginning of Alex's world, a strange and alien world. She began to understand why he was different from others his age. Alex and Peruche—the white boy and the old Indian—separated by gulfs of age and experience and yet united in friendship—in a world so far removed from her own that she still couldn't grasp it.

Now, slightly frightened, she looked at John Nicholson and saw Antonio leaning toward him, his face unusually solemn.

"Mr. Nicholson, when I wrote to you in New York, I asked you if the rather colorful details of Laura's past, as related by her, had any basis in reality. Well, were those details true or not?"

"The details were essentially true; the color was probably added by Laura. Regarding the main points: yes, she *was* the daughter of wealthy Hollywood parents—her mother a former actress, her father a producer of some repute—and her mother *was* highly neurotic, very impressionable regarding matters of the occult, and did indeed frequently boast of having spent a night—*one* night—with the Great Beast, Aleister Crowley, sometime during 1915. However, since Crowley, irrespective of his reputed charisma and occult knowledge, was unquestionably something of a charlatan, I think we can take it that Laura was not possessed because of anything that went on between Crowley and Laura's mother that particular night. Nonetheless, my own knowledge of Laura as a child and, later, as a fairly talented photographer in New York, convinces me that if Laura wasn't actually insane, she was certainly on the way to becoming every bit as neurotic as her mother had been; and that if she was not possessed by the forces of darkness, then she was certainly *convinced* that she was obsessed—so much so that it had a dramatically bad effect on her. Her neurosis, instilled in her by her mother and growing stronger as Laura became more emotionally unsettled, particularly during her teens, seemed to have taken her over completely by the time she arrived in New York, shortly after her separation from her husband and estrangement from her father.''

"So you don't think she was genuinely possessed?''

"No, Mr. Bozzano, I don't. What I believe is that Laura was so strongly convinced that she had been possessed, or cursed, that it eventually became the real thing to her, at least in the sense that she began to see signs of it in the most unlikely areas—''

"Such as Pearl Harbor and Hiroshima.''

"Exactly. Her identification with negative or destructive events really began when, as an emotionally insecure teenager with a neurotic mother and uncaring father, she became emotionally involved with an actress who subsequently killed herself. However, I should point out that that affair, much exaggerated in later years by Laura as further proof that she was possessed, was really no more than a passing infatuation on the part of a very insecure teenager for an older, more sophisticated woman, that they were never in fact found in bed together—the physical aspects of the affair were probably all in Laura's rich imagination—and that the actress therefore could not have killed herself because she was found in bed with Laura—a more likely motive was that her career was going downhill and she couldn't bear the thought of aging in anonymity. Given this evidence, should we not then accept that the connections Laura made between her own life and such destructive events as Pearl Harbor and Hiroshima were no more than exaggerated fantasies based on the most tenuous coincidences? The curse existed only in Laura's mind—and because she was always looking for signs of it, she naturally found them everywhere.''

Dark clouds were passing over the sun, heralding the coming of the daily afternoon rain. The slate-gray clouds appeared to Avril uncommonly ominous; her imagination seemed to be running riot, pushing her into a fear that had no solid foundation. Shivering, watching the bright light turning gray, she felt increasingly unreal.

"Do you believe in the occult at all?'' Father Benedict asked John Nicholson, his voice, ravaged by alcohol, sounding aggressive.

"Yes, Father Benedict, I do,'' Nicholson replied. "I am, if I may say so, something of an authority on Brazilian religions and cults— which is why it was within my province to assign Laura to this area. After years of study and investigation, yes, I have certainly come to believe in the remarkable powers of African voodoo and Indian witchcraft. My belief that Laura was *not* possessed in the manner she often recounted has nothing to do with my quite separate belief in unseen forces.''

Father Benedict nodded judiciously, then managed to straighten his shoulders, staring at each of them in turn and pursing his lips. "So," he said, "we might as well go back to Rio. We still don't know precisely what happened to Laura and we can never find out—but we *do* know that the demonic possession was all in her mind. The poor woman was driving herself into madness, and that's all there is to it. Her presence in the Amazon was an accident, no more and no less.''

"Not necessarily so," Alex said, leaning forward, his cheeks starting to show some color, his blue eyes bright again. "According to the Indians, if one believes oneself to be possessed, then one *is* possessed . . . and if one is in that particular state, he or she has opened the way for the forces of darkness to enter. If this is true, then what happened between Laura's mother and Aleister Crowley is irrelevant: what matters is that Laura believed that she was possessed and, in her belief, became exactly what she believed herself to be: a victim of the forces of darkness—a victim and instrument.''

The air was turning moderately chilly, and Avril shivered again, not sure if it was from the afternoon coolness or from the fear creeping over her. She studied Alex carefully, remembering all he had told her: about Peruche, about Laura, about the visions that had joined them all together. *A great ball of fire in the heavens; an umbrella of light.* Both Peruche and Alex had shared that dream—they had dreamed of the atom bomb the day before it fell—and that dream, no matter how tenuously, had connected them to Laura. Alex, as if reading her mind, seemed to echo her thoughts.

"It is my belief," he said, directing his attention at John Nicholson, "that Laura, by simply believing so strongly, conjured up the forces of darkness and was then posessed by them. The night before the atom bomb fell on Hiroshima, I dreamed about a great ball of fire in the heavens; and the old Indian, Peruche, who had had the exact same dream, told me it was a sign that someone was coming to point the way to my future. When Laura arrived—a woman obsessed with that same bomb—I knew that she was, as Peruche had indicated, the one chosen to guide me.''

"Guide you to what?" Nicholson asked.

"I don't know," Alex said.

"Since there is no way of finding out what happened to Laura," Father Benedict intervened, this time speaking in a hurried, breathless manner, "there is no way we can either prove or disprove your theory—which again merely emphasizes the fact that your mission is fruitless."

"It may not be," John Nicholson said. "We may have a witness."

Alex and Father Benedict were obviously startled by the remark, the pair of them sitting up in their chairs as if charged with electricity. They glanced briefly at one another, both flushed and oddly furtive, then returned their attention to John Nicholson.

"I received a cable yesterday," Nicholson said, "from one of my former acquaintances in Manaus, stating that a semideranged Indian girl located in a village in the rain forest could well be the daughter of the *seringueiro* who started the troubles—the girl who fled into the jungle with Mengrire and Laura."

Avril, hearing this, was finally smothered in the fear that had been creeping slowly over her for the past hour. Her heart beat with a dangerous rapidity and her skin seemed to be on fire: she didn't really want to know what had happened to Laura; she wanted no mysteries solved.

"Naturally I can't confirm whether or not this is in fact the actual girl," Nicholson continued, "but apparently the girl in Manaus was found wandering in the rain forest, is presently suffering from severe shock, and babbles a lot about the Yano Indians and a redheaded white woman. The girl is being held in one of the waterfront houses of an *igapo* in the Educandos district. I've drawn the location of the house on this map and I suggest you go find her."

Nicholson passed the small, hand-drawn map over to Antonio, who studied it carefully, then folded it in two and placed it neatly in his wallet. Nicholson sighed, looked at his watch, and said, "Sorry, but I fear my time is up. Is there anything else?"

"No," Antonio said. "You've told us enough to be going on with. We really appreciate it, Mr. Nicholson."

As they all stood up, Avril heard thunder rumbling in the distance and felt the start of the daily afternoon rainfall. She saw the drifting black clouds and saw their shadows on the bay. The thunder rumbled again, the wind blew, the water rippled, and the rain started coming down heavily, splashing noisily around them.

John Nicholson shook hands with each of them and said, "I'll go and pay the bill and then shelter indoors with the bar owner; meanwhile, I think you'd better get a taxi and head for the boat. Given the nature of the Brazilians, it might well leave early. Good-bye—and good luck." He waved his hand and hurried away.

Avril glanced over the railing at the market below. Buyers and sellers were crowding together beneath their stalls while the rain splashed on the sodden fruit, on the alluvial carpets of silvery fish, on the dark, rippling water that rose and fell in languid motions before cascading over the hulls of the numerous boats along the darkening, drenched jetties.

Alex tugged at her hand and smiled. Then she and Alex followed Father Benedict and Antonio down the hill. They were drenched in no time, but caught a taxi close by the market, the four of them crowding together in the back seat. As they wiped rain from their faces, Avril felt the warmth of her body against her wet clothes and knew she would soon dry out. Alex's hand fell on her knee, squeezing it lightly as he smiled at her. The rain was pouring down through gray light, splashing in a glistening tapestry off the walls of the ugly warehouses. The journey to the docks was brief, past the drab, ancient buildings, occasionally allowing glimpses of the bay's rippling, lightflecked water and the gray cumulus clouds above it. Avril wanted to see the forest, the green banks of the *igapos*, but the sheets of rain obscured the far side in a thin veil of drifting spray.

She huddled on the seat, crushed between Alex and Father Benedict, feeling their warmth seeping into her, their bodies pressing in from both sides with an oddly sensual effect. She was flushed, her heart was racing, and her feeling of unreality continued. Suddenly, she was overwhelmed by the presence of Laura, convinced that she was looking out of Laura's eyes at the men on each side of her.

Avril spiraled down into fear, into the bowels of bewilderment, unable to grasp what was happening. She saw the back of the driver's head, then glanced from Alex to Father Benedict to confirm where she was. There was one last burst of thunder, far away, across the river, then a shaft of sunlight dazzled her eyes as the taxi raced on.

Drums? Could she hear drums? The fear formed a scream inside her. She had a vision of Laura outstretched on the jungle floor, a mass of black men crowding around her, the lights rising and falling high above as the drumming, relentless and hypnotic, made the very earth shake. *No!* she thought. *No! I will not submit to this!* She felt her spirit reaching out to the faith she had once left behind her. The drumming: *Please stop it!* Who was she? *Laura Wellman.* No! *I am not Laura Wellman! I'm in a taxi! I'm Avril.* She shuddered and looked sideways, saw Alex, and reached out to him; she held his hand as the drumming filled her ears and the taxi braked to a halt.

Drumming? *What* drumming? She glanced out through the window, fearful of where she might be and what she might see. She saw a multitude of people around her, the docks beyond their heads, the boat at the jetty with the broad expanse of water behind it, a thin green line of forest far away where the *igapos* began. There was a group of Indian drummers near the boat, all playing ferociously, while the passengers, fighting their way through the people trying to sell their wares, climbed the gangplank to the lower deck, burdened down with their cases and boxes, none looking too elegant. The taxi had simply brought her to the Belém docks, and this was perfectly normal.

Avril felt dazed, rubbing her eyes and blinking repeatedly, but Alex tugged her gently from the taxi and pressed his lips to her cheek. She smiled automatically, hardly aware of him, her attention drawn to the crowds all around her as she walked toward the boat. There was the usual diversity of races, the usual ebullient, demonstrative activity, and everyone seemed to be shouting to defeat the sound of the drums. Alex now had his arm around her, holding her close in that dense mass, and she went with him, following Antonio and Father Benedict, her thoughts spinning crazily.

She wasn't sure what was happening but sensed what was causing it: she reached up with a visibly shaking hand and touched the blackstone amulet that lay on the stem of her throat and drew her into its opaque depths. In there was another world, defying all her former beliefs, pitting her against her hidden nature and setting fire to her faith. She felt frightened, disoriented, torn away from her stable roots. The image of Laura Wellman, that ghostly competitor, seemed to be wrapping itself around her more completely with each passing hour.

She glanced at Alex, her love making her spirit leap, but then she turned to see the band playing by the gangplank and her fear, first a chill in the humid air, became ice in her veins. She looked irrationally for the suitcases, wanting something familiar to cling to, knowing that they had been delivered earlier direct from the hotel, but convinced, in her high-strung condition, that something was wrong. The suitcases were there, piled up near the gangplank. Antonio was checking them carefully and giving instructions to the porters while Father Benedict, his face a parchment of pain, took a drink from his hip flask.

Avril felt claustrophobic, imprisoned by the jostling bodies, her head tightening because of the pounding drums and the dancing

Indians' strange singing. Then someone pushed her forward—she assumed it was Alex—and she found herself directly facing the band and one man in particular: a very tall Indian, a carved bone through his nose, liana vines and rodent skins around his forehead, his brown eyes gleaming brilliantly. He stared at the amulet on her throat and then reached out and grabbed it.

"This is not for white women," he said almost incoherently, holding it close to his face and studying it closely. "You must surrender it now or suffer the consequences—which for you might be terrible."

Avril heard herself laughing—a humorless sound—as she slapped the amulet out of the Indian's hand and pressed it back to her throat.

"Go away!" she snapped. "*Damn you!*"

Then she felt the pain and shrieked, jerking her hand off the amulet, realizing that the palm of her hand had been burned and seeing the circle of scorched flesh. Stunned, disbelieving, her heart racing as her fear increased, she tried to turn away from the Indian but felt suddenly paralyzed. She stood there, trembling helplessly, feeling cold in the returning sunlight, her senses scattering with the last of her strength.

"Magic!" the Indian replied. "*You must not have the power!*"

And then the ice fell away, she felt the warmth of the sun, looked down to see the Indian's hand sliding over her throat, then Alex's hand slapping it away as he snapped something in Portuguese. Avril blinked and rubbed her eyes, licked her lips and glanced around her, saw the Indian retreating into the crowd behind the band, and reached up, automatically, her heart lurching, to ensure that the amulet was still hanging around her neck. After she touched it, and feeling the pain in her hand, she realized that it had indeed been burned when the Indian medicine man stared at her.

"Give it up," Alex said, his blue eyes fearful. "Throw that damned thing away!"

"No!" someone replied—her own voice. "It's mine and I'll keep it. *Don't you ever dare touch it!*"

Her own voice? Not at all. Another voice, quite demented, raging with the venom of pure malice from some terrible, unknown place. Avril clapped her hand over her mouth, stepped back, glanced around her, saw Antonio, Father Benedict, and Alex, all shocked, staring at her as if seeing something they had lost.

Then, without another word, the pounding drums filling their silence, they stepped back to let her walk onto the gangplank and lead them up to the boat.

22

The first two days of the journey, upriver to Santarém, started in the grayness of a disturbing dream and led her, with a dreadful inexorability, into a living nightmare. The bad feelings had begun during the taxi ride to the Belém docks and had been deepened by her encounter with the Indian medicine man, and when the boat pulled out, its horn hooting, the crowds cheering, Belém shrinking behind it and the tropical forest coming closer, Avril felt herself sliding deeper into the embrace of an unyielding fear.

Remembering her strange behavior on the dock, shocked at how she had shouted at Alex, convinced that the venomous voice that had come from her had not been her own, she found herself avoiding the others, unable to look at them, and instead spent much time by the railing on the top deck, watching as the boat moved carefully through the narrow, gloomy *igapos* and as the forest, dark and silent, moved in and drooped over the boat.

The *igapos*, or *igarapes*, were the narrow, winding lanes of water formed by the partly submerged equatorial forest; the river wound around the tops of the submerged trees. Branches often actually fell over the boat or formed arches above it, casting their shadows on the deck, and flowers of yellow, mauve, and white fell off them to fill the air with a heavy perfume and form floating gardens between the riverbanks. They were beautiful but ominous, and Avril, opening and closing her scorched hand, could not help but feel threatened by them.

She knew she had changed, that her old beliefs had died, and that now, no matter how much she tried to convince herself otherwise, she could not help but believe in those powers that Alex had talked about frequently. He had once possessed those powers, but had lost them when he lost his faith, surrendering his innocence to Laura and then giving her the amulet that had protected him; now Avril had that same amulet, and had already been affected by it, taking power

from it and losing herself inside it in some strange, frightening
otherworld. As she stood on the top deck, surveying the narrow,
winding *igapos*, watching the chameleons slithering up the treetrunks
and disappearing as if by magic, she rubbed her dazed eyes and felt
that she was losing her senses.

"It's no use hiding," Alex said, coming up to her at the railing.
"This is going to be a seven-day trip, and you can't avoid us that
long. Besides, there's no point. We all know what happened back
there. For a moment you were someone else and didn't know who
we were."

"Who?"

"I don't know—and given the venom in that voice, I don't want
to know."

Avril shuddered to remember it, gazed at the yellow flood water,
imagined herself sinking down into it and finding oblivion. She
knew that what Alex was saying was true but didn't want to admit it.

"Are you suggesting that *I* was possessed?"

"Yes," Alex replied. "The amulet has magical properties, but
they're both positive and negative. You know as well as I do what's
been happening to you."

"Nothing's been happening," she insisted, feeling guilty. "Not a
damned thing."

"Nonsense. Why deny it? We're being haunted and you know it.
First it was me—that was the storm on the beach in Rio—but now,
because you're carrying that amulet, they're concentrating on you."

"Who?"

"The forces of darkness. The forces that brought me back here.
That amulet is a channel from this world to the other, and as long as
you insist on holding on to it, we will all be in danger."

"Rubbish. You're just trying to frighten me. You just want me to
get rid of the amulet, but it's not going to work."

"Why is keeping it that important to you?"

"I don't know. *I just want it!*"

She hurried away, ashamed even as she did so, striding along the
top deck, past the people slinging their hammocks, to the stern of
the boat, where two long tables, serving as bar and kitchen, were
already crowded. The sun was going down, the sky turning charcoal
gray, the boat moving in and out of shadows, its engines making a
muffled roar. Avril wanted to be alone, wanted silence for speculation,
but one look around the top deck told her that that would be
impossible.

The old boat had two decks and was divided into three classes, the upper deck consisting of first-class cabins and first-class hammocks, the lower deck holding the second-class hammocks and most of the cargo. The first-class hammocks on the top deck, all covered in mosquito nets, were slung around the outside walls of the tiny and extremely hot first-class cabins, with passengers already lying in them, or sitting beneath them, and others taking up most of the deck space with their boxes and bags. Avril saw no hope of privacy here and knew that the chance would be even less on the lower deck.

In desperation she had a drink, a *cachaça*, which she had bought at the cookhouse. She sat on some bales of straw and again stared at the forest as it slid past on either side of the boat, beyond the tops of the submerged trees of the *igapos*. The gray light was turning to darkness and the boat's lamps were turned on, casting their yellow glow over the noisily socializing passengers and the water below. The submerged trees looked eerie, the water swirling around their canopies, and the forest on the banks beyond the trees was turning from green to pure black.

She sipped her *cachaça*, touched the amulet, let time pass, heard the chattering of the forest, its constant, loud rustling, and then saw the stars in the sky through breaks in the treetops. Alex joined her again, determined not to leave her alone, and she heard her own voice talking to him as if from far away.

"I feel as if I'm being pursued," she said, "and you feel that as well."

"Yes, I do," Alex said.

"By the spirit of Laura?"

"No, by those who possessed her. We're being haunted by those forces I once viewed as lights over the jungle."

"The lights that rose and fell over that unknown area ruled by the Yano."

"Which is where we are going."

"Why, Alex? What are you really looking for? Do you really believe you're going to find the Yano by going into that jungle? No one has ever gone in there and come out again; what makes us so different?"

"You're wrong: Peruche was once their prisoner—and actually escaped."

"A one-time-only affair that has never been repeated. Even Laura didn't return from that jungle; why should you or I?"

"Because we've been called. Because my nightmares were the

same as Laura's. Because of the supernatural things that have happened since we arrived in Brazil. I've been pulled back here for some purpose. I'm not sure what it is, but I know, because of all that I've told you of Laura, that she's leading the way."

The boat was rounding a hairpin bend, the trees scraping it bow and stern, the branches bending and then whipping back up, sending their leaves flying into the air to rain down again upon the heads of those massed on the deck. The boat appeared to fill the *igarape*, grazing the trees on both sides, and the forest, within reach, actually meeting above her head, was a featureless blackness only broken by the shifting yellow light of the boat and emitting, with a frightening consistency, the jungle's macabre nocturnal chattering.

"I keep thinking the boat won't get through," Avril said. "I never imagined that the river could get so narrow that the trees could touch us on both sides. I keep thinking that some spider or snake is going to fall from the branches."

Alex smiled gently at her. "It often happens," he said. "It's best to keep away from the railing while the forest is this close."

"I thought the river was really wide."

"This isn't really the Amazon, Avril. These *igarapes* wind through the jungle for nearly a hundred miles, but in a few hours we'll reach the river proper where you'll find it's much wider."

"How *much* wider?"

"Up to seven miles. I hope that makes you feel better. And in the meantime, since everyone gets up early, you should try for some sleep."

"I don't really feel like sleeping, Alex."

"Come to bed," he said. "*Please . . .*"

Still thinking of snakes and spiders, she stepped away from the railing and noticed to her surprise that most of the passengers had either climbed into their hammocks or were in the process of doing so. Checking her watch, she was startled to see that it was midnight. A few people were still eating and drinking, their faces bathed in lamplight. Father Benedict was among them, talking drunkenly to a Brazilian, the fingers of one hand around a glass, a bottle of rum on the table.

"Shouldn't you stop him?" Avril said.

"It'll help him sleep," Alex replied. "I'd rather he sat there and got drunk than sneaked off for *epena*."

"Where's Antonio?"

"Almost certainly in bed—which is where we're now going."

He led her back to their cabin, which was as narrow as a tomb, one bunk placed just above the other, the bottom space not much larger than a coffin, the air hot and stifling. Avril felt claustrophobic but said nothing about it, aware that Alex was already disturbed by her recent behavior. He smiled at her, tentatively, as if no longer sure of himself, embraced her, kissed her fully on the lips, and slid his hands down her body. She felt herself responding, her flesh running in rivulets, her fear dissolving into the warmth of her quivering loins as he pulled her close to him. She wanted it—yes, to find oblivion from the fear—but the minute he had undressed her and pulled her down to the lower bunk, she felt that she was being buried alive, suffocating in darkness.

"What's the matter?"

"I'm sorry, Alex, I can't. It's too cramped and hot here."

He looked hurt but let her go. He climbed up to the top bunk while she, unable to offer a comforting word, lay just below him. She closed her eyes and tried to sleep, failed, and opened her eyes again. She looked at the porthole and saw a shirt-covered body pressed to the window. She blinked, looked again, and realized that the body was that of a passenger in a hammock—one of the many strung to the walls of the cabins out there on the top deck.

Her claustrophobia became more acute, making her sweat with discomfort. She closed her eyes again and thought of the priest out there on the open deck. Thinking about him increased her tension and brought a blush to her cheeks, resurrecting the memory of what she had felt in the taxi to Belém: a sensual attraction that had flowed out of her and warmly around her, touching both Alex and Father Benedict and then making them one. She had been shaken by her desire, by its force and ambiguity (ricocheting, as it had, from Alex to Father Benedict, not knowing where to finally lay its head). Now, thinking of the drunken priest out on the deck, she was convinced that in that taxi she had viewed him through Laura's eyes.

The bunk above her creaked as Alex tossed and turned. Avril touched the amulet and slid down through herself; she emerged from a curving tunnel of rushing, light-flecked darkness to that place where the lights rose and fell and the drums made a deafening noise. She was on her back—on her bunk?—no, on the shaking earth, looking up at a patch of stars, at a patch of sky surrounded by faces, all the faces, black and painted, topped with feathers and braided vines, staring down at her stripped and battered body as their hands reached out to her burning flesh. She took a deep breath, swallowing bile, and actually pushed herself up toward them, wanting it to be over quickly, to end and set her free, and then, as her spine curved and her body quivered like a bow, she let out a high, keening wail that reverberated in her ears.

She opened her eyes, staring wildly, terrified by that wail of anguish, and saw a bright light pouring into the dark cabin in wavering striations. She sucked her breath in and held it, remembering the man in the hammock, first thinking that he was shining a torch into the cabin, then realizing that the light, forming a quivering, inverted funnel, was actually splaying out around his body where it filled up the porthole. The man was still asleep in his hammock— and the light was beaming around him.

Petrified, wondering what the light was and only certain that it wasn't natural, she glanced at the bunk above her, desperately hoping that Alex had awakened. She saw no sign of movement and tumbled into a deeper fear. She returned her gaze to the porthole, to the brilliant, wavering funnel of light, rubbed her eyes but could not turn them away, and then felt the vibration. Yes, a vibration, a very fine, consistent sensation, rippling through the mattress, through the wood of the tiny bunk, then through every bone in her body until it made her head tighten. She heard a noise—glass on metal—and that helped her eyes to turn, widening in panic as the glass tumbler containing the toothbrushes bounced off the mirror on the wall and floated gently in thin air.

Avril stared, disbelieving, watching the tumbler float in the air, then saw the toothbrushes drifting away, spiraling gently as they ascended, then watched combs and bars of soap and items of clothing rising slowly and drifting up, or to and fro, in a bizarre, silent ballet.

She let her breath out, then held it in again, her body quivering as the sheets below her made a soft rustling sound and then, as if pulled by invisible strings, billowed up all around her.

"*Oh, Christ!*" she whispered without thinking, jerking upright on the bunk, knocking her head on the base of the bunk above her and closing her eyes from the shock. The light burned through her closed eyelids, her whole body was vibrating, she heard the silence—yes, *she heard the silence*—and then, just as the fear tightened her stomach and throat, the vibrating stopped, she heard things dropping all around her, and her closed eyelids went dark.

She opened her eyes and saw the porthole framing that portion of someone's body, glanced down through the darkness, the light no longer present, and saw the tumbler and toothbrushes and items of clothing lying there on the floor. The cabin was quiet—really quiet—except for the sound of breathing, and she realized, as she managed to control herself, that Alex had slept through it all.

Through what? What had happened? She shuddered and breathed deeply, feeling the fear, insulted by it; then, remembering the light, wondering what it had been, aware that it had emanated from the deck outside the cabin—not too far from the dining tables where Father Benedict had been drinking—she swung her legs off the bunk, stood up and hurriedly dressed, checked that Alex, still sleeping, was all right, and then left the cabin, closing the door quietly behind her and looking along the quiet deck.

She was at the wrong side of the cabins—the light had shone on the port side—and she stood there for a moment, trying to gather her courage, and then walked toward the stern of the boat, toward the area used for eating and drinking, passing the other cabins with the hammocks slung up outside them, the passengers all apparently sleeping, their belongings piled up below them. It was a very short walk, but it seemed to take forever, giving her time to notice that the boat had left the narrow *igapos* and was traveling into a broad expanse of still, moonlit water, the river banks far away on either side, the sky above clear and starry. The boat was moving very slowly, navigating the darkness with care, and the muffled, bass growling of its engine was the only sound in an oddly vibrant silence. Avril still felt frightened, her heart racing, her throat tight, but she forced herself around the end of the cabins and stepped into the almost deserted dining area.

Almost deserted, but not quite: Father Benedict was at one of the tables, pouring himself a drink, his face a picture of terror and despair, his whole body shaking.

"Father Benedict! What . . . ?"

"Did you see it? Oh, my God, child, did you see it? Did you see that accursed light?"

Avril followed his wandering gaze—down at the water, up at the stars—and then, seeing nothing, but forced to wipe sweat from her brow, looked back along the deck, along the port side where her cabin was situated, and saw nothing but another long line of hammocks and the piles of luggage beneath them. Letting her breath out, the sheer relief making her weak, she looked back at the priest who was waving one hand, indicating the still, moonlit river and the black line of forest over two miles away.

"It came from over there," he said. "At least I think it came from there. It seemed to materialize from that direction, but I couldn't be sure of that. Then it was hovering right above me, about fifty feet up—up there," and he pointed directly over his head, "right over the cabins."

He stared at her, his wide eyes reflecting the moonlight and looking like burnished stones.

"It was a light," he continued. "A single ball of light. It was blindingly bright but had a dark inner core, and the light seemed to be spinning around that core and sucking the air up. Yes, it took my breath away, scorched my lungs and left me gasping, and then it dropped lower, and glided straight along that deck, and stopped, hovering as if by magic, at one of those hammocks. It just hovered there, very bright, spinning rapidly and silently, shining its light around the man in the hammock and into the cabin, presumably your cabin. Then, like a flashlight being turned off, it just disappeared."

The boat was in the Amazon proper, and the river was wide, more like a lake than a river, both banks miles away. Still frightened, Avril studied it, her fear increasing at what she saw: that enormous expanse of perfectly black, moonlit water, fringed with black jungle and covered in the vast bowl of the starry sky. The boat was still traveling slowly, its engines comfortably muffled; the river was perfectly quiet and disturbingly eerie.

"That light seemed to be alive," the priest said, "to know what it was doing, and apart from sucking the air out of my lungs, it paralyzed me with terror. *But it knew what it was doing!* It was some form of being. And as it examined your cabin, as it hovered outside the porthole, I suddenly realized that it looked just like one of those strange lights that rise and fall over the rain forest when the Yano drums start to play. Yes, Avril, it was one of those lights—*and it came here to find us!*"

Avril knew what he was feeling, remembering her terror in the cabin, the fear gradually trickling away but leaving her shaken. The boat was pushing patiently against the current, the river splashing and rippling, its black surface reflecting striations of moonlight and the large, pearly moon.

"I saw it shining into my cabin," she said, "but didn't know what it was. Strange things started to happen in the cabin: objects rising and falling."

"Yes," Father Benedict replied, "rising and falling . . . like those lights in the jungle." He drank some *cachaça*, his hand visibly shaking, licked his lips and brushed the white hair from his forehead, and then rubbed his bloodshot eyes. "The forces of darkness," he said. "Just as Peruche described them: the forces of darkness as lights in the sky, rising and falling. . . . Yes, they know we're coming, why we're coming, what we want, and from now on they won't give us peace unless we turn back."

"Alex won't turn back," Avril said.

"I know that. God help us."

Listening to him, Avril finally understood fully that Father Benedict had come to believe in the reality of dark forces and the occult power of the Yano Indians. He was almost certainly blaming both for what he had himself become in his alcoholic, sometimes drugged condition: a man obsessed with the nature of the "otherworld" to which Laura had fled. A man who had gambled with his life—as he had been doing in the ritual in Rio; a man who had gambled with his very soul. Now, thinking about that ritual in Rio, she asked the question she had not dared ask before.

"Why were you taking part in those rituals, Father Benedict? Was it some kind of penance?"

"Yes," the priest replied, now too drunk to bother denying it. "I suppose I hoped that by letting myself be used in those blasphemous rituals, by challenging the forces of darkness to strike me down or possess me, I would be casting myself beyond the reach of God, thus paying penance with eternal damnation for what I had done."

"But that's what puzzles me," Avril said, sitting down facing him. "You behave like a man shouldering enormous guilt—and I can't work out why. Can you *really* blame yourself for what happened on the plantation when you know that what Alex's father was doing could not be prevented? From what Alex told me, you berated Frank Poulson many times, but received no help from the Manaus authorities when you tried to do more than that. Given that, I can't see how you can suffer so much for what finally happened. It must have been something else, Father Benedict—not the murders nor Laura's disappearance—something other than that."

The priest shuddered and turned away. "Yes," he said, "it was something else. Of *course* it was something else! It was the greatest of my many secret sins . . . my most lasting and scourging shame."

"*What* sin, Father Benedict?"

The priest looked left and right, obviously frightened of the light returning. He shuddered again, had another drink, and stared at her with haunted eyes.

"The betrayal of faith," he said. "That and rank hypocrisy. What happened on the plantation, if hideous and tragic in its own right, merely served to accentuate the extent of my dishonesty and my lack of faith. Oh, yes, I lacked faith—and had lacked it for years—never knowing if I was truly meant to be a priest and always questioning His nature. God's nature—and my own: for all my piety, I was filled with lust, and once, in an aboriginal station in the north of Australia, I almost lay in sin with an ignorant native girl who, having lost one of her arms, was easily exploited. Do you understand, my child? My secret desires were my crown of thorns. Preaching virtue, I yearned for vice; condemning sin, I flirted with it; and all the time, even worse, was the knowledge that when I preached the gospel, I was in truth questioning every word and doubting His divine nature."

Avril glanced across the river, her eyes drawn to the distant jungle, the dense forest merely a thin line of deeper blackness between the vitreous, black water and the dark, star-flecked, moonlit sky.

"Yes," the priest said, "in doubting myself, I doubted Him, refusing to accept that imperfection could be part of His nature. And that girl with one arm: for years her beauty would haunt me, a symbol of life's ironic cruelties and indifference to suffering. Had He created this world? If so, He had created its cruelties, including in His grand design the anguished cry of man's suffering: murder and rape and pillage and torture and death. Yes, this was life, the boundless nightmare of our history, and if I clung to my beliefs, not in peace but in desperation, I was stripped of my final illusions of faith during the war in New Guinea."

He closed his eyes and lowered his head. Pressing his temples with his fingers, he shuddered and took a deep breath, remembering what he had buried.

"My regiment recaptured a native village that had been held by the Japanese," he intoned, "and found nothing but the remains of burning huts and complete, hideous carnage. Every man, woman, and child had been killed in an orgy of violence. Oh, God, what a sight! I will never forget it! And from that day on I lived with the conviction that either God did not exist or, if He did, He was either impotent against the power of evil or was Himself its creator. So it was that when I came to the Amazon I was nothing but a pretender, outwardly living the life of a man of God, but truly doubting His ultimate nature and my own hold on virtue."

The large, yellow moon, reflected in the black water, appeared to be gliding just under its surface like some bright, shiny disk. Avril thought of the strange light that had hovered just outside the porthole, and shivered, remembering the lights that rose and fell in her vile, vivid nightmares. Again frightened by that vast, silent river, she returned her gaze to the priest.

"Yes," he said, "my hold on virtue, always tenuous at best, became, in the Amazon, no more than a pitiful pretense. I had the most licentious dreams, and during the day felt lust constantly, rarely able to look at a woman without secretly wanting her. Even the Indian girl, Mengrire's girl, that unfortunate victim and avenger— even she, in the innocence of her flirtations, was able to arouse my desire to the point where it blinded me. No reason for my guilt? I think that reason enough. There I was, in my hypocrisy, loudly condemning Frank Poulson's lechery, when in fact I had lusted after the very girl he so blatantly abused. Yes, my child, I was guilty—of lustful thoughts and hypocrisy—and then, when Laura Wellman arrived in the Amazon, those sins which already were tormenting me became even more grave."

Before going on, Father Benedict looked all around him, first along the chugging boat, then down at the rippling water, then in both directions across the river and up at the sky. The moon was bright and beautiful, the stars glittering, but thankfully there was no sign of that mysterious light which had come out of nowhere.

"So, my child," he continued, "I lusted for women and material things—and when Laura Wellman arrived at the mission, I began lusting for her. Yes, from the moment she set foot on the docks of Manaus—and irrespective of the fact that my good friend, Father Symonds, had tragically dropped dead from a heart attack—I was, just like Alex, bedazzled by her exceptional beauty, and so reminded once more that my clerical collar had not robbed me of my physical desires and relentless male vanity."

Avril sat up on her bench, trying to keep her face composed, slightly shocked, but also quite touched, by what she was hearing. She glanced all around her, helplessly searching for that mysterious light, but saw only the broad, moonlit river flowing in the opposite direction from the boat and disappearing in darkness. Then, leaning her elbows on the table, she studied the bleary-eyed priest, recognizing that even in his dissolute state he was impressively handsome.

"You've really surprised me," she said. "That's the last thing I was expecting. Alex told me that you didn't like Laura much and were often rude to her."

"Yes," the priest replied, "I was rude to Laura Wellman—but not for the reasons that Alex, in his innocence, supposed. The truth of the matter is that I very soon found myself wanting Laura with constant, tormenting hunger, and for obvious reasons, was frightened of showing it. So I was rude, sometimes distant, often angry, the anger stemming not only from her eccentric words and deeds but also from my own increasing frustration and hypocritical behavior. I suffered enormous guilt and shame—not only because of what I was feeling, but because I knew that Alex was infatuated with her in the most painful manner. My guilt, then, was horrendous, torturing me night and day, and was made even worse when I realized that now when I fought with Alex's father about his mistreatment of Alex or the Indians I could no longer be sure if I was arguing from genuine conviction or simply because I resented his sexual freedom with Laura. In short, I was in a quagmire of moral ambiguity and could no longer believe even my own words."

"So when you tried to talk Alex out of his infatuation for Laura, telling him that it would come to no good, you were actually only thinking of yourself?"

"No, I wasn't that bad—bad enough, but not that bad. I loved Alex like my own and was genuinely concerned for him, convinced that his passion for Laura could lead only to rejection and pain, and equally convinced that the differences in their ages would make such a rejection inevitable. When I spoke to him, I truly spoke from the heart—and repeated the same warnings to Laura, entreating her as someone much older and more mature to respond to Alex's adolescent infatuation with caution and to discourage him without causing too much pain."

"And all the time, when Alex was in love with her, you also wanted her, and felt that by even thinking that way you were betraying his friendship."

"Yes," Father Benedict said, his voice now almost a whisper, difficult to hear over the chugging of the boat's engine and the whipping of wind. "Oh, of course I tried to stop it, to kill that feeling in myself, but working in the mission, with Laura there night and day, I was naturally in daily contact with her and forced, whether I wanted it or not, to spend a great deal of time with her. Yes, I fell under her spell, wanting her and worrying about her, and soon found myself obsessed with her own unhealthy conviction that she had been possessed and had to go into the jungle to find the Yano and brave the forces of darkness. So I was drawn into her web and couldn't get out, trapped there as surely as Alex and wondering how it would end. Then, when Laura sent her letter of resignation to her employers and moved into Frank Poulson's plantation—and when I thought of Alex's infatuation and his father's licentious reputation—I was convinced that the worst of my fears would come true in a very short time . . . convinced, but unable to do anything about it, since I was paralyzed, both morally and mentally, by my own desire for her.''

There were tears in the priest's eyes. He sniffed and wiped them away, then poured some more *cachaça* into his glass and drank it dangerously fast. Breathing deeply, returning the glass to the table, he looked back at Avril.

"The betrayal of faith," he repeated. "I believe I mentioned that before. What I meant was the betrayal of my remaining faith in God and, perhaps more disgusting, the betrayal, even if only in my thoughts, of my friendship with Alex."

"Did you ever tell Laura what you felt for her?"

"Absolutely not. Never."

His voice trailed away into silence, leaving only the boat's rumbling noise, and then he shook his head vaguely from side to side and again glanced all around him. Scanning the river and sky, then examining both sides of the deck, he looked like a fugitive from justice, disheveled and fearful.

"Sleep," he said. "I've talked too much already. Where's Antonio Bozzano?"

"Sleeping in his cabin," Avril said. "Do you know where it is?"

"Yes, child, I do."

He walked away very quickly, not saying another word, showing clear signs of embarrassment on top of his fear. Avril watched him go, his feet ringing on the wooden deck; he passed three or four of the mosquito-netted hammocks and then turned left into the tiny corridor that led to his cabin. She stood up, planning to return to her own cabin, but when she took a step forward, the fear swooped down and grabbed her.

She stood there for some time, breathing deeply, controlling herself, looking around the boat, across to the jungle, down at the water, up at the glittering tapestry of the sky, and then along the great river. There was nothing—no lights—she was alone near the stern, but instead of going back to her cabin she curled up on a bench. The bench shook beneath her, the sound of the engine was comforting, and she lay there, the river breeze blowing across her, cooling the sweat on her face.

She slept without dreams and awakened surprised to find herself surrounded by people already waiting for breakfast. That day passed in a silvery haze, the sun high and fiercely hot, its brilliant light reflecting off the river and burning into her tired eyes. She talked to Alex and Antonio, had lunch, talked some more, and then realized that Father Benedict was avoiding her with a criminal's cunning. She understood his embarrassment—or at least tried to understand—but something about his determination to avoid her filled her with the conviction that "embarrassment" was too mild a word for it.

Nursing a drink, she studied the river in the brilliant light of day and saw the jungle more clearly. The forest came right to the river's edge, its trees enormous and dense, the two banks about five miles apart and curving away in the distance. Both banks were dotted with houses on stilts, with palm-leaf hovels and wooden jetties; then there were flat-topped mountains and small groups of stucco houses, and the boat docked at a small town called Monte Alegre. Some passengers left and others came on, natives came on board to sell their various wares—salted fish and fruit, snake skins and crocodile leather, Brazil nuts and rubber and jute. The boat took on supplies and gasoline and, as the sun began to set, headed upriver again.

Darkness came quickly, bringing with it the fear, and Avril, trying to forget the priest hiding up near the prow, sat at the tables near the stern and drank a considerable amount of *cachaça* with Antonio and Alex. The boat was closer to the jungle now; she heard the forest chattering and rustling and occasionally saw an alligator gliding through the black water where the wavering yellow beams of the boat's lights rose and fell with the current.

It was beautiful—and frightening—and her fear increased each minute, until, when midnight came, when most of the passengers had gone to sleep, when Antonio left for his cabin and Alex invited her to do the same, she refused, saying it was too hot in there and that she wanted to sleep out in the fresh air, as she had done the night before. Alex looked confused and wounded, but he shrugged and left her there. When he had gone, when she had unsuccessfully looked for Father Benedict, she shivered and curled up on the bench and stared into the darkness.

The light came from the jungle, flying out of the black trees, a pinprick of yellow that grew larger and became a silvery disk. It skimmed across the river, not moving very fast, almost gliding as it flew in a straight line, heading toward her. She sucked her breath in and held it, too frightened to breathe, finally gasping as she let her breath out. The light continued moving toward her, seeming to spin as it flew forward, its brilliance illuminating the black water in a great shifting circle. It made no sound at all, but kept spinning as it rushed forward; then, becoming an enormous, flaring cartwheel, it hovered over her head.

It took Avril's breath away, scorched her lungs and left her gasping, and she lay there, too terrified too move, too fascinated to close her eyes. It was a single ball of light—not solid: like burning gas—its outer reaches swirling around a darker core that seemed slightly opaque. She didn't know how wide it was—its edges disappeared into the darkness—but its dark center looked like the pupil of a great, staring eye.

Avril opened her mouth to scream, tasted scorched air, and gasped for breath. The light dropped down lower, swirling rapidly and vibrating, its striations forming an umbrella around her and temporarily blinding her. She closed her eyes and tried to scream, kept trying to scream as reality dissolved, and then she tumbled down through herself, through the well of terror that was her spirit, and then just as suddenly flew up again and broke through her own surface. She opened her eyes and saw the light, a flaring whiteness directly above her. Then it blinked out and darkness rushed back and let the stars shine upon her.

Avril lay there in a trance, hardly knowing where she was, only aware of drifting stars in a dark sky that went on forever. She lay there all night, her body shaking as if with fever. Only in the dawn light, when the stars had faded away, when the warmth of the new day started filtering through her chilled bones and the first of the early risers had emerged on the open deck, only then did she manage to sit upright and take control of herself. She was sitting there, drinking coffee, talking casually to some other passengers, when Alex, Antonio, and Father Benedict arrived to have breakfast.

She had to disguise her great relief when the boat docked at Santarém.

23

The fever returned just as Avril stepped off the gangplank; she broke out in a sweat and felt slightly nauseated. She was not helped by the heat, which increased rapidly as the sun ascended and blazed with unwavering brilliance. Santarém was a small, haphazard town, its waterfront littered with shacks on stilts; sturdier houses, faced with Portuguese tiles, stood on the slope that rose up from the river. Situated at the juncture of the Tapajós River with the Amazon, the town overlooked a yellow river that was mottled with greenish patches, giving it a leprous effect that was none too attractive. Avril glanced at it briefly, then turned away, her stomach heaving, and saw Alex reaching out tentatively to take hold of her hand.

"Are you all right?" he asked. "You don't look too good."

"I'm fine. I'm just tired."

"That's what happens when you sleep out on the deck: all that wonderful fresh air keeps you awake."

She smiled but felt awful, her body sticky with sweat and weak, her head tight and her stomach upset, a clammy fear hanging over her. She was being surrounded by the locals, most trying to sell their handicrafts, some with parrots on their shoulders, others displaying items of pottery, most of it speckled with designs of frogs and serpents, when she saw Antonio and Father Benedict outside the crowd. Antonio waved his hand at her while the priest just stood there, his face corpse-gray, his eyes glazed with exhaustion.

"Actually," she said to Alex, "I feel a bit off-color and could do with a lie-down. Where's the hotel?"

"It's a waterfront hotel," Alex replied, "just a few minutes' walk from here. Just how bad do you feel? Is it your stomach or what?"

"That's it," she replied, reassuring him with a lie. "It's just my stomach—it's not too fit today—but it's nothing to worry about."

"Something you ate?"

"Yes, that plate of *pato no tucupi* that I had yesterday."

"Ah, yes, that's a risky one."

He slid his hand up to her elbow and guided her through the crowd, following Antonio and Father Benedict up the slope toward the shacks on tall stilts. Avril saw the lines of laundry, the small verandahs high above her, the faces of the inhabitants, African, Indian, and Portuguese, gazing down from beneath the palm-thatch roofs over which, with a languid, seductive beauty, some white clouds were drifting.

The sunlight hurt her eyes, and she rubbed at them and looked ahead, the fear returning when she noticed the back of Father Benedict and remembered that mysterious light that had so terrified the both of them. Only now did Avril understand why: when it had hovered above her, spinning around its dark inner core, it had appeared to be an enormous, unblinking eye, hypnotic and pitiless.

Yes, it had paralyzed her and had seemed to resonate in her brain, convincing her that the silence was actually speaking in some magical manner. The ball of light had not been solid—she had seen the stars above it—but had in fact looked incorporeal, devoid of dimensions. Now walking up the hill, passing the soaring stilts of the waterfront shacks, with Alex by her side and Antonio and Father Benedict just ahead, she shivered and tried to shake from her head one frightening image: a consciousness manifesting itself from darkness and taking the form it required: an immense, searching eye.

Alex led her around a corner, turning right behind the waterfront, and then along a crude, busy street to the front of the hotel where, to Avril's relief, they were to spend a day and a night before continuing upriver to the port of Manaus.

"It's not much of a hotel," Alex said with a grin. "It's more of a primitive guesthouse, I suppose, but good enough for one night. At least you'll have a proper bed to sleep on—and you won't feel as suffocated as you do in the cabin."

The hotel was indeed primitive, being no more than a large house, its floor raised up on stilts, its roof thatched above wooden beams, the ventilation supplied by the open windows and slow-spinning fans, all of which made a constant squeaking sound but at least kept the moist air on the move.

There was no real lobby, just a lounge leading off to the rooms, and being small it gave Father Benedict no chance to avoid her. Today he looked ghastly, even more ravaged than before. As Antonio signed them in, Alex leaning across his shoulder, Avril tried to catch the priest's gaze, with little success: he examined the floor, then the fan whirring above him, then the Indian woman who was brushing giant ants off the steps; finally, almost defiantly, he took his hip flask from his pocket, unscrewed it, had a long drink, and then put it away again. Only then—just that once—did he glance at her, but his eyes were like mirrors, reflecting the fear that she, also, could not escape.

Having signed the tattered register, Alex and Antonio turned toward her, the former simply smiling with affection, the latter studying her carefully. She felt uncomfortable, wondering what Antonio had guessed, and nervously lit a cigarette.

"If your stomach's upset, that won't help," Alex said. "In fact, it might make it worse."

"I don't care," she replied, her voice edgy. "I just feel like a smoke."

"So," Antonio said, smiling broadly to ease the tension and, with a knowing touch of diplomacy, turning his attention to the puzzled Alex, "I think I will go and explore Santarém. What are your plans?"

"I think Avril should sleep," Alex said, "and then, if she feels a bit better, try to eat something tonight when we all meet for dinner."

"At eight?"

"That sounds fine, Antonio."

"See you then, my young friends."

Avril was glad when they parted, each going to their separate rooms, Antonio and Father Benedict each taking a single room, she and Alex sharing a double overlooking the river. It was a large room, plain and functional, matted carpets on the timber floor, the bed truly enormous and covered with taut white sheets, flanked by old mahogany cupboards and brass-based oil lamps. Giant cockroaches crossed the floor, enormous ants hurried over the cupboards, bloated flies buzzed in frustration beneath the fan as it made the air spin. She walked across to the window, saw more insects on the mesh wire, and looked through it across the green-stained yellow water to the far side's dense forest. There were floating shops and fishing boats on the river, casting very short shadows; the sun was almost directly overhead, turning the water to polished glass.

"Is the room all right?" Alex asked from just behind her.

"Yes," she said. "Fine."

She didn't know what else to say, so she turned around and faced him, letting him slide his arms about her and press his lips to her forehead. She shuddered and held him tight, writhing against him with sudden passion, wanting to lose herself in his embrace and let him crush the life from her.

"Oh, God!" she groaned. "Christ!"

And immediately felt ill again, the nausea rising to her throat, the fear impelling her out of his arms and across the room to the large bed. She fell onto it, face down, not bothering to remove her clothes, then rolled over until she was on her back and staring up at his pale face. He looked terribly wounded, but also bewildered, instinctively sensing that she had shivered with revulsion, trying to understand why. She wanted to tell him and tried to smile, but then the sunlight hurt her eyes, pouring in through the window behind him, spreading out like a fan, and dissolving him in silvery striations that framed a shimmering haze.

She closed her eyes and drifted away, lying just below sleep's surface, aware that her body lay on the bed while she roamed through her mind. She saw Alex kissing her forehead, his blue eyes close to tears, then he sighed and walked out of the room, closing the door very quietly. She was there and not there—on the bed, outside herself—and she wandered through the thickets of her own thoughts to get at the truth. The fear was still present, almost palpable, permeating her, but then she entered the priest's room, hovering just above his bed, and gazed upon him as he tossed and turned in sleep, his face pale and terribly lined, the skin almost translucent, as if his skull were being illuminated from within, letting the bones have dominion.

Father Benedict was a tortured man, his anguish eating him alive, but Avril knew, in her troubled thoughts, that what he had told her was not the answer, that it was at least incomplete, and that his secret desire for Laura Wellman, his great temptation and torment, could not alone account for the hell which he was putting himself through. No, it was something else, something infinitely more shocking, some sin which went beyond mere desire and scorched the roots of his soul. The priest groaned in his restless sleep, tossed and turned on the bed, and Avril, drifting away through a bright, shimmering haze, understood with a fierce, unwavering certainty that his buried truth was a nightmare.

Was she sleeping? She wasn't sure. She remembered Alex leaving the room. She tried to open her eyes but was blinded by a brilliant light that poured out of the inverted bowl of the sky and made her feel dizzy. Santarém was a jungle town, the river before it, the forest around it, the trees soaring above the houses on stilts and the

open-front shops. She saw Alex wandering through it, trying forlornly to pass the time, looking over the mighty Amazon, here a
patchwork of green and yellow, and thinking of the humus-darkened
Rio Negro to which they were heading. She joined him, *became*
him, felt what he was feeling as, surveying the river, watching the
fishermen cast their nets out, he was reminded of those similar sights
which had colored his childhood along the banks of the expansive,
black river which passed the plantation.

Yes, the plantation, his whole world for eighteen years, a world
so removed from the normal that it now seemed unreal: his father,
Rollie Thatcher, all those nights spent in that awful room, old
Peruche, squatting in front of his modest hut by the *verzea* lake,
offering magic and the promise of transcendence to the peace of the
other world. And then Laura, her stunning beauty, stigmatized by
neurosis or insight, leading him to the brink of madness, the others
to slaughter and flight, lowering the curtain, in the innocence of her
convictions, on the dying plantation.

Now Alex was going back there, following Laura's spiritual trail,
and each day, as he drew closer, as the jungle became more dense,
as he watched Father Benedict suffering and wondered what was
causing his pain, he felt the weight of what had been done creeping
back to torment him. Being him, Avril knew this, felt it eating at her
insides, but then, as the sun flashed off the water, she returned to
herself.

"Avril! *Avril!* Wake up! You're just having a bad dream!"

She awakened, groaning fearfully, Alex holding her waving hands,
trying to stop her from hurting herself as she tossed and turned on
the bed. The sun was shining no longer, the pale light came from the
oil lamps, and the fan in the ceiling, just above Alex's head, was
squeaking with aggravating insistence as its blades, turning slowly
and steadily, cast long black shadows on the walls where chameleons,
with a speed that made her blink, raced back and forth.

"What?" she cried. "*No!*"

Alex shook her awake, then calmed her down, holding her tightly,
and she felt his ribs through his thin shirt, her fingers pressing him
urgently. Her heart was beating fast, her skin was sticky with sweat,
and she realized that she had slept all afternoon, having the most
vivid dreams. Eventually, when her heart calmed down, she slumped
back against the headrest, studied Alex, noted the anxiety on his
delicate good looks, and forced herself to smile at him, not wanting
him to know just how frightened and haunted she felt.

"Oh. dear," she said. "bad dreams! I should never sleep in the daytime."

"You've been sleeping for six hours," he replied. "It's now seven thirty."

He was smiling. but his eyes were puzzled, as if he didn't quite know what was happening, and Avril, remembering the strange light—and the vivid dreams that had started haunting her—felt the need to protect him as much as possible from what she sensed might be coming: some truth which would not spring from magic but from Father Benedict's buried past.

"Lord!" she said. trying to sound as normal as possible, ashamed of her false smile. "I better have a very quick bath and get myself dressed."

"You won't find a bath here," Alex said, returning her smile, "but you *will* find a rather primitive shower just outside the room."

"I can brave that," she said.

The shower was indeed primitive, both taps offering lukewarm water, but it helped wake her up and feel more refreshed. She put on a simple dress, flat shoes, and a simple necklace, combed her hair, and applied a little lipstick but no other make-up. Alex watched her the whole time, sitting under the squeaking fan, his blond hair tumbling over his forehead, his collar fluttering a little; he didn't say a word, but she sensed his anxiety and was glad when they could leave the dimly lit room and join the others at the table in a small lounge overlooking the river.

Outside it was dark, the moon reflected in the water, candles flickering from the porches of the houses on the slope just below them. Avril glanced at the river and shivered, remembering the light above the boat, then stared at Father Benedict and saw that his condition hadn't changed. He had obviously been drinking and was looking quite ghastly, his face haggard, his eyes bloodshot and unfocused, his right hand shaking when he picked up his fork or, as he did more frequently, raised a glass of red wine to his lips. It was an uncomfortable dinner, with many strained silences. Finally. after too many attempts to lighten the evening, Antonio, glancing first at Avril and then at Father Benedict, sighed loudly and folded his hands under his chin.

"I've been watching you two," he said, "and you've been acting very strangely. There's something going on that Alex and I are aware of. What has happened?"

Father Benedict had just been having another drink of wine.

Hearing Antonio's question, he wiped his lips with the back of one hand, put the glass back on the table, and stared directly at Avril.

"Well," he said, "shall you tell him or shall I? Or are we keeping it secret?"

"There's nothing to tell," she heard herself saying, as she glanced appealingly at Alex, not wanting him to know that she felt that Laura was calling out to her. "We just saw a strange light over the boat and didn't know what it was."

"A *strange* light?" Antonio said.

"Yes, Antonio, a strange light. It looked like a ball of burning gas—and probably *was* something like that."

Suddenly outraged, Father Benedict slammed his open hand down on the table, making the plates and glasses rattle, forcing them all to look at him.

"Damn you, woman!" he exclaimed. "Why not tell the truth? We did *not* see a ball of burning gas, and you bloody well know it! We saw something unexplainable—something unearthly but controlled—a globe of spinning light that resembled an enormous eye and flew quite deliberately out of the jungle to hover right over us. It terrified the both of us, it sucked the breath from our lungs, and it looked just like those lights that rise and fall where the Yano are said to be. A ball of burning gas? Then why are you frightened, Avril? Damn it, *tell them the truth!*"

His hand slapped the table again, making everything rattle, while he remained there, leaning very far forward, glaring ferociously and trembling. Then Avril heard her own voice, startlingly angry and even venomous, bursting from her lips before she could stop it.

"*What* truth, Father Benedict? That a ball of light frightened us? What else can I say about what happened, except that we saw it? It could have been marsh gas, some reflection . . . *it could have been anything!*"

"That's ridiculous and you know it! That light searched for us and found us! That light—that thing, whatever it was—came to frighten us off! We're all trying to challenge the forces of darkness and we won't get away with it. We have to turn back—*turn back now*—before it's too late!"

"No!" Avril replied, slightly shocked by her own bitterness. "*We* don't have to turn back. You *want* us to turn back because there's something you're frightened of facing. It's *you* they're hunting—not us!"

The priest seemed to freeze at that, his body tightening like a bowstring, and he stared at Avril as if seeing someone else. Then he suddenly stood upright, his chair crashing back into the wall, and with a peculiar choking sound rushed away to his room. Avril looked from Antonio to Alex, then lowered her eyes, chilled by the silence that was only broken when Antonio sighed again.

"So," he said, "what makes you think they're pursuing Father Benedict?"

"I'm not sure," Avril said, this not being a complete lie. "I just think that Father Benedict is being haunted by something that he refuses to talk about."

"And the light?" Antonio countered carefully. "You really think it was nothing?"

"I think it was very odd," she replied, "and I admit it: it frightened me."

She glanced at Alex, saw his beautiful, bewildered face, and was relieved when she heard Antonio speaking again, his voice careful and kindly.

"Atmospheric phenomena," he said. "Shall we leave it at that?"

"Yes, dammit," Avril replied, despising herself. "That's all it was."

"And was there anything else?" Alex asked her, sounding strange. "Anything else that you experienced but kept to yourself?"

"No," she lied, "not a thing."

She felt guilty but simply couldn't mention her dreams (or visions) of Laura. Instead she simply stood up with as much grace as possible and said, "This whole business is exhausting me. I'm going to bed again."

She saw Alex glancing at Antonio before managing to meet her gaze, then he shrugged and also stood up, putting his hand on her shoulder.

"I'm coming with you," he said.

Leaving Antonio at the table, they returned to their room. Avril, frightened of going to sleep again, deliberately lit a cigarette. She turned her back on Alex, trying to conceal her fear from him, and crossed the room to stand by the window and look over the river. The sky was filled with low, heavy clouds. The river was an immense blackness that disappeared, both east and west, into the deeper blackness of the silent jungle. There was no chattering here— the animals, unless desperately hungry, stayed well away from human beings—and that lack of noise, encircling the retiring town, seemed to reverberate in some ghostly manner. Avril shivered and

blew smoke out, listening to Alex walk up behind her, then she felt
his arms slipping around her as he pulled her back into him.

"Are you *sure* there wasn't anything else?" he said. "If there
was, you can tell me."

"Why would I *not* tell you if there was?"

"Because you might try to protect me."

"Protect you from what?"

"I don't know. That's for you to tell me."

"There was nothing else . . . nothing."

"All right," he said, "come to bed. Let's try to forget everything
for one night—before we get on that boat again."

She knew what he meant and was touched by his need. She
stubbed out her cigarette in the ashtray on the cupboard beside her,
then turned around to slide her tongue between his lips and press
herself tightly to him, letting him know with every move of her body
that she also felt that way. He responded with a shudder, his hands
sliding over her breasts, his weight forcing her back into the wall as
his mouth bruised her lips. She pushed him away and unbuttoned his
shirt, heard the zip on her dress opening, felt the dress falling down
off her shoulders as she unbuttoned his trousers. Then her thoughts
went out of focus, were suffused by desire, and she found herself,
naked, limbs akimbo, stretched out on the bed. He was lowering
himself on top of her, the mosquito net fluttering around him, the
wooden fan rotating above his head, various insects being battered in
the minor turbulence its blades were creating. He entered her—Alex
entered her—flooding her insides with heat, and then whispered
some words she couldn't hear as she melted around him.

That noise! *What noise?* She thought she could hear the sound of
drums. She was jerked back to reality, to the awareness of their
separate bodies, cocking one ear as Alex moved in and out, wondering what she was listening for. She opened her eyes and saw a white
gauze, something whirling above it, recognized the fluttering mosquito net and the rotating fan. No, not the fan—it was turning too
fast for that—it was something else whirling above her, growing
brighter, expanding.

"Oh, God, Avril, I want you so!"

She closed her eyes and gripped him fiercely, clinging to him with
arms and legs, trying to hold back her nausea and dread at what was
happening again. She was Avril (*I am me!*) and she fought to retain
this knowledge, hearing the drums and seeing the lights rise and fall
over that great, star-flecked canyon. He was gasping, cleaving to her

(*my Alex, on top of me!*), thrusting deeply and expanding up through her insides to make her flesh turn to liquid. She wanted to do that—to dissolve, to find obliteration and freedom—but then Laura, her voice ringing with pain and fear, seared through the ether and touched her.

Someone screamed—Avril screamed—and tried to push Alex off her, opening her eyes to look up at his stunned eyes as he pulled himself out of her. He was supporting himself on his hands, his spine curved, his muscles tight, and above him, above the wildly fluttering white net, was a whirlpool of brilliant, shimmering light, its vortex like the pupil of a giant eye, dark and malevolent.

"Oh, my God!" she heard Alex say. "It's Laura! *You're Laura!*"

At that moment, as Alex let out a strangled groan and hurriedly rolled off her body, and as the whirling light above grew dark and faded away to leave only the revolving, squeaking fan, Avril remembered all the times in London when she and Alex had tried to make love—all those times when he had started and then cried out in horror and, because of the visions *he* had then suffered, was unable to finish—and, in that recollection, finally understood fully what it was that had affected him so badly.

"You saw Laura? You thought I was *Laura*?"

"Oh, God!" he groaned. "*Yes!*" He stared at her, looking dazed, and then, his eyes widening, reached out and grabbed her by the shoulder and squeezed till she hurt. "Dammit," he said fiercely. "I knew it. I just *knew* it! You've been having the same dreams as I had, and were frightened of telling me. You can see and feel what happened to her. *Dammit, isn't that true?*"

"Yes, Alex, it is."

He let her go and sat back, at once shocked and filled with wonder, but then a sudden hammering on the room door made the both of them jerk upright, Avril automatically covering her body with the sheet as Antonio's voice, exceptionally loud and frantic, rang out from the hall.

"Alex!" he shouted. "Avril! Come quickly! It's Father Benedict! *Come quickly!*"

They glanced briefly at one another and then jumped off the bed, hurriedly putting on the same clothes they had just taken off and then opening the door and running to Father Benedict's room. The priest was huddled up on the floor, in the corner nearest the door, his whole body trembling and his face bathed in sweat, the light of an oil lamp sending shadows across his wild eyes as he pointed a very shaky finger at the bed he had just fled.

"It was her!" he said. "Beside me! In that bed! *Upon my soul, it was Laura!*"

"*Your* bed?" Alex asked with a breaking voice. "She was there in *your* bed?"

"Oh, God, yes. *She came back to me!*"

Given the lacerating grief and despair in his voice, there could be no doubting what he had meant by those words. Alex, in the silence that dropped like lead among them, glanced from Avril to Antonio before reluctantly returning his gaze to the priest.

The priest turned away, burying his face between his knees, his body quivering until he managed to control himself and lift his head up again. He rubbed his bloodshot eyes, using a very shaky right hand, then sniffed and slowly looked up at Alex, silently begging forgiveness.

"I couldn't help myself," he said, his voice dry as broken bones, his hands weaving arabesques in the air, exorcising his demons. "Oh, of course I tried at first—both for myself and for you. Believe me, Alex, I loved you like my own and broke my heart worrying over you. Yes, I was concerned for you, hating your father for mistreating you, thinking of you as the son I never had but always secretly wanted. But that wasn't enough! I wasn't prepared for lust and vanity. I only knew that I was faithless, that I felt I had betrayed my life, and that the minute I laid my eyes on Laura, I wanted her desperately. Yes—oh, dear God!—and the wanting was like pain, something leading to self-deceit: a most pitiful belief that to have her would resurrect the strength I had lost and renew my dead spirit. I wanted her with the base and craven lust that comes to those who need new life."

The priest was breathing heavily and had to sniff his tears back, rubbing his eyes with the fingers of a shaking hand and taking a deep, hungry breath. The flickering light was bleeding over him, etching his eyes in deep shadow, covering his skin in darting black lines that looked like ants on an anthill.

"Did I betray you, Alex?" he said. "Yes, but not deliberately. There was no calculation in what I did: there was nothing but anguish. Indeed I suffered the fires of hell, wanting her desperately, thinking of my calling, thinking also of you and of the trust you had placed in me, knowing that the very desire to possess her was a betrayal not only of my faith but of my friendship and love for you.

Oh, yes, I felt guilty, and my shame was like purgatory, but the day after she had you—when you both lay on that raft—yes, the day she told me about it, trying to expunge her guilt and shame—for indeed, Alex, she sincerely felt both—that day, when I heard what had happened, was the day of my downfall."

He looked at Alex, and his eyes were like the moon: reflecting light that showed dead soil.

"Do you understand, Alex? I was hopelessly addicted to her. To the eyes of the world I was an ordained man of God, but to myself, in the penury of my nights, I was a man of the flesh. Yes, I lusted for the forbidden—for earthly luxuries and pleasures, for the satisfaction of all my frustrated desires and longings and needs—and then, in the presence of Laura, the one person who recognized me, who knew how weak I was and how far my faith had fallen, and who, like myself, was in need of the love that she had never been able to accept before—yes, in her presence, and totally blinded by her careless beauty, I understood that what I felt would be returned if I could just let it happen—for in truth, if she knew what I felt, I also knew what *she* felt. And so, Alex, when she told me what had happened on that raft—when she told me of your magic and of how she had lost control of herself—I, too, lost control of myself and surrendered to my lust."

He let his breath out, stopped breathing for a moment, then put his head back against the wall and took a very deep breath. His face was turned up toward the ceiling, but his eyes were now closed.

"And I a priest! Oh, yes, that was the rub! And what made it perversely ironical was that this woman, this creature I was lying down with, might be possessed by the devil. Oh, Lord, how I wondered about that—why her, of all women?—and often thought that perhaps it was because I was challenging the God I mistrusted. But, no, I couldn't accept that—my love was too deep for that—so I came to think that possibly the devil had given her to me to tempt me. I trembled with fear, then, but also knew a sly delight: for indeed, if I had lived in servitude to a God I had never truthfully accepted, then surely my unbridled passion for a woman who believed herself possessed by Satan merely confirmed, with diabolical exactitude, where my sentiments lay. Yes, Laura was obsessed with evil, and I was obsessed with her, and if, in embracing her, I embraced evil—well, then, so be it."

He leaned forward, breathing deeply, and pressed his hands against his temples, then spoke in a very low tone, directing his voice at the floor.

"When you came to me that night," he said, clearly referring to Alex, "when you told me that you loved her and wanted to take her to England with you, I knew that something had happened between you—something more than just words. And so, the next evening—knowing that Laura would leave the following day, inflamed by the thought of what she might have done with you, and, perhaps more violently, jealous at the thought of her staying in your father's house on the plantation—I demanded to know just what had happened on the raft; and, of course, when she told me, almost in tears and clearly ashamed of herself, I gave her a tongue-lashing—oh, my God, what a hypocrite! —emphasizing that she was twice your age and had no excuse for what she had done. She cried—oh, how she cried, her tears falling like rain—but then, when I reached out for her, about to pretend that I wanted to comfort her, she stepped back and looked at me with the most awful perceptiveness and said—I will never forget it—she said, 'What do *you* want?' And so, shocked to hear her ask that, humiliated by her intuition, I nonetheless blurted out what she had known all along—that I wanted her, no matter the cost—and then, hearing her reply that she also wanted me, pulled her to me where we stood in her room—the room where Father Symonds, that fine man, had spent so many years—and then we fell on the bed."

Father Benedict raised his head and looked directly at Alex, and his eyes, which before had looked like stone, were filled with a light that shone through tears and mutely begged for forgiveness.

"I had her, Alex," he said. "In shame and guilt, I had her. The first time was the night before she left the mission for the plantation—the very thought of you and her on that raft had inflamed me; and fear of her being near your licentious father fanned the flames even higher—and thereafter, during those times when she left the plantation, when she stayed away all night and later said she had been drunk, I had her on the ground of the forest around the mission, in the back of the mission's truck when I had driven somewhere to meet her, sometimes even in various hotels in Manaus where my face was unknown. Do you understand, Alex? She loved neither you nor your father. She and I had one another with a passion that obliterated all reason. Laura loved *me*—and I, her. . . . And may God forgive both of us."

24

Once the boat left Santarém it seemed to leave civilization completely, the river narrowing until nothing could be seen but the solid green wall of the great Amazonian jungle, the clouds thunderous and black, hanging low over the trees, making it appear that the boat was traveling forever through a silent, sullen, monotonous tunnel whose walls, shifting subtly through various shades of brown-veined greenery, offered little variety and gave rise to constant, oppressive gloom.

Either standing at the railing or sitting by the table to eat and drink, Avril felt that oppressiveness hanging over her and enslaving her spirit. She could not forget what the priest had told them, nor the sight of Alex fleeing the stifling hotel room, nor the rest of that sleepless night during which, with heavy heart, she had held Alex tightly in her arms while he wept over his betrayal by his formerly beloved friend, the priest, and vowed repeatedly that once the journey was over he would never see him again.

Now Avril was watching them both—as was Antonio—aware that they were both in a bad way and could behave unpredictably. Alex already seemed totally different—his silence as sullen as the passing jungle's, his hatred for the priest all too evident when his eyes lit upon him—while the priest, in a bad state anyway, was rapidly growing worse, hardly ever leaving his cabin, constantly ordering more *cachaça* from the bar, and according to Antonio, mumbling a lot to himself and even weeping in private.

She tried to talk to Alex, telling him the priest had not betrayed him, trying to explain that his, Alex's, particular brand of trust had left no room for human weakness, and that the priest, being no different from Alex, had been unable to help himself; but Alex's shock went too deep, his sense of betrayal was too acute, and he could only respond with a venom that disguised his true pain.

"I hate him," he said. "What he did to me was unforgivable. He acted like a surrogate father to me, and all the time, when I thought he was concerned for me, he was merely plotting to steal her."

"That isn't true," Avril replied. "And deep down you know it. He cared for you then—and cares for you now—and when he warned you against Laura, he did so because he knew that she was only trying to humor you, that she only loved you in a platonic fashion, that her real love was actually reserved for him and that sooner or later, if you didn't accept reality, you would get hurt way past what you could bear. In the event, he turned out to be right: she drove you almost insane."

"I almost went insane because of Laura and my *father*," Alex replied, "after I saw them embracing in his room and knew, contrary to what the priest said, that it was he whom she'd rejected me for. Oh, yes, Father Benedict wanted her—and no doubt he did what he said with her—but Laura also had an affair with my father, which is what haunts the priest."

"The priest is haunted with guilt because he thinks he betrayed you—and you, who should forgive him for what he did, are only making it worse."

"No, he's tortured because Laura betrayed *him*—for my father—as the three of them secretly betrayed me while pretending to care for me."

"You're exaggerating everything, Alex."

"I'm just facing the truth."

The truth seemed more elusive with each fresh revelation, retreating behind walls of human pain and distorted perspectives. What had Laura really felt? Whom had she really loved? Had she truly loved the priest and only dallied briefly with Alex's father, or had she simply played one against the other for amusement or spite? *Diabolical possession*, Avril thought. *Perhaps she* was *possessed, after all, and, as a devil's disciple, took pleasure in seducing the priest*. A possibility, just one—there were others just as likely. Avril found her thoughts spinning in circles. At her first opportunity she turned to Antonio for help.

"What do you think, Antonio? You were there. What pieces are missing?"

Antonio shrugged, a bewildered smile on his handsome face, his brown eyes gazing out at the passing jungle. "I don't know," he replied. "I only knew about Alex: that he was obsessed with a woman whom I felt might be insane and that she spent a lot of time with his father and that pig Rollie Thatcher. I didn't know about the priest—he kept his passion for her well hidden—and I certainly couldn't say with any conviction that Laura and Alex's father, no matter how much they teased each other, actually went as far as having an affair. But if Alex says he saw them embracing, then he did so: he isn't capable of lying."

The boat continued its journey, pushing against the lazy current, the faraway banks coming closer with each passing hour; but once past Óbidos, well away from Santarém, the river narrowed more dramatically, sometimes actually resembling an *igarape*, the trees almost touching both sides of the hull, with furred sloths, clearly visible, hanging upside down from the branches, and the black holes in the enormous trunks, which rose out of the water, housing the fierce, stinging fire ants or large, hairy spiders.

Avril blessed such sights, studying the forest to distract herself, taking pleasure at being cast from her urban roots to this equatorial forest. The high grass that lined the banks, Antonio informed her, was *canarana;* and in the dark pools of the swamps and tributaries she occasionally saw alligators, water birds, and *capybaras*—or, like something created by Walt Disney, the fat, ugly *manatee*. It was an alien, exotic world, one that cast a dark spell, and by the end of the first night, when the mysterious light returned, she knew, as Father Benedict had warned, that there would be no respite.

Alex slept like a log that first night, as if exhausted by his own bitterness, but Avril was awake when the light came to shine through the porthole. Since he had disembarked at Santarém, the passenger in the hammock could not block the view.

Once more she was terrified, her objectivity failing her, nausea rising up from her stomach. The light was powerful and dazzling, painting the tiny cabin in shimmering silver. Trying to scream but suddenly struck dumb, she again saw every loose object in the room drifting into the air.

She tried to sit upright but could not—she was completely paralyzed, and the air was being sucked from her lungs. As she stared above her, at the bottom of Alex's bunk, hearing him groaning in a troubled sleep, she sensed that she was being pulled up by some malevolent, unseen force.

Her terror increased, making her head spin toward delirium. Then her sheets started whispering. They rippled and rose up about her, and she started rising, floating mysteriously in thin air until she touched the bottom of Alex's bunk, her face pressed to the solid wood.

She remained there for a long time, pressed to the base of Alex's bunk, the sheets, wrapped tightly around her, feeling as hard as sheet metal, while the light, blazing fiercely through the porthole, seemed to spin like a whirlpool. Fear was the one reality—all the rest was hallucination: the cabin expanding and contracting, the stars spinning through the whirling light, the great hole that opened out in the wooden base of the bunk above her to reveal the receding funnel of a cosmos and the eternal darkness beyond. Avril tried to scream, her body shaking with the effort, and then she started to black out, to spiral down through her deepest self. She awakened back on her bunk, the rumpled sheets soaked in sweat.

If Alex hated the priest, his love for Avril was not diminished, and when he saw her that morning, soaked with sweat on the disheveled bed, the floor of the cabin littered with all the loose items—toothbrushes and combs and towels and their scattered clothing—his concern was clearly sharpened with the fear that she was truly in danger.

"Throw that amulet away!" he said. "That damned thing is what guides them here. As long as you keep it hanging around your neck, you'll be a magnet for trouble."

"No, Alex," she replied. "We have to finish what we've started—and this amulet, according to Peruche, can also protect us. Do you *believe* in the forces of darkness? Do you think they're pursuing us? If you do, then why are you complaining, since they're what we are seeking? Yes, I can hear Laura—and see her and feel her—and because of that, because she seems to be calling to us, I can't give up the amulet. Do you want to find the Yano, and possibly Laura? *Then I must keep the amulet!*"

That same morning the priest emerged, his face white as a sheet, shaking visibly as he queued up at the cookhouse for a mug of black coffee. He sat down beside Antonio, facing Alex and Avril, his fear helping him to ignore Alex's contemptuous glance as he stuttered his words.

"It gets worse," he said. "Every night it's more terrible. Last night, in that cabin—in that damned tomb of a cabin—I awakened to find the darkness like daylight and feel something on top of me. I couldn't see it—I just felt it—but my God, it was awful: something immensely strong and malevolent that seemed to be choking me. No air! I was choking! I had the feeling I was drowning. Either that or I was being crushed out of existence. . . . And then I saw her again— yes, Laura, right there beside me—and she was covered in slime—I think it was mud and blood—and she reached out and tried to pull me to her and then I blacked out. God, oh God, I need a drink! I won't sleep there again!''

He left the table and wandered away, taking himself to the prow of the boat, having little trouble wending his way past the other passengers since most of them had already disembarked, some at the larger towns of Santarém and Óbidos, a few at impoverished waterfront villages or at rickety jetties that appeared to lead to nowhere. Now the boat was almost empty, a pervasive silence hanging over it, leaving the priest with plenty of places to hide away and imbibe more *cachaça*. Avril watched him disappearing, the deck swaying gently under him, then she turned to glance at Alex, still sitting beside her, and finally fixed her gaze on Antonio at the opposite side of the table. The Brazilian was no longer smiling, and he seemed very weary.

''And what happened to you, Antonio?''

''Nothing, Avril. Not a thing. I slept like a baby all night and awakened refreshed.''

''Avril had a bad time,'' Alex said, ''but I slept through it all. I had bad dreams—about the jungle, about the rising and falling lights, and I think Laura was in it somewhere, but I can't be too sure. Apart from that, though, I kept sleeping and was untouched, while Avril actually levitated along with everything else.''

Antonio sighed. ''We can't ignore it anymore,'' he said. ''We're all caught up in something we can neither comprehend nor control, and given what I know of Indian witchcraft, it could be very dangerous.''

''Do you believe,'' Avril asked, directing her question at the both of them, ''that the Yano are actually involved with that light and what it can do? Do you really think they can reach us when we're here, hundreds of miles away from them?''

''Yes,'' Alex said instantly. ''I've no doubt about it at all. I know what *I* was capable of when *I* had the power—and I was, after all, just a beginner, on the ladder's first rung. But Peruche's powers were awesome, and even he was no master. According to him, the members of the Yano, the dispossessed ones near the Gateway, could, being the instruments of the forces of darkness, wreak diabolical havoc of the most frightening kind. So, yes, I think the Yano are behind this. I think they know we are coming.''

''And you, Antonio? What do *you* think?''

The Brazilian shrugged. ''I stand with Alex,'' he said. ''From what I know of Indian magic—and I saw a lot when I was younger—I'm convinced that they do have real powers of the kind we don't understand—and if, as is widely reported, the Yano's powers are greater than normal, then those powers could be remarkable indeed, capable of defying space and time to travel as far as need be.''

They all drank a lot that night, sitting together at the long table, Father Benedict obliterating himself in order to ignore Alex's contempt, Avril drinking to steady her nerves for the forthcoming night, and Antonio trying to draw them closer together with light conversation. The clouds returned to hide the stars, there was a quick, savage rainstorm, then the clouds moved away behind the silhouetted jungle canopy and let the moon illuminate the water and streak its black-flowing, alluvial surface with wavering silver lines.

Antonio went to bed first. Avril knew, as she watched him disappearing, that no matter how drunk she was, she would not be able to spend one more night in her cramped, haunted cabin. She told Alex and he flinched, glancing distastefully at Father Benedict, but the priest, possibly exhausted by fear and drink, was already asleep, his folded hands acting as a pillow for his forehead, his body, leaning across the wooden table, twitching spasmodically.

"Help him," Avril said. "Tomorrow. Try talking to him."

"No," Alex replied.

She slid away from him a little, then swung her legs onto the bench, and finally, turning her body sideways, rested her head on his lap. She felt him hardening against her cheek, and smiled, amused by it, then closed her eyes and let the night surround her with the promise of sleep.

This time, when the light came, Alex saw it as well, his shocked *"Oh, my God!"* making Avril open her eyes and look up to see that brilliant, spinning eye directly above her. Someone screamed and she jerked upright, staring wildly along the deck, and saw some members of the crew, standing close to the railing, waving frantically and pointing at the light as they backed away from it. She glanced at Alex, saw his wide eyes, saw the priest staring wildly, heard another scream, and looked across the deck at the panic-stricken crewmen. One of them was on his knees, gripping the railing with one hand, screaming dementedly as he stared up at the dazzling light swirling fiercely above. There was noise—no, vibration: a terrible *feeling* of noise—and then some oil lamps exploded, the flames racing over the deck, and the other crewmen bawled and jumped

overboard just before the flames reached them. The kneeling man
was engulfed, the flames seeming to explode around him, and then
Avril heard his screams drowned by her own as Alex jumped up and
ran away.

She followed him automatically, scarcely thinking about it, and
quickly joined him at the railing to look down at the men in the
water. The whirling light remained above them, illuminating the
river, and then it seemed to expand, stretching across the whole
boat, and the water in the river, which had been smooth, started
roaring and bubbling. Avril glanced to her right, saw the blazing
man falling over, his body just a bundle of charred rags in a pool of
small, flickering flames; then, as others appeared, as the fire
extinguishers burst into life, she looked back down at the river, saw
the water boiling furiously and then, to her horror, as the swimming
men screamed for help, saw a mass of gigantic snakes—all over
thirty feet long—coiling and uncoiling and wriggling over the electric eels which, racing through the boiling foam, managed to reach
the men first. The mens' screaming was truly terrible, lacerating
Avril's ears, and then she saw them catapulting, their bodies spinning like rag dolls, before crashing back down into that hideous
wriggling mass and disappearing beneath the snow-white foam as
the darkness returned.

She stood there, aghast, and then was pulled away by Alex,
letting him drag her back to the table where the priest was muttering
incessantly, only stopping, whenever he found the breath, to take a
drink from his hip flask. Avril looked up at the sky, blinked, and
rubbed her watering eyes, looked again, and saw nothing but the
clouds moving over the moon. There was shouting, more hissing,
the sound of feet on the deck, and the foam of fire extinguishers,
like milk on the boil, splashed over the flickering blue flames and
the charred remains of the dead man.

She was shivering and felt cold, but had to wipe sweat from her
brow. Alex was also dripping, his face as white as that of the priest
who was standing behind him. The shouting continued, there was
more foam on the dark deck, and the crewmen, all chattering
excitedly, were either staring over the railings at the water or
pointing up at the sky. Avril groaned, hardly knowing she was doing
so, and then leaned against Alex, this time resting her cheek on his
trembling shoulder and sliding her right arm around him. She remained there, not saying a word, until the dawn light broke through.

Antonio joined them for breakfast, looking the ghost of his former

self, listening patiently as Alex told him what had happened during
the night. He then explained that he, too, had seen the swirling light
but, when he tried to leave his cabin, could not open the door.

"It was locked securely," he said. "The key just wouldn't turn—at
least not until I tried it this morning, when it was working perfectly."

Father Benedict was eating dry bread and washing it down with
beer. As if talking to himself, he said, "God forgive me. It's me
they are after. I will never be forgiven for what I did until I give
myself to them—or until they manage to steal my soul."

Avril was startled, touched again with intuition, convinced that
his confessions so far were only part of the whole. And then, with a
sudden rage that surprised her even as she spoke, she hammered her
clenched fist on the table and shocked the priest to attention.

"Damn you!" she snapped. "Tell us the rest! Tell us what you're
still hiding!"

"No!" the priest exclaimed. "There's no more! *I've told all I can
tell!*"

He kicked his chair back as he stood up, swaying from side to
side, and then, with another choked sob, turned away and disappeared down the steps that led to the lower deck. Avril stared at
Antonio, at Alex, then at the river, noticing how colorless it looked
in the pearly light of the morning.

"God," she said, "this journey is interminable. I'll be glad when
tomorrow comes."

Later the sun came out, at first bleeding down weakly, then
breaking through the disappearing clouds to make the day dazzling
and fiercely hot. The river looked like a sheet of glass, a mirror
winding through walls of greenery, reflecting the great cecropia trees
and the bizarre, writhing lianas, the sunlight turning the gentle
ripples to silver where alligators, anacondas, and giant eels glided
close to the banks.

Avril felt that she was dreaming, that reality was dissolving
around her, making it difficult to distinguish between the actual and
what might be a mirage. She thought of the journals of Carvajal, of
his hallucinatory descriptions—royal highways through the jungle,
great white cities by the river bank, the fair-skinned female warriors
who fought with terrible ferocity and after whom Orellana had
named the river—and understood why he had written so: with the
sun overhead, blazing down in naked splendor, the reflections from
the vitreous water began to distort all she saw, making tributaries
and *verzea* lakes shimmer above the far horizon, turning odd collec-

tions of riverside shacks into gilded cities and domesticated animals in the forest clearings into giant prehistoric beasts. Toward evening, as Alex had prophesied, the happenings began to get worse and reality turned to a nightmare.

The river tapered away in the distance, curving between green walls of forest, and from out of the clear sky, above the canopy of the trees, came a great boiling mass of black clouds and a cold, whipping wind. Father Benedict saw it coming, his lips quivering as he groaned, and when Avril reached out to touch him reassuringly, he twitched as if whipped. The thunder roared as the clouds approached, lightning darting through boiling grayness, and Alex, as the wind whipped his face, shook his head disbelievingly. The thunder roared again, black shadows raced along the river, and the boat was plunged into a semidarkness. Then the rain fell.

The other passengers ran for cover, sheltering close by the cabins, as the rain came down in enormous, glistening drops that splashed heavily on the deck. Soaked, Avril cupped her hands across her forehead, protecting her eyes as she looked up, but the rain, turning into enormous hailstones, forced her fingers apart. She heard the sheltering passengers shouting, their voices clashing in Portuguese, and then they started to scatter, obviously frightened by the unfamiliar. A high-pitched, female scream lacerated her eardrums.

"Hailstones!" Antonio exclaimed. "*In the Amazon!* It must be starting again!"

She saw his brown eyes squinting, the hailstones exploding over his shoulders, then Alex grabbed her hand, shouted something about shelter, and started dragging her through the windwhipped, lamplit darkness toward the back of the cabins. She heard the woman screaming again, a sound of pure, mortal terror, and wondered briefly if it signified something much worse than this miraculous storm. Something light fell on her shoulder, dropped on her foot, and fell away; she glanced down and saw nothing but the dark deck. Then Alex pulled her toward him.

"Oh, Christ!" he said. "What—?"

The boat was shuddering violently, its engines roaring to no avail, and then its stern turned toward the port side until, with a violent, convulsive shudder, it came to a halt. Avril glanced over the railing and saw a wall of broken treetrunks, the water pouring over numerous gnarled branches and around the hull of the boat.

"I don't believe it!" Alex exclaimed. "The boat's stuck in those broken treetrunks. How on earth did they all bunch up there? It just isn't possible!"

The thunder roared and the lightning flashed, the hailstones changed back to rain, someone screamed, and again something light fell on Avril and bounced off her shoulder. She looked down and kicked at it—automatically, her skin rippling—and saw the scrambling legs of an enormous spider as it hurried into the darkness. Another appeared on the deck, then another, then another, someone screamed and something light fell on her shoulder and she slapped it away.

"Christ!" It was the priest. He was pressed against another cabin, wriggling frantically and slapping at his body as huge spiders fell onto him.

Revulsion made Avril burn and she quickly looked directly above her at the overhanging branches of the tall sapopema and acacuzeiro trees out of which, when the trapped boat hammered against them, the enormous spiders were falling. Another landed on her head, fell onto her shoulder and bounced away, and she started to scream, the fear and revulsion whipping through her, but managed to choke it back as Alex pulled her toward the prow of the boat, which was, from what she could see in the darkness, reasonably clear of the riverbank.

They found Antonio there, huddled up with some other passengers, the rain pouring out of the dark sky and splashing harshly upon them. He pointed obliquely with a wavering hand, and Avril looked up through the storm to see a pulsating, disk-shaped light shining through the black clouds.

The thunder roared again, the sound too loud to be natural, then jagged bolts of lightning, darting down from the stormy sky, seemed to explode over the funnel of the boat and crackle down toward the deck. Glass exploded, more people screamed, a lamp fell and burst into flames, and then a snake, long and heavy, its body smooth with river slime, slid noiselessly over Avril's foot and headed for those just behind her.

She tumbled into real terror, breaking free from Alex's grasp, the scream that she had stifled now daggering out of her throat as Alex's hands, having let go, managed to grab her again. Spinning around, she fell toward him, burying her face in his shoulder, unable to stop her body's panic-stricken convulsions and her loud, broken sobbing. He held her, rocked her, covered her ears as others screamed, as the thunder roared and the lightning flashed and more snakes dropped on the deck, their bodies making soft squelching sounds that made her skin crawl.

Then the thunder and lightning stopped, the rain stopped, the boat broke free, and she felt the deck heaving under her feet as the engines pushed it away. Alex was stroking her hair and murmuring, his hands squeezing her reassuringly, and then he led her away somewhere, set her down, kept talking to her, until eventually she managed to sniff back her tears and look fearfully around her.

The night around the boat was quiet, but the boat was still in chaos: people bawling or screaming, running this way or that, some shrieking and wriggling as they avoided spiders or snakes, the crew racing back and forth with sticks and brushes, sweeping the dangerous, revolting creatures off the decks and back into the river. Avril watched it all, mesmerized, hardly believing what she was seeing. She glanced up at the sky, saw the stars and a pale moon, then shuddered, closed her eyes, and pressed her face into Alex's shoulder, appreciating the warmth of his familiar skin as she drifted into uneasy sleep.

She dreamed of Laura in the jungle, of the Yano Indians crowding around her, of blood and mud dripping off tortured flesh as the lights rose and fell. Then she awakened, groaning softly, still shivering with terror, and looked up from Alex's lap to see Father Benedict staring down at her with eyes ruined by grief and the most terrible guilt, illuminated in all of their haunting tragedy by the pearly dawn light. He was shivering, but he reached down and touched her, stroking her cheek very lightly.

"Oh, my child, it's all my fault! *My fault!*"

"Then confess," she said quietly.

The priest jerked his hand away and stared at her in a startled manner, then, after glancing at Antonio and Alex, let his eyes roam around the boat and only slowly return to her.

"Confess?" he said. "To what? I can scarcely trust my own memory. But what is happening here—yes, all of it, these terrible hauntings—these things are the bitter fruits of my sins, of my lust and deceit. It is *me* they are after, Avril. I am absolutely sure of that. I have flirted with the devil in many ways, and now he has come for my soul. It was Laura and I—it was our forbidden love— that led to all this tragedy."

He glanced around the deck, which was quiet in the dawn light— the few remaining passengers either sleeping off the night's horrors or huddling together for comfort and glancing nervously about them—

and then, with an almost imperceptible sigh, turned back to Avril, his gaze lighting briefly upon her before passing on to Alex, at whom he stared very directly, his face luminous with pain.

"I was Laura's lover," he continued. "Yes, Alex, that is true: I first made love to her the night before she moved into your father's house, and from that night on we became secret lovers, meeting wherever we could. . . . Please, Alex, don't turn away! Can't you imagine how I felt? A celibate all my life, but suddenly fulfilled in love and desire, naturally I was inflamed, completely mesmerized by her, and could barely let her out of my sight, let alone out of the mission. Small wonder, then, that I soon ignored my doubts and gradually started falling to pieces because of what I was doing—for indeed, whether sane or insane, an innocent fool or a calculator, Laura, in giving herself to me, had destroyed my every foundation and laid waste my faith. And if, in dealing with you, I was no longer sure of my true motives, now, with Laura about to live on your father's plantation, I was even less sure of my reasoning and didn't dare think about it. No, I didn't want her to live there—not near you and your father—and when she did, my already possessive love became completely insatiable."

Avril looked across the water, squinting into the brightening daylight, trying momentarily to distract herself from the pain in the priest's voice. Here the river was about two miles wide and was growing wider every minute, the dense forest becoming a shrinking green line that curved away, both east and west, to where the sky met the jungle. A flock of herons flew beneath some gathering clouds: black spots merging with gray haze.

"Oh, God," she heard the priest saying. "The sordid deceit of it all: always meeting her in secret, praying we wouldn't be seen; and after it, the rancid taste of my hypocrisy and self-wounding shame. How ironic that when she was staying in the mission, when we were seeing each other every day, we had not been engaged in such an affair—not, at least, until the night before she left—but that once she moved into the plantation, thirty miles from the mission, we were obsessed with seeing one another to continue our profane, forbidden love; and could only see one another openly either when she visited the mission or when I, in my hypocritical role as priest and moral guardian, visited the plantation to attend to the workers or, ostentatiously, confront your father over his own, much more blatant, immorality." He leaned slightly forward toward Alex, trying to will his attention. "Oh, yes, Alex, I know: you think I was just using you; but such simply wasn't the case. Before meeting Laura and even during that terrible affair, my love for you never once wavered and only caused me more pain. . . . Did I cheat you with ease? Most certainly not! Rather, I was sick to the very depths of my soul, constantly questioning my own motives for all of my actions."

He sat back on the bench, took a very deep breath, and then, rubbing his cheeks in a distracted manner, stared at Alex again.

"My dilemma was acute," he said, "and perhaps a form of natural punishment: if I had initially advised you against falling in love with Laura because I was genuinely concerned that you would be hurt—and certainly that was the case—now, as Laura's lover, I could not give the same advice without suspecting that self-interest had become entangled in my formerly honest concern. Likewise, if I had previously fought with your father over his brutal treatment of his Indian workers, now, knowing that your father also had designs on Laura, I could not avoid the suspicion that what had once been genuine outrage was now merely a disguise for my resentment that he had her under his own roof and clearly wished to seduce her. There I was, trapped between two mirrors, each showing a different face."

Avril watched the river widening, the wall of forest visibly shrinking, the sky becoming an enormous inverted bowl that encased the great river. She studied it out of embarrassment, not wanting to see the priest's moist eyes, nor the anger and revulsion on Alex's face as he opened and closed his hands.

"And yet it continued—that soul-destroying affair—and if I lived with shame and guilt, I was also living with the fear that Laura, with her obsessive interest in the forces of darkness, was in fact possessed and, being the instrument of the devil, had been sent to corrupt me. And added to that—a very religious concern—was the more earthly fear that my relationship with Laura would sooner or later be discovered by someone and made known to your father—or, much worse, to you, which I felt would damage you in a manner that could never be undone. That concern, if you can believe me, was relentless—and was a concern shared by Laura."

Avril glanced at Alex and saw his delicate profile, his blond hair flopping over one eye, his head framed by the gray sky. He was trying to keep his face blank, to suppress his torn emotions, but the straight line of his lips was a sign that he was having some trouble.

"Laura cared for you, Alex—not in the way you wanted, but she cared for you deeply and suffered because, increasingly aware of your passion for her, her guilt over the affair she was having with me became quite unbearable. Did you think she found your father attractive? No, Alex, she did not. She flirted with him to keep him from guessing about her relationship with me, and also to distract him from thinking too much about your embarrassingly obvious infatuation with her—an infatuation that your father found either amusing or threatening, depending on how much he had had to drink or how nice Laura was to him. Yes, Alex, she cared for you, and made a point of protecting you, while you, in the blindness of your passion, could see only the opposite.''

Now Alex leaned forward, the anger draining from his face, leaving him pale but less grim, his brow furrowed in thought.

"Yes, Alex," the priest said, "you saw the opposite to what was happening. You thought that Laura was loving your father when in fact she was loving me, and that she didn't give a damn about you when in fact she was always protecting you. Why did you almost have a breakdown? Because your father was in her room. Because shortly after she had slapped your face—when you said she behaved like a whore—you saw your father in her room, placing his hand on her breast while she, just before you turned and fled, placed her hand on his hand and, as you so graphically remembered later, chuckled while doing so. You saw that and naturally assumed the worst, and then, with your worst fears confirmed, you almost went out of your mind.''

Alex blushed and lowered his head, obviously ashamed of that memory, while Father Benedict, speaking softly and nervously, revealed the truth to him.

"But you were very wrong," he said. "You saw what you wanted to see. Laura hadn't invited your father to her room that night: he simply turned up, very drunk, saying that he knew about your infatuation for her, that he was going to send you back to school the very next day, and that if she didn't come to bed with him that night he would throw her off the plantation. Laura just laughed at him, saying she didn't give a damn, and that she had anyway intended to move into Manaus and from there organize a trip into the jungle in hopes of finding the Yano. Her answer merely inflamed your father, making him want her all the more, but he was really terribly drunk, almost too drunk to stand, and so, when he pathetically put his hand on her breast, she laughed at him, humiliating him all the more, and then simply took hold of his hand and, as you turned and fled, removed it and pushed your father from the room. That's all that happened between them.''

Someone was shouting, and a bell was ringing from across the water. Avril saw that the land was closer, houses on stilts rising up to the edge of the forest, the stretch of river in front of them filled with fishing boats and *recreios*, with the floating filling stations known as *pontoes*, and even a large floating factory which, she assumed, was one of the refrigerating plants that Antonio had told her about. It was almost like civilization, and she wanted to see more, but the priest's voice, hoarse with whiskey and grief, forced her attention back to him.

''That was it, Alex: Laura was not involved with your father. This belief, I know, has been haunting you—so now you are free.''

Alex stared at the priest, started to speak, and then went dumb. He buried his face in his hands, and his body shook uncontrollably as he let the anguish pour out of him while Father Benedict touched his head with a trembling hand, expressing his sorrow.

''She truly loved you, Alex—as I, too, truly love you. A few weeks later, when you had gone to school in Manaus, both of us, shocked at the extent of your despair, vowed to terminate our affair and go our separate ways. Yet Laura knew that I couldn't do it—that I could not ignore her while she was near me—as she also knew that she had to follow her own course to her ultimate destiny. 'You won't be able to keep your word,' she said. 'Only I can set you free. And in doing that, I'll also set myself free from whatever is haunting me.' That same night, your father and Rollie Thatcher were slaughtered—and Laura, Mengrire, and the Indian girl all disappeared.''

He removed his hand from Alex's head, sighed loudly, and sat back, wiping his lips with the cuff of his shirt sleeve. Alex slowly sat upright. They stared at one another a long time, neither saying a word, while the clouds behind them shifted, letting sunlight break through, its silvery rays beaming down into the early morning's grayness and falling over the deck of the boat. The river here was busy, filled with canoes and other craft, the sloping bank, very close, littered with houses on stilts over which, in green equatorial splendor, the rain forest began. The priest surveyed it all, recognizing it with trepidation. Then he spoke softly to Alex.

''And why did she do it?'' he said. ''Why did she disappear that night? I think she did it on impulse, hardly knowing what she was doing, in a state of shock because she had walked into that room after the killing was finished. In a dazed condition, finding Mengrire and the girl there, and learning that they were going to flee into the jungle, she instinctively fled with them. Impulsively or instinctively, yes . . . but there were definite reasons.''

Father Benedict sat up very straight and then stared at each of them, speaking firmly and clearly.

"She did it to free me," he said. "She did it to save my soul: to remove her seductive presence from my sight and save me from further sin. And she did it, of course, because she was still convinced that she had to face the forces of darkness—those forces possibly known to the Yano—in order to regain her own soul and put Satan behind her.''

When Alex raised his head, pain whipped through Avril's heart: a pain mixed with the rage that sprang from her conviction that his feelings for her were merely a substitute for the love he had lost. Her hurt and anger fused together, setting her wounded heart to the flames, but she leaned toward the priest, feeling cold and self-destructive, determined to have it all out no matter what it might cost her—or, perhaps more relevant, what it might cost Alex who, sitting in front of her with his head in his hands, was trying to choke back the tears that he knew would enrage her.

"And that's when your downfall started?" she asked the priest, keeping her voice soft and calm.

"Dear God, yes," he replied. "My world ended that terrible night. When Laura disappeared, my soul went with her—and was lost in that jungle.''

Avril felt her own world ending, crashing into the dust of betrayal, and refused, even though her heart was breaking, to acknowledge Alex's tears. The boat shuddered and rocked and made a hollow drumming sound, followed by the sounds of squeaking rubber, then music and cheering. She looked over the railing and saw an enormous floating dock, a mass of people along the jetty where the hull was crushing the rubber tires, the dock's ramps leading away to a rising, bustling town which was encircled, as far as the eye could see, by the equatorial rain forest.

They had arrived at Manaus.

PART FOUR:

THE RAIN FOREST

25

If Father Benedict's revelations had left Alex in a daze, disturbing him and exalting him, offering shock and relief at once, being back in Manaus, in its haphazard, cluttered streets, merely agitated him all the more and resurrected, with an overwhelming vividness, every incident that had led to his premature departure. He felt split in two, the older Alex observing the younger, as if, looking back to what had happened just over a year ago, he was actually looking back a few decades to some unreal, remote period. And yet, given the feeling that time had stretched much further than possible, he also kept expecting to see some familiar faces, though he wasn't at all sure whose faces he was thinking about, apart from those of old school friends. Yes, he had practically just finished his schooling—and that knowledge, reverberating in his mind, again made him feel immature.

"It seems much smaller than I'd remembered it," he said to Avril, "as if I'd left as a child."

"You *were* a child," Avril replied tartly, "and in many ways still are."

He winced at that and felt a blush on his cheeks, glanced out of the hotel window at the tree-lined Avenido Eduardo Ribeiro, wondering if Laura and Father Benedict had ever stayed in this same hotel, and then, filled with shame, despising himself for his senseless jealousy, turned away from the window, suddenly aware of her anger and realizing the cause of it.

"Just what do you mean by that?" he said, hoping it wasn't what he had sensed. "It obviously wasn't meant as a compliment, so let's clear it up quickly."

"Don't act naïve," she replied. "You know damn well what I mean. You've been wounded to the quick ever since learning that Father Benedict was Laura Wellman's lover. You just can't stand the thought of it."

"It hurt," he replied. "Naturally. You *know* what I felt for her. I don't feel that way any longer, but Father Benedict betrayed me."

"Rubbish!" she snapped. "You just can't stand it that he had her. You can't bear to hear the priest mentioning Laura Wellman's name—and the thought that she actually loved someone else is simply too much for you. God," she continued vehemently, "what a damned fool I've been. You didn't come back here to set yourself free from your nightmares: you came back in the hopes of finding that bitch again—alive and in one piece."

"That's not true, Avril."

"Damn you!"

She had been taking her old clothes off, throwing them angrily on the bed, and now she turned away from him, her naked buttocks quivering, and walked across the bare boards of the floor to disappear into the equally Spartan bathroom. He looked out the window again, feeling flushed, his heart pounding, listening to the sound of water running into the tub and unable to shake off the guilt that her accusation had filled him with. Was there some truth in what she said? Did he still desire Laura Wellman? Had he merely used Avril as an emotional crutch when he most desperately needed one? Now, he wasn't sure, loving Avril, obsessed with Laura, on the one hand vastly relieved that Laura had not succumbed to his father, on the other still bitter that his good friend, Father Benedict, had turned out to be Laura's lover. He was still reeling from that revelation, not too sure of his own emotions, and now, faced with Avril's accusation, he had no honest answer.

"Christ," he said, talking to the window, "why did I bring her here?"

The road below was busy, cutting through the commercial area, and between some of the tall buildings, surrounding the shacks on the hills beyond, he could see odd patches of dense, tangled forest and scudding gray clouds. It was hot, but he shivered, the fear returning to settle upon him: an almost palpable fear that put a mist around his mind and made all his nerves feel on edge. They would soon be seeing the Indian girl, might soon learn what had happened to Laura, and that—which he desperately desired but was frightened of hearing—was only a prelude to their journey into the rain forest in search of the Yano. When he thought of that forthcoming adventure, and remembered what had already happened during the boat journey from Belém—the mysterious light, the hauntings, the inexplicable phenomena—he felt his heart fluttering with panic, his skin crawling with dread.

Avril returned from the bathroom, obviously still very angry, holding a damp towel around her body, and walked back to the bed. She let the towel drop to the floor and stood in front of him, completely naked, the fierce light in her eyes refusing to let him take too much pleasure from the sight of her.

"Well?" she snapped.

"What?"

"Did I tell the truth or didn't I?"

"I love you," he replied, his heart breaking as he said it. "I never knew what love was until I met you, but now I do—*yes, I do!*" His heart was pounding and he was flushed, his skin sticky with sweat, yet he knew through his fear and confusion that he was speaking the truth. "Damn you," he said, without malice, in desperation, "I just want to put all this behind me and then go back to England. *I want to live without doubt!*"

She rushed up to him and embraced him, pressing her naked body tightly to him, writhing against him, her fingers digging into his back as if trying to draw blood.

"God!" she said. "I'm just a bitch! I can't keep my bloody mouth shut. I've let Laura Wellman come between us and can't forget that she's there."

Alex held her in one arm, stroking her hair with his free hand, pressing his lips to her head as desire made him tremble.

"It's that amulet," he said. "You shouldn't still be wearing it. I don't understand why you want to keep it when you know what it's doing."

"I won't let it go, Alex."

"I know that, but why?"

"I won't let it go unless *you* take it—and promise to keep it."

"Why me?"

"Because all the bad things that happened to you only happened after you gave the amulet away—and because Peruche must have had a specific reason for giving it to you in the first place. I think that if the amulet has *positive* powers, they will only work through you, and that sooner or later, whatever your feelings, you'll have to take it back off me."

"No, Avril, I won't. I want nothing more to do with it. I gave up my magical powers when I left Brazil and I don't want them back.

I'm leaving all that behind me. Those powers only do good for those with faith—and I no longer have that.''

"Then I'll hold on to the amulet until you get your faith back.''

"That might never happen.''

"We'll see, Alex. We'll see.'' She slipped out of his embrace, offered a tentative smile, brushed her dark hair from her forehead with one hand, and said, "Father Benedict and Antonio are probably downstairs already, so I better put my clothes on and get you down there.''

She dressed quickly and attractively, wearing a simple white blouse and skirt, letting a long scarf hang down from her throat, her feet in sensible flat shoes. They walked downstairs together, Alex holding Avril's hand, a pulse beating nervously in his stomach when he thought of the Indian girl. Father Benedict and Antonio were indeed in the large lobby, which was, like so many of the buildings in Manaus, as baroque as the famous opera house, with the same seedy elegance. Antonio looked refreshed, having had a bath and changed his clothes, but Father Benedict, still wearing the same increasingly bedraggled shirt and slacks, had the appearance of a man who hadn't slept for three or four days. There were three glasses on the table in front of him, one still filled with beer.

"Lady's prerogative or not,'' Avril said, "I hope I didn't keep you *too* long.''

"Not at all,'' Antonio replied. "I've just come down—besides which, we don't have an appointment and can take our own good time.''

"We shouldn't be going at all,'' Father Benedict said. "Why dig up old bones?'' The remark was unintentionally brutal and he glanced up at them, embarrassed. Then, having a sip of his beer, he wiped his lips with his hand. "I'm sorry,'' he said. "I didn't mean to put it that way. But I beg you, Alex, to forget this obsessive mission, forget Laura and the past, forget that poor Indian girl and any distorted memories she may have, and let us all take a plane back to Rio and relative safety.''

"No,'' Alex replied. "I won't. You know damned well I won't. That Indian girl could tell us what happened to Laura, which I had assumed was something that even *you* would want to know.''

"No, I don't. I think the past should stay buried. Learning the doubtless unpleasant details of Laura's fate can do nothing but make us suffer all the more—and getting the story out of that demented

Indian girl could possibly damage her further. No, let's leave well enough alone and get out while we can."

Alex stared at Father Benedict for a considerable time, trying to work out what was bothering him about seeing the Indian girl. Of course it would be painful—for himself as well as the priest—but as he studied his old friend, again shocked by how much he had aged, he had the feeling that the confessions so far offered were, if accurate in their essence, still incomplete. Father Benedict was a frightened man—much more frightened than he should be—and neither the manifestations on the boat nor the reported powers of the Yano were enough to explain his reluctance to learn more about Laura.

"What good will it do you to return to Rio?" Alex said, feeling a lot less brutal than he sounded, but needing to get it out. "You're drinking yourself to death because of what happened a year ago, so don't tell me that finding the truth doesn't matter—it matters a lot to both of us."

"Speak for yourself, Alex. I don't wish to know more. I do not wish to dabble in things that we can't understand."

"You *were* dabbling in such things," Antonio quickly reminded the priest, "so your present attitude, to put it mildly, seems a little bit odd."

"Is there something you know that we don't?" Alex said. "If not, then why this fear—after all we've already been through—about discovering what actually happened to Laura when she left the plantation?"

"All right," the priest said, finishing off his beer. "Forget it! Let's go!"

He stood up very quickly, clearly very agitated, and actually led them all out of the hotel into the busy main street, turning left and heading downhill toward the cathedral square. Antonio hurried to catch up with him, obviously wanting to calm him down, and Alex took Avril's hand in his own and pulled her close to him. He appreciated having her near, taking comfort from her dark beauty—shoulder-length auburn hair, very finely lashed brown eyes, her white cheeks slightly burnt from the sun, her tight lips showing tension—needing the comfort as the city pressed in upon him with the weight of old memories.

All the streets sloped down gently over a series of *igarapes*, the roads becoming bridges that spanned the steep drops above the wooden shacks and stilted houses in the creeks filled with water from the Rio Negro. The whole town was remarkably shabby, with broken pavements, flooded drains, an unsightly conglomeration of open-front shops, cheap restaurants and rough bars, and derelict buildings that had once been elegant homes but now were as empty as plundered tombs. Seeing it all again, remembering how he had gone to school here, Alex couldn't help thinking of his father and the world that had shaped him.

"If you want to understand my father," he said to Avril, "you should study the history of this city, because my father was formed by this city and, just like the city, prematurely faded away when the rubber boom ended."

"Tell me about it right now," Avril replied, "since I'm actually walking the streets and might never come back here again."

"It's a riches to rags story," Alex said. "By the end of the nineteenth century, Amazonia had the largest known reserves of rubber in the world and rapidly became the richest region in Brazil. The two major cities—Manaus and Belém in that order—were transformed as the rubber millionaires, including my father's father, spent their fortunes on lavish mansions, hospitals, libraries, theaters such as the Teatro Amazonia, and all the ornate monuments and public squares of the kind we've been passing. The millionaires of that rubber boom were essentially unsophisticated men who, with their extraordinary, seemingly limitless, overnight wealth, became more and more profligate and, determined to mark their own existence in some suitably flamboyant manner, built much of this city at their own expense and without considering the cost: the opera house was built with marble imported especially from Italy, and the customs house with stones brought here all the way from Scotland. Likewise, food, wine, champagne, clothing, and furniture were all imported from Europe. Electricity and the telephone, which existed nowhere else in Brazil, were here taken for granted. So demented did the millionaires become in their need to prove just how wealthy they were that they even sent their laundry to Europe to be washed. Naturally, in both cities, but particularly here in Manaus, the sexual licentiousness was outrageous and the exploitation of the Indians and other lowly workers quite commonplace. As part of that singular world, a son of one of those millionaires, my father was very much a creature of his environment: spoiled, self-centered, sexually insatiable, and of course contemptuous of the Indians and his own *seringueiros*. In short, my father was made degenerate by a decadent way of life, and when that way of life died out, leaving him stranded, he took his revenge in worse cruelty."

"You mean after the rubber boom ended in 1929?"

"Precisely. I was about one year old at the time, my mother had died, and then, after what became known as the great crash, Manaus and the plantations around it started sinking back into impoverished neglect, something that made my father even more bitter and—if I may say so without sounding self-pitying—made him a terribly bad father who, when not ignoring me completely, was either raging at me or being sarcastic just to amuse himself. That's why I drew close to old Peruche and, later, looked upon Father Benedict as a surrogate parent."

"And now you appear to have lost both of them as well."

"Yes," Alex said. "Possibly."

"Does it disturb you being back here?"

"Right now it *all* disturbs me: seeing these streets again, thinking again of my childhood, my father, old Peruche, even the Indian, Mengrire—and, of course, the hauntings on the boat journey and what's been happening to you and me as Laura, whether imagined or not, more and more stands between us. Yes, it disturbs me—but in a strange way I feel better; even during our frightened and sleepless nights, I have the feeling that we're doing the right thing and will soon resolve everything."

"We'd *better* resolve everything," Avril replied. "We won't have a second chance."

They had reached the busy square by the cathedral and customs house. Alex wanted to walk around, to show Avril some of the sights, but Father Benedict had already hailed a taxi and was opening the rear door. When they had all climbed in, the taxi moved off past the rows of market stalls and headed away from the center of the city.

"It's only a five-minute journey," Father Benedict said tartly, "so I hope you can all manage to wait that long before torturing the unfortunate Indian girl with your questions."

That remark reminded Alex of how angry the priest was. He glanced at Antonio and received a small, knowing grin. The taxi was crossing the Educandos Bridge, and he looked down at the *igarape*, seeing the houses on stilts rising one above another on the opposing slopes. The Indian girl was down there, living in one of the fishermen's houses, and Alex, thinking of what she could reveal, felt a cold chill go through him.

It was very hot—much more so in the taxi—the late morning gray and humid, the heat held in by low black clouds, no breeze to cool them as the temperature climbed. Father Benedict coughed into his fist, his back shaking as he did so, and Alex, his own head filled with memories, knew what the priest was feeling: increasing anguish mixed with excitement, insatiable curiosity mixed with dread, the resurrection of love and its attendant doubts and subsequent grief. Yes, the priest would be suffering, unable to stop the flood of emotions, and Alex, glancing sideways at a pale, grim-faced Avril, was aware of just how strong and potentially destructive those emotions remained.

The taxi turned right and moved down toward the river, the slope becoming steeper and the street increasingly narrow as they passed open-front shops that were selling fruit and fish, warehouses filled with what seemed to be mountains of cardboard boxes, and shabby wooden stands piled high with sacks of flour, rice, *farinha*, and various nuts. The taxi stopped halfway down, unable to go farther, the water, filled with oil and rotten fruit and the remains of fish, lapping around the stilts of the houses that stood, one row on top of the other, on the slopes of the creek.

Father Benedict paid the driver and they all scrambled out, Antonio staring at the map which John Nicholson had drawn for him, then gazing up at the houses towering above him, wondering where to begin. The taxi reversed past them, turned around, and roared back up the street while Antonio glanced at the map again, scratched his head, and shrugged his shoulders.

"It's somewhere to the left as we stand facing the river," he said, "so let's take that path up behind the houses and then, if we get lost, just ask someone."

The filthy water of the *igarape* was lapping around the stilts of the house nearest to them, a tethered canoe bobbing up and down gently, its oar making a hollow drumming sound against the wet hull. Alex stared past the canoe, at the water running back toward the river, washing around the stilts of the other houses near the bottom of the wet, grassy slopes. Children were swimming beneath the houses, some men were casting nets from small boats, and the stench of rotten fruit and fish could not be ignored.

Alex took hold of Avril's hand, tugged it playfully, and smiled at her, then followed Antonio across the road and up a steep, winding mud track. Father Benedict was right behind him, panting heavily and muttering crossly, but Alex ignored him, squeezing Avril's hand for comfort, staring briefly at her to see her brown eyes and blowing hair, her face framed by the stilted shacks and the gray and black clouds above them.

The path led them between the stilts, below the dilapidated wooden houses, and soon they came to a group of *cafusos*—some fisherman's family—all squatting in the earth around the steps that led up to their house. There were two sullen teenage girls and a gray-haired woman, probably their mother, the children, all naked, scrabbling around them, covered in dirt. Antonio spoke to the gray-haired woman, showing her the crumpled map, and she smiled, showing toothless gums, spat languidly near his feet, then jabbered in illiterate Portuguese and pointed a bony finger up the dirt track. When she had finished talking, which seemed to take a long time, Antonio waved them all forward.

"We're on the right track," he said. "It's at the top of this hill. The house is painted green, it's owned by a fisherman—the girl's uncle—and the girl is said to be a bit crazy and never comes out. So be prepared."

They reached the top in a few minutes and found the house with no trouble but stood there uneasily, looking down along the creek to where the river, five miles wide, glittered darkly. Staring at it, Alex shivered, the immensity of it quietly shaking him. Then he turned and looked up at the flaking green walls of the house that stood high above him on bent, rotting stilts. Antonio was at the steps, putting the map back into his pocket, and as Alex walked forward, holding Avril by the elbow, he saw Father Benedict uncorking his hip flask and taking a very long drink.

"It's all wrong!" he said. "*Wrong!*" He stared at each of them in turn, his eyes red-rimmed and frightened, and then, screwing the cap back on his hip flask, stepped backward away from them. "I'm not going in there," he said. "I don't want to see that girl. If you want to talk to her, do so—but don't expect me to listen. I'm going back down the hill and I'll meet you afterward in the waterfront bar. *I just can't go in there!*"

He turned and rushed away from them, stumbling back down the rough track. Alex, frustrated and angry, wanting to drag the priest back, shrugged and shook his head. With Avril behind him, he followed Antonio up the steep wooden steps to the slightly tilting verandah. The verandah was deserted, but Antonio knocked on the door; there was the sound of shuffling within, the squeaking of a chair being moved, and then the door opened a little and an old man peered out, his face thin from lack of nourishment, the cheekbones high and very prominent, his lips being sucked back onto rotten teeth, his eyes rheumy and squinting.

"*Sim?*" he said, his voice cracked and suspicious, his gaze taking in each of them in turn, his right hand, its brown fingers surprisingly thick, preparing to slam the door shut.

"*Boa tarde,*" Antonio replied, this being just after noon, his smile geared to melt the man's suspicions and keep the door open. "*O meu nome e Antonio Bozzano. Pode ajudar-me, por favor?*"

The old man stared at Alex and Avril, sniffed and rubbed his rheumy eyes, then looked at Antonio again, considering him thoughtfully.

"*Desculpe,*" he said. "*Nao entendo.*"

There was noise from inside the shack, what sounded like a squeaking bed, and as the old man glanced over his shoulder and then looked back at Antonio, Alex felt the nerves tightening in his stomach, the dread falling about him. Antonio started talking to the old man, explaining what they had come for, but Alex, hardly listening, looked sideways at Avril and saw his own fears reflected in her brown eyes and tight lips, in the constant, restless movement of her fingers as they drummed on her thighs. He placed his hand on her shoulder, squeezed it lightly, received a trembling smile, then returned his attention to Antonio and the man in the door. They were having a mild argument, the old man trying to deny them entrance, explaining that his niece was very ill and could not talk about what had happened in the jungle without getting upset. The argument went on for some time, Antonio pleading, the old man refusing, but eventually, either charmed or defeated by Antonio's rhetoric, the old man shrugged his naked, bony shoulders and, stepping backward, opened the door wider to let them walk in.

The fear immediately swamped Alex, making him break out in a sweat, his heart quickening as he stared through the candle-lit darkness at the girl on the bed. She was sitting upright against the wall, her black hair falling over her shoulders, a loose dress of what looked like ordinary sack cloth unable to hide the full breasts of her young but prematurely wasted body. Alex stared at her, shocked, comparing her with the girl he had known a year ago: only her breasts retaining the fullness that he clearly remembered, while the rest of her, body and face, was now almost emaciated, her eyes terribly large above sunken cheeks, staring at him in panic. He experienced that same panic—perhaps catching it from her—and he wiped sweat from his forehead, felt stifled and glanced around him, noticing that the darkness was caused by the curtains that were drawn all the way across the windows and keeping the daylight out.

"She likes to feel that she's locked in," the old man explained in Portuguese, obviously knowing what was troubling Alex, "and that the outside world can't get to her: so she stays here all day in the darkness, usually seeing no one."

"How did she end up here?" Antonio asked him.

The old man looked melodramatically offended. "I am her *uncle*— that's why she was brought here."

"I understand that you're her uncle," Antonio replied with some impatience, "but this girl was thought to have disappeared for good, so *who* brought her here?"

"A priest." The old man shrugged. "That one who used to run the mission. He brought her to me one day—many months after she had disappeared—and said that he had found her wandering in the jungle, and that I had to look after her. I complained, saying that I had no money, but he left her here anyway. That priest, he looked like a madman—and has not been back since."

"*Father Benedict!*" Avril cried.

Alex couldn't believe his ears, the shock making him reel inwardly, but he looked down at Antonio's upturned eyes and realized it was true. He opened his mouth to say something, wanting to shout, perhaps scream, but nothing emerged but a kind of gasp, a choked expulsion of breath. He felt his heart pounding, the sweat pouring down his face; he took out a handkerchief and wiped his skin dry as he stared, completely dumbfounded, at Antonio. The Brazilian was leaning closer to the bed, staring into the girl's eyes, yellow light flickering over them both, painting stripes c the shadows.

"Can I talk to her?" Antonio asked.

"*Sim, Senhor*—but she may not be helpful."

The girl stared up at them all, her dark eyes reflecting the candlelight, while first Antonio, then Alex and Avril, moved closer to the bed, Antonio going down on one knee to talk to her while Alex and Avril just stood there, hardly daring to breathe. The girl took hold of the bedsheet, tugged it up to her chin, stared at each of them in turn, her beautiful brown eyes unnaturally bright, then giggled and gazed directly at Antonio, her smile almost flirtatious. Antonio talked to her in Portuguese, his voice infinitely gentle, introducing himself, reminding her who Alex was, and then, after introducing Avril, asking if she would mind conversing in English.

"*Sim, Senhor,*" she said. "Okay."

Antonio nodded at her, glanced at Alex and Avril, and eventually, after taking a deep breath, told her what they had come for. The girl's eyes grew bigger, her pupils yellow in the candlelight—like cat's eyes except for the fear that made them even more bright. She shuddered, huddled deeper into the wall, and pulled the sheet tighter to her.

"No!" she whispered. "*No!* I cannot tell you! *I don't want to remember!*"

She sobbed and jerked away, hiding her face against the wall, the shadows cast by the candles flickering over her shaking shoulders while the old man, sniffing loudly, scratching his chest with bony fingers, kneeled down and put his hand on Antonio's shoulder and spoke quietly to him.

"You have money?" he asked.

Antonio, at first startled, simply stared at the old man, but eventually, understanding the situation, nodded in assent, withdrew a fistful of cruzeiros from his jacket pocket and, his distaste hidden by the flickering shadows, pressed the money into an outstretched hand. The old man stood up immediately, hid the money in a ceramic jar, then dipped his fingers into a bowl, grabbed the girl's head with his free hand, held the fingers of his other hand up to her nose, and forced her to sniff at them. The girl relaxed almost immediately, letting out a loud sigh, her head falling back against the wall as her eyes opened again. This time she looked steadily at Antonio, the drug making her calm.

"Speak to him," the old man said harshly. "You must answer his questions."

"Questions?" The girl smiled at Antonio. "You want to question me, mister?"

"Yes," Antonio said, smiling back at her, "I want to ask a few questions—and first I want to ask if you remember me or the young man behind me."

Her eyes swung slowly up to Alex and she smiled flirtatiously at him. Then, seeing Avril, she abruptly scowled and looked back at Antonio. "*Sim, Senhor,*" she said. "The two of you I remember. You were the friendly one, the one who ran the plantation, and him, the one behind you, was the son of the pig, the big white chief who killed my father and stole me from Mengrire, shaming my honor."

Alex closed his eyes, wanting to die on the spot, but Avril's fingers, entwined with his own, lent some warmth to his frozen soul.

He opened his eyes again and saw Antonio staring at him, so he nodded, letting him know that he could continue, and then watched the girl. She kept gazing around the room, her eyes unfocused, distractedly chewing the bedsheet.

"Why did you run away from the plantation?" Antonio asked her.

"Because we killed the big white chief."

"You mean, you and Mengrire?"

"Yes."

"Anyone else?"

"No."

"Can you tell me what happened that night?"

"I feel good. I can tell." She sucked the sheet into her mouth, spat it out and stared at Alex, noticed Avril and abruptly scowled again, and then stared at Antonio, her brown eyes gradually going out of focus as she slipped back to that distant night. "It was Mengrire," she said. "He was avenging my shame. The big white chief killed my father, then used me as his whore, and Mengrire, who wanted me as I wanted him, told me that the pig had to die and that we must then run away. Oh, mister, I was frightened—when I heard that I was frightened—but Mengrire knew better—he had heard the drums of the Yano—and he told me that he could not live without me as his woman, that the only way he would get me was to destroy the white master and steal me away, and that he had sold his soul to the devil by sniffing *epena* and invoking the power of the Yano, and through this had finally found the courage to kill my tormentor. So, that terrible night, after we had both taken the *epena*—in the forest where we saw the gods of darkness and joined together as one—he came to the *fazendeiro*, to that awful room where I suffered so much, and then, following the instructions of a voice from the Otherworld of the Yano, killed the big white chief with a machete while he sat in his chair. And the other one, the fat one, oh how he shrieked and pleaded, but Mengrire, my man, paying for me with his soul, again raised the machete above his head and ignored all but his calling, after which, while the blood flowed, while their bodies were still twitching, I took the knife that he gave me—the knife blessed by the Dark Ones—and cut off what had made the pigs men and filled their mouths with their manhood."

"Oh, God," Avril murmured, her voice cutting through Alex's anguish, making him turn his head to see her covering her face with her hands. She was shivering, but there was little he could do since, given what he had just heard, his own pain was slicing through him as if, by some diabolical magic, the machete which had been wielded by Mengrire were being used against him.

"What about the American woman?" Antonio was saying. "Why did she run away with you?"

"She heard the screaming," the girl said, "and came running into the room: all the servants had heard the screaming, too, but were too frightened to enter. Also, they all hated the master and so blocked up their ears."

"So the American woman entered the room, and then she fled with you. Why did she do that?"

"We didn't wish it, but did not oppose it. We thought the woman was simply crazy. She rushed into that awful room, saw the blood and evil dead, was sick and dropped into a chair, and was calmed by Mengrire. Oh, my man, he was so kind—he was covered in blood but still kind: he told her about my great suffering, told her how my shame would only be erased by his actions, and how the Yano had talked to him. She was very interested in the Yano—hearing their name helped her recover—and then, as she looked around her, when she had groaned and wept some more, she said that it was terrible, that it was part of her curse, that it had all been written in the stars and so she had to come with us. Yes, mister, we thought her crazy—but we wanted a gift for the Yano—and knowing that they would like a red-haired woman we let her leave with us."

The girl glanced up at her uncle, who was standing behind Avril, his rheumy eyes peering out of a shrunken face, his tongue sliding on rotten teeth. He was stripped to the waist, his ribs showing through translucent brown skin, and the girl, scarcely recognizing his presence, let her gaze fall on Avril. Alex noticed that stare—its almost breathless intensity—and he shivered, seeing Avril doing the same, and wondered what was to come.

"What happened when you fled?" Antonio asked softly. "When you went into the rain forest in search of the Yano?"

The girl closed her eyes a moment, sucked the bedsheet like a dummy, then shuddered and opened her eyes again and stared straight at her raised knees.

"It was terrible," she said. "It was not what we had expected. We didn't have to find the Yano—they were waiting for us to come—and when we took the boat upriver, and then headed north into the forest, they observed us through lights that spun and sang with a noise beyond silence: a noise—even now it makes me tremble—

that seemed to shake us to pieces—a noise, perhaps a silence, just *something* that shook us apart. Yes, noise—or no noise—and lights that were not lights—and then—oh, I swear it—by the unmentionable that I renounced, they came, the forces of darkness, or the slaves of those forces—those cast out from the Yanoama to become the dreaded Yano—they emerged from the forest near Catrimani and took us into their camp.''

She kept staring at her knees, but her whole body seemed to ripple, waves of fear passing through her like sand blown by the wind, while the light, a flickering yellow streaked with black, made her flesh look like snake skin.

"We were already exhausted," she said. "The spinning lights had kept us from sleeping. We were weary and broken by the silence that seemed physical, and so, when the Yano took us to their village, we could not resist anything. And then—it was terrible, much worse than the most evil dreams—and even Mengrire, who had worshiped and obeyed them, was not spared from their diabolical practices.'' The girl took a deep breath, her eyes widening, the nightmare returning to life in her. "The village seemed ordinary—a collection of very large *malocas*, cooking pots steaming in the clearing, women weaving while the children played around them near the paddocks of livestock—but the men were like demons, their faces painted, their bodies pitch-black, their arms and legs covered in decorations that signified evil ones. They laughed a lot but were not good-humored, sang a lot but seemed to be groaning, and although they constantly sniffed from bowls of *epena* they received no joy from it. Mengrire told them why he had come—that he had heard them calling to him—but they only laughed at him, and slashed his body with their knives. And then, when he was bleeding, and biting his lips to stop his weeping, they tied him to a pole in the ground and made him watch what was happening.''

Alex felt completely stifled, the heat of the closed room getting to him, his eyes hurting from having to strain through the flickering candle-lit darkness, and also, he surmised, from the nausea that filled his stomach when the Indian girl, studying her knees with moody eyes, continued her story.

"We were stripped naked and beaten—myself and the American woman—then tied with thongs and staked out on the ground just in front of Mengrire's feet. There we remained all day, through the jungle's terrible heat, forced to endure the most unmentionable humiliations and taunts, constantly abused and tortured by the barbaric woman-hating Yano while Mengrire, my man, once so proud, shed his tears right above us. The sun moved across the sky, burned straight down on us at noon, passed on and let the afternoon cool us where our skin bled and burned—yes, they had done that, dropped hot ash on our slashed skin, rubbing pepper into wounds still seeping blood and urinating upon us—and finally, when it was evening, when the moon had replaced the sun, they started to pound their devil's drums and endlessly sniff the *epena*—and I knew then, when I saw their eyes grow bright, that they were turning into madmen.''

The girl sighed and stared at Avril, a hint of venom in her gaze, as if, in seeing this white woman's health and unmarked beauty, she were reminded of all that she had lost and could never recover. Then, with an almost imperceptible shudder, she again lowered her eyes to her brown, scarred knees.

''The Yano were demons, worshiping the devil and hating women, thinking women to be the handmaidens of the great unmentionable, creatures who could seduce them from the path of darkness and render them helpless; so, they enslaved their women, constantly abused and humiliated them, even made human sacrifices of them at certain times of each year. They were particularly fascinated by the American woman—by her fair skin and red hair—and that night, when they were crazed, when they were engaged in their diabolical rituals, when they had dragged us both into the center of a circle filled with their crazed brothers—all drumming or chanting or dancing or fornicating, sometimes with one another, sometimes with animals, never with their own women—when they had dragged us out there, our bodies burning and bleeding, they cast me aside, their attention drawn by the American woman, and then took turns at possessing her, holding her down while she screamed and sobbed, desecrating her body, that seductive instrument of the unmentionable, in order to invoke the forces of darkness and cause the Good to retreat. Oh, yes, they all had her—so many! so long!—and she passed in and out of consciousness many times, *many* times, her sobs drowned out by the pounding of the drums and the frightening shrieks of the crazed men.''

There was a sudden creaking sound and Alex turned his head a little to see Avril, her face a mask of horror, sinking onto a wooden chair. She held the chair with one hand, the other hand twitching in her lap, and she seemed to be breathing very heavily in the tense, too brief silence. The old man was still near the window, sucking his cheeks in, licking his rotten teeth, while Antonio, near the bed, gazing up at the Indian girl, looked like a quiltwork of light and shadow, bizarre and unreal. Alex also took a deep breath and wiped more sweat from his brow, his soul lacerated by what he was hearing, his fear seeming to choke him.

"So," the Indian girl continued, "the Yano had her—so *many* had her—while the drums beat and the others shouted and wailed and danced, and Mengrire, my poor Mengrire, still hung there and sobbed, his blood congealed where they had pressed burning torches against him and scarred him with hot stones. And then—oh, it was frightening!—when the last man had the American woman, when she was whimpering in her delirium and quivering like a bowstring, and as the drums reached a terrible, an almost unbearable crescendo, the Yano really went crazy—even worse than before—chanting and shrieking and jerking as if convulsed, their black bodies gleaming in the flickering light of the numerous fires, their feet kicking up the dust, the smoke swirling around them, as the stars—*yes, the stars!* —actually started to move—up and down, to and fro, in great loops and circles—and then changed into spinning lights like the ones that had haunted us, these lights rising and falling—falling as gently as bubbles, falling out of the shifting sky—the sky was tilting and turning around—and forming dazzling globes around us—a constant rising and falling of lights, at first above us and then below us— *yes, mister, below us:* a great lake of lights or stars where the ground had been, like staring *down* at the night sky—and then I looked across at the American woman, at her abused, naked body, and saw her writhing on the ground, her skin slimy with mud and blood, and groaning as ectoplasm came out of her mouth—perhaps a ghost, her spirit, some demon that had possessed her—and then I saw, all around her, in that upside down night, materializing out of the drifting lights and stars and tilting sky, something beautiful, something horrible—something beautiful *and* horrible—a vision that completely overwhelmed me and mercifully made me unconscious . . . *I saw God and the devil!*"

Avril released a choked sob and then jumped out of her chair, kicking it over onto its side as she fled from the dimly lit, stifling room. Alex watched her departing, too stunned to go after her, then heard the gasping of the Indian girl on the bed as Antonio leaned toward her. The old man had rushed forward and was also standing by the bed, tugging angrily at Antonio's shirt sleeve and spitting words into his ear. Antonio pushed him away with one hand, shook the Indian girl with the other, and said harshly: "What happened after that? How did you manage to get back here? *Talk* to me! What happened to the American woman? *You've got to tell me what happened!*'' But the girl simply shrieked hysterically and jerked away from him, turning her face into the wall and then praying dementedly. The old man started shouting, his hands waving above his head. Antonio pushed him away and rushed Alex out of the house.

"We'll get no more out of her," Antonio said, "but at least we've learned *something:* Father Benedict knows more than he's told us up to now—so let's find him and get the rest of the story before he also goes crazy."

They saw Avril ahead of them and managed to catch up with her near the bottom of the hill. Alex grabbed her hand and held it tightly, pulling her close to him and keeping her there as they walked toward the waterfront bar that Father Benedict had mentioned. Alex wiped sweat from his brow, aware of his racing heart, listened to Avril repeating brokenly, "I saw it! I *saw* it!" and felt that his senses were slipping away into a healing delirium.

The tall stilts were all around them, the shacks towering right above them, the water lapping nearby and bringing with it the soaked rubbish that littered the muddy ground around the shops and warehouses, around the fruit and fish stalls, around the door of the waterfront bar where they hoped to find Father Benedict. Alex followed Antonio in, still holding tightly to Avril, but when he squinted through the gloom, at the dusty tables and chairs, he saw no one but the fat, lethargic barman. When asked by Antonio if he had recently seen a white man, the barman simply raised his hands and shrugged his shoulders.

"Where *is* he?" Antonio asked.

26

The mission camp was small and desolate, made diminutive by the soaring trees, its few wooden buildings, now shuttered and empty, incongruous in the forest's green splendor and weird daylight silence. Father Benedict kept staring at it, his cigarette smoke stinging his eyes, his free hand, as he rubbed the tears away, shaking visibly and shaming him. What had he done? Why had he returned here? He looked across the clearing, at the empty medical hut, seeing the ghosts of his past there before him, still kicking up dust. Naked children had played there freely, chasing frightened ducks and geese, while their parents, most wearing shirts and trousers or shabby dresses, had milled around those mildewed wooden steps, waiting for treatment. Now, it was all closed, the mission as silent as a graveyard, while around it the rain forest, as usual ominously quiet and gloomy, let little sunlight penetrate through the trees, no breeze temper the clinging heat.

Father Benedict sniffed a little, inhaled on his cigarette, picked his hip flask off the damp earth, and had another long drink. He glanced at the sky, lugubrious, gray as slate, then turned away from the desolate, depressing mission and looked across the immensely wide, stippled river which, at this particular point, was perfectly empty and flat. The priest drank from his hip flask, trying to deaden the sound of silence, then leaned forward, his posterior hurting from the rusty barrel that supported him, and again stared at the jungle surrounding the mission, remembering when he had worked here.

Worked here . . . and loved here: just thinking of Laura choked him up, making him groan aloud and tremble with grief, lowering his gaze to the muddy earth. The rain forest, spread around him, was resonant with silence, forcing him back into himself where his worst fears were buried.

What had he done? Why had he come here? Those questions resounded in the forest silence and made his cheeks burn. The discovery of the Indian girl—that alone had been enough—and he had, at the very sight of that green-painted house, felt all of his deceptions come to light before man and God. So he had run, not even stopping at the bar, instead fleeing up the narrow street, away from the *igarape*, and then catching the first taxi that came by and huddling up in its rear seat. He had told the driver to bring him here, scarcely knowing the reasons why, and had spent that singular journey, through time and shrunken distance, haunted only by the thought of what the Indian girl back in that stilted shack might be saying at that very same moment to his insistent, bewildered friends.

He inhaled on his cigarette, watched the smoke rings drifting in front of him, gazed through one of the rings at the gray sky beyond, and felt the enormous weight of his guilt falling upon him like lead. The empty mission filled him with pain, with an almost unbearable, sweeping sadness, making him remember Father Symonds, Mengrire, all the others, in those days before Laura Wellman arrived and turned his world upside down, finally forcing him, through the abomination of his acts, to flee from the rain forest. Yes, he had been tempted, and had succumbed in his weakness: *Behold, the man is become as one of us, to know good and evil. . . . Therefore the Lord God sent him forth from the garden of Eden. . . .* In truth, he had fled from here, but had been banished from his own spirit, losing himself in the thickets of his guilt and shame, surrendering his soul to the devil. It was the price he had paid for love—for the release of his repressed desires—and now, when he thought about it, when his shame and horror returned in full measure, he nevertheless knew, with the certainty of the unredeemed, that if Laura were to appear here before him, he would do it all over again.

He covered his face with his hands, wanting to pray but unable to do so, groaned and had another drink, and slowly climbed to his feet. His eyes were wet, but he wasn't really crying; he sniffed and rubbed his nose, the desolation eating at him, then turned his back on the river and walked across the clearing until he reached the small raised hut that had once belonged to Father Symonds and had then, for a brief but traumatic period, been inhabited by Laura. He stood there for a moment, the toes of his shoes touching the bottom step. Then, carefully putting his hip flask into the pocket of his tropical jacket, he removed a clasp knife from his other pocket and walked up the few steps.

The silence was getting to him, and he felt slightly deranged, first glancing nervously over his shoulder at the eerily silent, deserted clearing, then opening the knife and slipping it under the metal base of the ring that was fixed to the door to secure the padlock. He pried the base loose from the wood, then slid the blade of the knife in further, bending it upward until the screws snapped loose and the padlock fell to the ground; then, closing the knife and slipping it back into his pocket, glancing again over his shoulder as if expecting to see someone, he walked into the small, gloomy room and stood there in silence.

He choked up almost immediately, waves of sentiment sweeping through him—grief, guilt, memories of brotherly love and respect, of sexual passion and shame—and he felt the emotions rippling through him as his eyes grew accustomed to the semidarkness and the contents of the room materialized before him as if from a ghost world: walls made of forest logs, open shelves along some of them (once crammed with books, but now empty), a hammock still stretched between one wall and a pole thrusting up from the floor, a mosquito net above the hammock and above the crudely made single bed; and, in the middle of the room, the same small wooden table where Father Symonds used to write his letters, a couple of matching chairs, plus three or four dust-covered oil lamps, their wicks dry and brown. Father Symonds had lived here, reading and preaching the word of God, but then, shortly after the mission had been closed, a singular desecration, a blasphemous sin, had perverted the hut's former sanctity. Thus did Father Benedict, in betraying his faith, also betray his old friend.

He stared at the bed, the mattress remaining though the sheets had gone, and slowly, almost dreamily, as if in a trance, he walked over to it, bent down a little, raised the mattress, found what he had been looking for and held it up in his shaking hand.

It was a pair of white panties, lightly laced, perfectly clean, and Father Benedict, remembering that night, when she had chuckled and given them to him, was shaken by a tide of love, by an onrush of desire and loss; closing his eyes, groaning again and trembling all over, he buried his face in that fine lace, letting his hungry lips moisten it.

He stood thus for some time, his face buried in the white panties, feeling her presence through the lace, his desire resurrected and setting his loins on fire, his skin glowing with a fine, tormenting heat while he trembled all over. Yes, he felt her through the panties, and smelt her and saw her—her green eyes bright and wild, her hair whipping like windblown flames, her thin body as smooth and white

as marble, opening to him like her painted, panting lips, arching up
to be touched by him—and he groaned again, this time very loudly,
and felt his whole body quivering like a live wire as the need made
his blood race.

Nothing could help him—he was possessed completely by her—
and with another cry of despair, his swollen flesh draining his
senses, he threw himself face down on the bed, his lips still pressed
to the panties. He touched himself with one hand, felt his pulsating,
insistent erection, and then let the spasms whip through his body as
his tears soaked the white lace.

He sank down, his spasms subsiding, to where the waves of
shame washed over him, below that to where sleep was the pale tide
that languidly lapped through the darkness. He rolled onto his back,
aware of his own dampness beneath him, and then saw Laura
coming through the door and walking up to the bed. She lowered her
head to stare at him, her lavish hair falling over him, then her lips
curved, smiling enigmatically, as she knelt on the floor. She seemed
vaporous, unreal, her skin glowing and translucent, and she gently
held his right hand and raised it to her lips, kissing it, licking it, the
ridged knuckles, the tingling palm, sliding her tongue sensuously
between his fingers to lick them and suck them.

I can't help it.

Forgive me.

She loosened the cuffs of his shirt, unbuttoned the shirt, then his
trousers, removed his clothes as if undressing a baby, letting them
fall to the floor. He burned with shame and love at once, writhed in
guilt and rising lust, felt her lips on his chest, on his stomach, all
around him, until, with a sigh—perhaps a sigh of sorrow—she ran
her tongue lightly along his legs and took his toes in her mouth.

He melted completely at that moment, dissolving down through
himself, hearing his own plea for forgiveness ringing sepulchrally
through the void as he found himself standing before an arched
gateway that appeared to have formed itself from vines and palm
leaves. *So he drove out the man . . .* and so saying, he went through
the gate and went east of the garden, where he saw a column of light
which, shaped like a great jeweled sword, turned into a pillar of
flames. He cried out, protesting his banishment, his shame equaled
by his rage, but then the cherubim materialized, winged creatures
with human faces, staring upon him from the swirling smoke of the
flaming sword and driving him away from the garden. He saw
knotted treetrunks, the tangled web of the giant lianas, saw green

vegetation and dark forest and trapped, dying insects—and then, suddenly awakening from his sleep, saw the hut's mesh-wire window.

He lay there, half dazed, still holding Laura's panties, aware that the damp patch on his trousers had already dried and that the gray afternoon light outside was surrendering to darkness. His shame was almost too much to bear, hurting his head, making his heart race, and he swung his legs awkwardly off the small bed and forced himself to stand up. He felt weak and was shaking, and the deepening gloom disturbed him, so after one last glance around the hut, he walked toward the door. Before he reached it he stopped again, suddenly remembering what he had dreamed, and suddenly, as he stood there, visualizing Laura in that same doorway—entering not as she, but as *he* had entered that night (the night before she left the mission to take up residence in the plantation) to join her in Father Symonds's old bed and to hell with damnation—yes, as he stood there, he almost believed he could actually see her, standing right there before him, and eventually, correcting himself, adjusting his clothing and shaking his head, he walked on through the door—through her ghost—and descended the steps to the clearing.

Every nerve in his body was shrieking, lacerated by his terrible guilt, and as he walked across the clearing, looking over the vast, darkening river, he thought of Alex and Avril, of his benign friend Antonio, and burned with the knowledge that he had cheated them and was continuing to do so. He was ashamed, but could do nothing, unable to go the whole way, to tell them, and thus accept himself, the full, hideous story. No, he couldn't do that—the very thought of it chilled his soul—and as he gazed at the water, watching the darkness descend upon it, turning river and sky into a rich, blood-red tapestry enclosed by an endless ribbon of blackening jungle, so, as he watched it, and heard the breaking of the silence, he understood that he could now run no farther and decided to kill himself.

The decision came with remarkable ease, encouraging the peace of resignation, and he shoved the panties into his trouser pocket and walked toward the river. He even smiled as he did so, and for the first time in a long time he actually thought of God, believing that He might indeed have His reasons and, as in this particular part of His great plan, was not beyond displaying a certain irony.

Father Benedict reached the river, filled with pain, but still smiling. When he stopped, looking down the sloping bank, surprised that the darkness had fallen so quickly and trying to find the best way to the river's edge, he suddenly realized that the silence, which had been broken gradually by the forest's nocturnal chattering, was actually filling up with something much more sinister: the beating of Yano drums.

The fear swooped down immediately, its vicious claws tearing at him, and he whirled around and looked up at the sky, dreading what he would see . . . the lights rising and falling.

The lights were like Catherine wheels, ascending and spinning rapidly, their brilliant outer rings swirling around a darker core, their silvery striations shooting out for miles and turning into great cobwebs. There were a great many of them, forming kaleidoscopes in the starry sky, shooting up from the jungle depths, far north, in the interior; and equally mysteriously, exploding out of the sky itself, first as pinpricks of light, then as dazzling fluorescent flares that descended in slow, elegant arcs and disappeared in the jungle.

He stared at them, horrified, convinced that his presence had roused them, and then, as the drums grew louder, turning into that familiar, bone-rattling bedlam, he sensed movement to his left, near the ground, in the tall rushes, and looked down to see two alligators lumbering awkwardly toward him. First startled, then terrified, forgetting his plan to kill himself, he turned and raced away across the empty clearing, toward the room that had once belonged to Father Symonds. He heard thunder (*Was* it thunder?). Lightning daggered down from the sky. With a gigantic ripping sound the hut burst into flames.

Father Benedict staggered back, his head reeling. He ran to the right, glancing sideways at the burning hut. The flames filled the night like fluttering yellow banners, illuminating the darkness at the edge of the forest. Breathing harshly, he kept running. He glanced up and saw the lights, looked the other way and saw the black river under its mantle of stars. He shuddered and stopped again. He took out his clasp knife, looked up at the door of his old hut, and started running toward it. The thunder roared again (*No, that isn't thunder!*) and then the lightning daggered down through the darkness and his old hut exploded, the flames leaping upward and outward in immense, dazzling loops and coils.

He turned in another direction, deciding to chance the jungle road, but then heard the thunder again, saw clashing fingers of lightning, saw all the mission buildings, one after the other, explode into great balls of yellow fire and swirling tendrils of inky smoke. He stopped running and glanced around him, let his eyes rest on the chapel, saw a pillar of fire take the shape of an upturned sword and then—or so he imagined—creatures materializing above it: gigantic but human— not *quite* human: with beating wings—and he stepped back, terrified, flinging his arm across his eyes, hearing his own trembling voice completing the tale that had been started, just an hour or so ago, in his bizarre, haunting dream:

"Therefore the Lord God sent him forth from the garden of Eden, to till the ground from whence he was taken. So he drove out the man; and he placed at the east of the garden of Eden Cherubims, and a flaming sword which turned every way, to keep the way of the tree of life."

Father Benedict fell down, crying aloud in his anguish, seeing the light of the flames filling the darkness above his head, hearing the Yano drums beating, reaching a crescendo and fading quickly, then falling away into silence and the peace of unconsciousness.

He opened his eyes some time later, his throat parched, his head ringing, to smell rancid smoke, see the stars above in darkness, and hear another sound—a Jeep braking with considerable urgency—at which, trying to swallow, wishing his racing heart would slow down, he managed to prop himself up on his elbows and stare fearfully around him.

Looking behind him, he saw the remains of the mission, the buildings now no more than piles of smoldering ash and thin, drifting smoke; looking the other way, he saw the Jeep parked near the exit, the vines and palm leaves forming a natural arch over the jungle road, Alex, Antonio, and Avril walking hurriedly toward him. He gasped and fell back, his head hitting the ground heavily, and lay there, defeated, thinking of what had just occurred, and accepting that it was all part of a pattern which was not yet completed. Nevertheless, he was still frightened, his body shaking, his head reeling, and when Antonio knelt down beside him, followed immediately by Alex and Avril, he understood that he had yet to find release from the pain of existence.

"So," he croaked, looking up at Antonio, "you managed to find me."

Antonio smiled gently. "It wasn't difficult," he said. "In fact, Alex was convinced that this was the first place you would come to."

"The second place being—?"

"The plantation. Which is where we're all going next." Antonio glanced around him at the smoldering huts and drifting smoke, then lowered his eyes again, looking thoughtful, and asked, "What happened here?"

"I'm not sure," Father Benedict said, pleased to hear his voice sounding normal. "I heard the Yano drums, saw the lights, became frightened, saw some *caimans*, and started to run. And then bolts of lightning—or what *seemed* like bolts of lightning—came down and systematically destroyed the mission. I think that I might also have seen some giant figures, but I probably imagined that."

"Strange figures?"

"Cherubim," Father Benedict said. "God's angels, no less."

"They must have been protecting you," Antonio said.

"Yes: from myself."

He pressed his elbows into the ground and forced himself to sit upright, looking left and right, then at Alex and Avril. Suddenly, with an intensity that was completely unexpected, he was filled with an anguish that shook him leaf and bough and again made him bury his face in his hands and weep like a child.

"You know!" he exclaimed, rocking back and forth. "She must have told you the truth! Oh, God, oh my God, please forgive me! *What did she tell you?*"

His sudden hysteria shocked him, slapping him back to self-awareness, and he immediately removed his hands from his face and sniffed back his remaining tears. His gaze fell on Avril, and her civilized, modest attractiveness soothed him, her brown eyes and auburn hair and pale skin making him feel strangely moved. He wanted to reach out to her—to touch that world he had left years ago—but instead he simply sighed and looked at Alex, thinking of how much he had changed in one year, of how his innocence had fled him. Alex, still handsome, had lost the mysterious beauty that springs only from the most rare kind of virtue but is easily scorched; like the trees around this clearing, he had been scorched very badly.

"Are you all right?" Alex asked him.

"Yes, Alex, I'm all right. A little bit shaken, but I'll survive. Did that girl tell you everything?"

"Not knowing what originally happened, I can't know if she told us everything: but she *did* tell us that you were the one who found her and brought her back to Manaus. If that's true, Father Benedict—"

"It is."

"—then why did you hide the fact?"

Father Benedict took a deep breath, looking across the dark river, the chattering of the rain forest in his ears, his eyes filled with swimming stars.

"I didn't want you to know," he said, "because I knew that once you discovered that fact, you would want to know how I found her."

"According to her uncle, you found her wandering in the forest weeks after she had actually disappeared. Is that true?"

"No, it's not."

He placed his hands on his head, the fingers interlocked on his skull, his palms pressing into his temples as if trying to crush them. He didn't know why he was doing that, but it gave him some comfort.

"All right," he heard Alex say, his voice soft but clearly trembling, "we know that you haven't told us all the facts—that you're holding back the full story—so you might as well tell it to us now and get it all off your chest. You couldn't have found the Indian girl as you described it—so what happened to Laura?"

"She was captured by the Yano—"

"We know that. What happened after that?"

Father Benedict felt hollow, stripped of pride and drained of life, and he wanted to lie down and die right here by the river. The jungle could have him—as the jungle had taken Laura—and even as that thought came to him, filling him up with her presence, he wanted to join her in the cold earth and share her great peace. He looked up at Alex, then at Avril and Antonio, saw the smoldering huts behind them, the enormous trees soaring above them, the stars sweeping over the trees and over the river with its glinting black surface; he was riven, torn, wounded beyond all hope of healing, but he knew that he would have to tell them the rest before the morning light came. Knowing this, he took a deep breath and let his words paint the awful truth.

"So," he said, "Laura didn't disappear that first time. She fled into the jungle with the Indian girl and Mengrire, but when she did so, she didn't disappear for all time: she actually returned five days later."

"No!" Antonio exclaimed. "She never returned! I was there! She did *not* return!"

Father Benedict waved his hand, a gesture designed to console Antonio, understanding that the Brazilian was frightened that Alex would think he was part of it.

"No, Antonio," he said. "You only *thought* she had disappeared

. . . but she actually returned five days later, coming to see me in the mission. And for reasons which I will endeavor to explain, I hid her away in the forest.'' He stared at each of them in turn, taking note of their complete bewilderment. Seeing the pain on Alex's face, he continued his story. ''After the murders, when Laura fled into the rain forest with Mengrire and the Indian girl, they were all captured by the Yano and, as you have doubtless heard, horribly humiliated and tortured, in Laura's case this taking the form of a truly appalling multiple rape which left her half crazy. However, the morning after that Yano orgy, when Laura had recovered sufficiently at least to have regained her instinct for survival, she and the Indian girl fled that hideous nightmare by simply walking away from the sleeping and very heavily drugged Yano. She was then led by the Indian girl—who had not suffered to the same degree at the hands of the Yano and was therefore more in control of herself—back through the jungle, south toward the Amazon, until they arrived, about five days later, at my mission. Luckily it was night and there was no one to see them. When I had sneaked them into my room, I learned the whole hideous story. I also noted that Laura was badly shocked— that she was, in fact, almost demented.''

He closed his eyes for a moment, shutting out the moon and stars, remembering that night of glory and horror when Laura returned: glory because it was a miracle that she was still alive and had returned to him; horror because of what she had been through and the state she was in. Even now he winced to remember, seeing her clearly in his mind's eye. They had knocked on his door after midnight, and when he had opened it he had been frightened, seeing the Indian girl first, her face covered in grime, her eyes gleaming with fear in the starlight as she muttered incoherently. And then he had heard the scuffling, fingers scratching on the outside wall, and as he took a step forward, about to peer around the door, Laura slid into view, her large green eyes clearly demented, shining out of a face that was covered in blood and mud, this slime also covering the tattered remains of her clothing and sticking to what remained of her red hair, which had, he was horrified to note, been mostly hacked off with knives. Clumps had actually been torn out by the roots, leaving ulcerated, bare skin. Of course he had taken them in, embracing Laura with anguished love, his tears mingling with hers as they both sobbed uncontrollably while the Indian girl, wolfing down some food, told him all that had happened. Later he managed to calm her—after managing to calm himself. As he studied her, shocked and outraged at the sight of her, she explained, her tongue tripping over the words, that it was all meant to be.

"She was convinced that the mass rape had been diabolical, that it had, instead of saving her, been designed to fill her with the spirits of darkness, thus making her a vessel for Satan and, by so doing, fulfilling the prophecy of Aleister Crowley. Anyway, there was that—and the terrible psychic scars from the experience generally—and so, that same night, before the dawn broke, I sneaked them back out of the mission and hid them in a local village, where they stayed for some time—and where, Alex, she was in fact hiding when you returned from school in Manaus to attend to your father's funeral and close up the plantation. After a few weeks, when I saw that she was getting restless—but not wanting to return her to her village—I took the Indian girl, who was also suffering from fits of dementia, to stay with her uncle in Educandos, where you found her; but Laura continued to live in that village, determined in the conviction of her madness never to leave it. . . . Yes, Alex, for the whole of that second week, when you were closing up the plantation, Laura was hiding out in that village, no more, I would imagine, than twenty miles from the plantation itself."

He watched Alex sucking his breath in, closing his eyes, shuddering slightly, and understood with a fine sense of woe just what he was feeling—just as he knew, by the fluttering of his own heart, that what he was about to recount would hurt the boy even more.

"So," he said, "you attended to your father's business and went off to England, but Laura remained right here in the jungle, in that small, relatively unknown Indian camp. She was in a terrible state, refusing to see anyone she had known, and the memory of that whole nightmare refused to leave her mind—particularly those visions she had had of God and the devil warring over her—and then, when she discovered that the impossible had occurred—that the mass rape had left her pregnant—she was convinced more than ever that it had all been preordained and that now she was going to give birth to Satan's child. Thereafter there was no hope of consoling her: that child was all she could think about."

This time Alex turned away, fixing his gaze on the wide, black river, a slight tremor rippling through his body and then leaving him still. He was breathing deeply but evenly, obviously fighting to control himself, and Father Benedict saw Avril staring at him with love and concern. *A fine girl*, he thought. *She is just what he needs: she is stable and knows what she wants, which is what that boy wants.* Not Laura, though: she had never known what she was seeking; so, when she found the Yano, when she found life's ghastly reality, she retreated into protective insanity and refused to come out of it. He remembered, and would not ever forget, how she spent day after day, night after night, in that small thatched hut, smearing her face with the dirt, stumbling to speak the Indians' language, mumbling constantly about Satan and his child and the forces of darkness and, like a jackal, like a hyena sniffing for blood, spending much time staring up at the moon and rubbing her taut, swelling belly. Father Benedict, thinking about that, caught Alex's returning gaze and, feeling as if he had been knifed, lowered his own eyes demurely.

"During her pregnancy," he continued, "when you, Alex, were back in England, Laura grew increasingly demented and was kept from a total breakdown only by my own devoted attentions when I determined to do everything in my power to make amends for my sins. Of course it wasn't that alone, not *merely* the need for penance, but was also an impulse that sprang from my continuing, most passionate love. Nonetheless, I was made to suffer, unable to forget what they had done to her, and, even worse, also suffering because, in her fear and anguish, she could no longer tolerate being touched, particularly in any manner suggesting intimacy. Yet, as I loved her, so too did she love me; and in her stumbling broken way, her eyes unfocused, her words faltering, she often tried explaining to me that her inability to let me touch her was caused not only by her still vivid memories of her abuse at the hands of the Yano but, perhaps more importantly, by the knowledge that she was pregnant and probably carrying a child of Satan. Her love for me—and her awareness that I was still a man of God—made her frightened that she might somehow contaminate me if she once let me have her. So, during those terrible months, when she lived like the lowliest Indian, when she smeared her face with mud and tried to obliterate her former character, retreating into another, more demented world filled with demons and ogres and tormenting Yano Indians—so, during all that, as I secretly stayed with her and cared for her, I nonetheless could not touch her, could not satisfy my relentless and undiminished desire until, in some miraculous way, perhaps understanding what she had been through and was imagining if not actually suffering, I found my desire for her turning into something different; that in fact, since I could no longer possess her physically, while still wanting her emotionally and spiritually, my desire was turning into the pure flame of a selfless, asexual love. It was the transcendental moment of my life—to know pure love for another—and I used it to try to protect Laura from her burgeoning madness.''

He stopped talking, glanced around him, saw the moonbright, starlit night, took some comfort from Antonio's steady, supportive gaze, then fixed his own eyes directly at Alex, letting the truth break the silence.

''Unfortunately, I failed. Laura gave birth to the child—a perfectly normal child of Indian extraction—and thereafter appeared *completely* to lose touch with reality. She simultaneously loved and feared the child, was devoted to it and reviled it—on the one hand in awe at the miracle of its actual existence, on the other terrified of its possible nature and reason for being—and so, inevitably, because of that *and* her past beliefs, all her hope was defeated by her increasing revulsion and mortal terror until—and I still can't say it without nausea—she came to accept that she had given birth to Satan's child.''

''This is horrible,'' Avril said.

Father Benedict glanced up and caught the full weight of her stare, the large, luminous brown eyes very steady, but filled with muted revulsion. He returned his attention to Alex, noticing how slight he still was. Alex slowly raised his head and spoke in a tentative whisper.

''Go on,'' he said. ''It isn't finished yet. I want to hear all the rest.''

Father Benedict told him, trying to keep his voice steady, but hearing it cracking as he talked more and more, every word like a separate stab in his vitals. As he told it, he relived it, seeing it vividly and becoming part of it, again squatting in that small, squalid hut through long nights and shimmering days. If the hut was squalid, so was Laura, her face caked with mud and grease, her red hair, once long and luscious, now like a piece of ragged carpet. The fingers that tugged her hair also pulled restlessly at her dress of sack cloth, hanging loose around her body, that once elegant frame now emaciated, her feet blistered from walking on stony ground, her emerald eyes wild and furtive. The hut stank of sweat and urine, the baby howled day and night, and Father Benedict, doing penance, and also demonstrating his love, fed the baby when Laura ignored it, washed it clean, kept its scabs to a minimum, tried to get her to love it. In fact, she *did* love it, often holding it and rocking it, just as often crooning to it, occasionally sweeping it up in her arms and crying for what it might be—but she was also frightened of it, the fear ascending to heights of terror. As she rebounded from love to terror, the latter gradually took precedence. Then, that awful evening, when Father Benedict found the baby missing, when he looked at Laura's eyes and saw their enormous, staring insanity, he was forced to step back in horror and disbelief as she told him what she had done.

"She killed it," Father Benedict said. "Plunging it into a barrel of water. She was sobbing, in despair, cursing the devil and herself, pushing the child down into the water, her fingers slipping and sliding off it, the baby bobbing up and down and howling and spinning over, being pushed down and springing up again and being forced down once more. She was never to forget that moment—she would recount the story repeatedly—of how the night swam all around her, the stars and firelight blending, as the baby screamed and rolled and bobbed up and down, Laura's tears dripping into the barrel in which her baby was drowning. . . . She killed it, Alex. Oh, dear God, she drowned her own child . . . and doubtless, in trying to thus destroy the devil, gave her soul over to him."

The pain was too much to bear, and Father Benedict burst into tears again, twisting his body away from them as he covered his face with his hands. He kept crying for some time, unable to stop himself, as if whole rivers of tears were pouring out of him to carry the pain away. Eventually hands fell on his shoulders, feminine hands, touching him lightly, and he turned back and pressed his face into Avril's breasts as she held him close to her. She was speaking very softly to him, almost crooning, her words like music, patting his shoulders and rocking him from side to side as if soothing a child. He felt ashamed, but also comforted, touched by human warmth and sympathy, and finally, when his tears had all dried, he mumbled his thanks and moved backward out of her arms, shame-facedly drying his sodden cheeks.

"I'm sorry," Alex said, "but I've got to ask you. What happened to Laura?"

"*That's* when she disappeared," Father Benedict replied. "After killing the child." He glanced up at the sky, at the wheeling stars in the heavens, stunned by life's beauty and cruelty, by its casual indifference; then, taking another deep breath, he looked back at Alex. "Murdering her own child was the last straw," he said, his voice like smoke, drifting through the darkness and coiling languidly around their shared grief. "She had buried the baby's body some-where deep in the rain forest, and a few days after that, during a night when the Yano drums were beating, perhaps as a form of penance, possibly suicide, she headed back into the jungle and was not seen again. I waited—oh, God, how I waited—but she never came back. She had gone for all time.''

He looked at each of them in turn, frightened of what he had done to them, seeing six eyes in the moonlight, three bodies breathing with great tension, and then one face, Alex's face, floating toward him out of a vast, star-filled backdrop.

''When was that?'' Alex asked him.

Father Benedict sat up straight, stared at Alex, stared right through him, saw the stars in a sky that went forever through silence and emptiness. Was the cosmos part of God? His mind? His projected vision? Or was it no more than a boundless, eternal emptiness without pity or love? Thinking about it, he shivered, frightened by what they might all be: the human being, with his burning hopes and aspirations and valiant dreams, with his love and compassion and hatred and anguish, the human being no more than a fleck of matter in an infinite nothing. Is that what it all came to? Was his love for Laura no more than that? Was the suffering of Alex no more than a spark in that endless night? He shuddered, denying this, letting his anguish course through him, threatening to break him, but also humanizing him and making of him a miracle.

''Last month,'' he said.

27

Finally, definitely. Avril knew what the jungle was like: not exotic and beautiful, the greenery lush in brilliant sunlight, the flowers blooming in a dazzling profusion, but alien and ominous, sunlight rarely penetrating to the forest floor, the humidity making everything outsize but preventing the more colorful flowers from growing, the ground marshy and treacherous. By day it was silent, its greenery brooding and sullen, the enormous trunks of the trees, wrapped in the giant lianas, bathed in a strange and forbidding light that seemed to tug at the senses. And the heat—oh, dear God, she had never known such heat—an unrelenting, humid, equatorial furnace that seemed to suck the breath from her lungs and leave her constantly gasping. And that (she could scarcely believe it) was only the day: the night was very different, but equally uniniviting, the heat giving way to cold, the humidity giving way to a pervading dampness, the silence giving way to a constant noise that scraped at her nerves: the mass croaking of giant frogs, the hissing of minor rapids, the jagged, cutting shriek of one bird to another, constant rustling, ghostly growlings, the slitherings of snakeskin on tree bark and, miraculously, unbelievably, but most frightening of all, the great silence that arched above the forest canopy like an invisible dome. God, how she hated it! And cast her resentful sweat upon it! And was, every minute of every day, both frightened and fascinated by it, letting her mind dissolve into it.

Every minute of every day? She had only been in it for two days. It seemed like a century.

She glanced ahead, saw a machete swinging through gloom, glinting briefly when it passed through the barest hint of sunlight and chopped into the dense, obstructive foliage—branches covered in revolting fungi, palm trunks bristling with sharp spines, enormous dark green leaves, various kinds of clinging liana—as the Indian guide hacked a path through it, his back glistening with sweat.

Behind the guide were the Indian porters, four men and three women, all the men short and stocky, their bodies rippling with muscle, the women, mostly young girls, almost as sturdy as the men, all of them carrying bundles and packing cases on their heads, constantly ducking and straightening up again as they passed under low branches. Behind them, and in front of Avril, were Alex, Antonio, and Father Benedict, all of them wearing long trousers and white shirts, all soaked in sweat.

They had started the journey from the plantation, after inspecting its shuttered buildings, first traveling by canoe about fifty miles upriver, then marching north into the rain forest as Laura had done. At first Avril had enjoyed it, treating it almost as a reprieve, the sheer physical effort and the extraordinary strangeness helping to distract her from the fear that had built up inside her.

She had not seen the lights since the night of Father Benedict's confession, but each time she closed her eyes, either to sleep or just to rest, she saw them in the darkness of her mind, their beauty exquisite and frightening. And so her enjoyment of the journey hadn't lasted long: it had passed as soon as they stepped off the canoes, fading quickly as they marched into the rain forest and were plunged into gloom. Then that first night in the forest, kept awake by the forest noises, then further prevented from sleeping when, closing her eyes, she saw the mysterious lights rising and falling, illuminating her fevered thoughts. Yes, Avril hated this journey—hated the heat, hated the gloom, and most of all, hated the silence, the silence that made her think about too many things that would be better forgotten.

"Are you all right?" Alex asked over his shoulder.

"What do *you* think?" she snapped.

She regretted it immediately, seeing the hurt in his blue eyes, and realizing that she wasn't just tense but also riddled with guilt. She was feeling guilty because she had accused him of still being in love with Laura; more guilty since seeing his finely controlled grief in that desolate plantation: all the doors boarded up, the windows shuttered, the grass overgrown, the former houses of the *seringueiros* rotting beneath the dripping palmettos, the gray light making it all seem like a ghost town, silent and eerie. She had felt haunted in that place, sensing the ghosts of those departed, and when he had shown her the *fazendeiro*, also boarded up and shuttered, she had turned and walked away without a word, unable to stand the sight of it—or of his anguish. She had been glad to leave that place, and now, in this filthy jungle, near the unknown Yano territory, she knew that her resentment of Alex was based on her love for him.

"God," she gasped. "Dammit, I'm sorry, Alex: I didn't mean it that way."

"I understand," he replied.

She swatted flies from her face, had to spit them from her lips, felt them coming back, attracted by her sweat, to crawl upon her again. She kept swatting them away, cursing softly, her shoulders aching, then adjusted the white felt hat on her head and gasped in the hot, steamy air. Up ahead, Antonio stumbled, falling against Father Benedict, and the priest, with a speed that surprised him, grabbed his elbow and held him up. Antonio thanked him and the priest grunted a reply, then they both kept moving forward, behind the porters, as the machete hacked out a path for them.

There was actually a track here, overgrown and barely visible, which indicated, as Alex had told her with a feverish look, that they might be nearing the Yano. Avril wondered about that, feeling exhausted and very nervous, then twitched and slapped a giant beetle off her shoulder and moved away from the trees, trying to keep to the middle of the track, her booted feet finding soggy earth.

"How much longer?" she managed to gasp. "I don't think I can take much more of this. Every bone in my body is aching, and my lungs are on fire."

"Tomorrow," he said. "Sometime tomorrow evening. And it's going to be dark fairly soon, so you can have a rest then."

She plunged down into despair, into pits of further exhaustion, unable to bear the thought of so much distance still to be covered, nor the thought of another night in this pestilent jungle, trying to sleep. More flies buzzed around her, she dodged a cloud of mosquitoes, shadows shifted in the brush and she jerked away, imagining snakes, then hurried forward to catch up with Alex, his sweaty back magnetizing her.

The forest light was strange, not just gloomy but weird, constantly changing in some manner she could not define but which unsettled her greatly. She rubbed sweat from her eyes, blew some flies off her lips, saw the line of men and women with bundles and cases on their heads, a machete rising and falling, the foliage cracking and springing sideways, whipping back into more foliage and causing green leaves to scatter. Green—it was all green—a green deepened in gloomy light; she had to look very carefully to see the other forest colors: the shadowed brown of the treetrunks, the whitish brown of the dangling lianas, the yellowish-white of the fungi that covered the entangled branches, the dark clusters of cannonball fruit, and the red petals and silvery-white fruit of the heisteria flowers that very occasionally lent color to the gloom. Avril expected a riot of colors—but now she knew that most of the color was high up in the forest canopy—up there, near the sun, with the true wealth of forest wildlife: the insects and monkeys and snakes and extraordinary variety of birds. Yes, the beauty was all up there, breathing the air, warmed by the sun; down here it was the gloom and the damp and the silence, with stinging flies and poisonous spiders and eighteen-inch rodents, with brown moths and sloths and large cats and man-eating snakes. Down here, where she stumbled and sweated, was a world to make the flesh creep.

She went into a minor trance, feeling nothing but her aching bones, some part of her slipping away to avoid passing time. She hardly saw the darkness falling—perhaps the change was too abrupt—but suddenly, with an immense sigh of relief, she was sinking down to the ground. Father Benedict unscrewed his hip flask, Alex slid down to the ground beside her, both of them leaning against an enormous treetrunk while Antonio dealt with the porters. Something crawled onto her hand, she twitched violently, then relaxed, feeling Alex's fingers slipping between her own as he pulled her toward him. Yes, it was almost dark, and the forest was starting to chatter around her, and she put her head back against the treetrunk and took deep, even breaths. After a while she felt better, sat up straighter, looked around her, saw the Indians, men and women, expertly hacking the foliage away, making clear spaces and stringing the hammocks up and then lighting a fire. The fire lent a soft glow to the night, and the soup, boiled in the cans, was quickly consumed and helped to wash down the bread.

Avril kept looking around her, hardly believing where she was, trying to reconcile this place with the world she had come from, feeling, as she gave up in defeat, that she was living a dream. The forest around her was suddenly noisy, filled with distant growling and shrieking, the rustling and snapping much closer as the darkened floor came to life. She shivered, her skin crawling, thinking of spiders and giant snakes, of pacas and kinkajous and stinging termites and poisonous ants, then she drank the *cachaça* that Alex had given her and put her head on his shoulder.

"I wish it was all over," she said. "I don't think I can wait till tomorrow night. Although we haven't seen anything, I still feel

we're being watched: that we've been followed every inch of the
way and that we're not alone now.''

"We haven't seen anything,'' he replied, ''and we haven't heard
the drums—yet I feel exactly the same as you do: that we've been
watched all the way.''

"I sometimes think it's this amulet. Then I think it's just the
forest: that strange light that has no warmth in it and constantly
changes.''

"The forest can certainly do that: light and shadow come alive.
But I don't think that's our problem at the moment: I think we're
under surveillance.''

"By the Yano?''

"Yes. They can see across time and space. And I dread to think
of what they might do if they decide to take action.''

"I'm surprised they haven't done it before.''

"So am I,'' Alex said.

She was glad to get into her hammock, soothed by its gentle
swaying, and then she looked up at the trees directly above her and
immediately felt dizzy. The trees were black in the black night,
black tunnels leading up to the sky, showing tiny patches of stars as
they would be seen through an inverted telescope, placing a strain on
her eyes as the sky seemed to spin. She closed her eyes immediately,
took some deep, even breaths, glanced around at all the others—that
intimate circle of people in hammocks—and then, managing to close
her eyes again, prayed that sleep would come to her.

It came, and she slid through dreams, the shifting darkness brushing her lightly, familiar faces floating out of the void around her to
offer her comfort. She saw London, the gaunt ruins, her parents'
house in Regent's Park, her father introducing Alex to the family,
Alex's blue eyes invading her. He was indefinably beautiful, beguil-
ingly distant, almost too gentle to be true, and she went to him,
naked, unashamed, and wantonly dragged him on top of her. He
dissolved, disappeared, the walls of the bedroom became a cabin, a
brilliant light swirling fiercely above her and drawing her toward it.
She screamed—or tried to scream—collapsing inward on her own
silence, emerged from a curving tunnel of darkness to the deck of a
boat, snakes sliding across her feet, giant spiders dropping out of the
sky, flames flickering blue and yellow beneath the enormous light
that swirled just above. She looked up and saw it changing, shrinking rapidly, becoming the moon, followed its silvery striations back
down to the earth and the sad remains of the mission: piles of

charred, smoldering wood, gray smoke drifting through starlit darkness, coiling around the bowed head of Father Benedict where he sat on the ground. She reached out to comfort him, glanced at Alex, traveled through him, saw the padlocked, shuttered buildings of the empty plantation, the silence total and eerie. Laura Wellman was there, her magnificent hair like windblown flames, her green eyes very direct, touched with madness, her smile enigmatic. She mesmerized Avril, raising her hands, calling softly to her, and then Avril groaned aloud, her fear jerking her awake, and found herself tossing and turning on the swaying hammock, feeling that something was wrong.

Directly above her was pitch-black darkness broken by tiny glittering patches, the trees forming tunnels up to the stars, with the odd cloud, faintly illuminated by pale threads of moonlight, drifting across gaps in the forest canopy and making the sky appear to tilt slowly. Feeling dizzy, she turned her head, gazed around the makeshift camp, saw Alex, Antonio, and Father Benedict sleeping in their separate hammocks, the Indian porters, men and women, fearlessly sleeping on mats rolled out on the damp earth. She tried to see between the trees, but the darkness was almost total, offering only the haunting sounds of the birds and animals deep in the forest: the odd jagged, staccato cry, a very distant, hollow growling, the sudden screeching of a large group of angry monkeys, branches breaking as fruit fell down. Nearer the camp, it was different: there were no large animals there; instead there was constant rustling, the snapping of twigs, the sound, whether real or imagined, of slithering and sliding. Avril shivered, thinking of snakes, of furred sloths and hairy spiders, and was unable to stop scratching herself as she arched her spine in the hammock.

Then she heard something different, something louder and closer, so close that it made her body twitch and sent a cold chill down through her. She jerked her head around, hearing the sound from another direction, saw nothing but the darkness beneath the shivering trees and then, almost instantly, but from the opposite direction, heard the bizarre sound again. Terror slashed swiftly through her, turning her cold and making her tremble, as she heard the sound again, then again, yet again, now emanating like a ghostly chorus all around her, the sounds—for they were many—obviously coming from different sources and seeming to call out to one another and then intermingle.

Not an animal sound—a human sound!—a human imitating some

kind of animal . . . or like a child blowing through a tiny horn: a sort of hollow, high-pitched, quavering cry that was now rebounding spectrally, with a regular, eerie rhythm, from one side of the clearing to the other, as if the camp were completely surrounded by creatures who, whether human or inhuman, were calling out constantly to one another in that weird, frightening manner.

Panic paralyzed Avril, letting her move only her head, looking left and right, between her feet, in all directions, to where the strange calls seemed to be emanating from at an ever-increasing speed. Human beings? Strange creatures? The sounds were well above the ground—five or six feet off the ground—so, yes, they were possibly human, though that didn't help much. And then—oh, dear God! —she saw and heard movement: some bushes springing apart, something racing around the clearing, someone running the other way —yes, people, shadowy forms, all suddenly racing to and fro around the edge of the small camp.

Eyes! (*Could she see eyes?*) She thought she was going mad. The terror made her burn as she stared left and right, again between her own feet, and saw the eyes racing around her—eyes painted in luminous rings, the paint looking like glowing circles that flew to and fro as the men—if indeed they were such—encircled the camp. And then—*please God, no!*—she heard a rushing sound right behind her and violently jerked her head back, letting it hang down over the hammock, and saw him towering above her, a tall, black-skinned barbarian, his body all muscle and bone, his sweat glistening in a beam of moonlight, the luminous circles around his large eyes, the rest of his face painted, his head covered in feathers and leaves, his teeth bared in a demonic snarl as he raised a machete above his head.

Avril's own screaming slapped her awake, making her suddenly jerk upright, glancing wildly around her as bushes parted and sprang back together and the floating, luminous eyes disappeared like lights being switched off. Everyone had awakened—her screaming had done that—and she gripped the edge of her hammock, shaking violently and ill with fear, as Alex rushed up to her, followed by Antonio and Father Benedict, Alex holding her wrists and talking to her, asking her what had happened, while the others stared at her in alarm and, behind them, the Indian porters chattered excitedly to one another. Avril tried to explain, stuttering and shivering as she did so, and eventually managed to get it all out and swing herself off the hammock, determined not to sleep again that night and wanting to feel Alex's arms around her, as they were at that moment.

"It was the Yano!" Father Benedict exclaimed. "It had to be! *It was them!*"

"Be quiet!" Antonio snapped. "Don't mention their name again! If the porters even suspect that it was them, they'll panic and leave us. I'm going to tell them you had a bad dream, Avril, so please don't contradict me."

"He—the one above me—was going to kill me with his machete." Avril was surprised by her trembling voice, ashamed to hear her own fear.

"No," Antonio said. "He only wanted to frighten you. If he'd wanted to kill you, you'd be dead by now. They want to frighten us all."

He turned to the Indian porters, waving his hands and speaking sharply, lying about Avril's dream and telling them to go back to sleep. At first they were uncertain, then puzzled, then amused, and finally one of them jabbed his finger at Avril and made a grinning remark, at which they all burst into laughter and returned to their mats. Avril refused to go back to her hammock, and Alex sat on the ground with her, leaning against a treetrunk and putting a blanket over them both to keep out the cold. Avril shivered for a long time but eventually managed to stop, feeling warmer and more secure in Alex's arms. Antonio had gone back to his hammock, but Father Benedict was kneeling beside them, drinking some *cachaça* from his hip flask and then pursing his lips. He glared through the moonlit darkness at Avril and then shook his head.

"You think *tonight* was bad?" he said. "Then just wait till tomorrow. Now that they've found us—as clearly they have—they won't leave us alone. They'll try to drive us crazy, and then, when we've no resistance left, they'll just come and take us. Tonight was just the beginning."

Avril huddled up close to Alex, taking comfort in his arms, still frightened and feeling like a child, now dependent upon him. She slipped in and out of sleep, the priest's words refusing to leave her, repeating themselves insidiously in her head as the night slowly passed. When dawn came, she felt dazed, disconnected from those around her, eating her breakfast with little enthusiasm, but relieved to see daylight. Then everything was packed away, Antonio gave the command to move out, the Indian porters piled the bundles and cases on their heads, and eventually everyone followed the guide through the undergrowth, away from the clearing.

"Today," Father Benedict mumbled, wiping his cracked, shivering lips, "is the day that we will all learn to pray—because today will be hell."

He was right. This time they progressed easily, moving forward with little delay, the guide sheathing his machete because the forest floor was clear, with the lower layers of the trees quite high above them and the air reasonably cool—but then the heat came, building up beneath the trees, turning the dew to steam and the crisp air to gross humidity, making the flesh sweat and the mind reel toward catatonia: Avril holding on to her senses by keeping her eyes fixed on the others; Antonio just behind the guide, looking amazingly cool; Father Benedict looking weary, but managing to walk straight; Alex staying by her side and trying to fight his natural frailness, making her heart beat when she saw him, her love pouring out to him. Then, with that heat and exhaustion, the latter arriving remarkably quickly, came a relentless, frightening feeling of unreality which left everyone (she assumed) as unprepared as she for the demented screaming that tore through the forest's silence and stripped her nerves bare.

Avril briefly lost her senses, the fear automatic and blinding, felt a hand, someone's hand, Alex's hand on her elbow and was pulled aside (What was he trying to hide from her?) as the screaming grew in intensity. She jerked her elbow free, scanning the gloom, the scattering porters, and gasped, shaking suddenly, her heart beating too dramatically, when she saw the woman, brown-skinned, her long black hair whipping, being crushed in the coils of the giant anaconda that had slithered out of the rushes by the exquisite *verzea* lake over which, like solemn monks, the trees were bowed, their trunks beautifully decorated with mosaics of peperomia and reflected in water as still as glass.

It was a scene so beautiful and terrible that it would change her forever, stripping away the remnants of her childish belief in order, and leaving her with nothing but that breach which only true faith could fill. The horror and the beauty—the lake and the scene beside it—Avril stared, disbelieving, knowing nothing but what she saw: the very young Indian woman, her long black hair whipping, one free arm waving frantically, her whole body and both legs imprisoned in the giant snake's body—a thirty-five-foot anaconda—its lower half crushing her, pulsating as it tightened, coiled around her and dragging her gradually breaking bones back down toward the lush vegetation of the lovely *verzea* lake. The girl screamed—an inhuman sound—and waved her one free arm, and then choked into silence, the arm dropping like a broken twig, and spewed blood and phlegm onto glistening, mottled snakeskin as the monstrous reptile slid back into the black water and took her down with it.

Bedlam reigned as the porters panicked, shouting loudly and waving arms, dropping down to their knees and letting the supplies fall to the ground, clearly getting ready to run but being stopped by Antonio who, with that experience gleaned from years on the plantation, bullied and cajoled them into submission and pushed them onward again. "What—?" Avril began. (Was that her own voice? Not really.) "Shut up!" Antonio snapped. "Don't say anything! Please God, just keep walking!" And so she kept walking, trying to control her shaking limbs, avoiding Alex's haunted gaze, watching the priest drink from his hip flask and hearing his constant, obsessive monologues, only truly aware of her own increasing fear as the heat suffocated her. Yes, the jungle was a furnace—or, more accurately, an oven—and as they skirted the *verzea* lake, and followed the water to its babbling source, she felt that she was being buried alive in the lush green vegetation.

The source of the lake was a rock-strewn river, a tributary of the Rio Branco, a curving stretch of black water that briefly divided the soaring forest and let the sunlight pour down between the trees in oblique, wavering lines. The morning had almost passed, the sun stood high in the sky, and the sunlight, now so rare, reflecting off the dancing water, dazzled their gloom-expanded pupils and made them half blind.

Avril blinked and rubbed her eyes, saw the dense trees of the far bank, looked again and saw a long line of Indian warriors, blinked again and saw nothing. She shook her head from side to side, remembering the Indian poised over her hammock, assumed she was imagining things and again scanned the far side and, as a black body melted into the trees, heard a grunting noise beside her, turned her head and saw a spear, heard a whimpering become a groan as the porter stumbled backward, his hands groping at the spear that sloped down through his stomach and emerged from one side of his spine, just above his left buttock. He managed to grab the spear and screamed—another quavering, inhuman sound—and then he suddenly rushed forward, as if pulling himself by the spear, and seemed to glide through his own blood, which squirted over his fellow

porters, and then plunged head-first into the river with a dull, solid
splash.

At that instant all the other porters were galvanized into action,
shouting out in terror, dropping their bundles and cases and fleeing
back into the jungle. Only the guide remained, bawling angrily at
them and waving his machete—but even as he did so, the water
behind him started bubbling, suddenly exploded into a frothing
mass, the white foam streaked with red blood and filled with silvery
streaks as a shoal of piranha savagely attacked the man who had
fallen into the river. The water boiled in terrible fury, blood and
foam splashing over the green bank, the piranhas forming a solid
mass that resembled a giant heaving lung as their razor-sharp teeth
stripped the flesh from the man's bones, and his skeleton, first the
ribcage and then an arm, was released to float off downstream with a
great many fish still tearing at him and loose bones drifting free.

Avril had to look away, her flesh rippling with nausea, and found
herself staring at the far bank, half expecting to see the Indians
again. She saw nothing but the trees, the ominous gloom beneath
them, and she stepped forward, when the guide moved toward the
river, automatically following him. Then she heard the screaming
behind her—a terrible wail of human pain—and as she looked back
over her shoulder, her whole body twitching violently, she realized
that it was one of the Indian porters who had fled into the jungle.
There was another, different scream, then another and yet another,
as the porters, men and women, were butchered by the Yano warriors,
and then, as Avril sobbed, as the fear made her feel faint, Alex
grabbed her by the arm and practically dragged her toward the river,
following the guide, Antonio, and Father Benedict, all of whom
were already knee-deep in the water, their bodies swaying from side
to side as they fought the strong current.

"The fish!" Avril heard herself exclaiming. "Oh, my God, the
piranhas!"

"It's all right," Alex replied. "They only go for the smell of
blood. That whole shoal will be following that porter's blood as the
current takes it downriver. It's safe, Avril. Let's go!"

The water came up to her waist and beat against her with some
force, breaking around her in black, glittering eddies and then
flowing on. She held tightly to Alex, staring nervously at the far
bank, still expecting to see the fearsome Yano warriors emerge from
the trees. Mercifully they did not appear, but she heard another
shocking scream behind her, emanating once more from the forest

they had left as, she assumed, some of the fearsome Yano warriors tortured one of the unfortunate Indian porters.

Another hideous scream made her cover her ears with her hands, turning her head as she did so and glancing upstream to where the river, flowing toward her, emerged from a sharp, tree-shrouded bend. Around that bend came two alligators—at least that's what she thought they were—but even as she cried a warning, and wildly indicated with a shaking hand, the loglike objects floated closer, being carried on the current, and then, to her horror, could be seen as what they really were: two of the butchered Indian porters, one man and one young girl, their flesh hanging in crimson strips from gleaming bone, large pools of blood forming garish patterns in the water around them.

Avril retched and was almost sick, but managed to hold it in as Alex tugged at her, urging her toward the opposite bank, shouting that they had to get out of the water before the piranhas arrived. The very mention of the dreaded fish was all she needed to energize her, and as she waded away from the drifting corpses, and from the approaching swathes of rich blood, she saw a triangular silvery mass—a large shoal of the flesh eaters—racing out from the shadows of the bank upstream and heading straight for the blood.

Panic propelled her forward, gave her the strength to move much faster, and with everyone shouting at her—Father Benedict and Antonio, the Indian guide and Alex—she was soon clambering up the muddy bank and falling, with her breath coming in heavy spasms, into Alex's waiting arms. The river behind her hissed and boiled, became a cauldron of blood and noise, but she only glanced fitfully at it, not wishing to see the horror, and even as the piranhas were stripping the bones of the corpses clean, she found herself heading, with the rest of the much diminished party, into the monstrously humid gloom of the forest that now belonged to the Yano.

It was another world, a darker and more alien place, the heat pressing down like an almost physical presence while the light, gray and shadowed, seemed to shift all around them, expanding and contracting reality in some indefinable manner. It had been raining and the trees were soaked, the rain turning to steam, and this steam drifted lazily to and fro and made them sweat all the more. The ground underfoot was marshy, but seemed alive with numerous insects, including very large stinging ants and a remarkable number of spiders. Avril watched the latter carefully, her flesh crawling like the ground itself, shocked at the size and quantity of the spiders, wondering where they had come from. Also, there were snakes, hissing and slithering through the wet leaves, not attacking but seeming to follow them as they forged on ahead.

"It's the Yano," Alex said. "They control the animals and watch us through them. We didn't lose them back there at the river: they're watching us right now."

"Faith," Father Benedict said, an unusual firmness in his voice. "They cannot defeat us if we have faith and hold strongly to it."

Yet faith was hard to come by in this soggy, brooding forest where spiders as large as dinner plates kept crossing the ground in front of them, and snakes, some small, some thirty feet long, slithered through the undergrowth at either side as if keeping pace with them. Avril's horror turned into acceptance, a protective feeling of unreality, as if what she was seeing was a dream that could not really touch her. Certainly time passed that way, the afternoon fading fast, the gray light becoming darker every minute as the unseen sun went down. A different fear now attacked her—the draining fear of the unknown—and she moved a little closer to Alex, who was walking beside her.

"Are we close?" she asked.

"We've arrived," he replied. "They must be all around us."

And indeed that was true, as they all found out brutally when, not five minutes later, as the grayness turned black, the guide hacked through dense foliage and they all emerged to another *verzea* lake and saw, hanging upside-down from a tree on the muddy bank, another of the Indian porters who had fled.

It was a large cecropia tree, its trunk hollow, filled with fire ants. The Yano had smeared honey on the head of the then-alive porter and, after making a small slit in his belly, applied the same honey to that bloody wound. The man's death would have been hideous, a catalogue of agonies beyond description, and even now, with thousands of ants racing in and out of his mouth and ears, his nostrils and empty eye sockets, and swarming in a glistening black mass over the gaping remains of his belly—yes, even beneath that mass of fire ants, and though hanging by his feet, the frozen contortions of his body and the anguished lines of his facial muscles were eloquent testimony to the living hell he had been through before death released him.

The Indian guide stepped back, letting his machete fall to the ground, flinging his right arm over his eyes as he let out a quavering groan of horror. Then he turned and fled, running around the still lake, suddenly stopped and jack-knifed, yelping in terror as he did so, and straightened up again and staggered back with a long lance sticking out of him. The lance was quivering up and down, piercing his belly at an angle, and as he screamed and tugged at it, his torn stomach pumping blood, the weight of the weapon pulled him forward, then made him spin and fall down, the lance breaking off as he hit the ground and rolled onto his back.

The darkness was descending quickly, but the Yano warrior was discernible, standing at the far side of the lake and staring directly at all of them. Avril studied him in silence, her mind reeling with shock, but then the man on the ground screamed and she found herself running toward him, Alex and Antonio racing after her, calling her name. The wounded man screamed, the Yano warrior disappeared, and someone managed to grab Avril, tugged at her, jerked her back, and she fell to the ground and heard the man screaming again, this time much louder than before—and in the most awful terror.

She rolled over and saw Alex—he was trying to hold her down— and she peered through the darkness and saw the wounded guide waving frantically, his lower half disappearing down the jaws of an alligator that was dragging him backward through the rushes and into the lake. Avril couldn't close her eyes—she was riveted to that terrible sight—and she lay there and watched, seeing everything very clearly: the darkness taking command, a patch of moonlight on the water, the tall rushes parting as the alligator backed through them, its jaws crushing and shredding the skin and bone of the Indian guide as he screamed one last time, his whole lower half gone, and then was dragged down the muddy bank, into a pitiless silence.

Avril sighed and sat up, numbed by horror and exhaustion, and let Alex pull her into his arms and rock her gently from side to side.

"Terrible, terrible," she heard Father Benedict murmur. "This is not like any jungle I've ever been in—and those Yano Indians aren't human."

"I've lost all sense of direction," Antonio said, "and the compass doesn't work anymore. No north or south; no east or west: the needle just spins."

"The Yano are all around us anyway," Alex replied. "So let's just sit it out."

No north or south; no east or west. Avril heard those words echoing in her head and understood what they meant. This jungle was unearthly, a soggy, humid hell, dripping and steaming and deceiving the eyes, playing tricks with shadow and light, making time become meaningless. *No north or south; no east or west.* Just the gathering darkness, the metamorphosis of sun to moon, the ghostly materialization of the stars in the distance, viewed obliquely through a gap in the forest canopy not too far away. She kept staring at that gap, no longer caring about the Yano warriors, realizing that she had automatically started stroking the amulet and that the ground, warm and soggy beneath her, had started to shake.

Father Benedict's head jerked up. Antonio and Alex stared directly at her. She looked at them and then returned her gaze to that patch of sky in the distance. Then she heard the drums, muffled at first, but getting louder, and as the ground beneath her shook—very distinctly, as in an earthquake—she saw a single light rising from the jungle and then dropping down again, forming a languid, elegant arc that took the shape of a question mark.

"There they are," Alex whispered.

First the one light, then another, then three or four more, all rising up from the jungle, climbing as if in slow motion, flaring out in brilliant yellows and purples and blues, expanding and spinning and looping over to drop down again, the ones falling passing those soaring majestically skyward, their dazzling luminescence hazing the stars and painting the night many colors.

"That's it," Alex said. "That's where we're going. So let's get to our feet."

They moved on, leaving the *verzea* lake behind them, trudging wearily or fearfully—there was no way of telling—through an eerie blue darkness that seemed to glide like smoke, often flowing around mosaics of shadow or treetrunks like gargoyles. The ground was warm and marshy, draining the noise from their footsteps, springing beneath them with the resilience of a mattress filled with feathers and eiderdown. Avril thought she was walking on air, on the sky, above the clouds, and when she looked all around her, through that shifting blue darkness, her feeling of being afloat just became that much stronger.

No north or south. No east or west. No way of telling what time it was—if time indeed still existed. Yet she sensed that she was being watched—not by Alex and the others, but by eyes that were moving in around them and pacing them silently. The hairs on her neck stood up, a ripple of dread passed through her, but she glanced at the sky, at that approaching break in the forest canopy, and saw the lights rising and falling in sublime, silent splendor. This time, instead of frightening her, the lights seemed to offer comfort, and she touched the amulet hanging around her neck and felt a sharp, tingling shock.

Although there were no lights, the Yano drums were beating, their insistent rhythms becoming more fierce, the noise growing louder every second and starting to make the trees shiver. Avril felt her head tightening, her thoughts streaming away from her, and she started to reach out for Alex's hand. Then she saw the night changing.

The break in the forest canopy was still a fair bit ahead of them, the lights more clearly visible as they rose and fell before the stars, turning that particular patch of nocturnal sky into a startlingly vivid circle of many colors. And now, straight ahead, in the area beneath those spinning lights, rose a large, fan-shaped, pulsating glow that made the treetrunks and tangled lianas shimmer. Treetrunks? Or human beings? Avril blinked and rubbed her eyes. She looked again and saw that great dome of shimmering light expanding as other lights, much smaller, silvery pellets on pulsating yellow, grew bigger as they glided through the trees, directly toward her.

Avril froze—they *all* froze—and just stood there as the lights surrounded them, drifting slowly through thin air, rising and falling on invisible waves, their outer edges spinning rapidly, all the colors of the rainbow, around inner cores that resembled the black pupils of huge, staring eyes. Avril studied them, fascinated, feeling awe rather than fear, and then noticed that their dark cores, which at first had appeared to be opaque, now, up close, looked like the entrance to small tunnels which stretched obliquely up to the sky and beyond to the stars.

The lights spun and bobbed all around her, black pupils revealing the cosmos, soothing her passage into another world beyond time and space. She felt divorced from herself, knowing awe instead of fear, and moved forward again, following Alex's hazy outline, toward that great, fan-shaped, pulsating glow beyond the trees straight ahead. She wondered what Alex was thinking, where Antonio and Father Benedict might be, and then glanced down at the ground and saw a mass of seething life: thousands of giant insects and hairy spiders and huge rodents, scorpions and snakes of every size, and gleaming black beetles, all moving forward with her, heading toward the shimmering dome, neither touching her nor causing her revulsion as they would have done previously. They were being drawn toward the light, as she was being drawn toward it, and she viewed them with eyes no longer shocked but now able, or willing, to recognize the beauty hidden in horror.

The ground, which had been warm and soggy, now seemed incorporeal: the mass of insects and furred creatures had turned it into a shifting sea, and it seemed, because her feet could feel nothing below them, that she was walking on air. The fan of light had become enormous, a great dome close ahead, its yellow striations beaming obliquely through the shimmering trunks of the trees and blending with the numerous smaller lights that were spinning and bobbing around her. It was like being inside a rainbow, in a multicolored, enchanted garden, and when she looked at the spinning lights and saw the distant stars through their dark cores, she felt herself being drawn up toward them, her soul leaping toward freedom.

Something touched her right hand—it was Alex, wanting to hold her—and as their fingers locked together, as they moved closer to one another, as they approached the forest clearing in which the great dome of light was pulsating, as the edge of the light touched them and seemed to make them dissolve, she felt an affirmation of faith, her doubts dropping away like chains, her love leaping on wings of rapture to wrap itself around Alex and carry him, enfolded and protected, to the shimmering light's dazzling vortex.

She lost Alex in there. He released her hand and raced forward. She blinked and rubbed her eyes, overwhelmed by what she was witnessing, and then, stepping forward, saw Alex and heard him, his voice exploding out of an abrupt, stunning silence and reverberating, as if magically amplified, through the dream she was living.

"*Peruche!*" he said.

28

Father Benedict heard that cry and was startled back to awareness, shaking his head and squinting sideways at Antonio, then ahead through the incandescent, dazzling light. He no longer felt afraid, but merely filled with curiosity, still unable to comprehend this new reality, wondering if he was dreaming. Yet he had just heard Alex shouting—shouting the name of old Peruche—and as the silence dropped abruptly (the drums had just stopped), he saw Antonio nearby, not moving, simply staring, then followed his friend's gaze and held his breath at what he saw just in front of him: two silhouetted figures, one standing, one sitting, both distorted in the pulsating light, neither saying a word.

"Oh, dear God," Father Benedict said.

He could scarcely believe his eyes and turned away in confusion, and thought he saw, just outside the immediate vicinity, not more trees but unobstructed, star-flecked sky and, on either side, at the edges of the bizarrely illuminated jungle clearing, great stretches of featureless darkness where the forest, by normal logic, should have existed. Further confused, a little dazed, he looked down at his own feet and saw, instead of solid ground, a shifting mass of forest wildlife—insects and spiders and beetles and slithering snakes—a sea of life on the move, neither touching him nor frightening him, simply existing, like himself, in the kaleidoscope of the shimmering, prismatic air.

Slightly stunned but not afraid, he glanced across at Antonio, wondering what he was thinking as he stood there, staring quietly in front of him; yet even as he studied him, Antonio sank to his knees, then lay down on the ground and curled up like a child in its bed, oblivious to that dark mass of insects, spiders, and snakes which, like a wave in slow motion, flooded over him and soon covered him completely.

Father Benedict was not concerned—what he had seen seemed

perfectly natural—and he stepped forward again, feeling as if he were walking on air, and eventually stopped close to the silhouetted figures who were, he felt, awaiting his arrival. Avril came up on his left, the light making her dark hair luminous, and then Alex was in front of him, dropping down to one knee, hazy and unreal in the streaming, glittering radiance, his gaze focused on the figure sitting in front of him: the old Indian, Peruche.

Father Benedict dropped to his knees, hardly knowing what he was doing, his thoughts vaulting back to the days of his mission, to when he still possessed the remnants of his faith and regularly visited the plantation. Yes, he had been a priest, then—indeed, was *still* a priest—and had involved himself deeply in Alex and his peculiar environment. Frank Poulson had been part of that—the black scar on Alex's childhood—and Peruche, also, had been part of it: a loving if exotically different guide through the thickets of childhood. He, Father Benedict, the priest devoured by doubts, had likewise tried to guide Alex—his surrogate son, the child he had never had, the emblem of the faith that he represented but could not quite accept—and had, in so doing, often resented the old Indian's teachings, thinking him a pagan or charlatan, certainly spiritually dangerous. And yet Alex had learned from him—not only magic, but virtue and strength—and now knelt before him in a blinding haze, as if their parting had never been. Was the old Indian a ghost? Was this golden light of the other world? Father Benedict wondered about that, his spirit stirring in currents of fear, and then he glanced at the figure who was standing just behind Peruche, blinked, and then looked again and recognized the young Indian, Mengrire.

"I can hardly believe that you're still alive," Alex said. "We all thought you were dead."

"No, my young white friend," Peruche croaked back in reply. "Right now, I am very much alive—but, alas, that must end soon."

"I don't—"

"I have come here to meet my end—and you to meet your beginning."

"My beginning?"

"In new faith or disbelief; what transpires will decide that."

Father Benedict glanced up at the young Indian, Mengrire, and noticed the terrible scars all over his body where the Yano had tortured him. Mengrire was staring straight ahead, as if he hardly knew they were there, an unusual machete in his hand, its handle embedded with gemstones.

"*Como está*, Mengrire?" Father Benedict said to him. "I'm delighted to see that you're still alive, but what are you doing here?"

"He cannot talk," Peruche said. "The Yano tore out his tongue. He is here because I called him to my side by using the wind."

"And what do you want with him, Peruche?"

"I am too old to carry what he holds in his hand: the jeweled sword which, turning to flame, will open the Gateway to the Otherworld. And through that Gateway, my friend, you must go before this night is finished."

Wondering what the old Indian meant by that remark, Father Benedict turned and looked behind him, through that iridescent light, and saw that the sea of insects, spiders, and snakes had stopped moving, but that it still covered the supine body of Antonio like a thick, living blanket. Strangely unaffected by this normally hideous sight, he turned his attention back on Peruche who, sitting there on the ground in front of him, was also bathed in the radiant light, his face looking even more wizened than before, his body nothing but skin and bone.

"Your words are just confusing me," Alex was saying. "Where are we? This place isn't the normal jungle. Where are the Yano?"

"You have arrived at your destination," the old Indian replied. "You have found exactly what you were looking for, but do not recognize it. You are illuminated on the rim of the Gateway to the Otherworld, and must either venture into it or turn away, thus changing your fate."

"The Gateway? I cannot see a gateway. I can only see this brilliant light, a clear sky beyond it, what seems like great darkness on either side. I think the light is playing tricks with my eyes, but that's all I can see."

"What you see is the true reality. You are at the Gateway to the Otherworld. There are many such Gateways scattered all around the world: small areas where space and time cease to have meaning, and through which lies the Otherworld, the Oneness of the Eternal All, where the finite meets the infinite, where past meets the future, and where good and evil wage the eternal war which, though necessary to balance the universe, tears the hearts of us mortals. This light illuminates the Gateway. Behind you is the mortal world. The star-filled sky you see behind me, and the darkness on either side, represent the farthest limits of your world and the beginning of, or entrance to, the Otherworld."

"And where are the Yano?"

"They are behind you—in the forest. The Yano guard this particular Gateway, keeping mortals at bay, acting on behalf of the evil ones who came here long ago. They live right here by the Gateway, existing only to practice evil, either killing or torturing those they capture, just occasionally enslaving them."

"They deliberately let us come here," Father Benedict said. "There must be a reason."

Peruche stared at him, his withered face revealing nothing, his ancient body as light as a feather and seeming to float off the ground.

"The Otherworld, or the Oneness," he said, "is where the finite meets the infinite, where the past meets the future, where evil meets good, and where you, the witnesses, the bridges between one world and the other, must choose between right and wrong, good and evil, not only for the sake of your own individual souls, but also for the struggling soul of all humanity. You have been called here for that purpose, to be tested in the flames, to choose at a terrible cost which way you will go. Thus, as a man may be asked to sacrifice his own child, so, too, will you have to make a great sacrifice to find your redemption. The Yano, who are behind you, but cannot be seen while you are in this light, allowed you to survive and reach here because they know you are needed."

Father Benedict gazed around him, first at Alex and Avril—both of whom were kneeling just in front of him, their eyes fixed on Peruche—and then past Peruche's head at the star-filled sky hazed by the light, and finally, at the frightening darkness on either side where silence reigned over nothing. Shivering, he withdrew into himself, casting his mind back to the plantation, remembering the day he had sat with Alex in front of Peruche, listening to the old Indian's description of this very place. At that time he had refused to even consider the possibility, yet now here he was in this brilliant light, the unnatural surrounding him.

He glanced around him again, at the smaller lights within the shimmering globe, watching them bob up and down, spinning fiercely as they did so, their outer layers all the colors of the rainbow, their inner cores, like large pupils, actually acting as other doorways to the stars that represented the Otherworld. So, staring at them, he vividly remembered Peruche's words: *"The lights represent the Good. They constantly war with the forces of darkness. The Yano, though mortal, are the slaves of the dark forces and exist on the perimeter of the Gateway that leads to the infinite. The lights, which we see rising and falling, pass in and out of the Gateway, which separates this mortal world from that place where time and space have no meaning.''* And here they were, on the glowing rim of the mortal world, about to either turn back or leap off into the boundless unknown. Father Benedict, studying the lights all around him, was very reluctant to make that leap.

"And now that we are here," he heard himself asking Peruche, "what happens if we decide to turn straight back? Will the Yano then murder us?"

"No, priest, they will let you go—by turning back you will have betrayed your faith—and in doing that, you will have given victory to the forces of darkness and let them enter your hearts. That's why they have let you reach here: because you represent the Good; and because, if you fail—as they think you will—they will have captured your souls—exactly as they have captured the lost soul whom you have come here to rescue.''

"Laura Wellman?" Alex whispered emotionally.

"Yes, Laura Wellman: she who was destined to bring you here and force you to choose.''

Father Benedict felt Alex's pain, and Avril's very human resentment, watched them glancing at one another, both slightly dazed, yet still clinging to the feelings that had sustained them in the material world. They could not let one another go, nor leave the past to bury itself, and their trust, through which doubt flowed like a river, was now about to be tested. Their trust—and his faith: his belief in God and love, having betrayed the former for the latter, and now possessing neither. Father Benedict shivered, the coldness of terror eating at him, the radiant light forcing him to stare into the prism of judgment day. That prism was Peruche's ancient face, now hazed by the shimmering light, being subtly altered and distorted as his quavering voice spoke again.

"Laura represented humanity in all of its imperfections, confused and thinking herself a sinner in need of redemption. You, Alex, were perfect innocence, the undefiled child who, like all children, eventually lost your innocence and the magic which that innocence had embodied. You, Father Benedict, were the disciple who betrayed his Lord, the one who, like the angel Lucifer, surrendered to vanity and lust, thus being condemned to wander in darkness and the pain of self-hatred. Together, you were one, working through one another, all part of that goodness which in various ways was corrupted in order that it might find greater purity in the light of redemption. Laura is in the Otherworld, her soul captured by the forces of darkness, and in order to set her free from that enslavement, you must first free yourselves. You have come here, where time and space no longer have meaning, where past and future exist in the one eternal present, to represent humanity, its whole history of doubt and fear, and in so doing either ensure that good shall endure against evil, or that evil shall have dominion over those not yet born. The war between good and evil goes on through eternity, and you, briefly plucked from time and space, must commit yourselves to it. You are here for that purpose."

Father Benedict glanced around him, again wondering if he was dreaming, the light dazzling his eyes, enclosing him in its dome-shaped radiance, holding back the darkness on either side and the hazed, star-flecked sky. He felt divorced from reality, betrayed by his senses, the ground as insubstantial as air, the light distorting all he surveyed, the carpet of insects and snakes perfectly, unnaturally still, as if indeed they had been frozen in time and space and would only spring back to life when he awakened to the real and familiar.

"And Laura's lost in the Otherworld?" he heard Alex whispering brokenly, his voice trembling between grief and simple confusion, tentatively begging for truth. "Does that mean she's dead?"

"Dead?" Peruche replied. "Of course she is dead. And her soul is crying out to be released from the first abyss of the darkness. She cries out, but you do not hear—because you gave away what you should have kept: the amulet that I gave you in trust and which now rests on *her* throat."

His rheumy gaze was fixed on Avril, making her flinch and sit back a little, her right hand automatically going up to her throat, her fingers covering the amulet. Peruche stared at her a long time, his eyes opening and closing slightly, before turning, with a visibly weary movement, to focus on Alex.

"When you gave the amulet away," he said, "you also threw away your strength: that virtue which, by being based on a total innocence, opened you up to the magic powers of the Good and kept you from evil. Thus, when you gave it away, you became sick and self-destructive, letting vain dreams and hopeless passions rule your heart and make you, like the priest, lust for the gratification of base desires which could have no lasting consequence. You and the priest are brothers, two sides of the same coin, both victims of the woman whose life had one real purpose: to seduce you into coming to this place to find either the abyss of damnation or the eternal flame of redemption. Her coming was preordained—as I had told you on the plantation—and her obsession with evil, which drove her into the arms of the Yano, has inevitably cast her into the first abyss of the darkness from which she can only be rescued by your subsequent actions. She brought you here and now you must release her—or condemn her to hell.''

Father Benedict started weeping, now understanding what he had done, his heart breaking when he saw the door opening to reveal his great sin. He could still not fully accept it—how she had gotten to that terrible abyss—but he knew that sooner or later he must face it or lose his soul in avoiding it. Yes, it had happened, and now he could see the sequence clearly: Laura's contact with the Yano had been her first step through that Gateway, her rape and humiliation happening there, just beyond the shimmering light, where time and space found oblivion. They had impregnated her by the Gateway, where the war between good and evil raged, and then cast her back into the mortal world where their seed would come to fruition. The forces of darkness *did* rage on earth, entering and leaving through various Gateways, and here, in this mighty jungle, a vast, unexplored territory, they have taken up residence in the hearts and minds of the unfortunate Yano, and through them are hoping to spread their blasphemous gospel to the rest of mankind. Laura *had* been possessed by them—they had impregnated her with their evil—and then, although she murdered her own child in an anguished attempt to destroy that evil, she actually, by so doing, committed the most unpardonable sin and innocently condemned herself to the first abyss of the bottomless hell of the Otherworld. Yes, Father Benedict wept, because he, too, had been tricked, his own crime, a reenactment of Laura's, the seal of doom on his soul.

''Why weep?'' Peruche said. ''Is that all you can do? I thought you had come here for more than that: to purge your separate souls—that single, human soul—and, in setting her free from the abyss, to let yourselves find redemption. Yes, your individual selves: you and Alex . . . raised on high before God.''

''I cannot . . . I cannot admit the truth.''

''Then she is doomed . . . and you will be.''

Mengrire suddenly rushed forward, snatched the amulet from Avril's throat, and darted away again. He dropped the amulet in Peruche's lap, glancing down as it was picked up, then resumed his rigid stance behind the old Indian, his machete slanting across his chest, one hand firmly gripping the jeweled handle, the other holding the blade. Peruche held the amulet up in front of Avril and waved it lightly from side to side, watching as her eyes moved left and right, growing bigger each second.

"You, too, have a purpose," the old Indian said to her. "Now stand up and walk past me and, unprotected, follow Laura Wellman's despairing cry into the unknown's great darkness."

Father Benedict jerked upright, forgetting his tears, his heart lacerated by the sound that distantly echoed around his head: the unmistakable sound of Laura Wellman in torment, crying out words he could not define, but which he well understood: words that represented a plea for help, cried over and over again.

"*No!*" he heard himself shouting—and heard Alex shouting the same—and then Avril jumped up, her taut body washed in white light, and rushed away past Peruche and Mengrire to disappear, with a startling, impossible suddenness, outside the great globe of light. Almost simultaneously, before Father Benedict could react, Mengrire jumped forward until he stood beside Peruche, then raised his jeweled sword above his head and spun it around. Its reflected light was blinding, enormous striations cartwheeling, and then the sword seemed to explode and became a pillar of fire. The globe of light disappeared, plunging them all back into darkness—and as Father Benedict jumped up, and saw Alex doing the same, he saw a stunning sweep of sky, the stars multitudinous and remarkably brilliant, not diminished by three great moons that beamed down through the night: over an immense, featureless black plain, over Mengrire's flaming sword, and—most terrifying—over the mass of Yano warriors who, painted and feathered, seemingly oblivious of all, were advancing in a great semicircle, jabbing at the dark air with long lances, their shields forming a solid wall.

At that moment he fused with Alex, sharing his every emotion and thought, and turned to scan that great flat plain toward which Avril had run. She was there, not far away, stretched out on the ground, face down with hands folded beneath her forehead, not moving at all, her white clothes fluttering in what seemed to be a modest breeze, the moonlight illuminating her dark hair where it blew out above her. Nothing else: just Avril—lying unconscious on the mysterious plain, the sky filled with stars that looked like silvery fruit, the three great moons staring down at her.

Alex stared at her, stunned, hardly knowing what he was seeing, wanting to run forward and help her but instead (as Father Benedict) turning his head to where the pillar of flames illuminated, in great strips of flickering yellow light, that fearsome mass of advancing, chanting warriors, all of whom had painted their faces in numerous demonic ways, emphasizing the wildness in their eyes and their bared, gleaming teeth.

Alex turned away from them, not understanding where he was, unable to reconcile this immense space with the jungle he had just traveled through before seeing Peruche. Where was Peruche now? Where had Antonio and the insects gone? He looked across the featureless plain, still feeling stunned by its total emptiness, and saw Avril as a fluttering white object in the encompassing darkness that only ended where the starry sky began, its chunky stars and three limpid moons looking too close for comfort.

He heard the Yano warriors behind him and suddenly started running—Alex or Father Benedict, it made little difference which—wanting to fling himself across Avril before the warriors got to her. The Yano chanting was very loud, but was magically enclosed in an outer silence, and then, out of that silence, came the sound of rushing water, and he looked back over his shoulder, stopped with shock and turned around, watched a waterfall pouring down out of somewhere high above the earth—out of some invisible source located mysteriously in thin air—to form a river that flowed obliquely across the earth just behind him, creating a natural barrier between himself and the massed Yano warriors.

What he witnessed was a miracle—either a mirage or a trick of time—and now, as he stood there, staring dumbfounded across the river, he heard a sound that chilled his blood and broke his heart simultaneously: the voice of Laura Wellman, now shrieking, now calling for help, now sobbing and groaning and choking and crying out, in agony and despair, "God! Oh, my God!" He looked across that rushing river, saw the jungle reappearing, lights rising and falling above the trees and illuminating the Yano. There was something unreal about them—they seemed slightly incorporeal—but the sound of the drums was clear enough, their pounding fast and vicious, and even as his head tightened, and Laura's wailings tore at his heart, he saw that the Yano had changed, that they were mingling with one another, some dancing, some chanting, spears whirling, shields clashing, and then—*Oh, dear God!*—he saw Laura on the ground beneath them, her body smeared with mud and blood, her long red hair tangled over her face, some of the warriors leaning over her and holding her down while others, their bodies gleaming with sweat and warpaint, brutally had their way with her.

Father Benedict and Alex wept—they both shared the same anguish; they had become one and the same—and even as their tears flowed, dropping into the silvery river, the water, as if anticipating that they were contemplating swimming across it, suddenly parted near the middle, roared and boiled into furious fountains, as a truly giant anaconda, wrapped around a struggling alligator, shot up into the air, twisting and writhing as it crushed the *caiman*, and then both animals fell back down, one snapping and whipping its tail, the other tightening its horrendous grip, and crashed back into the turbulent water to continue their fight to the death. And then the whole river went wild, turning into a nightmarish vision, filled with extraordinary beasts—six-legged lions and calves, flying eagles with human heads, a lamb with seven horns and seven glittering eyes, giant double-headed serpents and grotesque, jawless crocodiles, and manatees whose bodies were no more than bloody ribcages where the great teeth, also tearing at sloths and anteaters and deer and pumas, had stripped the flesh clean off the bone while the piranhas, massed together in a frenzy of bloodlust, devoured entrails and brains—all of this in the river that ran past the muddy bank upon which, her cries rising above the bedlam, Laura was being abused.

Alex and Father Benedict wept, and also trembled in mortal terror, aware that they were witnessing the first abyss of the eternal darkness, from which, if they had the courage of faith (that faith they had both renounced) they could possibly rescue Laura Wellman and thus set her soul free. Yet how could it be done? Could faith renounced be resurrected? Alex turned toward the front again, leaving Father Benedict behind, saw Avril lying there, and immediately raced toward her, seeing himself racing toward her from the opposite side, out of a vast star-flecked backdrop of the most vivid hues. Shaken, he slowed down, as did his opposite number, dropped his hands as did his opposite number, then started racing toward himself again, his approaching self terrifying him. A lone comet crossed the sky, casting its light upon the plain, and he stopped running, staring wildly at himself, afraid to go any farther. He stared straight at himself—at that reflection in thin air—and then felt the ground shaking beneath him and heard a deep, muffled thunder. Panic-stricken he rushed toward Avril—and then ran through himself. When he stopped, his stomach lurching, and spun around on one heel, he saw that where he had just been—and where Avril had been lying—had since become the near edge of an enormous, sweeping black hole filled with bright stars and giant, spinning moons. Avril had gone— she was nowhere in sight—and he found himself looking *down* at the sky, which seemed to go on forever.

Even as he did this, seeing that dizzying sky below him, he felt the ground shake again, heard the muffled bass rumbling, and found his eyes drawn up to that other sky where the three limpid moons, each ringed in pulsating crimson rays, began moving apart and then slowly crossed the sky until they were above the enormous, star-filled hole that had once been the flat plain. And then, as he stood there, his senses reeling at what was happening, some of the stars below him started flying up toward him, growing larger very quickly, their cartwheeling striations fencing with one another, the light exploding in silvery waves, and then they rushed out of the nothing where the earth should have been and ascended as fiercely spinning, multicolored discs to the sky directly above where, after forming elegant arcs, they started falling again, dropping back down to the sky below as others ascended.

He stood on the rim of the Gateway, looking downward through boundless space, looked up and saw the same space beyond a strange, brilliant sky. The smaller lights rose and fell, passing in and out of the Gateway, going to and fro between the world and the Otherworld in this zone where time and space had been rendered meaningless and all things became one. His human self should have been dwarfed, his emotions overwhelmed and obliterated, yet when he thought of Avril and Laura, two women, one soul, his pain was like the cry of all the world rising up from some lost dungeon of the self and squeezing the life from his heart. The world was love and pain, the rose wrapped within the thorns, and he gazed at the sky above him, saw moons shifting and colliding, saw beautiful stars exploding into even more beautiful rainbows, and understood that destruction and renewal were the bricks of all life, and that just as the faiths of childhood had to wither before maturity, so, too, could the sorry wisdom gleaned from experience turn into new faith.

Then he saw Avril. She seemed to be floating on air. She was still lying horizontally, her forehead resting on her crossed arms, her face, which before had been turned down to the earth, now turned down toward that awesome, alien sky at the other side of the Gateway. She was just lying there—on nothing—the smaller lights rising and falling around her, the lush stars and shifting moons spread out below her in that vast, awesome void. And at the other side of the hole (a hole or invisible surface?), about half a mile away, where the hellish river had been, flowing past Laura and the barbaric Yano who were torturing her, there was nothing but another plain of darkness that seemed to go on forever.

Swallowing his fear, he stepped forward, determined to risk all in reaching her—stepped forward off the rim of the black hole and stood over the sky below. Yes, he was standing, walking tentatively across the stars, out over that vast void in which the great planets wheeled, feeling himself to be less than a speck caught between hell and heaven. He kept walking, a sleepwalker, aware of himself as someone else, heading straight for the unconscious, white-clad figure of the woman he loved. The smaller lights rose and fell about him, beautifully colored and radiant, forming elegant arcs high above his head before dropping down again. He did not dare look straight down—that endless drop would have raped his senses—but instead kept his gaze fixed on Avril as he gradually approached her. She still seemed to be lying on air—as he felt that he was walking on air—and indeed, when he drew close, when he could actually distinguish her features, he noticed that her limbs and clothing were slightly flattened beneath her, as if she were truly lying on something solid but invisible—though the lights still rose and fell with unsurpassed grace all around her, passing easily, with no sign of obstruction, from one world into another and then back again.

Eventually he reached her and knelt beside her to roll her over, but just then the ground (*What* ground?) shook, and a deeper darkness seemed to surround him, and he raised his head and gazed across the dark plain as if he had sensed what was coming.

He saw it: a white horse, racing out of a rolling darkness, running across that boundless plain with a deeper darkness following it, blotting out the stars as it advanced like some boiling, black cloud. The horse was snow-white and magnificent, its mane blowing out behind it, steam emerging from its nostrils as it left the dark plain and ran across the hole above the stars as if running on glass. It made no noise at all—though the darkness behind it seemed to rumble—and as he rose to his feet in wonder (and wondering what was shaking beneath him) he saw another horse coming toward him, emerging miraculously from the east, a flaming red horse that sprang out of that vast darkness and also headed toward him. He glanced west and saw another, a magnificent black horse springing from blackness, and then, as if by instinct, glanced over his shoulder toward the north, and saw yet another horse, a spectral, off-white beauty, bursting out of a boiling darkness that advanced from a lighter darkness, and running with that dark cloud pursuing it across the great, star-filled Gateway.

Alex dropped to his knees again, resting his hand on Avril's head, then looked east and west, north and south (if such existed) and heard his own voice, clearly the voice of Father Benedict, whispering the only words he could think of as the horses raced toward him: "*And I looked, and behold a pale horse: and his name that sat on him was Death, and Hell followed with him.*" And so saying, he shivered, and turned to roll Avril onto her back; and when he had done so, found himself looking down at Laura, her flaming red hair entangled across her face, her eyes closed, her sun-tanned skin smeared with mud and blood.

She was obviously dead.

Alex groaned, as did Father Benedict, both inhabiting the same skin, and then looked in every direction, at the four horses racing toward him, and saw the great darkness rolling over the wondrous animals and then pouring over the rim of the Gateway to swirl around the lights that rose and fell in serene, silent splendor. His skin crawled with revulsion, he felt the evil coming toward him, and he knew that he was witnessing the forces of darkness moving against what was good. Lightning daggered out of the sky—the sky above and the sky below—and then he heard the roaring thunder, the terrible sound of dividing firmament, and then the moons became as blood and the suns as black as pitch, and the stars below seemed to roll back as the forces of darkness invaded them.

He knew they would come for Laura and carry her off in that approaching darkness, that they would cast her from this terrible abyss into hell's deepest pit; and even as he looked around him and was tempted to flee—seeing the black clouds rolling toward him, coming at him from all sides, bolts of lightning daggering through them, flame and smoke belching from them—the ground around her cracked and split—a ground that had just materialized—and the earth upon which she was suddenly lying began sinking beneath her.

Someone screamed Avril's name, and Father Benedict jerked his head up, seeing Alex at the other side of the splitting earth, reaching down toward Laura. "Avril!" he screamed. "*Avril!*" And then reached out toward Laura, his eyes wide and anguished, his jaw opening and closing mechanically, his hand falling too short as the ground on which she lay shifted and took her out of his reach, beyond the flames roaring up all around her. "Avril!" he screamed.

"*Avril!*" And then stared at Father Benedict, oblivious of the boiling black clouds that were swirling over his head.

Their eyes met for a brief moment, both dazed, uncomprehending, and then the clouds rolled over Alex as the flames pushed him back and Father Benedict, toward whom the broken earth was now moving, reached down and out to grab Laura. She was coming toward him, but sinking, something roaring right beneath her, her red hair lying across her closed eyes as the flames leaped up around her. Father Benedict clawed at her, his fingers opening and closing above her; then, as she sank lower, as the greedy flames climbed higher around her, he felt the full weight of his guilt—of the deed itself and his refusal to face it—and he recognized how she had died, and the abominable trick that had been played upon them, and knew that he must pay the price or forever be damned.

He stood up to go to her, to leap across that flaming chasm, to surrender himself to the flames that she might be redeemed. Then everything roared and spewed hail and fire around him as, in the Gateway, in the void between two worlds, in that place where past met future, where time curved back on itself, he saw her lifeless body sinking down between his own trembling knees.

Father Benedict sobbed, his spirit destroyed by guilt and grief, and then felt himself picked up and hurled backward through whirling dark heat. He hit the ground and rolled over, choking on loose soil and grass, saw tall trees directly above him, a few sections of starry sky, then heard the crackling of flames and smelt smoke and forced himself to sit upright.

He was back in the forest clearing, Alex lying unconscious beside him, his blond hair disarrayed, one leg bent at a peculiar angle, old Peruche not far away, stretched out on his back, what appeared to be a smoldering heap of rags near some still burning bushes, the whole clearing surrounded by a large ring of charred, depressed earth where the edge of the dome of light had been. Antonio was just outside that black line, sitting up and shaking his head, his body no longer covered in insects, the ground around him quite normal. There was no sign of the Yano—they might never have existed—but then, when Father Benedict studied the clearing once more, he found to his ineffable horror that there was no sign of Avril.

"Oh, dear God," he murmured.

Alex groaned and opened his eyes, started to move and gasped with pain, fell back, and looked around as best he could by just moving his head. Father Benedict moved over to him, smiled at

him, examined his leg, saw that it was broken and told him so as
Antonio joined them. Alex cursed in frustration, though obviously
still dazed, and Father Benedict, with Antonio, helped him to sit
upright against a tree, wincing each time Alex winced, murmuring
comforting words, while the beauty and horror he had just witnessed
returned to make his heart lurch.

"What happened?" Antonio asked. "What did I sleep through? I
dreamt that I was lying there covered in snakes and insects, and that
you two and Avril disappeared when that great light winked out.
Now old Peruche's lying there, apparently dead of natural causes,
and Mengrire seems to have been burned to a cinder where those
flames are still burning. What happened? *Where's Avril?*"

Alex's whole body stiffened as he stared around in rising horror,
and then, mumbling some inaudible prayer, returned his gaze to the
front. Father Benedict held his gaze, unable to tear his eyes away,
remembering what they had shared in that world beyond the Gateway when he—as Alex tried desperately to rescue Avril—had likewise tried to pull his beloved Laura from the consuming flames of
the abyss. Laura and Avril: had they been one and the same? Had
they, in that place where time and space had no meaning, been fused
together as one soul—as all souls must finally be one—in order that
he and Alex, two wanderers from the right path, could choose
between fleeing from the truth or finally facing up to it, no matter
the cost? Father Benedict stared at Alex, seeing the world's pain in
his blue eyes, and also, in that pain, seeing the steel of accusation,
the dawning of a truth that had been glimpsed in the Otherworld and
now, irrespective of the possibility of further pain, would need to be
confirmed in this mortal world.

"I know where Avril is," Alex said. "Damn you, Father Benedict,
I know. But this question I've got to ask you right now: *What really
happened to Laura?*"

And there it was: the question that Father Benedict had dreaded,
ringing out like a bell of doom in the silence of the forest clearing
where the darkness was giving way to dawnlight and dew glittered
like nature's tears. He glanced wildly around him, wondering if he
could find the courage, the soaring trees and tangled lianas seeming
to press down upon him, the weight of his guilt and grief crushing
him further and squeezing the breath from his lungs. He rocked back
on his heels, covered his face with his shaking hands, almost wept,
but managed to contain it and then dropped his hands again. He

glanced once at Antonio, hoping to steal some courage from him, and then, taking a deep breath, licking his dry, shivering lips, he forced himself to stare straight at Alex and tell him the truth.

"I killed her," he said.

29

The dawn light was breaking through and the jungle had fallen silent when Father Benedict, his anguished eyes fixed on Alex, made his final and most shocking confession, his words cleaving the chilly air.

"I killed her," he said. "With my bare hands, I killed her. I killed her because I loved her, because I feared for her soul, and because she begged me to prove my love to her by putting an end to her misery. . . . And I did what she asked of me. Laura never really returned to the Yano camp: I killed her and buried her."

He burst into tears, leaning forward and covering his face, pressing his hands against his temples as if trying to crush his own skull, while Alex simply stared at him, too stunned to respond, scarcely able to believe what he was hearing, let alone take it in. The tree was rough against his spine, the earth beneath him damp and cold, and he saw lines of gray light beaming down through the high, close-knit trees. He wanted to get up and run, to feel the cool air slapping his face, but when he thought of his leg, of where Avril was, and listened to the priest's sobbing, he knew that he would have to sit it out until the nightmare completed itself.

He said nothing, did nothing, letting his good friend cry alone, staring at him as his curved body shivered with his terrible anguish. Alex was not moved by pity, instead letting his rage have freedom, then encouraging that rage to turn to the hatred which alone could protect him. There could be no forgiveness—neither for friendship nor love—and as he watched the priest weeping, his tears falling upon the dew, he kept thinking of why they had come here, of his own guilt over Laura, and reminded himself that Avril was lost in the world that Laura had brought them to.

He said nothing, did nothing, letting his hatred defeat his pain; but as the priest choked back his sobs, wiping his eyes with a shaky hand, Antonio moved closer to him, kindly murmuring words of comfort, and then slid his arm around the priest's shoulders and gave him a hug.

"It's all right," he said. "It's all right. It's all over now."

He glanced pleadingly at Alex, but Alex made no move, keeping his eyes focused mercilessly on Father Benedict's face as he sat up, took a deep breath, and straightened his shoulders, a gray light falling over him.

"Oh, God, Alex," he said. "Please try to understand: you have to try to imagine how much I loved her and what her suffering did to me. Her suffering was terrible, beyond endurance for us both, and what I did, in the light of what I knew, I did as an act of pure love, seeking the mercy of God." He sniffed and wiped his nose, rubbed his eyes with his upturned palm, then put his head back and studied the sky, trying to find Laura's face there. "Oh, my boy, you should have seen her . . . I mean, after her hideous ordeal. When she emerged from the rain forest and fell into my arms—after her rape by the crazed Yano and her subsequent experiences beyond the Gateway—she was, at least by normal standards, an utterly destroyed human being, pregnant with what she thought was Satan's child and, because of that, surrendering to madness." He shook his head from side to side, displaying his bottomless, destroying grief, then lowered his eyes and fixed his gaze on Alex, his cheeks glistening with tears. "As I've already told you," he said, "I tried to save her from herself—hiding her away in that Indian village, looking after her all those months, even personally supervising the delivery of her child, all the time trying to talk her back to sanity— but then, when she killed the child, when she realized what she had done, she surrendered absolutely to a madness that was based on pure anguish. For indeed, if she had feared the baby—or at least feared what it might be—she found out, when she killed it, that her love was stronger than her fear, and that no matter how long she might live, she would never be able to forget her terrible deed, nor forgive herself for it. In a sense, when she buried that child in the forest, she also buried her mortal self."

Father Benedict leaned forward and hammered his fist into the earth, kept pounding at the grass like someone trying to smash his reflection in a mirror, until Antonio, slipping an arm around his shoulders, pinned his hands to his sides. The priest nodded and sighed, acknowledging what he had done, and eventually, when he seemed to have calmed down, Antonio released him.

He looked up, his eyes tortured, and Alex felt a pain go through him, remembering that this man had once been like a father to him, remembering his own pain over Laura's disappearance. He also remembered why they had come here and what had happened to Avril—and, in so doing, hardened his heart against the priest's suffering.

"Oh, Alex, the madness—you have to understand that madness: it came out of her like flame from a spit and soon scorched me as well. As she was mad with grief and fear, so I was mad with my love for her—a love that grew stronger and more unreasonable every day, because every day I was forced to observe her increasing helplessness, both mental and physical. Yes, I cared for her and tried desperately to understand her, and in doing that I surrendered to that reasoning which only the mad can know. Yet the reasoning of the mad has its own peculiar logic, and so, in that mud hut, in the daily squalor of her base existence, I found myself agreeing when she told me how her life had to end."

Alex closed his eyes briefly, traveling back down through himself, found a glimmering of sympathy in his depths, and came back up again, opening his eyes to the priest and staring at him with his thoughts well concealed.

"Madness," the priest said. "An insanity based on love: the kind of love that raises man from his body to a realm of transcendence. And so I listened to her, holding my breath at each nuance, and eventually understood that her grief and fear were like the fires of hell to her. Yes, having killed her child, she still felt she was possessed—felt it more so because she had developed the conviction that if, as she sometimes thought, her child might in fact have been normal, then Satan, in his diabolical cunning, had tricked her into committing the infanticide, thus truly stealing the soul that she had thought had already been stolen. Do you see what she was doing, Alex? Do you comprehend such a need? She had lived all her life with the conviction that she was possessed, and now, either way, no matter which way she looked at it, she would always find the proof for that conviction and suffer accordingly. And so, dear God, she suffered, and finally came to the end of the road; and knowing that I, loving her, could not bear to watch her suffering—knowing, also, that I wanted to pay for the sin of loving her—she begged me to prove my love to her by putting her out of her misery: by killing her, as she could not find the courage to do it alone, and then burying her—about this she was most adamant—beside her dead child."

A gray light poured through the trees, bringing warmth but little reality, simply framing the priest in a hazy dawn in which no birds were singing. The brief silence was acute, appearing to vibrate between them, and when the priest spoke again, squeezing his temples between his fingers, his voice was almost devoid of human timbre, at once sepulchral and tragic.

"So," he said, "she wanted to die—to make atonement for her sins; and also, I believe, to escape the anguish of her terrible guilt—and I, her lover, convinced that her case was just, believing that whether or not she had been diabolically possessed, her suffering at the hands of the Yano would not be forgotten, and that her sanity, in retreat from guilt and horror, would never return—yes, I, a priest, in an anguish equal to her own, held her in my arms one last time and agreed to do as she asked." He lowered his face to his upraised hands, sniffing a little, his body shaking, and eventually taking a very deep breath, raised his shoulders, straightened his spine, and kept his gaze very steady. "Laura never returned to the Yano. What I told you was a lie. I took her into the jungle and there, to prove my love for her, slit both of her wrists, embraced her and kissed her, and let her bleed to death in my arms, talking to her the whole time. Then, as she had requested, I buried her where she was lying—in that very same patch of earth in which her dead baby lay. I killed Laura to release her from the demons that were possessing her. I tried to free myself by setting *her* free . . . and I found only hell."

Alex closed his eyes again, traveling back down through himself, searching for the innocent love he had known a few years ago. He saw the broad swathe of the river, the trees and shacks of the plantation, that awful room in the *fazendeiro* where the blood had flowed too freely, the more placid and modest buildings of the mission at the edge of the forest. Seeing those, he saw his childhood, all the dark days he had numbered, all the pain and confusion he had suffered when his mother died and his father, in the bitterness of his failure, had treated him cruelly. Who had rescued him from that suffering? Antonio Bozzano and Peruche . . . and later, this priest, Father Benedict, with his humor and love. And then Laura: her witchcraft; driving him close to suicide. . . . Who had rescued him and offered him comfort, if not that same priest? Yes, the priest had loved him—loved him still, and suffered for him—and if indeed he had lied, or at least withheld the truth, he had done so in the hopes of preventing the further pain he thought it might lead to. That pain had not been avoided—Alex could feel it right now—but when he opened his eyes and saw the face of his friend before him, the innocent love that he had thought was gone forever rushed back to pour over him.

He leaned forward as best he could, feeling the pain in his broken leg, reached out with one wavering hand and gently squeezed the priest's shoulder.

"Oh, Father Benedict," he said. "My good friend . . . it's all in the past now. Forget it. Let's live again."

The priest quivered like a bowstring. Sitting upright, he closed his eyes, took a deep breath, and nodded his head gratefully. He let his hand lie on Alex's as he opened his eyes again and smiled, his haggard features brightening with relief.

"Yes," he said, "it's over, thank God. At last it's all done."

"No," Antonio said. "Not *quite* done. . . . I think Peruche's alive."

Alex looked across the clearing to where Peruche was a spreadeagled and saw one withered hand upraised, the magic amulet dangling from crooked fingers and swinging slowly from side to side like a pendulum. As Antonio rushed toward the Indian, muttering a joyful imprecation, Father Benedict started to say something to Alex, but Alex simply shook his head lazily and gave him a smile.

"Come here," he said. "Help me across the clearing. I have to talk to the old man."

Father Benedict did as he was told, dragging Alex across the clearing, and Alex gritted his teeth until he got there and could steady his leg again. He leaned against another tree, looking down at the wizened Indian, but Peruche, even at death's door, hardly gave him a glance, instead turning his rheumy eyes upon Father Benedict and nodding judiciously.

"I have been waiting for you," he said. "I am dying and wish to finish it—but I cannot go until the English girl is brought back to this world. Do you understand, priest? The two women share the same soul. Beyond time and space this doesn't matter, but here, in the material world, Alex suffers because of it. And you, priest, whose faith was weak, who killed your woman out of love, have yet to regain the faith you lost when you shoveled the earth on her body, thinking, as you committed that gross stupidity, that you were doing the right thing." Peruche shook his head wearily, a look of disgust on his withered face as he let the amulet swing from side to side. "You were cheated," he said. "The devil used your love to cheat you. By murdering the American woman, you handed her over to

the forces of darkness—and also paved the way for your own
downfall, which came soon enough. Yes, priest, you were cheated—
they used the American woman to enslave you to them—and now
you must reverse that position and regain your soul by defeating
them. Do you understand, priest? Set them free and thus free
yourself. Return to the Otherworld and face the forces of darkness
and, in so doing, release the woman you loved from the abyss into
which your love sent her. The two women share the same soul. They
lie together in that fiery pit. Release the American woman, letting
her enter the light of goodness, and the English woman can then
return to her own body and live out her natural span. Go, priest!
Return to God and find redemption. Walk back into the Otherworld!''

He held the amulet up higher, waved it to and fro gently, and
Alex, observing Father Benedict's face, knew what he would do. The
priest took a deep breath, but hesitated no more. He reached out with
a shaky hand, removed the amulet from Peruche's fingers and then,
hanging it carefully around his neck, climbed to his feet. He looked
up at the sky and at the forest surrounding him; then, without saying
a word, he returned his gaze to Peruche. The old Indian was pointing
toward the place where Avril had disappeared, and only when the
priest nodded and turned to walk across the clearing did the Indian's
hand fall back to his side, his fingers outspread on yellow grass.

At that moment Peruche died. His body shuddered and then was
still. And at *that* moment Father Benedict walked over Avril's
footsteps—and a great ball of fire, an umbrella of light, exploded
over the clearing.

Alex closed his eyes, blinded, and felt the heat washing over him,
then heard a crackling sound as the forest trees were ignited. He
opened his eyes again to see the flames flickering under a gray
smoke. The heat receded almost immediately but seemed to suck the
air up with it. Alex gasped and coughed as smoke swirled around
him and then mercifully passed on. Antonio was lying beside Peruche,
his hands cupped over his eyes, his body shuddering as the ground
beneath him began to shake violently and a rumbling came from
deep in the earth and exploded around them. The ground roared and
split, became a jigsaw puzzle of darting cracks out of which, as if
emanating from hell, came yellow flames and foul black smoke.
Alex thought he heard a wailing—the anguished cry of human
history—and then he stared across the clearing, through spewing
flames and belching smoke, and was drawn forward, out of his
human shell, to where the past meets the future.

The forest melted away, the earth turned to molten lava, the sun, black as ash, hovered beside a crimson moon, and hail and fire rained from the skies as they rolled back like carpets. Beyond the skies was the cosmos, filled with stars and colliding planets, the debris from galactic explosions forming tunnels through time. He descended—and rose again—and exploded out into the light, and saw himself through all the ages of his life, returning after his dying. He was young and then old, and then himself as he now was, and stood silently staring straight at the sun as it blazed down upon him. His dark-haired mother held him close—dressed in white just like the sun—and then she vanished with a gentle wave of her hand and left him in tall grass. He snapped the grass and it cried in pain, felt it squirming in his tightening fist, deliberately dropped it into the black *verzea* lake and watched the fish swarm around it. The water rippled across his face, erasing the features from his reflection, and he reached down, touching his own reflected fingers, and felt the water surrounding him. It was deep and very dark, filled with light, without end, and a pale moon, its soothing light wavering, gave life to the cosmos. There were stars all around him, both above and below him, and he saw the forces of darkness and light sweeping through one another.

Father Benedict was in that maelstrom, being swept through eternity, first crushed and then stretched between the forces of good and evil, his being spreading over the great void between heaven and hell. Above were cherubim with flaming swords, below were demons and ogres; thunder clapped and lightning spat and fire flowed in winding rivers in which, their cries fearsome yet tongueless, the damned suffered endlessly. Father Benedict rode the whirlwind, his body shredded and then devoured, his spirit reaching down in love and faith to pull Laura to safety. She was sleeping, unaware, existing neither here nor there, her flaming red hair sweeping out to disappear into the darkness, her body a pale flesh that flowed like a river, her eyes closed to the sky above and the mud below, to the light and the black pit. She was there—as was Avril—both borrowing the same form, and the abyss, spiralling eternally beneath her, began sucking her down. Father Benedict had to face it—had to stare hell in the face; had to look in the eyes of Satan and see only God's reflection; had to brave unmentionable horrors and vileness in order to redeem his faith—and he did so, destroying his mortal life, finding redemption in death, and then picked Laura up with his love and faith and carried her into the light.

Hell roared in its fury, hail and flame swept through the void, while the angels, resplendent in the light above, sang the song of redemption. Alex came back, returning, observing the fading of the Otherworld, his heart bursting with love, his spirit soaring, when silence reigned over chaos. Father Benedict had gone forever into that silence, his soul at last finding peace.

The sun died and became a cinder, the moon melted to dripping blood, the blood flowed across the floor and splashed on antique furniture, then congealed on the walls of that awful room in which his father had died. He saw them before that dying, since they all defied space and time: his father and Rollie Thatcher, Laura Wellman and Father Benedict, Mengrire shedding tears for the Indian girl before the blood stained their hands. They had lived—and still had life—and would never relinquish it, existing here, in Alex's mind, where space and time had no meaning, as he flew through his own pain, borne on the wings of his love, and descended back to the jungle, to the reality of the material world . . . and saw the flames in the forest clearing growing smaller and dying out, the smoke drifting like gauze and then gradually disappearing, and then heard the primeval silence filling his ears with the song of his sheltered heart.

Alex opened his stinging eyes, shook his head, trying to recover, then saw Antonio sitting up, also shaking his head, Peruche's dead body stretched out beside him, its weathered skin like brown parchment. Avril lay not far away, face down on the flattened grass, her smooth forehead resting on her crossed hands, the breeze rippling her white clothes.

She lay there without moving, the breeze making her dark hair dance, her spine rising and falling as she breathed in slow, even motions. Then her left foot kicked, her head shook, her hands parted, and she groaned and rolled onto her back and stared up at the sky.

Thus she lay in a drifting mist on the forest floor, sunlight touching her wakening eyes.

"She's all right," Antonio said. "She's just fine. I think she just needs a drink." He turned his head to grin at Alex, then withdrew a familiar hip flask from his pocket, swung it to and fro in a teasing manner, and smiled even more broadly. "Here," he said. "I got it from Father Benedict—and he left enough for the two of you." He grinned and threw it at Alex, expertly landing it in his lap, then stood up, glanced across at the exhausted Avril, and stretched himself.

Alex sat against the tree, feeling the pain in his broken leg, his spirit soaring on the wings of his love as his faith was renewed. He stretched one arm and spread his fingers, watched the grass rise up to touch him, turned his head, and poured his love at a flower and watched its petals unfold to him. He made the trees bend, made the branches shed their white and yellow flowers, and only then, when golden pollen was falling on Avril, did he lean back and smile. The sun hovered above the forest canopy, and he called its light to him.

"I'll have to leave you for a while," Antonio said. "You can't travel with that broken leg. I promise to bring back some stretcher bearers and all the comforts of home. You can survive here for a day or two: boil the water and peel the fruit. Father Benedict's gone—he won't come back—but you've got Avril now . . . and that's more than enough."

Alex looked across the clearing and saw Avril crawling toward him, shaking her head constantly to clear it, her lips tight and determined. The tall grass bent before her, bowed down as she passed, and as she moved, coming closer, occasionally rubbing dirt from her face, she seemed to take energy from the dawn light, her cheeks gaining a warm glow. She kept crawling until she reached him—the forest soaring high behind her, the gray clouds in the sky threatening rain, the brown lianas strangling the trees and themselves surrendering to green foliage—and then stopped, propping herself up on her elbows, and stared at him with puzzled eyes.

"What happened?" she asked him. "I saw light . . . and then I simply passed out."

"I'll tell you later," Alex replied. "We've got plenty of time."

Avril crawled into his arms and laid her head on his chest, and he sat there, stroking her dark hair, the tree rough against his spine, watching the white and yellow flowers fall all around him to carpet the forest floor. Antonio picked up his rucksack, slid the straps around his shoulders, and then, sniffing the fresh air, his *café-au-lait* face beaming, he put his right hand out, let it fill up with the falling flowers, and ceremoniously poured the flowers over them, offering nature's confetti.

"Peace be with you," he said. "I now go for the stretcher bearers. You know? Those *ordinary* people—the ones just like us—those poor mortals who live only to die, defying their terror with love . . . those who measure God's justice."

And with that he walked back into the forest.